If you

Eagerly watching the girl toss her blouse to the floor and unhook her bra, the Professor's eyes widened as she peeled the white silk cups away from her firm breasts. Topped with chocolate-button nipples, her youthful mammary globes were small but delightfully formed. *If her cunny was in proportion, it would be wonderfully tight!* he reflected as she tugged her skirt down her long legs.

Kicking her shoes and skirt aside, she stood in her ballooning red panties, gazing at the Professor as she slowly pulled the flimsy garment down. She was obviously revelling in her striptease act, gently easing the material down just enough to expose her unfurling blond pubic hair. A little further, and the top of her tightly closed sex crack came into view . . .

Doctor Sex

Ray Gordon

NEW ENGLISH LIBRARY
Hodder & Stoughton

Gordon, Ray
Doctor Sex
1. Erotic stories
I. Title
823.9'14[F]

ISBN 0 340 72813 2

Typeset by Hewer Text Ltd, Edinburgh
Printed and bound in France by
Brodard & Taupin.

Hodder and Stoughton
A division of Hodder Headline
338 Euston Road
London NW1 3BH

Chapter One

Naked netball teams, schoolgirls' bulging knickers, firm breasts topped with erect nipples, naked buttocks inviting the whip, tight teenage pussies well-juiced in arousal . . . Professor Sexton Snide was a fiendish sex maniac, his mind perpetually riddled with thoughts of perverted filth. One glimpse up a young girl's skirt, one flash of a triangular patch of ballooning panties, and his penis stiffened, his full balls heaved and rolled.

Professor Snide was far madder than any mad professor, far crazier than the infamous Baron Frankenstein, far more insane than insanity itself. He worked in his castle like a man possessed, only emerging from his laboratory to prowl around the local village in search of fresh young girls to lure to his dungeon.

Rumours concerning his diabolical work were rife, and the people of the village, who'd nicknamed him 'Doctor Sex', had come to regard him with suspicion and disdain. Teenage girls disappearing for a few days at a time, strange noises emanating from the bowels of the castle – the villagers locked up their daughters and gave the Professor, and the castle, a wide berth.

But, unbeknown to the villagers, Professor Snide had spent three years designing and constructing an ingenious device – a brainwave-transference machine that would ensure that their daughters pulled their knickers down and opened their girlie cracks for him as and when he desired crude sex.

1

His machine was designed to record the alpha waves emanating from the male brain and induce the patterns into the female brain. His seemingly crazy notion was that the female would then think and behave as the male, would perpetually crave sex as the male does. Once transformed, the village girls would flock to him in their droves, stripping off and demanding obscene, crude, disgusting, and highly illegal sex.

His meticulous research had revealed that there was a worldwide gap in the market for rampant, sex-crazed nymphomaniacs. If the device worked, he'd not only have his sinful way with the delectable village girls but would also earn a fortune from transforming men's prudish wives and girlfriends into sex-mad whores. There'd be no shortage of money, or of juicy pussies!

His machine ready for testing, the Professor sat at his bench in his disorganized laboratory, rubbing his chin pensively. His unruly black hair cascading over his lined forehead, his lips furling into a slight grin, he turned and gazed longingly at Hollie Hocks, his young assistant. Focusing on the girl's rounded buttocks billowing her tight skirt as she walked across the lab, he massaged his cock through his trousers, pondering on Hollie's incredible prudishness.

In her early twenties, her dark hair drawn back and tied in a ponytail, she had great potential, he reflected. With her hair let down and a little make-up applied to her pretty face, she'd be very attractive. Naked, her pubic hair shaved, her dripping sex slit gaping, she'd be horny in the extreme – extremely fuckable.

He'd have liked to sink his teeth into the alluring globes of her bottom, into the fullness of her firm breasts – but Hollie wouldn't have teeth anywhere near her beautiful body. Teeth, tongues, fingers, church candles, vibrators, cucumbers, penises . . . Especially penises! Hollie would tolerate nothing of the sort — yet!

She was single and undoubtedly a virgin, and he wondered whether she masturbated in her bed at night, slipping her slender fingers between her fleshy cunny lips and rubbing her swollen clitty to orgasm. Perhaps she pressed a vibrator against her solid clitoris and took herself to mind-blowing climaxes. *Probably not!* he concluded.

Many times he'd tried the subtle approach, wooing her, asking her out to dinner, suggesting that they have a drink in the village pub. He'd even offered to pay her the last six months' salary he owed her if she would accompany him to his living quarters in the west wing. But all to no avail. Hollie was determined to keep her knickers and bra firmly in place — and her hymen!

But the Professor was devious, insane, and maniacal in the extreme — and not one to give up easily. Driven by his insatiable thirst for perverted sex, he viewed Hollie as a challenge — a challenge that he'd taken on with dynamic enthusiasm and a neurotic obsession. He often slipped his cock out and wanked: as he imagined his penis driving deep into the girl's tight cunt, his spunk would shoot from his pulsating knob and splatter the floor. He imagined many things during his wanking sessions — schoolgirlies' hairless pussy cracks, rounded breasts firm in youth, his prick spunking down young girls' throats . . . But not least, he imagined slipping his solid cock between Hollie's beautifully rounded buttocks, driving his swollen knob deep into her tight bottom-hole and sperming her bowels.

His quest in life was to convert the girl from a reserved prude into a sex-crazed nymphomaniac — and then to fuck her senseless. Every day, he imagined her moist sex valley, his lapping tongue tantalizing her pink inner flesh, licking her ripe clitoris to massive orgasms. He imagined bending her over the bench, her thighs parted, his tongue licking the small bridge of skin between her lust holes. With the aid of his incredible machine, his fantasies, he hoped, were about to become reality.

Successfully recording his own alpha waves, he now needed a guinea pig, an unsuspecting woman on whom to test his equipment. Hollie, believing the machine to be a device for correcting the deranged brain patterns in the mentally insane, was the ideal candidate – the only candidate. But he had to convince the girl that no harm would come to her, that his intentions, for a miraculous change, were honourable. He had to lie to her, but lies came easily. Lies came as easily as spunk!

'Miss Hocks,' he said, rising to his feet as she walked towards him. 'Miss Hocks, I want to come . . . I mean, the time has come.'

'What time?' she asked, her sea-green eyes frowning as she stared at her crazy boss.

'It's half-past eleven.'

'No, what time has come?' she repeated, raising her eyebrows and shaking her head despairingly.

'The time for *you* to come . . . Er . . . The time of the revelation!' he chuckled, rather too excitely.

'I don't know what you mean, Professor Snide. The revelation?'

'The transformation, Miss Hocks. You are to be my first victim . . . Er, you are to test my equipment.'

'But I'm not mental!' she protested as he reached up to a shelf and grabbed a helmet sprouting a dozen wires. 'You told me that your machine will bring sanity to the insane. I'm not insane.'

'No, no . . . What I need to do is record your alpha-wave patterns. Being a highly intelligent, intellectual and mentally

4

unstable . . . stable young woman, your brain patterns will be the blueprint for my patients – for the mentally insane.'

'But . . . '

'I wonder why it's called a blueprint? Why not red or green?'

'But . . . '

'Blueprint. The word must be the product of a deranged mind.'

'But . . . '

'Your insanity will bring my patients sanity. Or is it the other way round?'

'But . . . '

'But, but, but. What's the matter with you, Miss Hocks? Don't you want to go down in history? You'll be in the *Guinness Book of Criminal Records* for playing your part in ridding the world of madness. Sit on the chair and I'll slip my helmet into your mouth . . . I mean, onto your head.'

Sitting down, her hands clasped, Hollie looked at the Professor with suspicion as he placed the helmet on her head. Working with him for three years, she'd learned never to trust him. She'd only been at his laboratory for two days when he'd asked her to slip her panties off and lie on the rack with her ankles and wrists chained, her legs wide apart. In the name of medical science, he'd wanted to measure the length and breadth of her vaginal canal. Had she not spied him masturbating in the rack chamber with a vibrator earlier that morning, shooting his sperm all over the flagstones – in her naivety, she'd probably have complied with his request.

Over the years, he'd come up with one excuse after another to examine her vagina. To help females the world over, to discover the root cause of hysteria in women, to establish a link between the size of the clitoris and clinical insanity . . . There wasn't one excuse he'd missed in an effort to get his hands up her skirt, his fingers up her tight pussy. But Hollie knew the Professor well: he was a full-blown sexual pervert, a first-rate sexual deviant. But did she know him well enough?

'I won't pass out, will I?' she asked nervously as he moved to the control panel, his long fingers hovering over a switch.

Only when I fuck you and take you to a shuddering orgasm!

'No, of course you won't pass out, Miss Hocks. All I'm going to do is record your brain patterns and then screw your tight . . . '

'I'm not sure that I want to do this. I might become a zombie,' she complained.

'Hopefully, you'll become a rampant . . . You'll feel no ill effects whatsoever. Now, to ensure that I won't be inducing corrupt brain patterns into my lunatical patients, I have to ask you a few questions before I begin. How often do you masturbate?'

'I *never* masturbate!' she cried, her hand held to her pretty mouth.

I do! 'Good, good. I wouldn't want my female patients to become hooked on masturbation, addicted to multiple orgasms and forcing church candles up their tight . . . I do apologize, my mind ran away with me. Tell me, when did you last have it off? What I mean is, when did you last have inter sex of course?'

'Inter sex of course?'

'I'm sorry, my brain's not working properly. I deduce from my deranged thinking that my brain *never* works properly during times of great sexual excitement.'

'Sexual . . . I've often wondered about you, Professor – about the workings of your brain.'

'As have I, Miss Hocks – as have I!' he sniggered wickedly. 'It would appear that I've inherited certain traits from my grandfather, Lord Sanatorium, which cause me to . . . I won't go into the illegalities of my peculiar sexual behaviour in public toilets. Tell me, when did you last have sex in a public toilet? Er . . . Sexual intercourse?' *When were you last fucked?*

'I . . . I've *never* had sexual intercourse in a public toilet, or anywhere else, for that matter!'

'You haven't lived, Miss Hocks!'

'Are you sure that this isn't one of your snide tricks, Professor Snide?'

'One of my snide tricks, Professor Snide? Goodness me, what *do* you think I am?'

'I don't think, Professor – I *know*!'

'Fuck me backwards! I mean . . . You have the golden opportunity to help women, and you're talking about snide tricks in public toilets? You leave me speechless – dumb-founded, even! Don't you want to go down on me . . . Go down in history?'

'Yes, but I know you of old.'

'Of course you don't, I'm only thirty-five.'

'Not that sort of old. The other day you asked me to expose my breasts so that you could take photographs. What normal man would ask such a thing of an innocent girl?'

All normal men! 'Not ordinary photographs, Miss Hocks. I wanted to take gamma-ray photographs to determine muscle development in the female breast. With my revolutionary tit . . . revolutionary breast developer, silicone implants will soon become a thing of the past, antiquated, antique – archaic, even, I must stress that my sole intention is a soul-felt intention solely to help women.'

'Your sole intention is to help yourself to women's . . . '

'Oh ye of little faith, Miss Hocks!'

'Talking of faith, that nun from the Our Lady of the Wretched nunnery will be here soon.'

'Ah, Sister Elizabeth. The poor child came to me out of desperation.'

'She came to you because she'd seen your advert.'

'Of course she didn't. The advert I placed in *Church Weekly* offering free hands-on spiritual healing to teenage girls had nothing to do with it. Her faith failing, her belief in God waning, she came unto me as a last resort before offering her naked body as a sacrifice to Satan.'

'She's mad!'

'We're all mad to a greater or lesser degree, Miss Hocks. In fact, I'd go so far as to say that some are madder than others and others madder than some.'

'I couldn't agree more, Professor!'

'Loosely translated, that means that we're all madder than each other.'

'That doesn't make sense.'

'Nothing makes sense, I'm afraid. Anyway, Sister Elizabeth will benefit greatly from alpha-wave engineering. Unlike you, Miss Hocks, she has great faith in me, unshakable faith, undying lust . . . I mean, trust. My machine will increase her devotion to the church, strengthen her belief in God and immeasurably enhance her good work.' *And have her begging me to fuck her wet mouth!*

'How?'

'Well . . . She'll become more . . . Let's get on, we're not here to discuss what nuns get up to in public toilets.'

'I don't want to be your guinea pig.'

'I must warn you that murder has crossed my mind, Miss Hocks.'

'Oh!'

'As my assistant, you'll assist me by assisting me.'

'I want a verbal agreement stating that . . . '

'Of course you don't. Verbal agreements aren't worth the paper they're written on.'

Flicking the switch on the control panel, Professor Snide rubbed his hands together as the machine whirred and streaks of blue light flashed around the dungeon. Wide-eyed,

Miss Hocks bit her lip and stared at her boss. Noticing the evil glint in his eyes, she was sure that she'd fallen into a trap. She should have known better, she reflected as her head began to spin, but it was too late to turn back. Whatever the devious fiend had planned for her, it was too late.

'There!' he grinned, switching the machine off. 'That wasn't too bad, was it?'

'No, no, I suppose not,' she murmured hesitantly as he removed the helmet. 'But I'm not sure . . . '

'Trust me, Miss Hocks. Trust me as you would the Devil . . . er . . . as you would God.'

'I feel . . . I feel sort of peculiar.'

'Interesting. Tell me, how's your libido?'

'My libido? What's that got to do with anything?'

'I omitted to mention that there might be a minute, minuscule, minimal, meagre side effect. To be correct, I should say a major, maximum, massive fucking side effect! Sorry, I . . . '

'What sort of side effect?'

'Er . . . You might feel uncontrollably sexual, horny, really dirty and perverted and beg me to . . . '

'What have you done to me?' she stormed, leaping off the chair.

'Done? I've done nothing, other than record your brain patterns.'

'I . . . I feel like a woman.'

'So do I! Preferably a naked schoolgirlie! You don't happen to know any naked schoolgirlie netball teams, do you?'

'God, I feel like a woman!'

'You *are* a woman.'

'Yes, but . . . '

'Silence, Miss Hocks!'

'Why?'

9

'What's that ringing sound?'

'It's the doorbell.'

'Ah, the bells, the bells. That's probably Sister Elizabeth. If it *is* her, show her into the lavatory . . . the laboratory. If it's not her, then don't show her in.'

'How can I show her in if it's not her?'

'You can't.'

'Then why say don't show her in if it's not her?'

'My mind works in mysterious ways, Miss Hocks.' *As will yours!*

As the young woman staggered up the stone steps, Professor Snide slipped his erect penis out of his trousers and pulled his foreskin back. Examining his swollen purple knob, he grinned. 'You'll soon be up her virginal cunny!' he chuckled wickedly, running his hand up and down his solid veined shaft. 'And when I've finished constructing my machine of all machines, my gamma-ray penis developer, you'll grow to at least fourteen inches long!'

Hearing footsteps and muffled voices approaching, he hurriedly concealed his twitching cock within his trousers. With a nun nearing the lab, this was no time to have a wank, to splatter the stone floor with his spunk. 'Later,' he murmured as Hollie led the young nun down the steps. There again, flashing his cock in front of a nun . . .

'Greetings, Sister Elizabeth,' he smiled, wondering how tight and wet her pussy was. *Do you fuck yourself with church candles?*

'Hallo, Professor Snide,' she replied, her pale face framed by her starched wimple. 'I haven't come too early, have I?'

'You haven't come at all – *yet*!' he chuckled in his devilment.

'I'm sorry?'

'There's no need to apologize.'

'I'm sorry?'

10

'Don't mention it. How's your faith today?'

'Waning terribly,' she replied sullenly.

'Good. Oh come off all ye unfaithful. Er . . . Sit down and we'll begin the treatment, the hands-on spiritual healing. You didn't tell the Mother Superior of your hazardous visit to my humble commode, did you?'

'No, I did as you suggested and said that I was going for a walk in the Forest of the Dead.'

'Wise, most wise. So, no one knows that you're here?'

'No one, only God.'

'I'm pretty sure you won't find Him floating around these parts. Miss Hocks, would you kindly leave me with my patient, please?'

'Yes, of course, Professor.'

'Make some tea for the horny little . . . for the Sister, and I'll call you after I've administered the healing.'

'Milk and sugar?'

'No, a cup of tea, Miss Hocks. Do try and pay attention.'

'Certainly, Professor.'

'Hollie put the kettle on, Hollie put the kettle on, we'll all have tea!'

'Are you feeling all right, Professor?' the perplexed nun asked.

'Er . . . Yes, yes, I'm fine. I have a tendency to display signs of acute clinical insanity during times of great sexual excitement.'

'Sexual excitement?'

'Er . . . I mean . . . It's nothing to worry about.'

Placing the helmet on the nun's head, Professor Snide pondered on Hollie. She'd not grabbed his crotch as he'd expected her to after the treatment. Disappointingly, she'd not changed at all! The nun might be more susceptible to the male brain patterns, he mused in his evilness, standing by the control panel and flicking the switch. These were early days, he concluded as the machine whirred and the lights flashed. There were bound to be teething problems, problems with sinking his teeth into Hollie's firm buttocks.

'Are you all right?' he asked Sister Elizabeth as she moved uneasily on the chair. *Would you care to suck my cock?*

'Yes, I think so,' she smiled nervously. 'Why do I have to wear a hat with wires coming out of it?'

'It's . . . it's part of the healing process. Have faith, Sister.'

'Will it be long?'

'About fourteen inches! Er . . . It's done!' he grinned, flicking the switch. 'God's work is done.' *The work of the Devil!* 'How do you feel about your religion? Has your resolve been strengthened by the spiritual healing?'

'I feel the same as before.'

'No change at all?'

'None.'

'Fuck it! Er . . . Please, excuse my obscene language – it's most unlike me to swear. It may take a while for the healing to have an effect,' he enlightened the naive woman as he removed the helmet. 'You'll probably find that you'll see God in the form of another person.'

'What do you mean?'

'You might see me as God's gift to . . . As I was made in the image of Satan . . . the image of God, you'll probably worship me as you do God.'

'Why would I do that?'

'Inexplicably, we all do inexplicable things at times, Sister. I blame religion.'

'Do you?'

'But of course. There's nothing like religion to spark off a few bloody wars and cause countless deaths and rape and pillage and looting and . . . '

'You shouldn't blame religion for . . . '

'Sit on the couch over there and Miss Hocks will bring you

a nice cup of milk and sugar. There's no charge, I always give my victims a drink – it's part of my impeccable service.'

Standing before the woman as she sat on the couch, the Professor projected his hips, displaying the bulging crotch of his trousers to the young nun. Scratching his head as he realized that she wasn't responding, he called for Hollie to bring the tea in. Something had gone very wrong, he concluded as the girl carried a tray into the laboratory. The females should be fighting over his cock by now, both desperate to suck his swollen knob and drink his sperm. *Back to the bloody drawing board!*

'The assistant will pour you a nice cup of tea,' he said, sure that some sort of change must have occurred within the women's brains.

'I'm not the assistant!' Hollie returned peevishly as she placed the tray on the bench.

'Of course you are.'

'I'm *your* assistant.'

'That's what I said, Miss Hocks. Please, don't try to complicate simple issues.'

'You said *the* assistant.'

'That's right, you're the assistant. Have you suffered a prolapsed brain?'

'No!'

'Then, pull your knickers . . . Pull yourself together.'

'I'm not an object.'

'Yes, you are.' *An object of carnal desire.*

'I'm a human being.'

'Define an object, Miss Hocks.'

'What?'

'If my pornographic mammary serves me incorrectly, an object is defined in the dictionary as a material thing that can be seen or touched. I can see and touch you, so . . . '

'You're not going to touch me!'

13

I'll fuck you in a minute! 'I was speaking metabollockally, Miss Hocks. This is getting us nowhere, the definition and etymology of certain words contained within the English language is not our concern. Please, sit beside Sister Elizabeth and calm yourself.'

'I'd like to fuck your wet cunt,' Hollie said unashamedly, turning to the nun as she sat down.

'And *I'd* like to fuck *your* wet cunt!' the sister grinned, provocatively licking her succulent lips.

'You can't fuck each other!' Professor Snide gasped. 'Good grief, you're both women!'

'A woman is quite capable of having herself fucked, Professor!' Hollie returned firmly.

'Yes, but only by a man.'

'I *am* a man,' the nun said.

'So am I,' Hollie rejoined.

'But you're both . . . '

His words tailing off as he realized what had happened, Professor Snide headed for his office. The women thought like he did, like a male, craving the female form, the girlie sex crack. 'Shit!' he murmured, sitting at his desk and swigging from a bottle of scotch. 'Shit and fuck!' Rubbing his chin, he pondered on the situation. They weren't lesbians per se, they were men in women's bodies. *What a cock-up. What a cunt-up!*

Holding his head, he realized that he should have had the insight to know what would happen. Male brain patterns induced into a female brain . . . 'I could be arrested for manufacturing lesbians,' he breathed, recalling an unfortunate incident involving the police and two young girls from the village. 'Locked up for creating female homosexuals. No, male lesbians . . . Fuck!'

There was no turning back, he mused, swigging from the bottle again. Hollie's brain patterns had been replaced with

his, hers were forever lost. And the poor unsuspecting nun
. . . *Fuck the nun!* 'Now there's a thought!' Grabbing the
phone, he rang his friend and confidant, Professor Spasm.

'Spaz, it's Snide,' he said as the Professor answered.

'Sexton, how are you?'

'Severely fucked.'

'Is that a Freudian petticoat, or have you had sexual
intercourse with another man?'

'What the hell are you talking about?'

'Have you had your arse knobbed by a man's knob?'

'No, no . . . I've transformed two women . . . It doesn't
matter what I've done, I need your help.'

'Anything, as long as it's not an arse-knobbing you're
after.'

'Of course I don't want a bloody arse-knobbing! What are
you, some kind of sexual deviant?'

'Of course!'

'I'm pleased to hear it. Do you know any nymphomaniacs?'

'Not off the wrist . . . I mean, offhand.'

'Fuck.'

'Are you saying that you want a fuck or that you've been
fucked?'

'I haven't been fucked, I do want a fuck, and I'm fucked.'

'Fuck me!'

'Certainly not. Do you know any nymphos?'

'There's our au pair, she's got huge tits and she's pretty
randy.'

'Excellent! Send her over to my lab.'

'Why?'

'I need her brain.'

'You can't take her brain, Sexton! How will she survive
without a brain? What devious and devilish plans do you
have for my young and not so innocent au pair?'

'I'm not going to remove her brain, you fool!'

'I could understand it if you needed her fanny, but her *brain*? You're not going to stick your cock in her ear and fuck her brain, are you?'

'Don't be ridiculous! Just send her over.'

'OK, I'll order her to repair to your dungeon forthwith.'

'Great!'

'With or without cunny-juiced wet knickers?'

'Without, preferably. I'll talk to you later, Spaz, much later – years later. On second thoughts, I might never talk to you again.'

'I'll look forward to that, Sexton.'

Banging the phone down, Professor Snide returned to the lab to discover the nun kneeling on the floor between Hollie's parted thighs, licking the girl's delicious vaginal crack. Gasping, her eyes closed as she reclined on the couch, Hollie was oblivious to the Professor as he gazed at the lesbian licking. This proved one thing, he reflected happily – although he'd made a cock-up, the machine certainly worked!

Watching the fanny-fingering and clit-sucking, Professor Snide pulled his solid penis out of his trousers and began wanking. Breathing heavily as his organ throbbed and twitched, he wondered whether, at long last, the time had come to shove his cock up Hollie's young cunt and sperm her cervix. But no, a man wouldn't want his cunt fucked by another man, he concluded. *What the hell am I thinking? She's a bloody woman!*

'Professor Snide!' a male voice echoed from somewhere above the dungeon.

'Fuck! Er . . . Coming!' he replied, slipping his cock into his trousers and dashing up the stone steps. *There's no peace for the perverted!*

'Professor Snide, I presume,' a uniformed police officer said as Snide walked along the corridor.

'Do you?'

'Do I what?'

'Presume.'

'Er . . . Yes, I presume that you're Professor Snide.'

'Intriguing.'

'*Are* you Professor Snide?'

'Without being presumptuous, presumably, your presumption is correct.'

'Yes, right. I'm DI Peel, I'm here in connection with . . . '

'That rings a bell!' the Professor chuckled.

'Pardon?'

'Peel, ring – as in rings a bell. Sorry, just my little joke.'

'Very droll, Professor. I'm here in connection with the big bad wolf.'

'The big bad . . . '

'I mean, a series of crimes.'

'Crimes of a criminal nature?'

'A series of crimes of a most serious criminal nature, Professor.'

'Er . . . There are no missing nuns here, if that's what you're looking for.'

'Missing nuns?'

'And I was nowhere near the public toilets yesterday.'

'No, no . . . It's been brought to my attention that you live here. Do you deny that?'

'No, definitely, emphatically and categorically not.'

'You don't live here?'

'Yes, in the west wing. The wing to the west, although it faces east – to be more accurate, east-west. I used to live in the north wing but I had to move out because of the south wind. I tried the east wing but when the wind was coming from the south-east, I had to . . . '

'Yes, all right, Professor. Have you heard or seen anything suspicious of late?'

17

'Apart from the headless lady who wanders around the castle in the dark of the night seeking revenge for the loss of her clitoris, no, I haven't.'

'The headless lady . . . Professor Snide, I have to tell you that there's a ruthless thief on the loose in this area.'

'My God, you mean to say that an employee of the Inland Revenue has escaped?'

'No, no! A ruthless thief has escaped from the prison on the wild and windy moor. We're dealing with espionage, Professor Snide.'

'Good grief, whatever next?'

'I have no idea, I'm not psychic.'

'Thank God for that. Not that I've anything to hide, of course.'

'Yes, quite. He – or she – steals company secrets, plans and drawings.'

'He or she?'

'Due to a phenomenal phenomenon, the gender of the escapee was never determined.'

'How odd.'

'Knowing that you carry out some sort of devilish and highly illegal research work here, I thought it best to bring the matter to your immediate attention immediately.'

'It's a shame you couldn't have brought the matter to my immediate attention earlier. Anyway, thank you for letting me know. I'll keep my flies open . . . my eyes open.'

'Give me a call should you suspect anything untoward, Professor.'

'I will. And thank you once again.'

'I'll see myself out.'

'Er . . . How did you see yourself in?'

'Your butler, he directed me to your laboratory.'

'Ah, Lucifer.'

'That's an unusual name for a butler.'

'He's an unusual butler.'

'Obviously! Good day, Professor.'

As the officer left, Snide rubbed his chin. *A thief on the loose?* he pondered. Why bother to go all the way up to the castle to say that a thief had escaped from prison? There was more to the Inspector's visit than met the eye, he concluded. What was the real nature of DI Peel's untimely, uninvited and unwelcome visit? There hadn't been any teenage girls missing from the village for a while, not since the ill-fated incident behind the reference shelves in the library involving . . .

'What the hell . . . ' he gasped as the nun flew along the narrow corridor in a state of disarray, crashing through the oak door leading to the castle above. 'Sister, come back!' Dashing into the lab, discovering Hollie flush-faced and looking extremely guilty, he frowned and scratched his head. Something was afoot, he mused – skulduggery, even!

'Why did Sister Elizabeth flee the castle in a state of disarray?' he asked.

'I . . . I suggested something terribly immoral concerning her bottom-hole and the broom handle, and she fled in a state of disarray.'

'Something terribly immoral, Miss Hocks?'

'I can't bring myself to talk about it. I behaved in a most uncharacteristic manner.'

'It's uncharacteristically unlike you to behave in an uncharacteristic manner, Miss Hocks.'

'I'm sorry, it won't happen again.'

'If it does, I have to warn you that your buttocks will be severely whipped.' *And your cunt severely spermed.*

'Yes, Professor.'

'Now, where were we?'

'I don't know.'

'Ah, the police officer.'

'Where?'

'He's gone, Miss Hocks.'

'Who has?'

'The police . . . Take a grip on yourself, woman. You're displaying acute signs of clinical insanity.'

'I'm sorry, Professor – I'm still feeling somewhat peculiar. What did the police want?'

You're supposed to be feeling somewhat randy. 'I've been talking to a police officer about the Inland Revenue. Allegedly, a thief . . . Ah, you must be the au pair!' he smiled, turning as a pretty teenage girl appeared in the doorway and trotted down the steps. *My next victim!*

'Yes, I am she. My name is Helga,' she replied. 'My master is telling me that you are wanting me to come.'

'Christ, yes! Er . . . I mean . . . Miss Hocks, will you leave me alone with this young tart . . . young lady for a while, please?'

'I'd rather *you* left *me* alone with her!' Hollie said huskily, her eyes transfixed on the ravishing beauty's deep cleavage.

'Miss Hocks, please restrain yourself! As it is, there's a ruthless thieving Inland Revenue employee on the loose, and espionage is rife. What with uncharacteristic behaviour, hermaphrodite thieves wandering the wild and windy moor, and nuns fleeing in states of disarray – I don't know what things are coming to!'

'Sorry, Professor. I . . . I couldn't help myself.'

Chuckling as Hollie left the lab, Professor Snide turned to face the pretty au pair. The job in hand was simplicity itself, he mused. Record the girl's brain patterns, induce them into Hollie's brain, and voila – the perfect female sex machine! As for the nun . . . *Fuck the nun!* Should any dreadful and highly illegal incidents arise from the nun's weird sexual cravings, he'd deny all knowledge of the woman. Denial was better than admission, he ruminated, recalling an incident behind the bike sheds at the approved school he'd attended. *It always pays to lie.*

'Now, Helga, what I want you to do is sit on my . . . Sit on this chair,' he instructed his gullible victim.

'My master is telling me that you are needing my brain,' she said as she obediently sat down. 'I am needing my brain, you cannot be needing it also as well.'

I'm needing your cunt! 'No, I don't want your brain, Helga – I have one of my own, thank you. All I want to do is record your brain patterns. I'll just slip this helmet onto your pretty head, like this, and we're ready. Old Spaz reckons . . . I mean, Professor Spasm tells me that you're randy, is that right?'

'Randy? What is randy?'

'Well, sexual.'

'Ah, sex! Yes, I am very sex!'

'Good, good!' *I'll soon have your knickers off and my tongue up your wet cunt!* 'Now, this won't take a minute.'

Flicking the switch to activate the helmet, Professor Snide decided to keep the little beauty prisoner in the castle for a few days in order to have his wicked way with her. She was in her late teens so she'd be tight, hot and wet, he mused as the machine whirred. As well as his cock, it was high time his King Dong vibrator saw the light of day – and the dark of a vaginal canal!

'Have you ever been thrown to the lions?' he asked, flicking the switch off and removing the helmet.

'Thrown to the lions?' she echoed, shaking her long blonde hair loose.

'It's an old English custom. What do you know of medieval English history?'

'I am knowing nothing of evil history.'

'You've not read about the rack?'

'What is this rack?'

'You'll see, Helga – you'll see. Follow me and I'll show you to the tearoom.'

Ushering the girl into the torture chamber, Professor Snide closed and locked the huge oak door, imprisoning the distressed young maiden. Ignoring her cries, he rubbed his hands together gleefully, chuckling wickedly as Hollie appeared in the doorway and asked what the commotion was about.

'She wanted to look around the torture chamber,' he grinned, his wide eyes darting between the locked door and Hollie. 'Sadly, the door closed behind her and seems to have locked itself.'

'We must release her!' Hollie cried, trotting down the steps.

We must fuck her! 'All in good time, Miss Hocks – all in good time. Procrastination is a virtue, remember that.'

'But . . . '

'There are no "buts". Due to your inexplicably inexplicable behaviour with Sister Elizabeth, you leave me no choice other than to administer my treatment again. Please remove your knickers and sit . . . I mean, please be seated.'

'I don't want . . . '

'Miss Hocks, I have to warn you that the rack hasn't been used for centuries. Well, for a few days. How tall are you?'

'Five eight.'

'Unless you wish to be six eight, I suggest you do as I ask without further delay.'

'But you said that procrastination is a virtue. That's why I was procrastinating.'

'You'll be masturbating by the time I've . . . Just sit down, Miss Hocks.'

'Yes, Professor.'

Inducing Helga's alpha-wave patterns into Hollie's brain, Professor Snide hoped that, at long last, he'd be able to slip his penis deep into her virginal pussy hole and fuck her

22

rotten. Three long years of planning, scheming, wanking, designing and building his machine . . . He couldn't wait much longer for the wet welcoming heat of her tight cunt!

Twiddling the controls as his heavy balls rolled, he eyed his assistant shrewdly. She'd obviously not yet realized what his machine was really for, but she'd soon find out. And she'd soon discover what her juicy cunt was for – and her tight bottom-hole and her succulent nipples and her mouth and her . . .

'All done,' he smiled, flicking the switch and removing the helmet from the dazed girl's head. 'How do you feel?' *Are you desperate for my cock?*

'I will be feeling strange inside,' Hollie replied with Helga's accent. 'Why do I not properly speak? What are you done with my mouth?'

'Don't worry about your mouth, it's your fanny I'm interested in! I mean . . . Tell me, do you feel sexy?'

'Ah, sex! Yes, I feel very sex!'

'So far so good,' Snide murmured, eyeing the swell of the girl's breasts billowing her tight blouse. 'Would you like me to fuck you?'

'I am lesbian!' she cried.

'You are *what*?'

'I am lesbian!'

'My God, Helga's a bloody lesbian!'

'May I be licking her cunny?'

'No, you may bloody not! You'll be thrown to the lions for your wicked lesbianism!' he yelled, dragging her across the lab and bundling her into the torture chamber. 'How the hell can I create the perfect female sexpot when I'm surrounded by bloody dykes!' *Back to the bloody drawing board!*

23

Chapter Two

Professor Snide's desire for perverted sex with a nympho-maniac was increasing dangerously. *Failure after bloody failure!* he cursed inwardly as he paced the laboratory floor. There was only one thing for it: he would have to venture into the village and nab a horny teenage girl, preferably an ignorant farmworker's ignorant sex-starved daughter.

As he walked down the steep cobble path and approached the village, several windows slammed shut and women gathered their children, ushering them into the small terraced cottages. Stopping as he noticed a teenage girl sitting on a wall with her legs apart, the tight crotch of her red panties bulging with her youthful sex lips, he flashed her a smile. Her long blonde hair cascading over her pointed breasts, her succulent lips pouting, she grinned salaciously at the Professor.

'You're Doctor Sex from that castle up there, ain't you?' she asked in her country-bumpkin accent.

'Indeed I am, Miss,' he replied, his cock twitching, his balls rolling. 'Tell me, what are your plans for today?' *Masturbation with a cucumber?*

'I ain't got no plans.'

I have! 'You're young, fresh, ripe, curvaceous in youth – ideally suited for my . . . I have a great cervical affection for young village girlies.'

'Cervical affection?'

'And a great mammary teat affection. How would you like to see my cock? I mean, my castle?'

'Me dad says I ain't to go nowhere near the castle.'

'Your father sounds like a wise man. But I'm sure he'd be only too delighted to have his delectable young daughter shown around the castle.'

'Me dad says that 'e'll fuckin' well kill me if I goes any-where near the fuckin' place.'

'He's obviously a man of many words, an educated man. Oh well, it's your loss, my horny little beauty – not mine.'

Walking on, Professor Snide stopped outside the village stores and post office, wondering whether to place a card in the window advertising free tours around the castle dungeon for horny young girls. Pondering on the idea as he entered the shop, he pretended to look at the souvenirs and gifts arranged on the shelves as two middle-aged women began whispering about him.

'That's that Frankenstein man!' one said excitedly.

'Doctor Sex, from the castle!'

'What's 'e doin' down 'ere in the village?'

'Looking for victims, I shouldn't wonder. You know, they never did find Mrs Gallbladder's pussy.'

'I reckon 'e took the poor thing. Cut it up, more than likely.'

'Is 'e a vivisexualist?'

'Yes, 'e must be. My Dennis reckons that 'e keeps young girls in 'is dungeon.'

'Really?'

'That's what my Dennis says, and 'e knows what 'e's talkin' 'bout – 'e knows lots 'bout young girls, does my Dennis.'

'Ladies,' Professor Snide grinned, turning to face the women. 'You don't know the half of it. I don't just keep young girls in my dungeon, I strip them naked and stretch them on the rack.'

'Oh, you evil man!' they shrieked in unison as they fled the shop.

'And then I eat their naughty bits for supper!'

'Professor Snide!' the fat Postmistress snapped from behind the counter. 'If you wish to purchase something, then do so, but please refrain from frightening my customers away.'

'The senile old bats asked for it.'

'That's as maybe, but you should learn to turn the other cheek.'

'With your ugly face, I'm surprised *you* don't frighten the customers away.'

'How *dare* you speak to me like that!'

'You should learn to turn the other cheek.'

'Er . . . yes. As you're here, you can take this. It's a telegram from London.'

'Oh, thank you. What does it say?'

'It's about your castle being a Grade One listed building and . . . I mean, I have no idea what it says. I don't read other people's telegrams.'

'Tell me, Postmistress – do you fuck?'

'Do I . . . Get out! Get out!'

Chuckling as he left the shop, Snide read the telegram as he ambled along the street. 'Professor Snide, stop. I have it from a reliable source that your Grade One listed castle is to be returned to the state, stop. The thieving fascist bastards are out to get you, stop. Your old friend, stop. The Purple Baron.'

Screwing the telegram up, the Professor walked along the cobble path in the direction of the castle. 'What dastardly deed is the government planning against me?' he breathed as he passed the young girl sitting on the wall. Stopping, he turned and gazed at her pretty face, her pouting lips. Lowering his eyes, he focused on her bulging panties as she deliberately parted her legs further.

'You shouldn't sit like that,' he smiled, his penis stiffening as he imagined pulling her panties to one side and tonguing

27

her young sex crack, lapping up her flowing juices of lust. 'There are fiendish sexual perverts roaming these parts.'

'I like sittin' like this,' she replied, provocatively licking her luscious lips.

'How old are you?'

'Seventeen.'

'Ah, seventeen! The sweet innocence of youth.'

'I ain't innocent.'

'Aren't you?'

'Course not. Your castle . . . You'll show me round?'

'But of course, my young beauty! Follow me and I'll show you far more than my castle. What's your name?'

'Clarissa.'

'Step this way, Clarissa.' *Like a lamb to the slaughter!*

'Me dad mustn't find out. If 'e does, when 'e sees me, 'e'll go mad.'

'I doubt that he'll ever see you again! What I mean is . . . Don't worry, my child, you'll be safe in my hands – believe me.'

Slipping off the wall, the girl followed the Professor up the hill to the foreboding castle. There was no way *she* was a lesbian, he mused, imagining her naked in a haystack with a farmboy's cock thrusting in and out of her tight cunt. An ideal candidate for the alpha-wave machine, he'd induce her alpha-wave patterns into Hollie's brain and create the perfect female sexpot. The horny dumb blonde was heaven-sent!

Leading Clarissa into the castle, the Professor was met by the tall, stooping frame of his butler. The man's beady eyes darting this way and that, Snide gazed at him with suspicion, wondering whether he'd been down to the dungeon and interfered with the prisoners. Lucifer knew the rules about interfering with young girls in the dungeon, and the punishment should he break them – non-surgical removal of his bollocks.

'I detect trouble,' the Professor said pensively. 'Have you been drinking again?'

'Only a little, sir. Just two bottles of vodka.'

'You really must stop getting pissed, Lucifer. What's happened during my absence?'

'Sir, there's been an intoxification . . . a communication,' Lucifer slurred, shielding his eyes from the shafts of sunlight streaming into the castle as he closed the doors.

'A communication? Are you saying that someone's contacted us from beyond the grave?'

'A mysterious gentleman calling himself the Prince of Darkness telephoned.'

'Ah, that'll be the Purple Baron. What did he say?'

'He's coming down from London on the next train. It seems that he has important news concerning the castle.'

'Despite your drunken state, from what you've told me I deduce that the Purple Baron is coming down from London on the next train bearing important news concerning the castle.'

'An amazing deduction, Professor.'

'I'm an amazing man.'

'Your powers of deduction leave me stunned.'

'My powers of seduction are pretty good, too. Right, I have work to do.'

'Er . . . Professor, may I ask whether you'd mind me going out again tonight?'

'Where to?'

'The village graveyard, sir.'

'Ah, the village graveyard. Of course, Lucifer – of course!'

'Thank you. I'll be back before sunup.'

'For your sake, I hope you are.'

'By the way, I've not seen Miss Hocks for some time.'

'No, no, she's . . . she's tied up at the moment. That will be all, Lucifer.'

'Yes, sir.'

Leading Clarissa down to the dungeon, the Professor rubbed his hands together as his penis twitched expectantly. This was more than a stroke of luck, he reflected, taking the girl's arm as they walked down the steps to the laboratory. Seventeen years old, tight, hot, juicy, wet . . . She really was heaven-sent – or hell-sent!

Deciding to determine her level of horniness before recording her brain patterns, he led her into the rack chamber. Her short skirt riding up her shapely thighs as she leaned over the awesome-looking rack and examined the chains and pulleys, her tight knickers following the contours of her rounded buttocks, clearly outlining her anal crease, he cast his eyes over her curvaceous young thighs and grinned.

'Tell me, Clarissa, what do you think of my dungeon?'

'It's creepy. Are you really mad, like what they say in the village?'

'Totally mad, completely and utterly insane!' he chuckled. 'What else do they say about me down in the village?'

'They reckon you're a sex pervert.'

'Their reckoning is most accurate.'

'What's that bangin' noise?'

'That's my assistant. She's locked in the . . . she's working in the torture chamber.'

'I thought you was gonna show me round your castle?'

'I will, Clarissa – I will. But first, I want to show you how the rack works. Climb onto the wooden frame and lie on your back.'

'You ain't gonna do nothin' to me, are you?' she asked, her panties disappearing up her bottom crack as she clambered onto the rack.

'No, I ain't gonna do nothin' to you.' *Apart from tongue your sweet cunt hole!* 'That's it, lie on your back and I'll fix the chains to your ankles and wrists. You'll enjoy this.'

Eyeing the girl's tight skirt outlining the slight swell of her sex mound as he chained her wrists and ankles, the sex-crazed Professor could barely contain himself. His cock solid within his trousers, his heavy balls full, he cranked the iron handle, stretching her arms and legs, spreadeagling her young body. Her mounds and crevices vulnerable to his every perverted whim, he grinned wickedly as she struggled and begged to be released.

'All in good time, Clarissa – all in good time. I'm going to pull your knickers down and have a look at your sweet pussy crack.'

'No! You ain't gonna . . . '

'I wouldn't want to be forced to turn the handle and stretch you until your vaginal canal is two feet long. Just allow me to look at your sweet cunny slit, and then I'll release you.'

'But . . . '

'I have to warn you that there's something very wrong with me, Clarissa,' he murmured mysteriously.

'What?'

'I have a peculiar obsession with teenage girls' hot, wet pussies. I love them!' he chuckled. 'God, how I love eating pussy and drinking cunny milk! On second and third thoughts, there's something very *right* with me.'

Lifting the protesting girl's skirt up over her stomach, he tugged her red panties down her firm thighs and gazed longingly at her youthful sex slit. Her sparse blonde pubes springing to life, her pink inner petals unfurling between her fleshy outer lips as she wriggled and squirmed on the rack, he leaned over her tethered body and kissed her swollen outer labia.

'Mmm, you smell nice,' he murmured, pushing his tongue out and licking her moist, pink inner lips. 'And you taste wonderful!'

'Stop it!' she cried as he parted her swollen sex hillocks,

31

exposing her ripening clitoris. 'You mustn't look at me fanny!'

'I must! I have never seen such beauty! And you're so wet!'

'I'll tell me dad!'

'Of course you won't. Besides, he's not here.'

'When I get 'ome, I'll tell 'im!'

'When you get home? Who said you were going home, Clarissa?'

Tearing her flimsy panties in half, he tossed the garment to the floor, laughing uncontrollably as his perverted male desires got the better of him. Whipping his solid penis out of his trousers in his sexual frenzy, he climbed onto the rack and positioned himself between the girl's splayed thighs. Pressing his purple knob between her warm love lips, he drove his shaft deep into her tight sex hole, gasping as her wet inner flesh gripped his organ like a velvet-jawed vice.

'God, you've got a tight cunt!' he breathed.

'And you ain't 'alf got a big cock!'

'All the better to fuck you with, as the well-hung wolf said to Granny Smith. I reckon that Little Red Riding Hood fucked rotten, don't you?' he asked, wondering what the Inspector had meant when he'd mentioned the big bad wolf.

'You're weird!'

'Indeed, I am. Ah, ah! How sweet your cunt! Tell me, Clarissa, have you ever been fucked before?'

'Loads of times. But I don't want *you* fuckin' me!'

'But I *am* fucking you, my girl. I'm going to fuck your sweet cunt and spunk up you.'

'No!'

'Yes!'

Ramming his glistening shaft in and out of Clarissa's tightening sex sheath, his swinging balls slapping her tensed buttocks, he looked down at his pistoning solid cock. The girl's love lips spread wide to accommodate his massive penis, her swollen clitoris exposed, the beautiful sight sent a shudder through his body, a tremor through his heavy balls. Impaling her completely on his granite-hard cock, he ground his pubic bone against hers, his knob massaging her young cervix as she whimpered and writhed in her sexual ecstasy. Unable to hold back, his sperm suddenly gushing, jetting from his pulsating plum, he repeatedly withdrew his glans and drove into her spasming cunt, gasping as the girl reached her own mind-blowing climax.

'You beautiful little tart!' he cried, battering her hot cervix with his purple-headed warrior. 'Christ, you dirty little sex-pot!'

'Oh, oh, me cunt!' she gasped as he repeatedly thrust his cock deep into her spasming vaginal canal. 'Oh, me lovely cunt!'

'You'll have a bloody good bottom-thrashing after I've fucked you!'

'No!'

'Yes!'

His balls draining as his jackhammering cock squelched within her drenched cuntal duct, he finally stilled his trembling body, breathing deeply in the aftermath of his crude fucking. With Clarissa's brain patterns, Hollie would open her legs and beg him to screw her, there was no doubt about it! But, even though he'd have Hollie to fuck, he'd hang on to Clarissa for a few days – or a few years!

'Professor Snide!' Lucifer called from above. 'Professor, there's a policeman here about a missing girl!'

'Fuck and shit!' Snide cursed, pulling his cunny-juiced cock out of the girl's spasming vaginal sheath and leaping off the rack. 'Er . . . Tell him that I'm out on important business!'

Zipping his trousers as he left the rack chamber, the Professor leaped up the steps and locked the door to the dungeon. Wondering what to do as he descended the steps, he scratched his head and rubbed his chin. What with Clarissa, Hollie and the au pair all taken prisoner, he knew that he'd gone over the top. And where the hell had the nun got to? *Fuck the nun!*

'He won't go away!' Lucifer called, tapping urgently on the door. 'He says that he knows you're down here with the girl!'

'Fuck and shit! Tell him that I'm dead! Better still, tell him to shag off!'

'I can't do that, sir! I'll be arrested for gross misuse of the English language.'

'Think of something, Lucifer – use what's left of your brain and bloody well think of something!'

After spending two hours in hiding, Professor Snide unlocked the dungeon door and ventured cautiously upstairs to the banqueting hall. The police officer had gone, but the only way to ensure that he wouldn't return was to send Clarissa home. 'What a tragic waste of a fine teenage fanny! Of all the rotten luck!' he breathed, pondering on Clarissa's tight, hot, wet cunt. 'Fuck and double fuck!'

'Ah, there you are, Lucifer!' he growled as the man materialized in the doorway. 'Why are you staggering? Are you drunk again?'

'Only a little, sir.'

'Only a little? Look at the state of you, you're completely pissed.'

'Yes, sir. I do apologize.'

'Don't let it happen again, and don't get pissed either – and you can lay off the drink, too. Did the police officer leave or did you murder him to death?'

'He left, sir.'

'Fucking bollocks! I do wish you'd show a little initiative, Lucifer. You should have thrown him to the lions.'

'We don't have any lions, sir.'

'How observant of you. Listen, I have a minor problem – to be exact, a fucking major problem. In the dungeon, there are three females – Miss Hocks, a well-spermed girl from the village, and an au pair from a far-off land.'

'Really, sir?'

'Yes, really. I took it upon myself to stretch the village girl on the rack, rip her knickers off and fuck her rotten.'

'Would she be the girl reported missing from the village, sir?'

'Yes, and to make matters worse, she's the village girl who's been reported missing from the village. Miss Hocks and the au pair aren't a problem because, firstly, they're not missing from the village, secondly, I haven't fucked them, and thirdly, I have a shrewd idea that they want to fuck each other.'

'Is that possible, sir?'

'Physically, no – mentally, yes. I can only come up with one answer concerning the village girl: I'll have to hook her up to my machine and erase her memory.'

'Remove her breasts?'

'Her memory, you damned fool!'

'Is that wise, sir?'

'It's most unwise, but I can see no other option.'

'This is rather a mess, if you don't mind my saying so.'

'It's a tragic tragedy. If only I hadn't allowed my rampant thirst for perverted sex with young girls to get the better of me . . . It's no good looking back, what's done is done. The girl's been stretched, her knickers torn asunder and her cunt well and truly fucked and spunked.'

'The police officer said that he'd be back later, sir.'

'Shit! I blame *you* for this, Lucifer.'

'*Me?*'

'You should have murdered him, or killed him – or both.

However, all is not lost. When he returns, lock him in the keep.'

'Not the *keep*, sir!'

'Yes, the keep.'

'Satan, have mercy on us!'

'Just do it, Lucifer. And stop talking bollocks. Satan have mercy on us, indeed. Right, I have things to attend, namely, the village girl's wet cunt. What's that ringing sound?'

'The telephone, sir.'

'Is it? Ah, yes. I'm not stupid, I realized that it was the phone. What do you think I am, senile?'

'No, sir.'

'Where are you going?'

'To answer the phone, sir.'

'Yes, yes . . . Good man, you're efficient in the extreme.'

There was no time to waste on police officers, the Professor mused as Lucifer answered the phone. There was work to be done, the transference of Clarissa's brain patterns to Hollie's brain. Although he'd enjoyed fucking Clarissa, it was Hollie he wanted, her body he had craved for three years. A conquest, a challenge . . .

'Sir, the call is for you,' Lucifer said, holding his hand over the mouthpiece.

'Who is it?'

'DI Peel.'

'Fuck!' he breathed, grabbing the receiver and slapping his butler around the head for not telling Peel that he'd gone out. 'Professor Snide here.'

'Ah, Professor. Does the name Clarissa mean anything to you?'

'Indeed it does, Inspector. It's a girl's name.'

'Yes, but do you know a girl of that name?'

'I know a girl named Hollie. My mother's name was . . . What *was* my mother's name?'

'That wasn't what I asked you, Professor. There's a girl missing from the village. She was seen walking towards your castle with you earlier today.'

'With *you*?'

'No, with *you*.'

'That's what I said, Inspector. If she was walking with you, then how come you don't know where she went?'

'She was seen walking with *you*, Professor. Not me as in me, but you as in you.'

'Me as in you? Oh, you mean, you as in me. Yes, that was my assistant, Miss Hocks. We'd been into the village to buy a jar of Vaseline, several large candles and a length of rubber hose.'

'The witness assured me that the girl was Clarissa.'

'No, it was Miss Hocks.'

'Clarissa.'

'Miss Hocks.'

'This is getting us nowhere, Professor. I intend to come to your castle with a search warrant later today.'

'You don't need a warrant to search the castle, I'll take you on a guided tour. Ten pounds, and I'm losing money.'

'Right, I'm on my way. Goodbye.'

Turning to his butler as he replaced the receiver, Professor Snide pondered on the secret tunnel running through the castle walls. DI Peel would never find the concealed entrance, he mused – Clarissa would be safe in the tunnel. The au pair hadn't been reported missing so she wouldn't present a problem. He'd free her after he'd fucked her, he decided. It was only fair to fuck her as she'd travelled from afar to experience the delights of England, English nobility – or knobility.

'Lucifer, prepare to prepare the secret tunnel in preparation for a prisoner,' Snide grinned.

'Prepare to prepare . . .'

37

'A devious change of plan. We're not sending the police officer to the keep, we're hiding the missing village girl in the secret tunnel.'

'Yes, sir. I'll prepare to make the necessary preparations right away.'

'When the Inspector arrives, he's bound to search the keep. It might be an idea to have a timely haunting by a gruesome ghoul, if you get my meaning.'

'Yes, of course. Leave it to me, Professor.'

'Good. I'll go and get the girl.'

Dashing down to the dungeon, Snide decided to release the au pair and Miss Hocks before dragging the village girl upstairs to the concealed tunnel entrance. Fucking the au pair wasn't a priority after all, he concluded. He could have her sent to the castle at a later date, then stretch her on the rack and fuck her senseless. Unlocking the torture chamber door, he peered inside to discover the two women entwined in lust, their mouths locked in a passionate kiss.

'Er . . . Miss Hocks,' he frowned. 'Would you be kind enough to retrieve your tongue from the au pair's mouth and return to your duties, please?'

'Why are you having locked me in here?' she asked, pushing past the Professor and storming into the lab.

'Because of your uncharacteristic behavioural patterns. It's my unconsidered opinion that you're utterly and completely mentally unbalanced.'

'I am wanting my own voice.'

'Yes, and I am wanting your . . . All in good time, Miss Hocks. Er . . . Helga, you may return to Professor Spasm's residence.'

'I am not wanting to return, I am wanting to stay here with sexy Miss Hollie.'

'Bloody lesbians!'

'I am lesbian!' Hollie cried.

'Me also is lesbian!' Helga rejoined.

'Christ! Two bloody women with the same accent and sexual preferences! Right, I have to take a girl . . . I mean, both piss off upstairs while I . . . while I do something of a criminally criminal nature.'

When the women had gone, the Professor slipped into the rack chamber and gazed at Clarissa's curvaceous body, her parted thighs, the well-spunked blonde down covering her sex mound, her yawning vaginal crack. There was no way he was going to let this little beauty go! But it was Hollie's cunt that again attracted him, that had become an obsession with him – haunted him. Once Hollie had Clarissa's brain patterns . . . Sheer bliss!

'You 'ave to let me go!' Clarissa spat.

'But I haven't sucked your nipples yet,' he grinned.

'You ain't gonna suck nothin'!'

'Clarissa, I have never met such an ungrateful girl as you. I bring you here out of the goodness of my heart and show you my dungeon, allow you to try out my rack, give you the pleasure of a damned good fucking terminating in an orgasm – and you protest when I suggest that I suck your nipples.'

'What's suckin' me tits got to do with showin' me round the bleedin' castle?'

'Everything! You don't seem to appreciate the fact that you've fallen into the hands of a sex fiend, a sexual pervert, a sexual deviant.'

'When me dad comes . . . '

'Your father's orgasms have nothing to do with us, Clarissa. It's not right to discuss other people's orgasms, it's bad form.'

'I mean, when 'e comes 'ere!'

'I certainly don't want your father coming all over my dungeon! Now, that's enough about your father's cock and his masturbatory habits. You're to be holed up.'

'You ain't puttin' nothin' up me 'ole!'

'Not your sex hole, you foolish child! You're to be hidden in the secret tunnel so that the police can't find you.'

Grabbing a pair of scissors and cutting the struggling girl's T-shirt and skirt in two, the Professor went on to snip through her straining bra and free her full breasts. Her elongated nipples surrounded by the chocolate discs of her areolae were extremely inviting, he observed, licking his lips – most inviting and suckable. But, with DI Peel on his way to the castle, there was no time for nipple sucking. Releasing the girl's hands, he grabbed a pair of handcuffs from a hook on the wall and cuffed her wrists.

'You can't fuckin' do this!' she hissed as he removed the chains from her ankles and bound her feet together with rope.

'I've done it,' he smiled, lifting her off the rack, her shredded clothing falling away from her curvaceous young body as he stood her on the floor. 'When the police officer has satisfied himself that you're not here, I'll satisfy myself by buggering your tight bottom-hole.'

'You ain't gonna do nothin' of the bleedin' sort!'

'Your protests are futilely futile, Clarissa. Now, if you'll hop this way.'

Helping the naked girl up the steps, Snide led her through a maze of dank, stone-walled corridors to the keep where Lucifer was waiting in the shadows. A section of the wall drawn back, revealing the entrance to the secret tunnel, the girl was bundled through the hole and ordered to settle on the mattress Lucifer had placed on the floor.

'I don't wanna go in 'ere!' she cried as Lucifer leaned on the wall, pushing it back into place. 'Let me out, you fuckin' bastards!'

'No one will hear her behind two feet of solid stone!' Snide chuckled, rubbing his hands together. 'Right, you go and wait for Peel and I'll have a quick wank. No, on second thoughts, I'll return to the lab. When Peel arrives, he'll discover me working hard and believe that the only thing I have to hide is my cock.'

Things were hotting up, he mused, returning to the lab and sitting at his bench. But girls had gone missing from the village before, it was nothing new. Teenage girls had a habit of disappearing when the Professor was around, but always reappeared a few days later – albeit stripped of their virginity and pubic hairs!

Hearing Lucifer instructing DI Peel to go down to the laboratory, Snide busied himself at his bench. Seeing him working hard to cure the clinically insane, to rid the world of madness, Peel would believe the Professor to be the epitome of innocence – well, not quite. Turning as the police officer entered the dungeon, he noticed suspicion mirrored in the man's beady eyes as he looked around the lab.

'What is it you do down here?' Peel asked, eyeing the alpha-wave machine, the helmet and wires.

Wank, get pissed, smoke dope, and fuck young girls to orgasm. 'I'm working madly like a madman to cure madness,' he replied, rising to his feet. 'Where would you like to begin the search?'

'What's all this, then?' the sleuth murmured, wandering into the rack chamber and picking up the remnants of Clarissa's bra and panties. 'Torn clothing – female clothing, by the look of it.'

'Ah, yes . . . They belong to Miss Hocks, my assistant.'

'Does she normally rip her clothes off and leave them on the floor?'

Sadly, no. 'She . . . she was ravaged by a fiendish monster.'

'A monster?'

'The diabolic thing roams the castle in the dark of the night. Legend has it that it returned from the dead four hundred years ago.'

41

'I find that difficult to believe, Professor.'

'So did Miss Hocks, until the thing ripped her clothes off. He has a rapier.'

'She was raped?'

'No, she managed to escape.'

'This is a rack, isn't it?'

'Yes, it came with the fixtures and fittings. The bloody estate agent tried to charge me extra, the thieving bastard.'

'When was it last used?'

'Earlier to . . . Early in the last century.'

'The wooden planking is creamy-wet and stained. Can you explain that?'

'There's no explanation, it's inexplicable.'

'I see. This work you do . . . What caused you to try to cure madness?'

'I'm a rampant alcoholic. Trying to cure the clinically insane keeps me out of the pub. Does clinical insanity run in your family, Inspector?'

'It's rife. Schizophrenia, paranoia, manic depression, psychotic . . . I'm not here to discuss insanity in my family. Shall we begin the search?'

'Yes, you've seen the rack chamber so if you'll follow me, I'll show you the torture chamber.'

Following the Professor into the other chamber, Peel looked at the chains and handcuffs hanging from the walls, the whips lined up on a shelf. Focusing on a row of hand-carved wooden phalluses, perfect copies of huge erect penises, he scratched his head and frowned. But there was nothing he could say. After all, this was an original torture chamber, there was nothing unusual about the equipment.

'It'll take some time to search the castle,' Peel said, turning to face the Professor. 'I'll leave you to carry on with your work and take a look around.'

'Don't get yourself lost, Inspector. The castle's a big place, and there's the headless lady and the fiendish monster to consider.'

'I very much doubt that I'll discover headless women and monsters. It's the girl I'm hoping to come across.'

'I wouldn't mind coming across her again! I mean, discovering her whereabouts. She's not here, I can tell you that much.'

'We'll see, Professor – we'll see.'

Watching the Inspector climb the stone steps, Snide rubbed his chin. The sleuth would never find Clarissa, but the Professor didn't like the idea of having the man roaming around the castle. There again, when he entered the keep, he'd have the shock of his life if Lucifer had organized the haunting. Never again would Peel dare to venture into the castle!

Spending an hour working on his penis-developing machine, the Professor pulled his cock out, stuck it through the hole in the wooden box and flicked the switch. 'Ooh, ah!' he gasped as the machine sucked on his organ. Turning the control to full power, he grimaced as the vacuum increased, his penis expanding to three times its normal size.

'Gamma ray on!' he chuckled, pushing a button. If the machine worked, he'd be hung like a horse, his cock permanently enlarged. Clarissa would be the first to sample his wares, he mused as his shaft tingled and his knob pulsated. She'd have her teenage cunt stretched to capacity by his magnificent member – and as for her tight rectal duct . . . !

After five minutes, a light flashed and a buzzer sounded, indicating that his penis was ready for inspection. Slipping his cock out of the hole, he gazed at his organ, his face beaming as he switched the machine off. 'My God!' he gasped, stunned by the sheer size of his tool. 'That's bloody incredible!' His purple knob larger than an egg, his veined shaft like a baseball bat, he hurriedly tucked his equipment into his trousers as Peel descended the steps.

'Well,' the Inspector murmured, wandering across the lab. 'There would appear to be no sign of the missing village girl reported missing from the village.'

'Of course there's no sign of her, she's missing,' Snide returned. 'If she was here, she wouldn't be missing, would she?'

'If she was here . . . '

'God, my cock!' Snide gasped, the crotch of his trousers bulging, his zip almost bursting open.

'Your cock?' Peel frowned.

'Er . . . The ballcock in the upstairs toilet needs looking at.'

'Oh, I thought for a minute that you meant . . . The keep, Professor – there's something in there that . . . '

'You didn't dare to venture into the keep?'

'I only looked through the door.'

'My God, you're more of a man than I!'

'There was a . . . I was unable to search the keep as there was a presence, a ghostly presence and eerie howling and blood-curdling screams.'

'That'll be the headless lady, or the fiendish monster – or all three.'

'All *three*? I have to go to the village, Professor. The girl might well have returned home by now.'

'I'm sure she has, Inspector.'

'By the way, I came across two naked women in a bed together.'

Lucky sod! 'Not to worry, they can have a wash later.'

'Er . . . Yes, right. Well, good day, Professor.'

'Good day.'

That was that prying git out of the way, Snide mused, his penis threatening to tear his trousers open as it stiffened in readiness to penetrate Clarissa's tight cunt. The time had come to test his magnificent organ on the girl, to force his weapon up her young vaginal canal and fuck her senseless with his King Dong.

Bounding up the steps, he made his way to the concealed tunnel entrance and was about to slide the stone wall back when Lucifer emerged from the shadows. The butler had a habit of creeping around the castle and materializing in doorways like a ghost. There again, the man was hardly human!

'Sir, the Prince of Darkness telephoned again,' Lucifer intoned, his stooping frame towering above the Professor.

'He telephoned again?'

'Yes, sir. He's at the station.'

'Has he been arrested? Good grief, he really ought to stop wanking in public.'

'He's at the *railway* station, sir. He'll be here shortly.'

'Ah, good! When will he be here?'

'Very soon.'

'As soon as that?'

'If not sooner.'

'If he's any sooner, he'll arrive before he rang from the station.'

'A time warp, sir?'

'Possibly. Right, go and dig a pit and then ring the pet shop and order half a dozen lions.'

'Lions, sir?'

'You know, those four-legged animals with big teeth that growl a lot. It's high time we threw a few people to the lions – bloody Christians!'

'Right away, sir.'

'I'm going to drag the missing village girl down to the dungeon and fuck her bottom. When the Purple Baron arrives, send him down.'

'The death sentence, sir? That's rather a strong punishment for wanking in public.'

'No, send him down to the dungeon! And lay off the bloody vodka!'

'Yes, sir.'

Sliding the stone wall back as Lucifer faded into the shadows, the Professor grabbed Clarissa and dragged her out of the tunnel. She was a rare beauty, he mused, observing her sperm-dripping cuntal crack as he pulled her to her feet. Spinning her round, he gazed longingly at her exquisitely rounded buttocks as she demanded to be released. The time was nearing when he'd have the base of his shaft between her firm bottom globes, he reflected – his knob spunking deep in her hot bowels. *Sheer perversity!*

'I had a word with your father,' he said, leading her in the direction of the dungeon. 'He sold you to me.'

'What? Me dad would never . . . ' she gasped, hopping along beside the Professor, her firm tits bouncing.

'Five pounds: he said you weren't worth any more.'

'Five bleedin' quid? The tight-fisted fuckin' bastard!'

'You belong to me now, my horny little sexpot.'

'You can't buy people!'

'Of course I can. I'm completely insane, so I can do what I like. Right, the first thing I'm going to do is record your brain patterns.'

Dragging the girl down the steps into the lab, Snide sat her on the chair and bound her naked body with rope. Hollie's transformation was nigh! he thought gleefully, placing the helmet on his struggling prisoner's head. Moving to the control panel, he flicked the switch and then slipped into the rack chamber to prepare for the mother fucking of all fuckings.

Taking a huge church candle from a shelf, he decided to open up Clarissa's cunt with the waxen phallus before forcing his massive penis into her tight pussy duct. The candle would arouse her, induce her sex milk to flow and lubricate her

46

vaginal cylinder in readiness for his incredible penile piston.
His heavy balls full, his penis twitching expectantly, he placed
the candle on the rack and kicked the girl's clothes into the
corner of the room.

Preparing the rack for his naked victim, he again pondered
on Hollie Hocks. At last, she'd offer him her tight, wet cunt
and beg him to fuck her. Never again would she shun his lewd
advances: she would rip her knickers off and open her legs
wide as and when he wanted to fuck her. He might even be
able to entice her to leave home and move into the castle as
his live-in sex slave – his live-in dirty, filthy, disgusting,
perverted, horny little tart.

'Shit!' he breathed, dashing into the lab as he remembered
that the machine was still running. Flicking the switch, he
removed the helmet from the dazed girl's head and asked
whether she was all right. Her eyes glazed, she said nothing as
he again asked her whether she was OK.

'Say something, Clarissa!' he yelled, waving his hand in
front of her expressionless face, her staring eyes. 'Fuck, I
seem to have overdone it – she's lost her mind!'

'Who is having lost her mind?' Hollie asked as she wandered into the lab.

'Ah, there you are, Miss Hocks,' he smiled, releasing
Clarissa and helping her to her feet. 'Sit on the chair and
I'll give you your voice back.'

'I am wanting that naked girl. She is lesbian, no?'

'No, she's *not* a bloody lesbian! Right, let's get the helmet
on your head and sort your brain out.'

Inducing Clarissa's alpha waves into Hollie's brain, the
Professor rubbed his chin pensively. He'd have to do something about Clarissa, he mused. He could hardly send her
home as a zombie. There again, if she was now unable to
speak or recall her time at the castle, perhaps it wasn't such a
bad idea! No, it would be best to reinstate her brain patterns

and somehow erase her memory of the illegal events at the castle.

'Can I take this bleedin' thing off me 'ead?' Hollie asked in Clarissa's country-bumpkin accent once the alpha-wave transference was complete.

'Of course, Miss Hocks,' Snide grinned. 'Tell me, would you like me to fuck your tight cunt with my fucking great penis?'

'Course I bleedin' wouldn't! And me name ain't Miss bleedin' 'Ocks, it's Clarissa.'

'Oh dear, I seem to have overdone it again,' he sighed. 'Er, wait there while I take this young girl into the disgustingly perverted sex den . . . I mean, the rack chamber.'

Leading Clarissa through the doorway, the Professor untied the ropes, lifting her naked body onto the rack and chaining her wrists and ankles. She'd be safe there until there was time to reinstate her brain patterns, he mused, his penis stiffening as he focussed on her pinken inner lips protruding invitingly from her gaping sex crack. *God, I need to come!* Wondering where the au pair had got to, he returned to the lab to find Miss Hocks climbing the stone steps.

'Where are you going?' he asked.

'I'm goin' 'ome!' she returned, dashing through the doorway.

'Shit, that's all I need!'

'I want me mum and me dad!'

'Bloody hell, what a cunting fuck-up!' *Back to the bloody drawing board.*

Chapter Three

Having waited an age for Hollie to return, the Professor finally gave up all hope. Slipping into the rack chamber, he gazed longingly at Clarissa's curvaceous naked body. Although he was beset by problems, the time had come to test his magnificent cock.

'Can you hear me?' he asked the zombie-like girl as he slipped his trousers off. 'Oh well, hear me or not, you're going to have your sweet cunt fucked rotten!' he chuckled, grabbing the candle and parting her fleshy pussy lips. Driving the wax shaft deep into her tight cunny sheath, her lower stomach rising as her vaginal cavern bloated, he grinned as his huge organ rose and stood to attention.

His bulbous glans reaching high above his navel, he realized that, if he lowered his head, he could suck himself off. *I might try that later!* Gazing at his huge knob, his sperm slit, he projected his hips, his superb penis pointing skyward as a proud monument to the male species. If he could modify his gamma-ray machine to accommodate a clitoris . . . *Now there's a thought!*

Slipping the dripping candle out of Clarissa's pussy sheath, he turned an iron handle below the rack, watching as the chains clanked and the girl's legs parted further. Her vaginal crack opening invitingly, he eyed her exposed sex hole, the pink flesh surrounding the wet entrance to her lust sheath. Her thighs almost at right angles to her naked body, he leaped onto the rack, his huge weapon swinging from side to side, his ballooning knob hovering over her bared vaginal portal.

'Here it comes!' he cried in his devilment, slipping his solid glans between her splayed inner petals. Grabbing the base of his gigantic cock, he moved forward, watching as his purple plum parted the girl's fleshy sex hillocks. Stretching her vaginal entrance open, his silky-smooth glans drove into the wet heat of her tight cunt. 'God!' he breathed, pushing inch after inch of his shaft into her creamy duct. 'Is she tight or am I fucking big?'

His knob pulsating, Snide forced half the length of his organ into Clarissa's vaginal canal, grimacing as her muscles spasmed, rhythmically crushing his rock-hard shaft. Wondering whether to slip his bollocks into the gamma-ray machine and enlarge them to the size of tennis balls, he withdrew his girlie-wet penis and drove his member into her well-juiced cunt again. Her naked body jolting with each penile thrust, her face remaining expressionless, he quickened his rhythm, fucking her with his jumbo cock.

'What are you having done with the girl?' Helga asked as she entered the rack chamber and gazed in disbelief at the Professor's magnificent cock.

'Ah, there you are. I am having fucked her,' he chuckled.

'You are like horse!'

'And she is like mare. Or she will be, when I've finished with her!'

'Has she deaded?'

'No, she's zombied. Would you like me to fuck *you*, Helga?'

'I am not wanting horse cock up me! Nevertheless, I am lesbian.'

'Yes, so you keep saying. Why don't you suck her tits while I fuck her?'

'I have better idea. I kneel on her head and she lick my cracky.'

Grinning as he watched the au pair slip her wet panties off and climb onto the rack, the Professor knew that the girl's time was near. Lesbian or not, she'd soon have his giant cock up her cunt, his swollen knob spunking her cervix. Holding her fleshy cunny lips wide apart, pressing her exposed pink inner flesh against Clarissa's open mouth, she rocked her hips. Gasping as her clitoris throbbed and swelled, she watched the Professor's cunny-drenched weapon thrusting in and out of the village girl's pussy, his solid shaft glistening with her lust juices.

'I will be coming!' Helga cried, massaging her throbbing clitoris against Clarissa's creamy-wet mouth. 'Oh, I will be coming!'

'And me!' Snide breathed, driving his knob deep into the tethered girl's stretched vaginal sheath. 'God, now!'

His sperm jetting from his massive plum, he rammed his cock into the young girl's cunt with a vengeance as Helga attained her lesbian climax. The old rack creaking, the chains clanking, the room resounding with pussy squelching and cries of orgasm, Snide and Helga rode Clarissa's naked body to their respective sexual heavens.

With a naked zombie as his plaything, the Professor wondered whether it was worth bothering with Hollie. There again, his original quest had been to have his wicked way with the woman, and it would be a shame to have wasted three years developing and building the machine. And DI Peel would be back with his eyes peeled unless Clarissa returned home before long. Hollie would have to be fucked, he decided – at any cost!

His balls draining, the last of his spunk pumping into Clarissa's convulsing cunt, the Professor finally withdrew his glistening organ and clambered off the rack. Helga was still gasping, enjoying orgasm after orgasm, and Snide left her to her crude lesbian ways and staggered into the lab. Looking down at his cunny-wet cock, he again pondered on enlarging his balls. Far too small for such a huge penis, they'd *have* to be enlarged, he decided, managing to push them through the hole in the gamma-ray box.

'God!' he cried as, switching the machine on, his bollocks were sucked into the box. 'Jesus F. Christ!' To the accompaniment of Helga's orgasmic cries of lesbian lust, he pressed the gamma-ray button, grimacing as his testicles swelled. Enduring the pain until the light flashed and the buzzer sounded, he switched the device off and tried to pull his balls out of the box.

'Shit!' he cursed. 'They're too bloody big!' Struggle as he might, he couldn't retrieve his massive bollocks. Opening the lid of the box, managing to force one ball out through the hole, he eased his other ball out of the top of the box and fell back, staggering around the lab with his huge testicles dangling below his awesome, cunny-dripping cock.

'Fuck me!' he gasped, looking down at his equipment. 'I've never seen anything like it!'

'Like what?' a man asked as he descended the steps.

'The Purple Baron!' Snide grinned. 'You've arrived.'

'Most observant, my friend.'

'How the devil are you?'

'From the size of your cock, I'd say not as well as you! What the hell have you done to your tackle?'

'My gamma-ray machine, it's enlarged my cock and balls.'

'You could earn a fortune from such a machine.'

'I intend to!'

'You received my communication, my friend?'

'No, but I received your telegram. What's all this about my castle?' the Professor asked, closing the rack-chamber door as Helga cried out again in the grip of a shuddering multiple orgasm. 'Sorry about that, it's an au pair and a zombie girl

enjoying filthy, perverted, highly illegal lesbian-induced
orgasms.'

'There's no need to apologize for filthy, perverted, highly
illegal lesbian-induced orgasms.'

The Purple Baron perched himself on the edge of the
couch, tossing his black cloak over his shoulder and removing his three-cornered hat as he gazed at Snide's amazing
cock. Taking a cigar from his pocket, he lit a match, reclining
on the couch as he puffed on the cigar.

'The government's out to get your castle,' he said, blowing
smoke high into the air.

'The bastard fucking bastards!' Snide yelled, brushing his
dark hair away from his forehead. 'What a bunch of bastard
fucking bastards!'

'There's more, my friend,' the Baron added mysteriously,
his dark eyes focusing on the Professor. 'Word has it that
they're planning a siege.'

'Fuck me! How do you know this?'

'More to the point, how do they know so much about you?'

'What do they know?'

'Everything, from your sexually deviant ways to your
abduction of young village girls – they know everything.'

'How?'

'There's a mole in your midst.'

'Yes, on my left bollock – I must have it surgically
removed.'

'Not that sort of mole.'

'My God, there's only one person who . . . '

'Exactly, my friend. Young Hollie Hocks is a government
agent.'

'The bitch! The fucking bitch of fucking bitching bitches!'

'She's been radioing information to her contact in Westminster concerning your activities. She has a shortwave
transmitter concealed in her dirty-underwear drawer.'

'How do you know?'

'A shrewd guess. Where is she now?'

'Christ, she's gone . . . No, no, it's all right – she's not herself.'

'Who is she?'

'She has the brainwaves of a village slut. She believes herself to be Clarissa, a seventeen-year-old strumpet with the most beautiful cunt you've ever laid eyes upon. Or shoved your cock up, for that matter.'

'Silence!' the Baron cried.

'Why?'

'I'm thinking.'

Eyeing the Purple Baron, Snide felt a draught around his swinging bollocks and slipped into the rack chamber to retrieve his trousers. He was relieved to have the Baron as a friend, he reflected, watching Helga tongue-fucking Clarissa's cunny hole. They'd met at a seminar in Transylvania for like-minded devilish fiends and had become good friends. Which was just as well because enemies of the Baron seemed to meet with untimely gruesome deaths! *I'm too young to die*, he mused, tugging his trousers up and returning to the lab.

'Are you still thinking?' he asked, buckling his belt as he stood before the cloaked man.

'No, I'm still deep in thought. I've got it! We'll hold the village to ransom.'

'We can't do that, Baron!'

'Why not?'

'We'll rouse the wrath of the evil postmistress. As it is, she despises me.'

'Damn the Post Office! Have you abducted any young girls of late?'

'Yes, there's one in the rack room – as we speak, even.'

'Good, good. Have you fucked her?'

'I've stretched her on the rack, torn her panties asunder, opened her vaginal crack and fucked her rotten.'

'Perfect! If my evil plan is to work, we'll have to shave her pubic hairs.'

'What is your evil plan?'

'We'll send her pubes to her parents with a ransom note. Either the government keeps away from you and the castle, or the girl dies on the rack.'

'That's a bit strong, isn't it?'

'The fascist pigs leave us no choice, my friend.'

'Hobson's choice.'

'No, our choice. I feel somewhat sweaty around my crotch, particularly my scrotum – I'd better have a wash and brush-up after my tedious journey from London.'

'Fucking trains! Right, Lucifer will show you to your quarters.'

'We'll discuss the matter further on my return from the bathroom.'

'We'll also discuss your plan, Baron.'

As the Purple Baron left the lab, Snide rubbed his chin. He reckoned that DI Peel was also a government agent, his story of an escaped ruthless thief being just a ploy to gain entry to the castle. And as for Miss Hocks . . . He couldn't believe that his prudish assistant was working for the fascist pigs. 'Miss Hocks, of all people!' he gasped. Hearing the doorbell, he bounded up the steps and made his way to the castle doors.

'Oi, bastard face!' a man yelled as Lucifer opened the door.

'That's a nice greeting, I must say!' the Professor returned, standing by his butler. 'My face is not a bastard.'

'Where's me fuckin' daughter?'

'From what you tell me, I deduce that she's fucking somewhere.'

'Don't come the clever dick with me, mate!'

'Shall I evict the commoner, sir?' Lucifer asked, staggering backwards and almost falling over.

'Shut it, Frankenstein!'

'I wouldn't talk to my butler like that,' Snide warned the man. 'He has a black belt in karate of the bollocks. And he's very drunk.'

'I don't care what 'e's got.'

'I could remove his balls with one chop, sir.'

'No, it's all right, Lucifer. His mental derangement isn't his fault. I blame his derangement on his deranged mentally deranged mother.'

'Me deranged mother ain't got nothin' to do with this. Where's me bleedin' daughter?'

'I have no idea where Clarissa is.'

'How d'ya know 'er name?'

'Er . . . You told me.'

'No, I never!'

'The police told me.'

'Fuckin' bastards! If I find out that she's been 'ere, I'll rip your fuckin' bollocks off!'

'You'll have a job!'

As the man left, Snide pondered on the whereabouts of Miss Hocks. With Clarissa's brain patterns, she wouldn't go to her own house – she wouldn't know where it was! *Shit, she said she was going home!* But, when she arrived, Clarissa's family would believe Hollie to be clinically insane and send her packing. Hopefully, she'd return to the castle, but the Professor couldn't bet on it. Turning to his butler, he instructed him to go to the village and forcefully drag the woman back to the dungeon.

'But the sun's out, sir,' Lucifer murmured, his face grimacing.

'Dusk is falling, you'll be all right. It's imperative that Miss Hocks is brought back here as soon as possible, if not before or even sooner.'

'I'll go immediately, sir.'

'No, time is of the essence – you must go now.'

'Yes, sir.'

As Lucifer left, the Professor returned to the dungeon. The Baron's plan to shave Clarissa's fanny was good, he mused, wandering into the rack chamber and dragging the au pair off the village girl's naked body. *It might be an idea to shave the au pair, too. Might as well shave every woman in the land!*

'What are you having doing with me?' the struggling girl asked as Snide dragged her into the torture chamber.

'I'm going to look at your cunt, Helga!' he chuckled, holding her arms above her head and cuffing her wrists to the steel rings set in the wall.

'I am not torturing!'

'Of course you're not torturing,' he grinned, ripping her blouse open and lifting her bra clear of her full breasts. 'But *I* will be fucking!'

'No!'

'Yes!'

Her nipples elongating in the cool air of the chamber, her areolae darkening, Helga's breasts were fine specimens, Snide observed – suckable specimens. Tugging her skirt down, he dropped to his knees and gazed longingly at her inflamed and very wet vaginal crack. Her inner petals unfurling, he focused on the globules of opaque liquid clinging to her pink sex folds, his cock solid as he licked his lips. Her cunt was a fine specimen too – kissable, lickable, suckable, fuckable, spunkable . . .

'You cannot be touching me there!' she complained as he parted her swollen pussy lips and gazed at her ripe clitoris.

'But I *am* touching you there, Helga. Not only am I touching you, but I'm going to fuck you.'

'I am lesbian, I am not being fucking!'

'You'll be fucking and that's the end of the matter.'

'But . . . '

'I'll rip your clitty off.'

'Oh!'

Eyeing the girl's open vaginal entrance, the wet flesh surrounding her pink sex hole, the Professor stood up and slipped his erect penis out. The time had come to fuck Helga rotten, he decided, pulling his foreskin back, revealing his bulbous purple glans. Gazing in awe at his heavy balls, his rock-hard shaft, the au pair protested wildly as he positioned his ballooning knob between her swollen pussy lips.

Hearing movements in the lab, Snide told the girl to shut up as he hurriedly concealed his cock within his trousers. *Bollocks! Just as I was about to screw her!* Surely Lucifer hadn't returned already? he pondered, adjusting his solid cock as he left the torture chamber.

'Ah, Baron,' he smiled as the man crossed the lab. 'Are you refreshed after your journey?'

'No, I only had a wash and brush-up. We must remove the abducted girl's pubic hair forthwith, my friend. Do you have any shaving equipment?'

'No, not actually about my person, but you'll find all you need on the bench over there, between the anal speculum and the vaginal syringe,' the Professor replied. 'There's a razor, shaving foam and a flannel.'

'Good, good.'

'Clarissa's on the rack: naked, chained, and ready for you.'

Following the Baron into the rack chamber, Snide watched as he massaged shaving foam into the zombie girl's blonde bush. There was nothing like a schoolgirlie-lookalike pussy, he reflected, recalling an illegal incident on a netball pitch that, on reflection, he thought it best *not* to recall. *Christ, I'm a sad pervert!*

'And now for the razor!' the Baron grinned, dragging the blade over the gentle curve of Clarissa's young mons.

'I see that you're a teenage-fanny-shaving expert,' the Professor commented, watching the girl's pubic curls fall away.

'Yes, I was trained at a Swiss finishing school by a naked lacrosse team.'

'Admirable.'

As the Baron stripped the pubic hairs from Clarissa's fleshy outer lips, Professor Snide adjusted his massive penis. He'd been so close to fucking Helga, he reflected. But there was plenty of time to shaft her pussy and spunk her young cervix after he'd fucked Clarissa's shaved cunt. And when Hollie returned, she'd have her virginal cunny shagged rotten!

Finishing the fanny-shaving, the Baron wiped away the foam and curls with the flannel, revealing the girl's smooth, hairless cunt. 'God, it's beautiful!' Snide gasped, eyeing her pink inner lips protruding invitingly from her naked sex valley. 'What I'm thinking is highly illegal!' His knob throbbing, he knew that he had to slip his cock into her lust hole and loose his spunk before he creamed his trousers. But the Baron had other ideas.

'Before committing any illegal acts, we must separate the pubic curls from the shaving foam,' the Baron said, passing Snide the flannel. 'Strangely, there appears to be a copious amount of spunk and girl come mixed with the foam.'

'As I told you, Baron – I fucked her rotten and spermed her cervix.'

'Ah, yes, of course.'

'Her vaginal muscles must have contracted and squeezed out the products of our orgasms. I'll take the flannel into the lab and separate the pussy hairs.'

Leaving the rack chamber, Snide walked to his bench and dropped the flannel into a beaker of water, chuckling as the hairs floated to the surface. Taking a filter paper, he scooped up the blonde curls and placed the paper and pubes on the bench to dry. When the girl's parents received the cunny hairs and a ransom note, they'd tell the government of their daughter's predicament. The fascist bastards would have no choice other than to leave Snide and his castle alone.

Grabbing the ringing phone as the squelching noises of a cock fucking a wet cunt emanated from the rack chamber, the Professor grinned. *The Baron hasn't wasted any time!* he chuckled inwardly as grunts resounded around the dungeon. Once she'd been well and truly spunked, she'd be well and truly spunked again.

'I'm in the phone box by the village stores and post office,' Lucifer announced. 'I thought it best to ring you, sir.'

'Why?'

'I can't remember.'

'Have you been in the pub?'

'Er . . . Well, sort of.'

'Bloody piss-head! Think, man, why did you phone me?'

'I didn't phone you.'

'You're phoning me now, you fool!'

'Ah, so I am. I'm calling because there are a dozen or so police officers making their way up to the castle.'

'Fuck and shit!'

'And they have sniffer dogs.'

'Double fuck and treble shit! I'd better hide the cannabis. OK, head them off at the pass.'

'There is no pass.'

'Right, I'll wind the drawbridge up.'

'There is no drawbridge, sir.'

'Fuck it! I know, I'll lower the portcullis.'

'There is no port—'

'Shut up, Lucifer! I'm trying to wank . . . I mean, think.'

'Yes, sir.'

'I've got it! Tell them that you saw the girl walking in the opposite direction with her wet knickers around her ankles. That should put them off the scent for a while.'

'I'll do it right away, sir.'

'If you succeed, you can shag a shaved cunt on your return.'

'Thank you, sir – you're too kind.'

'Kindness has nothing to do with it. It'll cost you fifty pounds.'

Replacing the receiver and turning to the Baron as the man staggered out of the rack room with spunk running down his trousers, the Professor told him of the latest developments. Zipping his trousers, the Baron held his hand to his head, appearing to be deep in thought. Frowning, he was no doubt devising a deviously wicked plan.

'Supper!' he finally cried, making the Professor jump.

'Supper?' Snide echoed.

'If your butler succeeds and the police go off on a wild-goose chase, they won't be here for hours. I've just had a wash and brush-up, enjoyed a bloody good fuck, and now I'm hungry – let's eat.'

'My God, what a fucking brilliant plan! To the banqueting hall!'

The sun rising over the castle, Professor Snide emerged from his living quarters and yawned. 'Another day, another fuck,' he murmured, trying to adjust his massive cock within his tight trousers as he walked to the banqueting hall.

'Ah, Lucifer!' he greeted his butler as he entered the hall. 'What happened last night?'

'After my intervention, the police headed off in the opposite direction in search of a girl with wet knickers around her ankles,' the butler announced triumphantly.

'Excellent!'

'And I've returned Miss Hocks to the dungeon, sir.'

'Good man!' Snide cried, rubbing his hands together. 'OK, this is the plan. We've shaved the village girl's fanny and I'm going to put her pubes into a plastic bag along with a ransom note and send it to her parents. What I want you to do is . . . Shit, there's the phone.'

Grabbing the receiver, Snide knew there was trouble in store as a man introduced himself as the Minister of Castles and Dungeons. The fascist bastards were closing in and he had to think quickly. The last thing he wanted was an all-out war with the state. There again, if that's what it took – that's what they'd bloody well get!

'You're not having my castle!' the Professor snapped.

'You have no choice in the matter,' the Minister replied. 'Your castle is to be returned to the state without delay.'

'You'll be returned to your mother's womb without delay unless you . . . '

'That's no attitude to take, Professor. The castle belongs to the state and . . . '

'My great, great, great, great, great . . . One of my ancestors built this castle back in the early something hundreds.'

'That's simply not true.'

'Of course it's true, simply or otherwise.'

'You purchased the castle from a local estate agent five years ago.'

'Big-mouthed fucking bastard!'

'Castles should be open to the public. As part of our heritage, it's only right that all castles should belong to the state. Apart from that, Professor, the government is gravely concerned about your illegal activities.'

'Illegal activities?'

'We've had reports of young girls going missing from the local village, as well as strange goings-on in the dungeon of your castle.'

'Fucking bollocks! What have young girls got to do with me?'

'Everything, by all accounts. And don't swear over the telephone.'

'I swear over what I fucking like.'

'I'll be sending a representative to see you concerning the return of the castle to the state. You'll be rehoused, of course.'

'I don't want to be re-bloody-housed!'

'A poky council flat in a tower block would suit you admirably.'

'Fucking bollocks!'

'No, a tower block. I hope we can work together towards the smooth transaction of your castle's return to the state, Professor.'

'The only smooth thing around here is Clarissa's . . . I mean . . . '

'There'll also be a senior police officer calling to inspect the dungeon and to look into the mysterious disappearance of village girls.'

'Marxist fucking bastards!'

Banging the phone down as the Purple Baron walked across the hall, Snide rubbed his chin. With years of work in jeopardy, there was no time to lose. Clarissa had to have her brain patterns reinstated and given her freedom before the police arrived, and the au pair had to be returned to Professor Spasm's residence. Hollie's brain patterns were forever lost: all Snide could do was induce his own brain patterns into the woman and hope for the best.

'Good morning,' the Professor said, turning to the Baron.

'Indeed, it is.'

'A change of plan, Barron. Lucifer has brought my traitorous assistant back and locked her in the dungeon. We must release the au pair, induce my assistant's brain patterns into the zombie village girl and release her too, and induce my patterns into my assistant.'

'Somewhat confusing,' the Baron replied, rubbing his chin. 'Give your assistant your brain patterns, give the village girl your assistant's patterns, and release the au pair.'

'That about sums it up. Lucifer, while we're buggering about with people's brains and . . . '

'You're not going to fuck their brains, are you?' the butler asked, swigging from a hip flask.

'Not "bugger" as in bugger like Catholic priests and choir-boys – "bugger" as in fuck about, piss around, fart about.'

'Yes, sir.'

'I want you to prepare for the invasion of the castle. Check the cannon on the turret and make sure there's plenty of gunpowder and bollocks . . . I mean balls – as in cannon balls. We'll blow the communist pigs from here to kingdom come, wherever that is.'

'Right away, sir.'

'OK, Baron, there's work to be done. To the dungeon!'

While the Baron busied himself transferring brain patterns from Hollie to Clarissa, the Professor entered the torture chamber and gazed longingly at the au pair's naked body, her swollen pussy lips, her gaping girlie crack. It was a great shame to have to release the girl without shaving her pubic hairs, he mused – and an even greater shame to release her unfucked.

'You are to return to Professor Spasm,' he enlightened the girl, his magnificent penis swelling within his trousers.

'I have been stood standing here all night!' she complained. 'I am tiring and hungered.'

'You'll have to speak with the au pair agency if you're unhappy with your diet and sleeping arrangements.'

'The agency is saying nothing about nakedness and tor-tured chambers.'

'Put your complaint in writing. Before you go, you must be severely fucked.'

'I am not wanting severely fucked!'

'Of course you are. What do you think your pussy is for?' Snide laughed, hauling his massive penis out of his trousers and displaying his bulbous knob.

'I am not wanting fucked by horse!'

'I'm not a horse, you stupid girl.'

'You are looking like horse!'

'What do you know about horses?'

'I like riding horses.'

'I'll bet you do!'

Standing before the girl with his erect penis waving from side to side, Snide grabbed his shaft and guided his solid glans between her fleshy pussy lips. Gasping as he penetrated her, forcing her tight cunt open, he grabbed her hips. His cock gliding deeper into her sex duct, his knob finally coming to rest against her cervix as she spat her protests, he chuckled wickedly.

'You like my horse cock?' he asked, pulling her naked body closer.

'I am not liking horse!' she cried. 'I am splitting closed!'

'You really should speak to your English teacher about extra lessons. In the meantime, I'll give you extra fucking lessons.'

'I am not wanting extra fucking lessons!'

'Then you'll never learn the language properly. OK, let's fuck!'

His swollen glans absorbing the wet heat of her young cunt, the Professor withdrew his shaft and then propelled his weapon head back deep into her vaginal sheath. Her wrists cuffed to the steel rings above her head, her body jolting with the enforced fucking, she whimpered as her tight sex duct stretched to capacity to accommodate the Professor's swelling organ. Her lust milk flowing, her outer lips engorged, gripping his wet pistoning shaft, she cried out as her orgasm neared.

'Oh, I am going! I am going!' she shrieked.

'Coming, you stupid girl!' the Professor corrected her.

'I have coming! The horse made me coming!'

'I'll fuck your bottom after I've spunked up your cunt!'

'I am not having bottom fucking!'

'Oh, yes, you are!'

His huge balls swinging as he thrust his giant cock in and out of the girl's youthful vagina, the Professor finally loosed his sperm. Gasping, his knob pulsating, his spunk jetting, he repeatedly thrust into the young beauty, taking her to her mind-blowing climax with his superb organ. Crying out in her pleasure as she hung from the handcuffs, Helga swung her hips, meeting his penile thrusts as her orgasm gripped her naked body, taking her to her sexual heaven.

'I have comed!' she sang, squelching sounds emanating from her sperm-brimming cunt as the huge cock shafted her. 'Ooh, I have comed!'

'God, you're tight!' Snide breathed, his copious spunk overflowing from the girl's sex sheath and streaming down her inner thighs. 'And your bum will be even tighter.'

'My bum is not being tighter!'

'Of course it is. All young girls' bums are tight.'

'Ah! Ah, my sex! I am lesbian, I am wanting girl!'

'You'll have horse and lump it.'

Finishing his vaginal pistoning, the Professor finally staggered back, his glistening cock gliding out of the girl's drenched pussy with a loud sucking sound, swinging from side to side as his erection slowly dwindled. Well and truly fucked, Helga hung limply from the steel rings, her cunt pumping out the creamy mixture of spunk and girl juice. Sadly, the time had come to free the little sexpot, Snide mused, tucking his cunny-wet, snake-like penis back into his trousers.

Releasing Helga's wrists, he supported her naked body as she staggered into the lab. The Baron had completed the brainwave transference and sent Clarissa packing, but Hollie still had the village girl's brain patterns. At least Clarissa was her old self, the Professor mused, propping the au pair up against the bench. All he had to do now was transfer his alpha-wave patterns into Hollie's brain and she'd return to comparative normality.

'I don't wanna wear no fuckin' 'at!' Hollie protested as the Baron tied her to the chair and plonked the helmet on her head.

'You'll do as you're told!' Snide ordered her. 'You don't want to spend the rest of your life as Clarissa, do you?'

'I wanna be bleedin' me!'

'You'll never be you, your brain patterns are forever lost. You'll have to put up with my alpha-wave patterns until I can record the patterns from a suitable girl, a sex-crazed nymphomaniacal whore.'

'What am I having to do?' Helga asked, covering her sperm-dripping sex slit with her clasped hands.

'Get dressed,' the Professor instructed her. 'What's left of your clothes are in the torture chamber.'

'I am telling Professor Spasm what you are done to me!'

'If you do that, he'll probably fuck you!'

As Helga dressed in her torn clothing, Professor Snide watched the Baron complete the brainwave transference. Hollie was now thinking like a male again, asking whether she could fuck the au pair. This was a right mess, the Professor thought. If he wasn't careful, he'd have several people with each other's alpha-wave patterns all thinking they were each other. Or the other way round!

'That's a thought,' he murmured pensively.

'What is?' the Baron asked.

'The copper who's been annoying me, I could erase his memory.'

'If we could somehow transmit and receive alpha-wave patterns without the need for the helmet . . . '

'It's funny you should say that, Baron. I've been working on a device to transmit and receive alpha-wave patterns without the need for the helmet. So far I've failed.'

'Damn and blast failure! But things aren't so bad. The village girl's gone, your assistant is now your old self, and the au pair is about to leave.'

'Surrounded by juicy cunts one minute, and the next . . . '

'Worry not, my friend. There's a plan so devious and wicked that we'll have a constant supply of juicy cunts *and* get the government off your back for good.'

'What is this incredible plan, Baron?'

'I don't know, I haven't thought of it yet.'

'Shit and fuck! Ah, Helga, you're dressed,' he grinned as the flush-faced girl emerged from the torture chamber. 'Return to Professor Spasm's residence and say nothing about your perverted time here.'

'I am telling agency that I was being fucking.'

'You do that and I'll rip your clitoris off!'

'You leave my clitty alone. I am coming home now. Hallo!'

'What?'

'Goodbye!'

As the girl climbed the stone steps and fled the dungeon, cannon fire rocked the castle. 'Bloody Lucifer!' Snide stormed as another blast resounded throughout the dungeon. 'I'll bet he's firing at the fucking sparrows again.'

'You should report him to the RSPCA, my friend.'

'I'll have him report to the nearest mental home if he carries on like this.'

'He certainly is a strange one.'

'Indeed he is. And he'll be even stranger when I've torn his bollocks off. But there's no time for a bollockectomy now. We must release Miss Hocks and try to bring an air of abnormality to the dungeon.'

Releasing Hollie Hocks and helping her off the chair, Snide ordered her to go about her duties. The scene was set, he mused – the missing village girl was no longer missing, the au pair had gone, and the castle was back to normal. But his dastardly plan to convert Miss Hocks into a rampant nymphomaniac had so far failed. *Try and try again,* he mused, his cock aching to penetrate his assistant's tight cunt. Cannon fire shaking the foundations of the castle again, he left the dungeon, dashing along the corridor and up the winding steps to the turret.

'What the fuck are you firing at?' he asked as he joined his butler on the windswept turret.

'A bat, sir.'

'A bat? Are you under the influence of alcohol?'

'I've been on the meths.'

'That's no excuse for shooting bats.'

'But it keeps flying around, trying to dive-bomb me. I believe it to be my insane vampire grandfather.'

'Why try to kill your grandfather?'

'He screwed my mother's bottom-hole when she bent down to pick something up.'

'My God, the perverted filthy pervert! Load the cannon, Lucifer – I'll blast the sex fiend out of the air!'

'I'm out of gunpowder, sir. And there's one other smallish problem.'

'What's that?'

'My grandfather was flying in the direction of the village and . . . and I sort of missed him and inadvertently destroyed the village stores and post office.'

'Fuck!'

'I really shouldn't drink so much, it blurs my vision.'

'I'll blur your bollocks in a minute! You know what this means, don't you?'

'I'm to be sacked forthwith, sir?'

'No, it means that we'll no longer be able to buy supplies from the village stores and post office. Fuck me! Look down there, towards the village. If I'm not mistaken, that's DI Peel – and he's coming this way!'

'Oh, dear. I feel terribly responsible, sir.'

'And so you should, Lucifer – you should feel fucking immensely responsible. I'll have your bollocks for this. Right, you stay up here and I'll go and wait for Peel to arrive. To be on the safe side, in case the bastard comes sniffing around up here, push the cannon over the side of the castle.'

'Yes, sir.'

Dashing down the winding steps, Snide made his way to the castle doors, brushing his dark hair back with his fingers as he waited in anticipation for DI Peel. There was one problem after another, he reflected as the phone rang. Leaping into the banqueting hall, he grabbed the receiver, wondering what the hell would happen next.

'Professor Snide!' he snapped agitatedly as the doorbell rang out.

'Professor, this is the Reverend Mother Horgasm from the Our Lady of the Wretched nunnery.'

'The wretched mammary? What's wrong with your . . . '

'Nunnery, Professor.'

'Ah, yes, right . . . '

'Sister Elizabeth visited your castle, did she not?'

'Er . . . No, she did not.'

'She did, Professor. She now believes herself to be a man, and she's wreaking havoc among the nuns in the nunnery.'

'You can't have none of that with the nuns in the nunnery!'

'Exactly. What did you do to her?'

'*Me?* I did nothing, Mother Orgasm.'

'Rather than involve the police, I'll be visiting you in connection with the matter.'

'Don't put yourself to any brother, Mother . . . Bother, Mother.'

'It's no bother at all.'

'I have to go, the doorbell's ringing.'

'I'll be seeing you later, Professor.'

'Much later, I hope!' *Fucking old hag!*

Replacing the receiver and dashing to the door, Snide invited DI Peel into the castle. Grinning sheepishly as the Inspector frowned at him, he knew there was trouble ahead. But there was no proving that the damage to the village stores and post office had anything to do with anyone in the castle. The cannon ball could have come from anywhere. Well, almost.

'What unremarkable weather for the time of year,' Snide remarked.

'The unremarkable weather is not my concern, Professor,' Peel returned. 'The village stores and post office have been badly damaged by a cannon ball.'

'Bloody vandals! I blame the parents.'

'A cannon ball that, on working out the trajectory, was fired from your castle.'

'No, no, you're wrong.'

'If A is the height of the cannon, B the distance from the cannon to the stores and post office, C the speed of the cannon ball . . . '

'Bollocks. If A minus C equals X, plus B divided by D, then Y is where the cannon is sighted, Inspector – in the grounds of the Our Lady of the Wretched nunnery.'

'Nuns don't have cannons and balls, Professor.'

'I know nothing about nuns' balls. There again, from what I've heard, they're probably male perverts dressed as nuns. Bloody transvestites.'

'I'm not here to discuss the gender of nuns. The cannon, by my reckoning, is situated atop your castle. I wish to inspect your turret.'

'You leave my turret out of this, Inspector!'

'The castle turret.'

'Oh, I see. Er . . . Well, I suppose you'd better follow me.'

A huge thud resounding throughout the castle, the Professor realized that Lucifer had managed to heave the cannon over the wall and send it crashing to the ground. Following the Inspector through the doors, he stood next to the sleuth, gazing at the cannon embedded in the grass bank of the moat.

'A cannon,' Peel murmured pensively. 'Most odd.'

'It's been there for ten thousand years,' Snide grinned.

'Ten thousand . . . Professor, cannons weren't invented ten thousand years ago. And the moat wasn't there ten thousand . . . '

'Of course they were. The Ancient Chinese invented gunpowder long before . . . '

'I put it to you that the cannon was thrown off the turret up there, probably by your butler.'

'My butler wasn't alive ten thousand years ago.'

'Ten minutes ago, Professor.'

'Yes, he was alive ten minutes ago. In fact, he's probably alive now, as we speak.'

'Where is he?'

'Down in the village, purchasing ladies' underwear.'

'Ladies' . . . As I approached the castle, I noticed the tall stooping frame of your butler atop the turret.'

'I can assure you that he's not atit the torrid.'

'This is getting us nowhere, Professor. I'm going up to the turret,' Peel said, walking back into the castle.

'Take the corridor to the dungeon, turn left and climb the winding steps to the turret. And mind you don't fall over the wall. I wouldn't want you to break your neck.'

'Thank you, I'll be careful.'

'And look out for the headless lady!'

Rubbing his chin, Snide gazed at the cannon, wondering why Lucifer hadn't pushed it over the back wall rather than the front for all to see. 'Oh well, what's done is fucking done,' he mumbled as he walked into the castle. The village stores and post office destroyed, DI Peel atop the turret, Miss Hocks with male brain patterns, Clarissa with a well-shagged and shaved cunt, Helga fucked rotten . . . 'What's done is fucking done!'

Wondering when the Reverend Mother Horgasm would arrive with her accusations of interfering with nuns, Professor Snide decided to strip the woman and shave her fanny. The old bat was probably in need of a good bottom-rogering, he mused, turning as DI Peel finally returned from the turret and walked across the banqueting hall.

'Did you find everything in order, Inspector?' he asked.

'You told me that your butler was in the village, and I found him atop the turret.'

'I lied. Well, not lied, exactly – I forgot. Retention loss, that's what it is.'

'I'll be taking the cannon away for forensic tests, Professor. I'll have my men pick it up later today, if not earlier.'

'Right, I'll make sure it's gone . . . I'll make sure it stays in the moat.'

'You'll be hearing a lot more from me.'

'I'm delighted to hear it, Inspector.'

'You haven't heard it, yet.'

'No, but I'll be delighted to hear it when I hear it.'

'Yes, I see. Good day, Professor.'

'Is it?' *Shit, fuck and treble fuck!*

Chapter Four

The cannon had to be removed forthwith, Snide decided after enjoying lunch with the Baron. When Peel returned with his men, the Professor would deny all knowledge of the cannon's timely disappearance, putting it down to the headless lady. There'd be nothing Peel could do without the evidence – no cannon, no balls, no bollocking!

'Baron, would you find Lucifer and ask him to meet me by the moat?'

'Of course, my friend.'

'Perhaps you'd help us to remove the cannon?'

'Indeed. We'll meet you outside by the cannon.'

'No, meet me outside by the moat by the cannon.'

Standing by the moat, the Professor noticed a young girl walking towards the castle. Her long blonde hair flowing in the breeze, her firm breasts billowing her tight blouse, her gymslip following the contours of her curvaceous young body, he assumed that she was from the village school.

What's she doing up here? he wondered as she approached, his penis twitching as he thought of something totally perverted and highly illegal concerning her bottomhole. With the Professor's reputation in the village, no young girl would dare to wander up to the castle. Not unless she wanted a damned good anal fucking!

'Are you lost?' he asked as she ambled up to the door.

'I'm new around here, I'm exploring,' she replied, her pretty face smiling sweetly.

I wouldn't mind exploring up your skirt!

'Is this your castle?'

'Yes, it is. So, no one's told you about me?'

'Told me what?'

'Er . . . nothing, nothing. I'm Professor Snide, Sexton Snide.'

'I'm pleased to meet you, Professor. I'm Angelica.'

'That's a lovely name. Would you like to come off . . . come in?'

'Thank you. I've never been inside a castle.'

And I've never been inside your knickers! 'I'll show you around.'

His evil mind brimming with wicked ideas as he closed the doors, Snide wondered where to take the girl. Deciding to hide her in his living quarters, he grabbed her hand and led her through the banqueting hall. The last thing he wanted was Peel returning and bumping into the intended abductee! The Inspector was a bloody nuisance, he reflected – Lucifer should have had the initiative to throw him over the turret wall and kill him to death. But there were more important things to think about – namely, the schoolgirlie's pouting pussy lips, her sweet sex crack.

Pondering on the girl's knickers as he led her through a door at the far end of the hall, he knew they'd be bulging with her young fleshy cunt lips, her firm mons. Her sex slit would be tightly closed, inviting a tongue to part the outer hillocks and delve into her moist valley of carnal desire, drive deep into her young vagina and taste her sweet honeydew.

'God!' he breathed, his heavy balls rolling as he imagined fucking the young beauty's bottom-hole with his horse-like cock.

'I'm sorry?' she smiled as they walked along a gloomy corridor.

76

'It's all right, I was just thinking about something highly illegal. If you'll follow me, I'll show you the west wing.'

'How old is the castle?'

'How old are *you*? Er . . . It was built in eleven hundred and something or other. When did you move into the village, Angelica?'

'I don't live in the village, I'm from Plonkton-on-the-Moor.'

'Ah, that explains why you've not heard about . . . So, you're into exploring?'

'Yes, I love the countryside. You won't tell anyone that I've been here, will you?'

'Of course I won't fucking tell . . . I mean, that's the last thing I'd do!'

'I should be at school, you see.'

'Ah, you're playing truant. Tell me, do you have many girlie friends at school?'

'Oh, yes.'

'You'll have to bring them here for a good . . . for a good look round. I'll bet they'll bend over backwards . . . I'll bend over backwards to help schoolgirlies.'

'You're very kind, Professor.'

'Kindness is a virtue, as is chastity. Are you chaste?'

'No, I've never been chased.'

'I'm pleased to hear it. This is the west wing, my living quarters. Actually, it's the east wing. To be correct, it's the east wing which faces . . . Shit, I can't go through all that bollocks again. This is where I live.'

'It's very big.'

'You haven't seen it yet. Oh, I see what you mean. I'll leave you here to have a wander while I make a quick phone call. I won't be long.'

'Thank you.'

'There's a shower in the bathroom. I expect you'd like to strip off and freshen up before I . . . After your long walk.'

'I'm fine, thanks.'

Fuck!

Closing the door as the girl walked into the huge room, the Professor turned the key. Before any schoolgirl-fucking commenced, he had to remove the cannon from the moat. It was probably a good idea to keep the girl secret from the Baron and Lucifer, he mused, making his way to the castle doors. It wasn't every day that sexy young schoolgirlies walked into the castle, and he wasn't going to share her with anyone!

'Right!' Snide said excitedly, clapping his hands as he joined the Baron and Lucifer by the moat. 'The cannon must be removed forthwith.'

'Where, to sir?' Lucifier asked, swigging from his hip flask.

'Somewhere well out of the way of DI Peel. I know, we'll dig a pit and bury it.'

'I don't see how we're going to lift it out of the moat,' the Baron said pensively. 'It must weigh a ton.'

'We'll get the Inspector's men to help us,' Snide replied.

'But we're supposed to be hiding it from the Inspector's men, sir,' Lucifer pointed out.

'Yes, I realize that. Er . . . I was testing you. Right, what we'll do is . . . '

'What about plastic explosive, sir?'

'What about it?'

'We could fill the barrel with explosive, and blow the cannon to pieces.'

'An excellent idea, Lucifer. But we don't have any plastic explosive.'

'Perhaps the village stores and post office stock it, or dynamite,' the Baron suggested.

'A good suggestion, Baron, but the shop no longer exists.'

'I have some explosive in my room, sir.'

'Really, Lucifer? What do you use it for?'

'Anal stimulation . . . I'd rather not say.'

'OK, get the explosive and destroy the cannon. Baron, would you mind assisting Lucifer with the blowing-up of the cannon? I have something hot and wet to attend in my living quarters.'

'But of course, my friend.'

That was that major problem solved, Snide mused as he hurriedly made his way to the west wing. Unable to stop thinking about the schoolgirl, his penis solid, he unlocked the door to his living quarters and slipped inside. And now to solve another problem, and drain his huge balls!

'Ah, there you are,' the young girl smiled, walking towards him.

'Indeed, I am.'

'I was wondering whether the castle has a dungeon?'

And I was wondering whether your cunt's tight and wet.
'Yes, it has. And a torture chamber and a rack and . . . '

'A torture chamber?'

'Yes, would you like to see it?'

'Ooh, yes!' she squealed excitedly. 'God, a rack! I just love the idea of torture!'

'Well, you're in luck.' *And so am I!*

'I *am* in luck. We're doing a project at school about castles and dungeons and torture.'

'What a coincidence. Your project will be the best, I'm sure. With what you're about to experience, you'll be top of the class.'

'Do you torture people?'

'Good God! No, no, no, no . . . Yes.'

'Great!'

'Isn't it just? Follow me, my horny little . . . Follow me, Angelica.'

This was too good to be true! Snide thought gleefully, taking the girl's hand and almost dragging her to the dungeon. Shave her pussy, and then screw nipple clamps onto her young milk teats and force a candle up her bum and spunk down her throat and finger her cunt and give her the buttock caning of her young life and . . . *Thank God for perverted sex!* he chuckled inwardly as he led the girl down the steps to the lab.

Too good to be true? he ruminated. A young schoolgirlie happens to walk up to the castle, she happens to be doing a project about castles, dungeons and torture, she happens to be overly keen to see the rack . . . Snide smelled something very fishy about the girl, and it wasn't her cunny-wet knickers!

'This is the rack,' he smiled, pulling her into the chamber.

'I've never seen a real rack. How does it work?'

'The victim is stripped naked and placed on the rack with the chains fixed to the wrists and ankles and . . . I'll tell you what, why don't you give it a try?'

'Really?'

'The best way to discover how it works is to try it for yourself. Or try it for me, or both.'

'What, take all my clothes off?'

Sheer bliss! 'It would be a shame if your gymslip gets torn when I stretch you, Angelica.'

'But my knickers and bra . . . '

'If you really want to experience the rack, discover exactly what it was like for the victims hundreds of years ago, I don't see that you have a choice.' *Either way, you don't have a choice!*

'It would help me with my project, but . . . '

'On open days, when I conduct guided tours, I charge twenty pounds to anyone wishing to try the rack but . . . Well, seeing as this is a private tour, I won't charge you. In fact, I'll pay you.'

'Will you?'

'Er . . . No, I won't. You'd better strip off.'

'You mean to say that people take *all* their clothes off?'

'It's in the castle rules, which are obtainable on written request. The management wouldn't want to be held responsible for torn clothing and, as I'm the management, neither would I. Members of the public use the rack at their own risk. It's the same with car parks and hotels and condoms.'

'Yes, I've seen the notices.'

'And swimming pools. Members of the public drown at their own risk.'

'All right, I'll try the rack.'

'Good, good! While you're undressing, I'll prepare the candle . . . I mean, the chains.'

Watching the girl out of the corner of his eye as he toyed with the rack, Snide felt his penis twitch as she pulled her gymslip over her head, revealing her sex-bulged navy-blue knickers, and unbuttoned her white blouse. This was incredible luck, he mused as she opened her blouse, exposing her tight bra. It wasn't every day that schoolgirlies wandered up to the castle and stripped naked, desperate to try the rack! If she really *was* a schoolgirlie.

'I think I'll leave my bra and knickers on,' she smiled, climbing onto the rack and lying on her back.

'The prerogative's yours, Angelica,' Snide replied, deftly fixing the chains to her wrists and ankles. *Get out of that, my little beauty!*

'It's not really right to take all my clothes off in front of a stranger, is it?'

'No, it's not.' *Especially someone as strange as I!* 'There, now I'll turn this handle and your arms will be stretched behind your head and your legs pulled out of their sockets. Well, I won't go that far.'

'Ooh, this is fun!'

81

'Indeed, it is! Now, if I turn this other handle, you'll find that the chains pull your legs wide apart.'

'What's the idea of that?'

So that I can look up your cunt once I've shredded your knickers! 'In olden times they used to put young girls on the rack and pull their legs wide apart in order to . . . Well, in order to torture them.'

'Oh, I think that's enough!' she cried. 'My legs won't open any further!'

'You're right, that's more than wide enough for what I have in mind . . . I mean, for the time being.'

Eyeing the girl's young body, the slight curve of her smooth stomach, the neat indentation of her navel, the swell of her mons beneath her tight knickers, the Professor could barely contain himself. He'd fuck her young vaginal sheath and sperm her cervix, he mused, gazing at her sex crack clearly defined by the tight material of her knickers. Then he'd shag her bottom-hole and fuck her cleavage and spunk down her throat and . . . But first, a little torture was in order – purely to show who was boss.

'Hundreds of years ago, young girls were placed on the rack and their nipples were clamped,' he said, watching for her reaction.

'Their nipples were clamped?' she echoed, lifting her head and focusing on the Professor.

'Yes, it was one of the most popular methods of torture – girls queued up for it. I have photographs of girls in the thirteenth century queuing up outside the castle doors: they're quite valuable. The photographs are worth a lot, too.'

'Photographs? They didn't have cameras in . . . '

'Er . . . I mean, oil paintings. As I was saying, nipple clamping was so popular that the king ordered all young girls to be clamped.'

'What do you mean, *clamped*?'

'I can't explain, I'd have to show you. Of course, as you won't allow me to remove your bra, I can't show you.'

'Well, I'd like to try it, but . . . '

'It's a great shame because it would really help you with your project. I don't see how you can write about teenage breast and nipple torture during the thirteenth century unless you experience the delight for yourself.'

'All right, you can pull my bra up.'

'Excellent! A most unwise . . . A most wise decision, I must say.' *Not that you had any choice.*

His hands trembling, he slipped his fingers beneath the cups of her bra and pulled them clear of her young breasts. Her succulent nipples standing erect as they were given their freedom, he licked his lips, imagining sucking on her beautiful teats, spunking over the brown discs of her areolae.

'I'll prepare your nipples by kneading your breasts,' he said, squeezing each mammary sphere in turn. Her tits were beautifully, youthfully firm, he mused, flicking her milk teats with his fingertips – firm, hard, fresh . . . Her areolae darkening as her nipples grew, he wondered whether she was enjoying his intimate attention. *He* certainly was!

First, the nipple clamps, and then the clitoris clamp, he decided in his rising wickedness as he reached to a shelf and grabbed the metal clamps. And then the vaginal speculum, the anal speculum, the outer vaginal lip clamps, the whip, the cane . . .

'Remember to take mental notes for your project,' he smiled, placing a clamp over her nipple and tightening the screw. 'I've always found that the best way to learn about history is to relive it.'

'Oh, I agree,' she replied, her wide eyes focused on her brown teat as he turned the screw a little more. 'Ouch! I think that's tight enough!'

'Yes, of course. I'll just clamp your other nipple and give you a while to experience the sensations.'

Clamping her hitherto neglected milk teat, Snide focused on Angelica's bulging navy-blue knickers, picturing her swollen outer lips, her pink sex valley. His King Dong vibrator would drive the girl wild, he mused, tightening the clamp. Forcing her young vaginal canal open, the vibrations inducing her sex milk to flow, he'd prepare her tight quim for a cuntal invasion by his massive cock.

'That hurts!' she complained as he turned the screw again.

'That's the idea, Angelica. Of course, to experience the rack properly, you'd have to allow me to remove your knickers.'

'Remove my knickers? Why?'

So I can fuck you. 'In the old days, young girls were sexually tortured to correct their wicked ways.'

'What wicked ways?'

'Do you masturbate?'

'Well, I . . . '

'Girls were punished on the rack by perverted Catholic priests for masturbating with cucumbers. It's a great shame that you won't allow me to show you. Your project won't be complete without . . . '

'OK, you can do it.'

'Great! I mean . . . Right, I'll rip your knickers off . . . *slip* your knickers off.'

Easing his fingers between the tight elastic of her panties and her firm stomach, he slowly pulled the material down, revealing the blonde down covering the gentle rise of her mons. Pulling the garment down further, his eyes widening as the top of her sex crack came into view, he couldn't hold back any longer and tore the material from her curvaceous young body.

'Oh!' she gasped as he tossed the remnants of her knickers to the floor. 'You've torn my knickers!'

'Yes, a slip of the hand. Sometimes I don't know my own strength. Or my weaknesses, come to that! Er . . . Not to worry, you won't be needing . . . I mean, I'll find you another pair later. My butler has several spare pairs of . . . '

'What are you doing now?' she asked as he parted her teenage vaginal lips and gazed at her succulent inner folds, the glistening pink flesh surrounding her inviting sex hole.

'I'm helping you to relive history,' he smiled. 'I'll just ease my finger up your cunt . . . er . . . into your vagina, and then I'll begin the sexual torture.'

'Oh! Oh, no one's ever done that to me!' she breathed as his finger glided deep into her hot cunt. 'Oh, I really don't think you should be doing this!'

'Of course I should!' he laughed wickedly.

'There's a funny look on your face, Professor. And . . . and a strange glint in your wide eyes. Are you feeling all right?'

'Yes, I can feel you perfectly.'

'Your eyes have gone very big, and they're glazed.'

'Naked schoolgirlies have a peculiar effect on me, Angelica.'

'What sort of effect?'

'I have a great vaginal affection for schoolgirlies. Whenever I see a young girl's cunt, I have this overwhelming urge to shove my cock up it and fuck her rotten.'

'Oh! But . . . '

'I have no idea why my mind works in such a peculiar way.'

'Perhaps you need help?'

'No, I'm quite capable of fucking you single-cocked . . . single-handed. You do want to be fucked, don't you?'

'Will it help me with my project?'

'Of course it won't . . . it will. But first, you must experience the age-old custom known as "appeasing the executioner".'

'What do I have to do?'

85

'It's quite simple: all you have to do is open your mouth and suck my cock until I . . . '

'OK, Professor Snide! You've been sussed!' she grinned triumphantly. 'I'm a government agent and I've been sent here to expose you!'

'I thought as much. It comes as no surprise since there's a fishy smell about you, and it's not your knickers – or my finger.'

'I'm arresting you in the name of the king.'

'What? We don't have a king.'

'The queen, then. You have been exposed!'

'It would appear that *you*'re the one who's been exposed, Angelica – if that's your real name,' he returned, slipping his well-juiced finger out of her love duct.

'You'd better release me, Professor. The punishment for chaining innocent naked schoolgirls to racks is . . . '

'But *you*'re the one who's going to be punished, my little beauty!'

'I have to warn you that under the 1951 Innocent Schoolgirl Act, it is illegal to chain naked schoolgirls to racks and insert fingers into their vaginas, or suggest that they suck you off. Furthermore, it is illegal to . . . '

'Furthermore, there's nothing you can do about it. And furthermore also as well, I'm going to fuck you.'

'And furthermore to that, under the Innocent Schoolgirl Act, it is illegal to fuck innocent schoolgirls.'

'And further to furthermore, how are you going to stop me?'

'I didn't come here alone, Professor. The castle is surrounded by the king's men and . . . the queen's men.'

'The only thing surrounding the castle is a moat. There's one major flaw in your plan, Angelica,' he grinned, hauling his solid penis out of his trousers. 'You are *not* a schoolgirl, innocent or otherwise.'

'Ah, yes, well . . . '

'The 1951 Act doesn't apply to anyone working for the fascist pigs and *posing* as an innocent schoolgirl. You're far from innocent, so you shall be fucked rotten.'

'No, you mustn't fuck me!'

'I must! Schoolgirlie-fucking is an age-old tradition originally thought of by King Turpentine in order to appease the carnal cravings of dirty old men.'

Turning the iron handle, his solid penis sticking out of his trousers as Angelica's legs parted further, Snide focused on her yawning sex valley, her open vaginal entrance. Schoolgirl or not, she was a rare beauty to be fucked senseless. Struggling to free herself as her legs spread wider, she spat expletives and threats at the Professor. But she could do nothing to halt the violation of her fresh young body as he grabbed his King Dong vibrator from the shelf and slipped the rounded end into her beautifully tight cunt. Turning the device on, the vibrations transmitting deep into her quivering pelvis, running through her solid clitoris, he pushed the shaft fully home.

'You have a nice cunt,' he murmured, eyeing the fleshy cushions of her outer lips stretched tautly around the buzzing phallus. 'Tell me, what do you normally fuck yourself with?'

'I'm warning you . . . Ah, God, that's . . . '

'Nice?'

'No, no, it's . . . Ah! Oh! I'm warning you, Professor. If you force me to have multiple orgasms . . . Ah!'

'Your cunt milk is flowing nicely,' he said, observing the opaque liquid dripping from the plastic shaft as he thrust the vibrator in and out of her tightening pussy.

'Ah, God! No, you mustn't . . . '

'Mustn't what?'

'You mustn't make me come!'

'Of course I must make you come, you silly girl. What do you think your clitoris is for, show?'

'No, no! Ah! Oh! No!'

'Yes!'

Taking a smaller vibrator from the shelf, Snide parted the girl's tensed buttocks and pressed the end against her anal ring. Twisting, pushing, he drove the shaft deep into her rectal duct to the accompaniment of her gasps of pleasure and protest. Switching the vibrator on, he stood back and gazed at the two pink shafts emerging from her bloated sex holes. Her nipples clamped, her sex ducts stretched to capacity, all that remained neglected was her pretty mouth.

'OK, suck this,' he grinned, standing by her head with his horse-like cock wavering from side to side. 'Suck my knob and drink my spunk.'

'No, no, I can't!' she cried, eyeing his bulbous knob.

'You can.'

'I mustn't!'

'You must!'

Pressing his silky-smooth glans against her succulent lips as she turned her head to face him, he slipped his purple plum into her gasping mouth. 'God!' he breathed, his cock twitching as Angelica's tongue rolled around his knob. 'God, that's good!' Sucking and licking his huge glans as the vibrations ran through her quivering pelvis, her contracting womb, her eyes bulged as her orgasm erupted within her pulsating clitoris. Her chained body twitching violently, her breasts heaving, she moved her head forward, taking his knob to the back of her throat.

Moaning through her nose as her orgasm peaked, she shuddered as the vibrator slipped out of her cunt as her muscles spasmed. Pushing it back home, the Professor withdrew the shaft and rammed it into her drenched vagina again, fucking her young cunt with the plastic phallus as she gobbled his throbbing knob. Her firm stomach rising and falling as she rode the crest of her orgasm, she moved her head back and forth as his shaft swelled and his sperm gushed from his pulsating glans. Licking, sucking, swallowing, she drank his flowing spunk as her own orgasmic juices issued from her vibrated vagina, spraying her inner thighs.

On and on the waves of sexual ecstasy rocked their trembling bodies, the rack chamber resounding with gasps and cries of orgasm. Continuing the vaginal pistoning with the vibrator, Snide rammed his throbbing knob in and out of Angelica's hot mouth, his heavy balls swinging, his spunk jetting to the back of her throat as she sustained his orgasm with her snaking tongue.

The last of his sperm finally shooting from his swollen knob, the Professor embedded the vibrator deep within her cunt and left it there as he leaned on the rack to steady his quivering body. She was good, he reflected, watching her mouthing his glans, desperate not to waste one drop of spunk. But she was a government agent, and there was only one thing to do with government agents.

'And now for my next prick . . . trick,' he grinned, slipping his dripping purple bulb out of her sperm-drenched mouth. 'Centuries ago, young girls were chained to the rack and their tits were thrashed with a leather whip.'

'What?' she gasped, licking spunk from her lips as he slipped the vibrator out of her inflamed vaginal sheath.

'Their tits were thrashed with a leather whip,' he repeated, a heavenly sucking sound echoing around the chamber as he pulled the second vibrator out of her tight bottom-hole.

'You're not going to . . . '

'Of course I am.'

Watching him zip his trousers as he moved to the shelf and grabbed a whip, her eyes widened. He was a maniac, she decided as he placed the whip on the rack – a deranged madman. Releasing her ankles, he pulled two chains down from the ceiling, chuckling uncontrollably as he fixed one chain to her left ankle. Protesting as she struggled to free her naked body, she knew that she was in for the thrashing of her young life.

Ignoring her threats, he fixed the other chain to her right ankle and moved to the wall. Turning a handle, he watched as her legs rose high into the air, her feet parting as the system of pullies squeaked and the chains clanked. Her legs straight, her feet wide apart, positioned high above her head, her cunt crack gaping, she lifted her head and gazed at her blatantly exposed vaginal entrance. Standing at the end of the rack, Snide ran the leather tails over the taut skin of her rounded buttocks, delighting in her plight as she struggled and squirmed.

'Before a tit thrashing, the girls had their bottoms thrashed,' he said, his dark eyes focused on her small anal iris.

'You just dare to . . . '

'Their naked bottoms were whipped until their buttocks burned a fire-red.'

'I'm warning you, Professor! If you . . . '

'Have you ever been thrashed?'

'If you thrash me with that whip, I'll . . . '

'Yes, I know – you'll scream.'

'I'll do more than scream!'

'There's not a lot more you *can* do, Angelica. I'll tell you what, after I've thrashed your schoolgirlie bum, I'll allow my eccentric butler to fuck you.'

'You'll do no such thing!'

'I won't, but *he* will. Enough idle chitter-chatter: let the thrashing commence!'

Bringing the whip down, the thin leather tails lashing her taut buttocks, leaving thin weals fanning out across her pale skin, the Professor grinned wickedly as the girl screamed. Again and again, he lashed her firm bottom orbs, delighting in her sobbed protests as her buttocks began to glow a beautiful shade of crimson. The tails cracking loudly across her burning flesh as he repeatedly brought the whip down, he noticed her girl juice pouring in torrents from her bared sex hole. Running down to her brown anal eye, her juices glistened in the light, inviting a lapping tongue. Her bottom-hole was more inviting, he observed – inviting his bulbous knob! But there was plenty of time, he mused, repeatedly lashing her anal orbs. A buttock-thrashing connoisseur, he wasn't going to rush the job.

'Please, no more!' Angelica sobbed, her twitching buttocks glowing scarlet. Her thighs wide, her cunt lips bared, the leather tails caught her exposed vulval flesh. 'Argh!' she cried as the tails lashed her vaginal lips again. 'Argh, not there!' Totally out of control, the Professor continued the merciless buttock whipping, the vaginal lip lashing, until her cunt milk issued from her open hole in torrents, spewing out like spunk and streaming down her anal crease.

Finally discarding the whip, he turned another handle on the rack, her body moving down until her rounded buttocks were lifted high, positioned over the end of the wooden planking. Her small brown hole crudely bared, he slipped his erect cock out and pressed his glans against her cunny-wet anal entrance.

'You'll enjoy this,' he smiled, pressing his knob harder against her delicate brown tissue.

'No, you're far too big!' she screamed as her ring yielded, allowing his penile eye to peer into her dank rectal duct.

'You can take it.'

'You'll tear me open!'

'Of course I won't. This has been practised since something or other million BC. It's another age-old custom developed by the Greeks, the fathers of bum-fucking.'

'No, you're too big!' she cried again as his purple plum slipped past her defeated anal sphincter muscles.

'God, you're tight!' he gasped, her brown ring taut around the base of his helmet. 'Jesus, do I like fucking naked schoolgirlies' tight bumholes!'

'I am *not* a schoolgirlie!'

'I'll pretend.'

A huge explosion rocking the castle as he drove his massive shaft deep into her spasming arsehole, Snide looked up at the ceiling and grinned. That was the cannon blown to smithereens, he mused. No cannon, no balls, no bollocking! A celebration was in order, he thought, grabbing his King Dong vibrator and parting the girl's swollen outer pussy lips. Driving the pink shaft deep into her tight cunt, her anal duct constricting as her vaginal canal bloated, he switched the device on.

'God!' she cried, her velveteen rectal sheath tightening around his massive shaft as he began his double pistoning. 'God, I've never . . .'

'Never been double fucked before?'

'I . . . Ooh! Ah, no!'

'Ah, yes!'

'Oh, my, my . . . Oh, my cunt!'

'Oh, my knob!'

'Oh, my bum!'

'Oh, my God!' the Baron grinned as he bounded into the rack chamber and gazed at the lewd coupling.

'Ah, Baron, you're just in time to give me a hand,' Snide sniggered, embedding his organ deep within the writhing girl's bowels.

'By the look of it, *you* don't need a hand!' he chuckled. 'But *she* does!'

'She needs a fucking great cock spunking in her mouth!'

'That's where I come in, my friend. Or, I should say, come off.'

As the Purple Baron slipped his erect penis out and pressed

his purple knob against the gasping girl's lips, she sucked him into her wet mouth and gobbled for all she was worth. Two hard cocks swelling her orifices, the King Dong vibrator stretching her cunt to capacity, she squirmed and writhed on the rack, her naked body contorting like that of a snake. Eyeing the nipple clamps, the Baron decided to increase the girl's pleasure and tightened the screws. Her sensitive milk teats painfully squeezed, adding to the lewd sensations coursing through her naked body, she moaned through her nose as she took the Baron's knob to the back of her throat.

'Who is she?' the Baron asked as he drove his cock in and out of her wet mouth.

'She's a Greek goddess of anal sex from the thirteenth century.'

'Really?'

'Well, not quite. If the truth were known, she's a government agent,' Snide replied, his balls slapping the girl's taut buttocks as he arse-fucked her.

'Thank God I don't know the truth!'

'But you do. I've just told you the truth.'

'Bollocks, so you have!'

'Sorry, Baron – I should have kept my mouth shut.'

'It would seem that my knob's keeping *her* mouth open. You've done well, my friend. To capture a government agent, a Greek-goddess-of-anal-sex government agent, is quite a feat.'

'I agree, she does have nice feet. I might suck her toes later.'

'I might suck her clitoris. You really have done well, my friend.'

'Even though I say it myself, I did plan the abduction with expertise.'

'When she's been suitably spermed, I suggest we sperm her again.'

'Good thinking, Baron. In the meantime, I suggest we sperm her without further ado.'

His spunk exploding from his orgasming knob, Snide rammed his cock in and out of the girl's tight anal sheath, filling her bowels with his orgasmic spend. The Baron's knob erupting in orgasm, his sperm bathing her sweeping tongue, jetting down her throat, he swung his hips, fucking her hot mouth for all he was worth.

The girl finally attaining her own sexual climax, she quivered uncontrollably, the chains clanking as her naked body rocked. Her young womb rhythmically contracting, her lust juices flooding past the buzzing vibrator and running around her taut anal ring, lubricating the Professor's pistoning shaft, her multiple orgasm rolled on. Reaching incredible heights of sexual ecstasy, her long blonde hair matted with the perspiration of carnal pleasure, she repeatedly swallowed, drinking the Baron's copious flow of spunk.

Finally stilling their exhausted bodies as their orgasms waned, the men breathed heavily in the aftermath of the lewd three-way coupling. The Professor's cock embedded deep within the girl's spunked bowels, the Baron's organ absorbing the heat of her wet mouth, the vibrator buzzing loudly within her young vaginal canal, the girl had been well and truly fucked. But another thrashing was in order, the Professor reflected. A government agent should be thrashed again and again for her treachery.

'Baron, the time has come for a thrashing,' Snide grinned as he slipped his penis out of the girl's well-spermed arsehole.

'I don't fancy a thrashing, my friend,' the Baron replied, his cock leaving their prisoner's spunked mouth.

'No, *you*'re not to be thrashed – *she* is.'

'Ah, I see. In that case, I suggest that we thrash her without further ado.'

'No, not again!' she protested as Snide withdrew the

buzzing phallus from her hot cunt, a delicious sucking and squelching sound reverberating around the chamber. 'Please, I'll say nothing to my boss in Westminster!'

'I've got it!' the Baron cried as he concealed his dripping cock within his trousers. 'We'll send a ransom note to the fascist bastards. We failed miserably with the village girl, but this time . . . '

'I have a better idea,' Snide grinned. 'Let's send a ransom note to the fascist bastards.'

'Brilliant, my friend. We'll need pen and paper.'

'We'll also need proof of the girl's imprisonment. I suggest we cut her clitoris off.'

'No!' she screamed.

'You're overlooking one important point, my friend. Without her clitoris, she won't be able to come the next time we double-fuck her.'

'OK, we'll send a fake clitoris. There are some mouldy peas in the fridge, we'll dip one into some pink paint – they'll never know the difference.'

'If we dip another two into some brown paint, we could say that they're her nipples.'

'Perfect, Baron. What's that ringing sound?'

'I'd say it's the doorbell.'

'Fuck! I'd better go and see who it is. I'll leave you to shave her pubic hair off.'

'Right, and I'll shave her pubic hair off while I'm about it.'

'No!'

'Yes!'

Leaping up the stone steps, the Professor pondered on the identity of the caller. If it was DI Peel and his men looking for the cannon, they'd be out of luck, he reflected. If it was the distraught postmistress, he'd fuck her rotten – on second thoughts! It might be Angelica's band of men, he mused, making his way to the castle doors. If they really had surrounded the castle . . .

'Ah, Lucifer!' he bellowed as the man walked towards the doors. 'Where's Miss Hocks? I haven't seen her for some time.'

'I don't know, sir. The last time I saw her she was in the banqueting hall looking through a men's dirty magazine and mumbling something about not having a penis.'

'That's because she has my brain patterns. She's obviously perplexed by her cunt and tits. Who's at the door?'

'I can't see from here.'

'Then open it.'

'Yes, of course.'

The Reverend Mother Horgasm stood with her hands on her ample hips, frowning at the Professor as Lucifer opened the doors. This was trouble, Snide mused, wondering whether she had a cunt or not – and finally deciding that she hadn't. With male brain patterns, what Sister Elizabeth had been up to with the nuns in the nunnery he dreaded to think!

'Welcome to my humble commode,' the Professor smiled innocently.

'I'm here about . . .'

'About a nun visiting my castle when, in fact, she didn't visit my castle.'

'She did come here, Professor – she told me.'

'I can't think why she's lied to you, Mother Orgasm. I've always been led to believe that nuns never got laid . . . never lied, or laid.'

'She didn't lie. She told me that she came here and you hooked her up to some sort of machine. She now believes herself to be a man.'

'Have you checked her genitalia?'

'What?'

'If I were you, I'd check her genitalia. If she believes herself to be a man, there's only one way to make her unbelieve it, inbelieve it, disbelieve . . . Look inside her knickers and point out that she has a . . . '

'I am *not* in the habit of looking into nuns' knickers, Professor!'

I am! 'You're in the habit every day.'

'Not that sort of habit. Sister Elizabeth told me that your female assistant suggested doing something disgusting with a broom handle and . . . I can't bring myself to repeat the dreadful words.'

'My assistant was probably asking her to help sweep up.'

'Ah, so you now admit that Sister Elizabeth was here.'

'Of course she was here.'

'But you said she wasn't.'

'Did I? How odd.'

'You suggested that she'd lied to me.'

'I'm sorry, but I have no recollection of the suggested conversation whatsoever.'

'There's something very wrong with you, Professor.'

'Yes, I quite agree. Shall we put it down to retention loss on my part?'

'Retention loss? I'm not at all happy, Professor.'

'I know the feeling. Have you tried turning to drink?'

'I *beg* your pardon?'

'Or drugs. There's nothing like sex, drugs and rock and roll – especially perverted sex, cannabis and Jimi Hendrix.'

'You're obviously demented, Professor. There's no point in continuing this conversation.'

'Which conversation was that?'

'I intend to take Sister Elizabeth to a psychiatrist and discover exactly what's going on in her mind.'

'Ah, er . . . I don't think that's a very good idea.'

'Why? Is it because you'll be proved guilty?'

'I'm sorry?'

'Is it because . . . '

'Yes, it is a lovely day. We've been so unlucky with the weather recently.'

'Professor Snide, I really don't think . . . '

'Neither do I, I've heard that it's not good for the brain. In fact, I was talking to a Martian the other day and he reckoned . . . '

'I'll be in touch, Professor.'

'Is that local?'

'What?'

'You said you'll be in touch, I just wondered where touch was as I've never heard of the place.'

'Good day, Professor!'

'Yes, it's all down to the beautiful weather.'

Rubbing his hands together as the woman left and Lucifer closed the doors, Snide again wondered where Miss Hocks had got to. The Reverend Mother Horgasm was out of the way for a while, the Baron was shaving the schoolgirlie government agent's beautiful fanny . . . Everything was being dealt with nicely, apart from Miss Hocks.

'Lucifer, did the destruction of the cannon go according to the destructive plan?'

'Yes, sir. The only sign of anything untoward is a massive crater in the bank of the moat.'

'That's OK, we'll put it down to an alien spacecraft attack.'

'A letter arrived for you, sir.'

'Where is it?'

'In my jacket pocket.'

'Give it to me, then.'

'Give it to you? Isn't that illegal, sir?'

'The letter, you fool!'

'Yes, of course. I took the liberty of steaming it open, but you won't know because I've been to great pains to carefully reseal it.'

'Good man. Your resourcefulness leaves me speechless.'

'Thank you, sir.'

Reading the letter, Snide frowned. It was from MI5 to a female agent posing as a mobile hairdresser, but it had been incorrectly addressed to the Professor. *They've made a right cock-up!* he mused, discovering that the agent was going to infiltrate the castle and take photographs of not only the dungeon but, hopefully, of young female prisoners, too.

'Do you need a haircut?' he asked Lucifer.

'Why do you ask, sir?'

'Because I wondered whether you needed a haircut. Why else would I ask you whether you needed a haircut?'

'No, I don't.'

'I do. If a mobile hairdresser happens to call, ask her in.'

'Yes, sir.'

'She'll be easily recognizable by her photographic equipment. You know the sort of thing, cameras, lighting, tripods and the like. Don't let on that you've seen the equipment, just ask her in and then call me.'

'Yes, sir. By the way, I owe you fifty pounds.'

'What for?'

'I shagged a shaved cunt, sir – as you said I could.'

'Shagged a shaved cunt? Who did this shagged shaved cunt belong to?'

'A woman in the keep.'

'There's no one in the keep.'

'There was, sir. She had no head and . . .'

'That's the headless lady, you fool!'

'Oh, dear! I thought it rather odd that she had no head.'

'She has no clitoris, either. Was she any good?'

'Her cunt was as cold as ice.'

'I'm not surprised. Don't let it happen again, Lucifer. I'll not have you screwing ghosts, it's immoral. I'll let you off the fifty pounds. In fact, no, I won't.'

'I'll pay you later, sir.'

'Right. In the meantime, I want you to set up a hair-dressing salon in one of the chambers upstairs. You know the sort of thing, a chair, sink, mirror, hair spray, scissors, handcuffs, lengths of rope, fucking great dildos and . . . '

'Handcuffs and . . . '

'To capture the hairdresser, Lucifer. We'll tie her to the chair and torture the truth out of her.'

'I'll see to it straightaway, sir.'

'Blast, there's the fucking doorbell again. You carry on and I'll see who it is.'

'Yes, sir.'

Waiting until the butler had made himself scarce, the Professor moved to the castle doors. Who was it this time? he wondered. DI Peel and his men, more than likely. There again, it might be the mobile hairdresser. Opening the door, he frowned as he gazed at a besuited man with a copy of *The Times* folded over his hand.

'May I help you?' Snide asked.

'No, I'm quite capable of knocking on the door, thank you.'

'What?'

'Oh, you've opened the door. Er . . . I'm looking for one Professor Snide.'

'How many are there?'

'One, I believe. Are you he?'

'Am I he? No, of course I'm not he – I'm me.'

'Who's me?'

'I have no idea who you are. I think you'd better identify yourself before I make some wild and completely wrong guess and have you thrown to the lions.'

'My name's Potter, I'm from the Ministry of Castles and Dungeons.'

'Ah, one of the fascist bastards!'

'You must be Professor Snide.'

'Why must I?'

'Because I say so.'

'Wait there and I'll get the Professor.'

'You're not the Professor?'

'If I was, I'd hardly go and get myself, would I?'

'No, I suppose not.'

Chasing after Lucifer, Snide ordered him to go and tell Potter that he was the Professor. 'But, sir . . . ' the man protested. 'You're Professor Snide, not me.' Slapping him around the head, Snide kicked him in the bollocks for good measure before dragging him to the castle doors.

'This is Professor Snide,' the Professor said as he approached Potter.

'You must accompany me to Westminster, Professor.'

'But . . . ' Lucifer began.

'I must warn you that there's a gun beneath this newspaper folded over my hand.'

'You'd better go with him, Professor,' Snide said, kicking his butler in the shin. 'You'll be all right. Do your usual stuff once you find a suitable spot.'

'But . . . '

'This way, Professor Snide!'

The mistaken-identity trick would allow time to send the ransom note and the mouldy peas to the government, Snide mused as his butler was led away. Of course, if Lucifer did his job, Potter would disappear before they reached the village, never to be seen again.

'Time for tea and cucumber sandwiches!' he grinned, making his way to his living quarters. 'And then find the headless lady and . . . ' *I wonder what it's like?*

Chapter Five

'Where have you been?' the Baron asked as the Professor staggered out of the keep the following morning with his clothes in shreds. 'I've been searching everywhere for you.'

'You shouldn't have bothered.'

'I didn't bother much.'

'To be dishonest, I had a spot of bother with the headless lady last night. The dirty bitch tried to drag me off to the astral planes and sexually assault me. I'll murder the cow.'

'She's already dead, my friend.'

'Fuck, so she is. Has DI Peel been with his men?'

'Is he gay?'

'I have no idea, Baron.'

'I can't say whether or not he's been with his men, but he's not been here.'

'Thank God for that. So, what's been happening?'

'Your butler seems to have disappeared.'

'Yes, I know about that. How's the schoolgirlie government agent?'

'Angelica has been shaved and she's still on the rack. Oh, and she's been fucked rotten several times.'

'Excellent!'

'I've also sent the ransom note to the government.'

'And the mouldy peas?'

'And the mouldy peas.'

'Pink and brown?'

'Pink and brown.'

'Have you seen Miss Hocks?'

'No, my friend, I haven't.'

'Fucking woman, I'll have her clitoris for this. OK, I'm going to do something really perverted to the government agent. I think I'll start by shoving bananas up her bumhole and then . . . I don't know, I'll think of something. Baron, I'd like you to do me a small favour.'

'Anything, as long as it's illegal.'

'It's highly illegal, and probably against the law. I want you to go into the village and rape the postmistress, give her a length right up her bum.'

'There *are* limits, my friend!'

'Shit, I suppose there are. OK, nab a horny young girl and drag her back here. I'll force the agent to endure crude lesbian sex with her.'

'I'll get off straight away.'

'No, get a girl from the village first.'

'Right you are.'

The schoolgirlie government agent was in for the perverted time of her young life, Snide mused as he took a shower and donned another set of clothes. Her bottom-hole was to be abused beyond belief, and her cunt and her mouth and her tits and . . . 'God, I'm a sad pervert!' he breathed as he approached the dungeon. 'I should be arrested for gross indecency.'

The Baron had left Angelica chained to the rack lying on her stomach, her arms and legs stretched, her rounded buttocks perfectly positioned for a damned good whipping. Her hairless cunny lips bulged beneath her brown anal entrance, fleshy, smooth, lickable – and he wondered whether to drink the juice from her tight cunt. A good arse-fucking was in order first, he mused, parting her tensed buttocks and eyeing the small portal to her bowels.

'Get away from me!' she screeched as he ran his fingertip over her sensitive brown hole. 'If you dare to . . . '

'God, here we go again!' he laughed. 'One minute you're enjoying two cocks spunking you, and the next you're complaining.'

'I've been here all night! You can't do this, it's illegal!'

'Just about everything I do is illegal, Angelica – if not against the law. By the way, your men don't seem to be doing much to save you.'

'They . . . they'll be coming soon.'

'Lucky for them! Are you going to suck them off or allow them to fuck your tight cunt?'

'Don't be disgusting.'

'Sorry, I can't help it. It's a trait I picked up from my mother.'

Pressing the tip of his finger into her tight bumhole as she wriggled and squirmed, Snide pondered on the girl. Working for the government, he reckoned that she'd have no back-up. If an agent was captured by the enemy, the government would probably deny all knowledge, leaving the agent to die a gruesome death – or worse. There were no men, king's, queen's, or otherwise. She'd be listed as a missing person, and no one would come looking for her.

'Your bum's nice and tight,' he murmured, forcing his finger deeper into her hot duct. 'Did you enjoy me fucking your bum?'

'No, I did not!'

'Do you enjoy lesbian sex?'

'No, I don't!' she spat.

'That's a shame, because you're going to have some.'

'Unless you release me, you'll find yourself in deep trouble.'

'The only thing I'll find myself deep in is your cunt!' he sniggered.

'I'll do a deal with you.'

'Ah, now you're talking.'

'I'll tell you about the government's plans.'

'Go on.'

'What do I get in return for the information?'

'I won't fuck your bum.'

'Oh.'

'What's the matter?'

'Well, I . . . I thought you might offer me breakfast in return.'

'If you have breakfast, I'll have to fuck your bum.'

'Oh, good! I mean . . . Yes, it's a deal.'

Even government agents enjoyed a bum-fucking, he reflected, forcing a second finger into her dank anal canal. Wondering whether the Baron had managed to nab a village girl, he pondered on lesbian sex, dreaming of forcing his victim to push her tongue into a girl's wet cunt and lap up her lust milk. But first, he wanted information.

'Do you know anything about an MI5 agent posing as a mobile hairdresser?' he asked.

'No, I don't,' she sighed as he forced a third finger into her anal canal, stretching her duct wide open. 'I have nothing to do with MI5, I work for shag.'

'Shag?'

'S.H.A.G. The Secretary for Horribly Abducted Girls.'

'You're rather young to hold such a job.'

'I was abducted from school by the government. They needed a schoolgirl to pose as a schoolgirl to catch sad perverts who abduct schoolgirls.'

'What else can you tell me?'

'Only my name, rank and number.'

'In that case, I'll fuck your bottom.'

'What about breakfast?'

'Fuck breakfast.'

Whipping his trousers off and climbing onto the rack, Snide parted Angelica's weal-lined buttocks and pushed his bulbous glans against her delicate brown tissue. Whimpering as her tight portal yielded, his mammoth knob slipping into her hot duct, she gasped, her naked body quivering in her lewd pleasure. His solid shaft gliding into her rectal tube, her brown tissue stretched to capacity, he yanked her firm buttocks further apart and gazed at the lascivious sight.

'You should see your bumhole,' he said, driving his penis deeper into her bowels. 'God, you've taken a good eight inches, and it's still going in!'

'Ah!' she gasped as her bowels opened to accommodate his giant cock. 'I feel as if . . . as if I'm going to explode!'

'Another few inches, and I'll be right in. Here it comes, hold tight!'

His veined shaft driving further into her bloated duct, his balls finally came to rest against her naked vaginal lips. His throbbing knob absorbing the dank heat of her inner core, he slowly withdrew his solid penis. Watching her brown tissue pulling away from her anal crease, clinging to his rock-hard shaft, he rammed into her again. Increasing his rhythm, his balls slapping her swollen pussy lips, his lower belly smacking her crimson buttocks, he breathed heavily as his orgasm neared. Her naked body jolting, her clitoris swelling, pulsating, she let out gasps of pleasure as he crudely arse-fucked her. But it wasn't pleasure she was going to experience once he'd spermed her bowels – it was the agony of the leather whip!

'God, I'm coming!' the Professor breathed as his knob swelled within her spasming anal sheath. 'Ah! Oh! God!'

'Oh, my bum! Ah! I'm going to split open!'

'Coming! Ah, ah!'

His heavy balls swinging, his shaft thrusting in and out of her velvety rectal sheath, his spunk shot from his pulsating knob, filling her bowels. Cries of lewd sexual gratification resounding around the rack chamber, Snide continued his crude anal fucking, slapping her rounded buttocks as he rode her like a horse. Finally slowing his pistoning as his flow of sperm stemmed, he stilled his huge organ, his knob deflating deep within her well-spunked bowels.

'That was good,' he murmured, slowly pulling his gigantic shaft out of her inflamed arse. 'Christ, I needed that.'

'God, you're so big!' she gasped as his knob emerged from her bottom-hole with a loud sucking sound. 'Oh, ah! My . . . my bum!'

'Talking of your bum, it's high time you received another severe buttock whipping.'

'No, no, I can't take another . . . '

'Of course you can,' he grinned, climbing off the rack and tugging his trousers up. 'All government agents can take a good buttock-whipping, they've been trained to endure such lewd delights. You'll endure a good bum-thrashing, and then a tit-whipping, and then . . . Fuck, there's the doorbell. Don't go away, I won't be a minute.'

'I can hardly go away!'

It was either Lucifer returning from his murder trip or the Baron returning with an ignorant village slut, Snide mused as he climbed the steps. Unless Miss Hocks had returned from wherever she'd been. *I really must give that woman a damned good fucking,* he thought as he opened the castle doors.

'Hallo, I'm a mobile hairdresser,' a young woman smiled. 'I was just passing and I wondered whether you'd like a haircut.'

'A haircut? Of course I don't want a bloody haircut. What do you mean by coming here and asking me whether I'd like a fucking haircut? Good grief, a haircut, indeed. If I needed a bloody haircut I'd go to the fucking village and . . . Ah, you're the mobile hairdresser! Er . . . Yes, I'd love a haircut. Please, come in.'

Helping her carry her photographic equipment into the

banqueting hall, Snide scrutinized the young woman. Around six feet tall with long jet-black hair, she was model material. Her breasts perfectly outlined by her tight white blouse, her long shapely thighs revealed by her red micro-skirt, she was also extremely fuckable. She'd be an ideal candidate for the rack, he mused, picturing her curly black pubes. A vulval shaving wouldn't go amiss, either!

'So, you just happened to be passing?' he asked.

'Yes, quite a coincidence, isn't it?'

'Is it? Oh, er . . . Yes, yes, it is. I was only saying to my butler last year that I really must get my hair cut. How much do you charge?'

'Nothing, I do it because I love cutting hair.'

'Oh, so do I!'

'You're a hairdresser?'

'I'm a shaving artist, a piss artist . . . Er, what I mean is . . . Where do you want to do it?'

'Well, preferably on your head.'

'I thought as much. Shall we go down to the dungeon?'

'What for?'

'To cut my hair.'

'Oh, yes. You haven't mentioned my photographic equipment.'

'No, I thought it best not to.'

'Don't you find it odd?'

'There's nothing odd about cameras. Right, let's get the equipment down to the dungeon and we'll begin. I'm Professor Snide, Sexton Snide.'

'And I'm Gigi.'

'What a lovely name. I once fucked a horse . . . I mean, I once *rode* a horse named Gigi.'

'How nice for you.'

'The horse rather enjoyed it, too.'

Forewarned was forearmed, Snide mused, wondering what

to do with his forearm as he lugged the equipment down to
the dungeon. It was best to play along with her for a while,
and then pounce and chain her to the wall in the torture
chamber. Play it by ear before playing with her pussy.

'Where would you like me?' he asked, dumping the equipment on the floor.

'I'll set up here and then we'll get started. What do you do
down here? It looks like a laboratory.'

'No, the lavatory's upstairs, on the left by the . . . '

'A *laboratory*.'

'Ah, yes, it is. I'm working to cure the clinically insane.'

'How uninteresting. What's in that room?'

A naked government agent. 'That's the rack chamber.'

'And that one?'

'That's the torture chamber. Would you like me to show
you?'

'Do you have the time?'

'No, my watch has stopped. I really must call a plumber in
to repair it. Before I do that, I'll show you the torture
chamber.'

Opening the door, he led the young woman into the
chamber, pondering on her vaginal lips, her hot, wet cunny.
Wondering, as she gazed at the chains and ran her fingers
over the leather whips, whether she masturbated with a
cucumber, he decided not to waste any time and to get
straight down to the job of abduction and severe sexual
abuse.

'Allow me to show you what these steel rings are for,' he
smiled, turning her round and lifting her hands above her
head.

'What are you doing?' she asked as he cuffed her wrists to
the rings.

'I'm capturing an MI5 agent.'

'A what?'

'Capturing you, an MI5 agent.'

'But I'm a mobile hairdresser!'

'You're no more a mobile hairdresser than I'm a Swiss watchmaker.'

'But . . .'

'Whatever you are, you're now *im*mobile. To take stock, I have a schoolgirl agent posing as a schoolgirl, and another agent posing as a mobile hairdresser. All agents must be severely fucked and spermed, it's in the rule book. Right, I'm going to rip your knickers off and take a look at your cunt.'

'You can't do that!'

'Why not?'

'Well, it's not the done thing.'

'Of course it is, Gigi. It's perfectly normal to rip women's knickers off and look at their cunts.'

'No, you can't do it – it's obscene.'

'You'd be surprised by what I can do, obscene or otherwise!' he smiled, kneeling down and parting her feet as wide as he could.

Cuffing her ankles to the steel rings set in the bottom of the wall, he stood up and was about to rip her blouse open and expose her mammary spheres when he heard movements in the lab. Leaving the girl cursing and complaining, the Professor went into the lab to discover the Baron standing next to a naked young girl. Eyeing her firm breasts, the triangle of dark curls below her smooth stomach, Snide reckoned she was ripe for a severe anal fucking. Her dark hair in a ponytail, her hands tied behind her back, her young body vulnerable, he was pleased with the Baron's work.

'Baron, you've done well,' he grinned. 'She's a rare beauty.'

'Her beauty's pretty rare, too. I happened to discover her walking out of the village police station. It's the ideal place to nab a young girl because no one in their right mind would do such a thing under the eyes of the law.'

111

'Fiendish, I must say.'

'Had a police officer seen me, he'd have thought nothing of it.'

'Ingenious. So, my horny little angel, what's your name?'

'I'm not telling you,' she returned.

'What's in a name, anyway? You've done extremely well, Baron. She's stripped and ready for . . .'

'I didn't strip her, my friend. She was naked with her hands tied behind her back when she left the police station, but she won't tell me why.'

'Misplaced her clothes and got her hands caught up in a length of rope, I would imagine – it's easily done. Tell me, my horny little angel, do you enjoy parting your cunt lips and frigging your clitty off?'

'Don't be disgusting!'

'Sorry, I can't help it. Right, down to business. We've a schoolgirlie agent in the rack chamber and a mobile hairdresser agent in the torture chamber. I really don't know what we're going to do with this little sexpot.'

'A mobile hairdresser?'

'Yes, she cuts hair. Actually, she doesn't.'

'Might I suggest that we force this little beauty into lesbian sex, my friend?'

'Better still, we'll force her to lick the mobile hairdresser's cunt. I'll give you a shout when I've prepared the girl.'

Slipping into the torture chamber and kneeling before the squirming hairdresser, Snide tugged her tight red microskirt down her long legs and ripped the garment in two. Although she protested wildly as he tore her knickers off, revealing her thick pubic bush, there was nothing she could do to halt the violation of her curvaceous young body.

'This is rape!' Gigi screamed.

'MI5 agents are well aware of what they'll have to endure should they be caught by the enemy,' Snide returned. 'You must have been prepared for this. I'm sure you've had in-house training.'

'I'm a bloody hairdresser, not an agent!'

'Yes, and I'm the Pope's left bollock. OK, let's have a look at your tits.'

'You can't do that!'

'Why not? Haven't you got any tits?'

'Of course I have.'

'Then I can look at them.'

Tearing her blouse off and ripping her bra apart, Snide gazed longingly at the girl's beautiful mammary spheres, her elongated, wedge-shaped nipples. Tweaking her sensitive milk teats as she stared at him in disgust, he ran his finger down over the gentle rise of her smooth stomach and pushed it between her swollen vaginal lips. Grinning wickedly as he parted her inner sex petals and located her vaginal entrance, he pushed his finger deep into the creamy heat of her tight cunt. Again insisting that she was a hairdresser as he massaged her soft inner flesh, she looked down at the Professor as he sucked her erect nipple into his wet mouth.

'Unless you release me and allow me to carry on with my hairdressing job, I'll . . . '

'Look, I know what you are and you know what I am. I mean, I know what you are and you know what you are,' he said, withdrawing his finger and slipping it into his mouth. 'Mmm, you taste nice. I'm rather partial to a drop of cunt milk. I have a great vaginal affection for vaginal milk.'

'Will you get it into your thick head that I am *not* a bloody hairdresser . . . I mean, an agent.'

'Ah, a slip of the tongue. There'll be a slip of *my* tongue in a minute, slipping up your hot, tight, well-juiced cunny hole. And if you're really lucky, there'll be a slip of my cock, slipping up your hot bum.'

'I have *never* met anyone as crude as you, Professor Snide.'

'A second slip of the tongue. How do you know my name?'

'You told me.'

'Ah, so I did. My bloody memory's going to pot.'

'You're insane.'

'That's most observant of you, Gigi. Now, where was I? More to the point, who am I? Ah, of course, I'm Professor Snide.'

'You should be locked up.'

'I will be later. OK, let the lesbian cunny-licking commence. Baron, bring the girl off . . . I mean, in!'

Dragging the young maiden into the torture chamber, the Baron was about to force her to kneel before the naked agent and order her to lick her cunny slit when Lucifer materialized in the doorway. Turning to face his butler, Snide frowned, immediately realizing that something was very wrong.

'What is it, Lucifer?' he asked.

'Sir, DI Peel is here with his men.'

'Fuck it! What happened to that man from the Ministry of Castles and Dungeons?'

'Mr Potter has been unavoidably detained.'

'Unavoidably detained?'

'He accidentally dropped his gun when I karate chopped his bollocks off. He's now naked, and tied to a tree in the Forest of the Dead.'

'Well done, Lucifer. OK, I'd better go and see Peel. Er, Baron, I'll leave you to force the girl to commit a vile and highly illegal act of rampant lesbian filth.'

'Of course, my friend.'

DI Peel wasn't at all happy, Snide observed as he went out to the moat. Standing with his men behind him, the Inspector gazed at the crater where the cannon had been, shaking his head in disbelief. Apart from pieces of shrapnel scattered here and there, there was no evidence. No cannon, no balls – no bollocking!

'What a lovely day, Inspector,' Snide said. 'It really is a good summer.'

'Where is the cannon, Professor?'

'The cannon? I'm sorry, I'm not with you.'

'Of course you are, you're standing in front of me.'

'So I am, how remiss of me.'

'What have you done with it?'

'It's in my trousers.'

'The *cannon*, Professor.'

'I would imagine he's in the cathedral. Knobbing a choirboy's bum, more than likely. You know what these church people are like, bloody perverted, disgusting, filthy, hypocritical . . . '

'Don't play games with me. You've destroyed the evidence.'

'Have I? I have no recollection of evidential destruction.'

'You'll have to accompany me to the station and explain yourself to the Super.'

'It's a super idea but I'm entertaining at the moment. Could you pop back a little later?'

'No, I could not!'

'Next year, perhaps?'

'No!'

'OK, just let me nip up to the toilet and I'll be right with you. I have to check my ballcock.'

Slipping into the castle, Snide locked the huge doors and rubbed his hands together. There was no way Peel could get into the castle, unless he had a cannon handy – which he hadn't. What with the Inspector stumped and Potter tied to a tree in the Forest of the Dead, things were looking pretty good. But there'd be more police officers and more agents, he knew – they wouldn't give up. Pondering on the ransom note as Lucifer approached, he wondered what the government's reaction would be.

'Sir, I took it upon myself to stock a cache of arms atop the turret,' Lucifer intoned.

'A cache of arms? You've not been digging up graves again, have you?'

'No, sir – firearms. Machine-guns, rocket launchers, hand grenades . . . '

'Excellent, Lucifer! You have insight.'

'No, they're well out of sight.'

'Good, good.'

'I did try to nab an F16 from the secret air force base at Plonkton-on-the-Moor, but the RAF were none too pleased.'

'Stuck-up fucking snobs!'

'Apparently, they'd nicked it from the American Air Force and didn't want it nicked from them.'

'Bastards! By the way, have you seen Miss Hocks?'

'No, sir.'

'Where is the bloody woman? What's the point in having an assistant if she's never here to assist me? I've spent three long years creating my alpha-wave transference machine, and failed in my quest to turn her into a rampant nymphomaniac – and now she's buggered off somewhere. I'll have her womb for this! Right, I'd better get back to the dungeon.'

'Yes, sir. I'll go to the turret and set up the firearms.'

'Right. Fuck, there's the phone. I'll get it, you go atit the turret.'

As DI Peel hammered on the doors, shouting and yelling, Snide grabbed the receiver, wondering what he was going to be confronted with next. 'I'm sorry, you have the wrong number,' he said, slamming the phone down before the caller could speak. Ignoring Peel's threats as the man continued to hammer on the doors, Snide looked at the phone as it rang again.

'What is it?' he snapped, pressing the receiver to his ear.

'Sexton, it's Spasm.'

'Spaz, how are you?'

'A little concerned about my au pair.'

'Why, what's wrong with her?'

'She returned to the house, and then disappeared.'

'Have you checked the bathroom?'

'I've checked every room. I was wondering whether you've seen her?'

'I've seen her fanny. I . . . I mean, no, I haven't. Have you tried the Foreign Office?'

'What would she be doing there?'

'Well, she's foreign, isn't she?'

'Yes, but . . . You didn't fuck her brain, did you?'

'How the hell could I fuck her brain?'

'Fuck, as in fuck up – not fuck, as in fuck fuck.'

'Fuck fuck?'

'Shag shag.'

'Shag . . . '

'Screw, squelch, spurty spunky.'

'What *are* you talking about, Spaz?'

'Did you fuck up my au pair's brain?'

'No, of course I didn't. Hang on a minute, my assistant has also gone missing. They got on well together, *very* well. Fucking lesbians!'

'Are you putting two and two together, Sexton?'

'No, why would I do that?'

'I just wondered.'

'I reckon they've run off together – eloped, even.'

'Ah! Ah, yes! Oh!'

'What's the matter?'

'Oh, my God!'

'What is it, Spaz?'

'I don't know how I'm going to explain this to my wife!'

'Explain what?'

'I've been wanking while we've been chatting and I've just spunked all over my new trousers.'

117

'Doesn't life stink at times?'

'Yes, it bloody well does. Oh, well, not to worry. Look, if you happen to come across my au pair, would you tell her to come home?'

'Once I've come across her, of course I'll tell her to go home.'

'OK, I'll talk to you later.'

'Yes, much later. In fact . . . '

'Don't start that again, Sexton!'

'Sorry, Spaz. Bye for now.'

Frowning, the Professor pondered on Miss Hocks and Helga. He was pretty sure that they'd run off together and were probably licking and fingering each other's cunts. Miss Hocks was in for the tit-whipping and arse-shagging of her life when she returned, *if* she returned. 'Fucking lesbians,' he murmured as the Baron approached.

'I have an idea, my friend.'

'What's that?' Snide asked, rubbing his chin. 'I really must stop rubbing my chin.'

'Your machine, I might be able to modify it.'

'Tell me more.'

'Not now, I want to tell you about my idea.'

'Go on.'

'If I can increase the power, it might be possible to use the helmet as a satellite dish. We could aim the dish at a passing young girl and suck out her brain patterns, or induce someone else's patterns into her brain.'

'It could be fucking dangerous, Baron.'

'Life's dangerous.'

'Good point. OK, see what you can do.'

Making his way to the turret as the Baron returned to the dungeon, Snide had an idea. If he recorded the alpha waves from a young girl and somehow rearranged them, increasing the libido and erasing inhibitions, it might be possible to create a custom-made whore. *Bring the patterns up on the computer screen and amplify the libido peaks*, he mused as he climbed the stairs to the turret.

'Ah, Lucifer,' he grinned. 'My God, you've got a lot of arms!'

'Only two, sir.'

'The guns, you fool!'

'Ah, yes.'

'Fuck it! Look down there!' Snide bellowed, leaning over the wall. 'It's Peel and his band of not so merry men. I'd have thought they'd have fucked off by now. I'll bet they're all fucking homosexual Marxists.'

'I've been watching them, sir. They've been pointing at the castle as if they're planning something – a raid, I would imagine.'

'Air raid? They haven't got any planes.'

'No, *a* raid, not *air* raid.'

'Fucking communist sods. Chuck a grenade at the bastards, just to show them that we mean business.'

'Yes, sir.'

There'd be no way Peel could prove where the bomb had come from, Snide mused as his butler grabbed a grenade and pulled the pin. No one could prove that it wasn't another alien spacecraft attack. As Lucifer dropped the grenade, Snide leaned over the wall and watched it splash into the moat. The explosion rocking the castle, water showering the Inspector and his men, he grinned.

'Perfect!' he chuckled as Peel ran for cover. 'Look at them, scurrying off like frightened rabbits!'

'The grenade *was* rather effective, sir.'

'Indeed, it was. I don't suppose we'll be seeing Peel for a while.'

'They might return with reinforcements, sir.'

'If they do, they'll have the alpha-wave machine to contend with.'

'You have a devious plan in mind?'

'I do, Lucifer – I do. Right, you stay up here and bomb the bastards if they dare to come back. I'm going to have a wank. No, I'd better go and help the Baron first.'

Discovering the Baron in the dungeon with a cigar in his mouth, Snide looked at the alpha-wave machine. Working with a screwdriver, mumbling to himself, the Baron had the machine in pieces. If the idea worked, they could aim the satellite dish at any passing young girl and have her open her legs and beg to be fucked, he mused, his cock twitching as he imagined something completely and utterly immoral – let alone against the law!

'How did the lesbian licking go?' the Professor asked, turning and gazing at the nameless girl tied over the bench, her feet wide apart on the floor, her rounded buttocks perfectly positioned for a good whipping.

'Very well, my friend,' the Baron replied.

'Good, good. Lucifer has bombed Peel and his men so we won't be hearing from them for a while.'

'I heard the explosion.'

'While you're working on the machine, I'd better familiarize myself with this little beauty's bottom-hole.'

'I thought you might wish to familiarize yourself with her bottom-hole, that's why I tied her over the bench.'

'Good thinking, Baron. Great minds think alike, as do perverted minds.'

'By the way, I've discovered her name.'

'Jesus Christ!'

'No, it's Penny.'

'For your thoughts!' Snide chuckled, sitting on a chair behind the girl's rounded buttocks.

Examining her fleshy vaginal lips nestling between her parted thighs, Snide peeled her sex hillocks apart and gazed longingly at the glistening pink flesh surrounding her open hole. As she writhed and squirmed and yelled expletives, he grabbed the anal speculum from the bench and parted her tensed buttocks. Carefully inserting the speculum, driving it deep into her rectal duct, he squeezed the levers together, watching excitedly as her brown hole slowly opened.

'Please!' she cried as her secret hole opened further. 'You're hurting me!'

'Of course I'm not!' the Professor chuckled. 'I'm just having a look up your bum. I enjoy looking up young girls' bumholes.'

'That reminds me, I have to go into the village for something,' the Baron said, bounding up the stone steps as Snide twisted the speculum.

'I'll see you later, Baron. Now, my little beauty, let's have a look deep inside your bowels.'

'No, stop it!'

'Be honest, you love it.'

'Love it? You're insane!'

'A shrewd observation, Penny. You should consider psychiatry as a profession. Damn, there's the bloody phone again. I do wish everyone would fuck off and leave me in peace.'

Leaving the anal speculum in place, Snide moved to the phone, wondering whether to answer it or not. Surprised that he'd not been cut off for non-payment of the bill, he finally grabbed the receiver. He wasn't in the least surprised to hear DI Peel's angry voice. Coughing and spluttering, the man was *more* than angry!

'You're really in trouble this time, Professor!' the Inspector yelled.

'Don't be ridiculous,' Snide replied. 'It wasn't my fault that an alien spacecraft attacked you.'

'Alien . . . What *are* you talking about?'

'The alien attack wasn't my fault. If you want to go

hanging around an area well known for anal activity . . . I mean, alien activity, then what do you expect?'

'I'm not calling about that! Where's my daughter?'

'I didn't even know you had a daughter, Inspector. How old is she?'

'Eighteen.'

'Wonderful! I'll bet she's really . . . Er . . . '

'She was abducted from the police station steps by a strange man in a cloak.'

'How odd.'

'What have you done with her?'

'It wasn't *me*. I am neither strange nor cloaked. What was she doing on the police station steps?'

'She was a plant.'

'Cannabis?'

'I'm fresh out of . . . No, you fool! In the line of duty, I got her to hang around the police station steps, naked with her hands tied behind her back, as a trap – as bait to capture the fiendish sex pervert.'

'I really don't see what this has to do with me, Inspector.'

'Professor, whenever a teenage girl goes missing from the village, it has *every*thing to do with you. Especially naked teenage girls with their hands tied behind their backs.'

'I couldn't disagree more. How will you explain the abduction of your abducted daughter to the abducted girl's mother?'

'I know she's in your dungeon so there's no point denying it.'

'I can assure you that her mother isn't here.'

'My daughter, not her mother!'

'Her brother?'

'Listen to me, Professor Snide – unless my daughter is set free within ten minutes, I'll call the army in to blow your castle up.'

'I wouldn't do that, Inspector. Hypodermically speaking, you'd blow your daughter up in the process.'

'Ah, so you admit that she's there?'

'I said, hypodermically speaking.'

'Are you on drugs, Professor?'

'Of course I'm not. Well, only slightly.'

'There's another thing. Apart from the destruction of the village stores and post office, and the missing village girl whose father wants to sue you for shaving a certain area of her body, and the hand grenade thrown at my men, and the wilful destruction of police evidence . . . '

'I had nothing to do with the cannon. You know very well that it was another alien attack.'

'And resisting police arrest, and the abduction of my naked daughter, there's the question of . . . I'll have to call you back, my other phone's ringing.'

Replacing the receiver, Snide gazed at the girl's brown tissue crudely stretched open by the anal speculum. *The Inspector's daughter?* he mused, wondering what terribly perverted things he could do to her. He was sure that the army wouldn't be called in, not all the time young Penny was in the dungeon with her bumhole stretched open. There was all the time in the world to abuse and use the girl's curvaceous naked body. But he knew Peel wouldn't give up. Grabbing the ringing phone, he decided to bargain with the Inspector.

'I'll tell you what I'll do, Inspector,' he began.

'It's all right, forget all I said.'

'What?'

'Forget that I rang you just now.'

'But what about your naked daughter?'

'She shouldn't have got herself into this mess. It's her fault that she's in this predicament and I hope she learns a lesson from it.'

'What about the shaved village girl and the village stores and post office and the grenade and resisting . . . '

'Forget it, it doesn't matter. All charges and investigations have been dropped as from now. Good day, Professor.'

Now that was a turn-up for the cookery books! Snide mused. Suddenly realizing what had changed the Inspector's mind, he rubbed his chin. The man had obviously had a call from someone in a high place. *Someone on top of a wardrobe?* he pondered. *No, the government, more than likely*. They must have received the ransom note and . . .

'What's my father going to do?' Penny asked.

'Nothing. He said that, as far as he's concerned, it's your own fault that you're going to be sexually abused and fucked rotten.'

'He'd never say that!'

'Well, not in those words, exactly. But he did tell me that you need psychiatric help.'

'Of course I don't!'

'Any young girl who walks down police station steps naked with her hands tied behind her back must need psychiatric help, it stands to reason.'

'But I was a plant.'

'And anyone who believes that they're a plant *definitely* needs help! As it happens, I'm an unqualified psychiatrist, so I'll help you by trying to unearth the root of your cannabis plant . . . the root of your problem.'

'No!'

'One thing I've learned about the clinically insane is that a damned good anal fucking usually helps. It gets right to the bowels of the problem . . . the root of the problem.'

'No!'

'I do wish you'd stop shouting. I'd better fuck your cunt first in order to lubricate my cock in readiness for your beautiful bumhole.'

124

'No!'

'Yes!'

Unzipping his trousers as he stood up, the Professor hauled out his magnificent penis and rolled his foreskin back. This was what psychiatry was all about, he reflected, parting the girl's fleshy vaginal hillocks and pressing his bulbous glans against the pink flesh surrounding her drenched sex hole. Fighting clinical insanity with a damned good vaginal fucking followed by a bloody good anal rogering was the basis of sound psychiatry.

Chuckling as she squirmed and wriggled, he propelled his swollen knob into her tight vaginal canal, gasping as the welcoming heat of her young cunt permeated his huge glans. She had a damned good body, he observed as she trembled and quivered, and the tightest cunt imaginable. Dressed in a white blouse and gymslip with ankle socks and navy-blue knickers, she'd be an ideal schoolgirlie lookalike.

'No!' she cried again as his shaft glided deeper into her tight sex duct, stretching her creamy-wet vaginal walls. 'Please, you can't do it!'

'I *am* doing it!' he returned excitedly as his cock drove further into her spasming cunt. 'God, you're hot!'

'I'm a policeman's daughter, for goodness sake!'

'All the better! There's nothing I like more than fucking policemen's daughters. 'Allo, 'allo, 'allo! What's comin' off 'ere, then?'

'You're insane!'

'Why, thank you so much. Evenin' all – 'allo, 'allo, 'allo.'

Eyeing the anal speculum protruding from her abused bottom-hole, his arousal soaring, Snide withdrew his horse-like cock and rammed into her hot cunt again. She was bloody tight, he mused, watching his glistening shaft repeatedly emerge and drive deep into her well-juiced sex sheath. Her naked body jolting, he pondered on his next perverted move in the violation of her sex holes. An anal fucking, and then . . .

'I've got it!' he cried, sliding his cunny-wet penis out of her vaginal sheath. 'The gamma-ray machine!'

'What?' she gasped, clinging to the bench as her dripping pink petals closed, concealing her hot sex hole.

'How would you like your clitoris extended?'

'No!'

'Three inches long!'

'No!'

'Yes!'

Zipping his trousers, he decided to fuck her and fill her cunt with spunk after he'd lengthened her sex nodule. She'd have the orgasm of her young life after he'd finished with her! Grabbing the wooden box, he knelt on the floor behind her and parted her succulent cunt lips. Pressing the box against her wet sex flesh, he hoped that the vacuum would suck her clitoris in through the hole just enough for the gamma rays to do their job. It was certainly worth trying. *Better to have tried and failed*, he mused, switching the machine on.

'Argh!' she gasped as the vacuum built, sucking her clitoris into the box. Ignoring her protests, he pressed the gamma-ray switch, his mind riddled with perverted thoughts as he imagined what he could do with a three-inch clitty. Jamming the box in place with the back of the chair as the phone rang, he grabbed the receiver.

'Professor Snide,' he replied, watching the girl quivering, trembling like a leaf in the wind.

'This is the Minister of Castles and Dungeons.'

'Not again! Look, I am not going to be re-bloody-housed!'

'I'm not calling about that. Did Mr Potter visit you?'

'Mr who?'

'Potter, I sent him to see you.'

'I've never heard of the man.'

'That's odd.'

'What is he, a lavatory salesman?'

'No, he's a . . . He hasn't made contact since he left London.'

'Made contact with whom?'

'With me. Are you sure he didn't visit you?'

'I'd hardly forget it if a potty man visited me, would I? Besides, I don't need a new lavatory. I could do with a new ballcock, though.'

'I wonder where he could have got to?'

'He's probably tied up somewhere. Or gone round the bend.'

'While I'm on the phone, I might as well tell you that the return of your castle to the state is now out of my hands.'

'Thank God for that.'

'It's been referred to another department.'

'Bedding or hardware?'

'I'm sorry?'

'Look, I'm busy,' the Professor snapped, watching the girl shaking violently.

'Yes, of course. Should Mr Potter turn up, would you be kind enough to ask him to call me?'

'Certainly not! I can't abide kindness.'

Replacing the receiver, Snide grabbed the wooden box, switching the device off as he moved the chair aside. Gently pulling the box away from the girl's yawning sex crack, a loud sucking sound resounding around the lab as the air rushed in, he gasped as her clitoris came into view. At least three inches in length, the pink pencil-like shaft was long enough to slip into a girl's cunt and fuck her. *Now there's a thought! A new meaning to lesbian sex?*

'You'll be pleased to know that you now have a penis-lookalike clitty!' he chortled.

'No, I don't want . . . '

'Too late!' he cried, kneeling behind her and removing the anal speculum from her stretched rectal duct. 'God, just look at it! I'd better suck it to orgasm.'

'No!'

'Yes!'

Briefly releasing the ropes, he turned her naked body over and bound her to the bench again. Her legs hanging over the bench, her cunny crack crudely gaping, her amazing clitoris pointing skyward, he pulled the chair up and sat between her splayed thighs. The pink protrusion erect in arousal, he tentatively licked the sensitive tip as the girl lifted her head and gazed in awe at her twitching clitty.

'God!' she gasped as he sucked the glistening shaft into his hot mouth. 'Ah! Oh, God!' Her miniature penis-like clitoris pulsating as he parted her pussy lips and slipped his finger deep into her tightening vaginal orifice, she writhed and squirmed as the incredible sensations permeated her quivering pelvis. She'd be an ideal candidate for the alpha-wave machine. Transferring her brain patterns to Hollie, if the bloody woman returned, he'd have his assistant begging for obscene sex.

Wailing as her orgasm approached, her cunny juice pouring from her tightening sex duct as he fanny-fingered her, Penny watched the Professor move his head up and down, sucking on her pulsating clitoris. 'Coming!' she sang, her naked body rigid as her climax erupted. Sustaining her orgasm, licking and sucking her solid clitoris, fingering her hot juicy cunt, he decided to shave her pubic hair before fucking her. *The more schoolgirlie-lookalike hairless pussies the better!*

'Oh, please! No more!' she cried as her orgasm peaked, her beautiful clitoris swelling and pulsating within the Professor's wet mouth. 'Please, I can't take any more!' Her climax finally receding, her naked body convulsing, Snide gently sucked out the last ripples of sex from her clitty. Wondering whether to stick her nipples in the gamma-ray box, he withdrew his wet fingers from her spasming vagina and slipped her clitty out of his mouth.

'What do you think of your clitoris?' he asked as she writhed and twitched uncontrollably.

'God, it's . . . it's fantastic!'

'I should charge you five hundred pounds for the treatment, but I don't suppose you have any money. I know, I'll fuck your bum instead.'

'No, not my . . . '

Hearing machine-gun fire, Snide leaped up the stone steps, bumping into the Baron as he dashed through the door. 'What's going on?' he asked.

'It's your butler, my friend. He's shooting the birds.'

'Bloody hell! The man's crazy!'

'So is the postmistress.'

'What?'

'I went into the village and . . . and I fucked her over the post office counter. Or what's left of the post office counter after the cannon ball ripped through the building.'

'Great! Was she tight?'

'As slack as Alice.'

'Did she come?'

'Yes, several times. But the postmistress's slack cunt is of no importance.'

'Why isn't it?'

'As I left the post office, I thought that things were rather quiet in the village. There was an uncanny silence, a strange hush, an air of desolation, a . . . '

'OK, so it was pretty quiet.'

'Indeed, it was. On further investigation, I discovered that the village had been evacuated.'

'How odd.'

'There's more. There are tanks gathering at the foot of the hill.'

'The army?'

'Yes, the army.'

'Oh, my God! We're fucking doomed!'

'I agree, my friend. I suggest we fuck the prisoners.'

'How will that help?'

'It won't, but it'll be enjoyable.'

'We shall fuck them on the benches, we shall fuck them up their cunts, we shall fuck the dirty wenches, we shall fuck them up their rumps. We shall never surrender!'

Chapter Six

Atop the turret with a pair of binoculars, Lucifer focused on the village, the tanks at the foot of the hill. Their guns turning towards the Forest of the Dead, he wondered what their plan was. Whatever their plan, it was best to annihilate them, he decided. The rocket launcher set up, aimed at the tanks, he was about to begin the attack when the Professor joined him.

'What's happening?' Snide asked, snatching the binoculars hanging from Lucifer's neck.

'They're aiming their guns at the forest, sir,' he replied, the binocular strap cutting into his throat as the Professor swung round and focused on the forest.

'Socialist pigs! It's a shame we don't have nuclear weapons, we could irradiate their bollocks. Wait a minute, they're firing at the forest!'

'Sir, do you mind?' Lucifer spluttered. 'Sir, you're . . . you're strangling me!'

'Take the strap off, you incompetent fool!'

'I . . . I can't, sir. Argh, help me! I'm having a near-death experience!'

'Here, let me do it. You'll be having a *real* death experience in a minute.'

'Ah, that's better. I almost swallowed my Adam's apple.'

'I wouldn't mind swallowing Eve's cherry.'

'Why are they firing at the forest, sir?'

'A good question. I'd also like to know why they're firing at the forest. Look, they're on the move, going towards the forest.'

'Mr Potter's in the forest, sir.'

'Shit, so he is. He'll have his cock blown off if he's not careful. Christ, imagine having a tank shell whistling between your legs and ripping your cock off.'

'I'd rather not, sir.'

'Neither would I, Lucifer – neither would I. Right, we'd better find out what their game is. As my intelligence agent, I want you to go down to the forest and discover what's going on.'

'I'm not very intelligent, sir.'

'You don't have to be. All you have to do is go and ask them what they're up to.'

'What if they won't tell me?'

'Karate-chop their bollocks off.'

'The sun's rather high.'

'Take an umbrella.'

'But . . .'

'Good God, man! Stop whingeing! Report back to me when you've found out what they're up to. I'll be in the war office.'

'Where's that, sir?'

'The lab, you fool!'

'Yes, sir.'

As Lucifer left, Snide focused on the tanks again. Still travelling towards the forest, it appeared that they weren't interested in the castle. Perhaps they were going to regroup under cover of the trees, ready to attack? he mused. Hoping Lucifer would come up with something intelligent, he returned to the lab to discover the Baron sitting on the chair between Penny's parted thighs, shaving her pubic hair.

'Her clitoris is amazing,' the Baron smiled as Snide joined him.

'It's fucking brilliant, if not better. I might stick her nipples in the gamma-ray box and lengthen them by two inches.'

'Let me go!' the girl cried.

'Shut up!' the Professor snapped.

'Why not stick your tongue in the box, my friend? With an eight-inch tongue, you could lick . . . '

'Certainly not, Baron. An eight-inch tongue? Good God!'

'It was just a thought. What are the army doing?'

'They're coming to rescue me!' the girl yelled.

'Unless you shut up, I'll shove my cock down your throat,' Snide returned. 'The tanks have gone into the forest, Baron – but I don't know why. I've sent Lucifer to find out what their plans are.'

'They'll soon be here to set me free!'

'Right, that's it! You've had plenty of oral warnings, and now you're about to be orally fucked! Baron, do you mind shoving your cock down her throat? I really can't abide her shouting for a moment longer.'

'I'd be delighted, my friend!'

Finishing shaving the girl's fanny, the Baron clambered onto the bench and whipped his erect cock out of his trousers. Snide paced the floor, rubbing his chin pensively as the girl yelled expletives, threatening to chew the Baron's cock off as he tried to drive his knob into her mouth.

The army might be looking for Potter, the Professor mused. But, there again, they'd have no reason to fire on the forest – not unless they wanted to murder Potter for his incompetence. As the Baron finally managed to slip his purple plum into the protesting girl's mouth and peace reigned once again, the Professor grabbed the ringing phone.

'DI Peel here,' the Inspector said.

'Ah, Inspector. How for art thou?'

'Pardon?'

'How are you?'

'I'm not calling to discuss my well-being, Professor. You'd better leave the castle.'

'Why? What dastardly plan have you planned now?'

'The village has been evacuated and the tanks are moving in.'

'Yes, I've seen them. But we're ready for the fascist bastards.'

'They're not after *you*, Professor.'

'That's a relief.'

'I reported the alien activity to the Ministry of Alien Activity and the tanks have moved in to . . . '

'Alien activity?'

'The aliens bombed me and my men, they destroyed the cannon, and I believe they also attacked the village stores and post office with their destructive weapons of destruction.'

Ignorant git! 'Yes, there's been a lot of anal activity of late – flying saucers, abductions . . . '

'Abductions, Professor?'

'My abducted assistant was abducted by aliens, I saw it happen.'

'You saw it happen?'

'I was there when my abducted assistant was abducted. A flying saucer hovered above the castle grounds and beamed her up.'

'My God!'

'Many village girls have been abducted over the years, as has your daughter, I would imagine.'

'I owe you an apology, Professor. I'm sorry I blamed you for . . . '

'It's all right, Inspector, a simple case of mistaken identity – not that I look anything like a Martian. I hope the army rids the forest of aliens.'

'I'm sure they will. By the way, word has it that a couple of government agents have mysteriously disappeared.'

'Not mysteriously, Inspector. Obviously, the aliens have them.'

'Good God! Right, I'd better get onto the Ministry about this.'

'Indeed you had, Inspector.'

Rubbing his hands together as the Baron fucked Penny's mouth, Snide pondered on the alien scam. The Inspector was a right prat, he reflected. Fancy believing that aliens had bombed him. And as for reporting alien activity to the Ministry, the man was crazy! A flying saucer seen streaking across the night sky would help, he mused, watching the Baron's purple knob driving in and out of the girl's gobbling mouth. It might be an idea to dress Lucifer up as a Martian and . . . The doorbell ringing, he dashed up the steps.

The castle wasn't the same without Miss Hocks, he reflected as he made his way to the doors. No doubt the bloody woman was licking and fingering the au pair's fanny! Inwardly cursing himself as the bell rang out again for cocking up the alpha-wave transference, he opened the doors to find a pretty young girl standing on the step, surrounded by photographic equipment.

'Hallo,' she smiled. 'I'm a mobile hairdresser. Snip, snip, snip.'

'Not another mobile fucking . . . I mean . . . '

'My name's Rebecca, I was just passing and I wondered whether you needed a haircut. Snip, snip.'

'What a coincidence. As it happens, I *do* need a haircut,' he grinned, realizing that the fascist bastards must have thought that their first agent had been lost in action.

'Oh, good. Would you help me with my equipment?'

'Yes, of course, Rebecca. I'm Professor Snide, Sexton Snide.'

Capturing one agent after another, Snide wondered how many more would be sent to the castle in an attempt to expose him. With Gigi, Angelica and Penny already in the dungeon, he pondered on what to do with them. He could

RAY GORDON

hardly imprison a dozen or more agents. There again, twelve
naked girlies lined up, twelve hairless pussies to fuck, twenty-
four nipples to suck . . . *Heavenly!* Picturing Rebecca's
clitoris, imagining her slender fingers masturbating her solid
sex nodule to orgasm, he scrutinized his latest abductee.

She was a right little beauty, he observed. Her long blonde
hair cascading over her firm breasts, her succulent red lips
smiling sweetly, she'd be a good lay. Chained to the rack, her
young sex crack bared, her wet inner lips parted . . . A damned
good fucking and buttock-caning was definitely in order!

Eyeing the girl's shapely thighs as he carried her equipment
into the banqueting hall, he decided to shave her fanny before
peeling her succulent pussy lips apart and forcing his magnificent cock deep into her tight cunt. But he'd play along
with her for a while, have a little fun before the enforced
debauchery commenced. Watching her pull a chair across the
floor and set it in the centre of the hall, he frowned and asked
her what she was doing.

'The chair's for you to sit on,' she smiled, opening a bag
and taking out a pair of scissors and a comb. 'Snip, snip,
snip.'

I'd rather you sat on my face. 'You're really going to cut my
hair?'

'Of course, what did you think I was going to do?'

Strip off and masturbate. 'Er . . . Nothing, nothing.'

Making himself comfortable on the chair, Snide pondered
on the girl. She was acting the part of a mobile hairdresser
very well, but could she really cut hair? Wondering whether
to ask her to trim his pubes as she placed a sheet around him,
he focused on her firm breasts billowing her white blouse.
Leaning over and combing his unruly hair, her breasts
dangerously close to his face, he imagined her nipples – erect,
lickable, suckable. He'd soon have the delectable beauty
stripped and chained to the rack! And once she'd been

136

hooked up to the alpha-wave machine . . . Pondering on the idea of turning all his prisoners into zombies, he asked her how long she'd been a mobile hairdresser.

'Since I was eighteen,' she smiled. 'I've been hairdressing for three years now. Snip, snip, snip.'

Working for MI5 for three years. 'Do you enjoy it?' he asked as she snipped away with the scissors. 'Hairdressing, I mean.'

'Yes, very much. Goodness me, your hair's so long! Snip, snip.'

'I haven't had it cut for twenty years. Do you have any friends who are mobile hairdressers?'

'No, I don't. Snip, snip, snip. This is a lovely castle.'

'Would you like a guided tour?' *My stiff cock guided up your wet cunt?*

'I'd like that very much. Snip, snip.'

'Excuse me, sir,' Lucifer said as he walked across the hall with a machine-gun slung across his back.

'Ah, Lucifer, this is Rebecca – she's a mobile hairdresser.'

'Yes, you said that a mobile hairdresser was going to call.'

'No, I didn't,' Snide returned, making odd facial expressions and winking at his butler.

'But, sir . . . You told me to turn one of the chambers into a hairdressing salon so that we could capture the hairdresser and tie her up with rope and torture the truth out of her.'

'My butler's a card!' Snide laughed, kicking the man's shin. 'Capture a hairdresser and torture her, indeed!'

'You were expecting me?' Rebecca asked, her blue eyes frowning.

'No, of course not. How could I possibly have known that you'd be passing by and would happen to call in to see whether I needed a haircut? I'm not psychic.'

'Your butler knew. Snip, snip.'

'Yes, the Professor told me that you'd be calling, Miss.'

'Lucifer, shut up!' Snide returned angrily. 'Have you done anything intelligent?'

'I've done something rather unintelligent.'

'I realize that!'

'Snip, snip, snip.'

'I was on my way to the forest and I thought I'd pop into the off-licence to buy some vodka. The shop was closed . . . In fact, all the shops were closed.'

'Yes, the village has been . . . Go on, Lucifer.'

'I was so desperate for a drink that I lost control of my senses.'

'And?'

'I sprayed the shop window with bullets, sir.'

'Snip, snip.'

'Bloody hell! I'll have your . . .'

'Snip, snip.'

'Rebecca, why do you keep saying *snip, snip*?'

'I can't help it. Snip.'

'Are you mad?'

'No. Snip.'

'My butler's mad, completely insane.'

'Not completely, sir.'

'My father's insane, and my mother. Snip, snip.'

'*Every*one's insane, if you ask me!'

'Snip.'

'Look, let's forget the bloody haircut and get on with the guided tour.'

'OK. Snip, snip.'

'Rebecca, will you stop saying . . . Lucifer, show this young lady around the castle. Start with the dungeon, if you get my meaning.'

'You mean, start with the dungeon.'

'You know, the dungeon. Nod nod, wank wank . . . wink wink.'

'Yes, the dungeon, sir.'

'Snip, snip.'

'The dungeon, if you get my drift.'

'Drift, sir?'

'Good God, man! Do you know what I'm saying?'

'You told me to start with the dungeon, sir.'

'The first and last call. Do you understand?'

'What about the rest of the castle?'

'Excuse me for a minute, Rebecca,' Snide breathed angrily, tossing the sheet to the floor and leaping out of the chair.

'Snip, snip.'

Grabbing the butler by his lapels and kneeing him in the bollocks, he whispered in his ear. 'Lock her in the fucking dungeon!'

'Argh! That hurt! Lock her in . . .'

'Shush, she'll hear you! Take her prisoner!'

'Oh, I see.'

'At last. Right, my butler will show you around the castle, Rebecca.'

'Great! Snip, snip.'

Shaking his head as Lucifer led the young woman away, Snide began to wonder whether she really was an agent. She was insane, that was for sure! But it didn't matter what she was – she had a fanny and a nice pair of tits, so what the hell? And a bottom-hole and nipples and a wet mouth and a fuckable cleavage and a clitoris and . . .

'Ah, there you are, my friend,' the Baron grinned as he approached.

'So I am, Baron.'

'There's a phone call for you.'

'Right, I'll take it in here.'

'I'll go and replace the phone in the dungeon.'

'Good man. While you're down there, perhaps you'd replace the receiver?'

'Certainly.'

Walking to the phone, Snide massaged his twitching cock through his trousers as he imagined slipping his knob deep into Rebecca's tight cunt. Hairdresser, agent or whatever she was – she'd be stripped, stretched on the rack, shaved, and fucked and spunked rotten.

'Snide speaking,' he said, grabbing the receiver.

'Ah, Professor Snide. My name's Brass, I'm the president of ARSE.'

'Arse, Mr Brass? Are you saying that you're an arsehole?'

'No. A.R.S.E. Alien Reports, Sightings and Encounters.'

'Of the third kind?'

'Of any kind. Word has it that there's been alien activity close to your castle.'

'Has there? Oh, I mean . . . Yes, there has been some activity. I believe the alien visitors to be Martians from Venus.'

'Martians from Venus? That's absolutely incredible! I was wondering whether you'd mind me coming to see you.'

'Certainly, Mr Arse . . . Brass.'

'I'd also like to bring a couple of members of ARSE along.'

'Members? I don't mind arses, Mr Brass, but not penises.'

'No, not penises. Members, fellow members of ARSE.'

'Oh, I see. Yes, of carse . . . Of course.'

'About six ARSEs in all.'

'No problem.'

'Tomorrow, if that's OK?'

'Right, I'll see you tomorrow, Mr Arse, with your other arses.'

Replacing the receiver, Snide wondered whether Mr Brass was another government agent. An arse would make an unpleasant change from a mobile hairdresser's cunt, he mused, wondering how Lucifer was getting on with Rebecca. A schoolgirl, two mobile hairdressers, Sister Elizabeth with male brain patterns, Clarissa's father threatening to sue, the postmistress fucked and spunked . . . And now Mr Brass from ARSE was going to start arsing around!

The time really had come to make some concrete plans, he reflected, dragging the chair from the centre of the hall and clearing the hairdressing gear away. The government's response to the ransom note would be interesting but, in the meantime, there were several prisoners to be dealt with. Turning as Lucifer wandered into the hall, Snide decided that the prisoners should be tied over the bench, their bottoms nicely positioned in a row for a good whipping, their legs apart and their cunts exposed, inviting a fucking.

'Sir, I've imprisoned the latest prisoner in the dungeon,' the butler said as he stood before the Professor.

'Why did you do that?'

'Because you told me to, sir.'

'Yes, I realize that. I'm not a fool, Lucifer.'

'Of course not, sir.'

'As long as we agree on that.'

'Yes, sir.'

'Right, well . . . What's the Baron doing?'

'He's playing around with your devilish machine.'

'Modifying it, I would imagine. OK, I want the prisoners tied over the bench, feet on the floor, legs wide apart, buttocks jutting out . . . Got the idea?'

'Over the bench, feet on the floor, legs wide apart, buttocks jutting . . . Right, I'll see to it straightaway.'

'No, do it now.'

'Yes, sir.'

'I intend to fuck the prisoners. I'll fuck them one after the other and . . . '

'Surely that's stating the obvious, sir?'

'What are you talking about?'

'Well, you couldn't fuck them simultaneously. Not unless you were the proud owner of several penises.'

'Shut up, Lucifer! The proud owner of several penises, indeed. I intend to compare the tightness and wetness of their cunts. After that, I'll do the same with their mouths and bumholes. Then I'll whip them and then I'll . . . God, isn't life great!'

'Indeed, it is, sir. Might I suggest that we . . . I do hope you don't think me too perverted and disgusting, but might I suggest that we force two penises into one girl's bottom-hole?'

'Good thinking, Lucifer. Your perverted and disgusting mind is admirable – enviable, even. We'll start with the second mobile hairdresser. Tie the other girls over the bench and drag out the double-bum-fucking chair from the keep.'

'Yes, sir.'

'Put it over there, by the wall, and then bring the first victim up.'

'Straight away, sir. Er . . . Which one's the second mobile hairdresser?'

'Rebecca, the one you've just taken down to the dungeon.'

'Oh, yes, how silly of me.'

'Have you been on the vodka again?'

'Just a little, sir.'

'Fuck it, there's the doorbell. Get the chair and I'll be with you in a minute or two. Maybe three, or possibly four or . . . I really must stop talking bollocks.'

'Yes, sir.'

Phone calls every five minutes, the doorbell ringing incessantly, a constant flow of agents . . . *Is there no peace for the perverted?* Snide wondered as he headed for the door. Whoever it was this time was in for a severe bollocking! Yanking the doors open, he frowned as he gazed at an attractive young girl dressed in a turquoise satin bikini. There was no way *she* was an agent, he mused, eyeing the bulging material of her tight bikini bottom.

'Hallo,' she smiled, dumping her bag on the ground. 'My name's Kirsty – I'm a mobile hairdresser.'

'And I'm a nun's left nipple.'

'Are you? You don't look like a nun's left nipple.'

'Of course I'm not a nun's bloody nipple, you stupid girl!'

'Oh, I see. Actually, I don't see.'

'What do you want?' *Apart from a good anal rogering?*

'I'm a mobile hairdresser and . . .'

'And you happened to be passing and wondered whether I needed a haircut?'

'Yes, but . . . How ever did you guess?'

'Intuition. Mobile hairdressers don't usually wear bikinis.'

'I like to be different.'

'So do I. Where's your equipment?'

'In my bag. Where's yours?'

'In my trousers . . . I mean, your photographic equipment.'

'I don't have any photographic equipment, I'm a hairdresser, not a photographer. Do you need a haircut?'

'Desperately. I'm Professor Snide, Sexton Snide. You'd better come off . . . come over my face . . . come in.'

Closing the doors as the girl entered the castle, Snide focused on the tight material of her bikini faithfully following the contours of her rounded buttocks. Three mobile hairdressers to sexually abuse and fuck rotten, he mused, imagining his solid cock embedded deep within her anal duct, his teeth sinking into her firm breasts. *There's coincidence, and there's fucking skulduggery!*

'I do like your bikini,' he grinned.

'It needs washing, I'm afraid. I haven't taken it off for five days.'

'God, I'd love a sniff . . . I mean, I'd love a quiff. Do you do quiffs?'

'Quiffs, perms, short back and sides, short sides and back,

143

top and tails, crew cut, short cut, quick cut, throat cut, subliminal cut . . . I do the lot.'

'Great. As it happens, my butler is setting up a hairdressing chair in the banqueting hall. If you'll follow me, we'll get started third, fourth or fifthwith.'

Leading the girl into the hall, Snide chuckled inwardly as Lucifer dragged the double-bum-fucking chair across the floor and positioned it by the wall. Her blue eyes frowning as she eyed the strange-looking chair, the girl was obviously wondering what it was for. With stirrups, leather straps, a seat with a bench slung beneath it – the chair certainly was odd.

'What's that?' she asked, standing before the contraption.

'Er . . . A hairdressing chair,' Snide replied. 'It's a brilliant innovation, a new concept in hairdressing chairs for discerning perverts . . . hairdressers.'

'But the seat's at an angle. Anyone sitting on that would find themselves virtually on their back.'

'That's right. The idea is that the victim's . . . the client's hair will hang down, away from their head, making cutting and styling easier. You have very long hair, why don't you try it?'

'I'll try anything once.'

So will I! 'Er . . . Lucifer, will you give the young lady a hand?'

'I'd be absolutely delighted to give her a hand!'

'No, just help her.'

'Yes, sir.'

Grabbing the ringing phone, Snide watched his butler take the girl's arm and guide her curvaceous body onto the chair. This was going to be fun, he mused, eyeing the tight strip of bulging material between her parted thighs as she took her position. One bumhole stretched to capacity by two cocks . . . Sheer bliss!

144

'Snide speaking.'

'Professor, my name's Al Coholic – I own the village off-licence.'

'Oh, fuck!'

'Pardon?'

'Er . . . Sorry, I just stubbed my toe. How can I help you? Of what assistance might I be to you in your time of greed?'

'Your butler blasted my shop window with a machine-gun.'

'Really?'

'Yes, really. I'll be sending you the bill.'

'I don't want your bills, I have enough of my own. Not that I bother to pay them. Fucking water authority, fucking electricity . . . '

'The plate-glass window, seven bottles of whisky, twelve bottles of wine, two bottles of vodka, five bottles of . . . '

'That's awfully decent of you, Al. I'll have two bottles of . . . '

'I am *not* offering you drink, Professor. I'm asking for compensation for my loss.'

'Why, what have you lost?'

'What have I lost? Your butler wrecked my . . . '

'Sorry, I have to dash. Speak to your insurance company about it. It's been nice talking to you.'

Hanging up, Snide turned to face the struggling bikini-clad girl. Strapped to the chair on her back, her ankles high in the stirrups, her thighs wide, she was ready for a double bum-fucking. Scowling as she lifted her head and gazed at the Professor, her face flushed with anger, she demanded to be released.

'What about your hair, Kirsty?' he asked, kneeling between her thighs. 'Don't you want a haircut?'

'A haircut?' she echoed. 'I came here to cut *your* hair.'

'No, I'm going to cut *your* hair – your pubic hair.'

'What?' she gasped as he pulled her bikini to one side, revealing her gaping vaginal slit.

'Your cunny hair, your curly sex hair, your fanny down, your pussy fur, your . . . '

'Stop it! How dare you . . . '

'My God, you have a nice cunt!' he chuckled. 'Lucifer, take a look at her cunt. With her feet in the stirrups and her thighs apart, her cunt's wide open.'

'Mmm, very nice, sir. I do like her pink fleshy folds. Might I suggest that we tear her bikini off?'

'You just dare to . . . '

'Better still, we'll tear her bikini off. Will you do the honours, Lucifer?'

'I'd be delighted, sir.'

'Unless you let me go, I'll . . . '

Ripping her bikini bottom in two as the Professor moved aside, Lucifer tossed the torn garment to the floor and gazed longingly at the girl's swollen outer lips, her pinken sex slit. Her buttocks parted, her neat brown anal mouth exposed, hungry to swallow a solid cock, this was going to be a brilliant double fucking. *Two cocks up one bum?* Snide mused. Yes, why not? Two cocks, three cocks . . . There *were* limits!

Removing her top as she squirmed and spat expletives, Lucifer tweaked the struggling girl's erect nipples, remarking on her darkening areolae. The cleavage between her firm rounded breasts was reminiscent of taut buttocks, and could have been designed to take an erect penis. There was nothing like cleavage sex! Snide ruminated, picturing his spunk splattering the girl's slender neck.

'She's a fine specimen,' Lucifer said, turning to the Professor.

'Indeed, she is.'

'I don't suppose you'd allow me to wank over her tits?'

'Certainly not, Lucifer! Good God, that's obscene.'

'You can't do this!' Kirsty hissed as Snide stroked the blonde down covering the gentle swell of her mons.

'Why is it that mobile hairdressers don't enjoy sex? Every hairdresser I've met has done nothing but complain when I've stripped and fucked them. I just don't understand it.'

'You're not going to fuck *me*!'

'Of course I'm going to fuck you. Good God, what do you think I'm going to do?'

'This is rape!'

'Here we go again, the same old thing – moan, moan, moan.'

'*You*'d moan if you were about to be raped!'

'*Moan? Moan?* Christ, I'd be only too pleased if a couple of sexy young birds raped me and forced me to spunk up their cunts.'

'I don't want to be spunked!'

'Shut up, for goodness sake. Right, Lucifer, if you position yourself on the bench beneath the chair and shove your cock up her bum, I'll take her fanny hole.'

'Of course, sir.'

'Not my bum!' she squealed.

'*Now* what's the matter? Good God, you're about to enjoy a double fucking, and you're . . . '

'If you dare to . . . '

'Enough! OK, let's do it!'

Watching Lucifer slide onto the bench beneath the chair, Snide grinned as the man pulled his erect penis out of his trousers. Pressing his swollen knob against Kirsty's brown ring, he manoeuvred his hips, his purple glans forcing her tight hole open to the accompaniment of her gasps and screams. His knob gliding into her rectal duct, he drove the entire length of his veined shaft into her tightening sheath.

Three mobile hairdressers? Snide reflected, focusing on the girl's brown tissue stretched tautly around the base of

Lucifer's solid cock as she writhed and squirmed. There was a chance that two of the girls were agents, but all three? One must be a genuine hairdresser, he decided – but which one? Two had photographic equipment, but Kirsty didn't. There again, Rebecca had started to cut the Professor's hair, so she might well be authentic. *Bollocks!* he thought, his penis stiffening as he gazed at Kirsty's gaping vaginal entrance. *Hairdresser or agent, what the fuck?*

Kneeling between Lucifer's legs, he hauled his granite-hard cock out of his trousers and pulled his foreskin back as far as he could without ripping his fraenum. Slipping his purple glans between Kirsty's yawning vaginal lips, his knob sucked into her hungry sex sheath, he shuddered in his ecstasy. His fully-laden balls resting on Lucifer's rolling testicles as he propelled his shaft deep into the creamy heat of the girl's cunt, he looked down at her swollen sex lips gripping the base of his huge cock.

'I'll tell you what I think, Lucifer,' he murmured, gazing at the girl's erect clitoris.

'What's that, sir?'

'This double fucking brings the Prime Minister to mind.'

'Why?'

'Because he's behind all this fucking.'

'I don't follow, sir. Ah! God, her bum's tight!'

'Please, take your things out of me!' the girl cried as the penises withdrew and rammed into her lust holes.

'Shut up, Kirsty. Take it like a woman,' Snide returned. 'As I was saying, the Prime Minister is behind all this agent-fucking, it's his fault. I reckon we should shoot him.'

'His wife would be none too pleased, sir.'

'I don't suppose *he*'d be too pleased either! Now's not the time to be talking of coups and revolution and murder, let's fuck!'

'I quite agree, sir.'

'I don't!' Kirsty screamed as her holes tightened around the invading cocks.

'You're an ungrateful girl,' Snide said. 'You have two magnificent cocks shoved up your lust ducts, and you're complaining.'

'I don't *want* two cocks shoved up my . . . '

'What you do or don't want doesn't matter. The point is that you *have* two cocks up your holes and that's that. Prepare yourself for a double fucking, inevitably terminating in a double spunking.'

Withdrawing his penis and then plunging it back inside her, he repeatedly drove into her vaginal canal, finding his rhythm with Lucifer's pistoning cock. The girl's naked body jolting with the double fucking, she gasped her protests as her spasming cunt spurted out its creamy lubricant, spraying the men's rolling balls. The opaque liquid trickling over the butler's thrusting cock, she whimpered as the first wave of preorgasmic spasms coursed through her trembling body.

'I'll shave your fanny fur after we've spunked you,' Snide grinned as his cock thrust into her squelching sex sheath.

'No, I don't want . . . '

'Of course you do,' he returned. 'All girls should have hairless pussies, especially mobile hairdressers.'

'Why?'

'Because it's aesthetic to perverted old men who delight in schoolgirlie-lookalike cunts. OK, my cock's well juiced for the double bum-fucking.'

'No! No, you can't . . . '

'Of course I can!'

Slipping his glistening penis out of the girl's dripping pussy, Snide positioned his cock against the butler's erect shaft. Opening her anal ring with his fingers, he forced his bulbous knob against her taut brown tissue, gasping as her anal sphincter muscles suddenly yielded and his purple globe slipped into her hot rectal duct. Screaming expletives as the Professor drove his weapon head alongside the butler's cock, sinking his member into her bloating bowels, she lifted her head and scowled at Snide.

'You're a bastard!' she cried as the two cocks withdrew and thrust into her anal duct, stretching her delicate brown tissue to capacity. 'Please, I can't take it!'

'If you don't mind my saying so, Miss, you *have* taken it,' Lucifer murmured.

'What with Lucifer's cock and my fucking great horse-like penis stuffed up your bum, I'm surprised you're not thanking us for the exhilarating experience!' Snide chuckled.

'I'll tear open!' she cried as her body rocked with the double bum-pummelling.

'Of course you won't. I once knew a girl who could take two fists up her arse.'

'Please, stop!'

'OK, let's rump her and spunk her!' the Professor grinned as his knob swelled and throbbed within her dank bowels.

The men's pulsating purple plums rubbing together as they arse-fucked the young beauty, their spunk finally shot from their slits, filling her spasming rectal sheath. Eyeing the girl's open vaginal entrance, Snide forced four fingers deep into her well-creamed cunt to add to her debased pleasure. His pistoning hand massaging her solid clitoris as he crudely fanny-fingered her, bringing out her orgasm, she shuddered as her climax gripped her.

'God, I'm there!' she cried out in her sexual ecstasy. 'Oh, God!'

'And me!' Lucifer breathed as his spunk jetted into the girl's bowels.

'What a beautiful arse!' the Professor chortled, ramming his horse-like cock in and out of her bottom sheath. 'We'll both fuck your mouth next!'

'No! Oh, God! God, it's . . . it's heaven!'

The banqueting hall resounding with cries of sexual satisfaction as the men fucked the young beauty, only Kirsty noticed the apparition hovering above the chair. Squeezing her eyes shut and then opening them, she gazed in horror at the naked headless lady. The ghost's vaginal crack clearly visible as she drifted down, her cuntal opening close to Kirsty's gasping mouth, the tethered girl screamed.

'My God, what's that?'

'It's my spunk,' Snide returned.

'No, up there!'

'It's my cock right up your bum, along with Lucifer's.'

'No, above me. Look!'

Ignoring the delirious girl, Snide continued his anal fucking, draining his heavy balls, his sperm mingling with Lucifer's as the girl ranted and raved about ghosts and dripping sex cracks. The last of his spunk jetting from his knob-slit, the Professor finally stilled his twitching cock, breathing heavily as he recovered from his massive climax. Easing his penis out of the girl's gripping anal canal, her brown ring closing around Lucifer's sperm-drenched member, he slipped his dripping fingers out of her burning cunt and sat back on his heels.

'That was something else,' he grinned, watching Lucifer's sperm-dripping balls rolling.

'There's a ghost!' Kirsty cried, her eyes wide, her mouth gaping as she desperately tried to slip her feet out of the stirrups. 'Help me!'

'The double bum-fucking really *has* blown your mind!' Snide laughed as the doorbell rang out. 'When I get back, I'll spunk down your throat.'

Walking to the door as Lucifer struggled to clamber off the bench beneath the seat, Snide pondered on the three agents, again wondering whether one of them really was a hairdresser. What with three mobile hairdressers and the school-girlie agent, the castle was filling up. If this was another hairdresser, he'd have to put up a No Vacancies sign.

'Ah, Miss Hocks!' he grinned as he opened the door to discover his assistant standing on the step in her bra and panties. 'Er . . . Where are your clothes?'

'I lost them,' she replied, stepping into the castle.

'Lost them?'

'I stripped off to look at my beautiful body because I fancy myself. I was in the forest and . . . Well, I lost my clothes.'

'What do you mean, you fancy yourself?'

'I prefer women's bodies to men's. The sight of my naked body turns me on.'

'Ah, that's because you think like a man . . . I mean . . . Where's Helga?'

'In the Forest of the Dead. She's taken up with a naked man tied to a tree.'

'That'll be Potter. Hang on, I thought she was a lesbian?'

'She's changed.'

'Most odd. Where the hell have you been?' he asked, closing the doors.

'Something's happened to my mind. I feel like a woman, like having sex with a woman, but I'm not a man.'

'I can see that!'

'But I feel like a man.'

'*I* feel like a woman.'

'No, I feel like a man who wants a woman. I wish I had a penis.'

'Er . . . I think we'd better get you down to the lab and sort your brain patterns out. You go down and I'll join you in a minute.'

At least she was in one piece, Snide reflected, eyeing her panties clinging to her rounded buttocks as she walked away. The time really had come to spunk up her bottom-hole, he mused, returning to the double-bum-fucking chair. Hairdressers and schoolgirlie agents were all very well, but it was Miss Hocks who really needed a good anal rogering.

Standing before the chair and gazing at Lucifer's cock embedded deep within Kirsty's bowels, Snide grinned. Writhing and squirming, the butler was obviously enjoying the welcoming heat of the girl's tight rectal duct, he mused. Focusing on the girl's gaping vaginal entrance, he pondered on slipping his magnificent cock up her tight vagina and sperming her young cervix.

'Sir,' Lucifer groaned, breaking the Professor's reverie. 'Sir, I don't seem to be able to withdraw my equipment.'

'What? You mean your cock's stuck up her arse?'

'It won't come out, it's lodged in her anal tube, stuck up her rear passage. I think it must be the vacuum.'

'You must take it out!' Kirsty screamed.

'All right, don't panic,' the Professor said, kneeling between Lucifer's legs and grabbing the base of the man's cock. 'Right, one good wank . . . I mean, one good yank should do it.'

As much as he twisted and pulled on Lucifer's penis, Snide couldn't retrieve it from the girl's bottom-hole. Again and again he pulled on the man's cock, but his efforts only caused the girl's rectal sheath to tighten and suck the organ further into her hot bowels. There was only one thing to do, he reflected, dashing down to the lab and grabbing a length of rubber hose.

'I'll blow her up,' he said, returning and kneeling between Lucifer's legs.

'I don't want to be blown up!' she protested, her eyes wide as she lifted her head and gazed in horror at the rubber hose.

'Not blow up as in "bang", you silly girl – blow up as in allow air into your bum.'

Easing the end of the hose past her tight anal ring, he pushed it deep into her bowels. The air rushing in, the Professor pulled on Lucifer's cock again. The girl's muscles still gripping the butler's organ like a vice, there was no way he was able to uncouple the pair. Scratching his head, he finally stood up and gazed down at the lewd union.

'I don't know what to do,' he sighed. 'I reckon you're stuck up there for good.'

'Sir, might I suggest that you blow down the hose?' Lucifer said. 'The pressure might force my cock out of her bum.'

'I don't want you blowing air up my bum!' Kirsty whined.

'You want to spend the rest of your life with a penis stuck up your arse, do you?' Snide asked.

'No, but you mustn't blow me up – I might burst!'

'That's a good point,' Lucifer murmured.

'What about plastic explosive?' Snide ruminated. 'A small amount set off up her bum would blow your cock out.'

'You just dare to set off an explosion in my bum!' she gasped.

'Only a small explosion.'

'No!'

'We could give her a Vindaloo curry,' Lucifer suggested.

'Don't be disgusting!' Snide returned. 'All I can do is give up. If at first you don't succeed, then fucking well give up.'

'You can't leave us like this!' Kirsty cried.

'All right, I'll see what I can do.'

Having spent half an hour trying to ease the butler's cock out of Kirsty's arse, Snide finally gave up. Holding his head as he made his way to his living quarters, he pondered on the multitude of problems. With Lucifer's cock stuck up Kirsty's bum, Rebecca to deal with, and Gigi, and Angelica and Penny and Miss Hocks . . . As for the nun . . . *Fuck the nun!*

There was only one thing for it, he decided, grabbing a bottle of vodka. Flopping onto his bed, he hauled his erect penis out of his trousers and examined his egg-sized purple knob. There was definitely only one course of action to take – have a wank, get pissed, have another wank, and then have a kip.

Chapter Seven

Woken by the phone the following morning, the Professor rubbed his eyes, wondering who it was this time. The Reverend Mother Horgasm? DI Peel or the Minister of Castles and Dungeons? Perhaps it was Mr Brass from ARSE? Whoever it was, he'd tell them in no uncertain terms where to go.

'Fuck off!' he bellowed, pressing the receiver to his ear. 'Fucking well fuck off!'

'Fucking well fuck off? But it's me, my friend,' the Baron replied. 'What do you mean, *fucking well fuck off*?'

'Sorry, a slip of the tongue. Or a tongue of the slip.'

'Wonderful! I have good news, my friend.'

'That makes a change. Where are you?'

'In the lab.'

'Baron, why are you ringing me from the lab?'

'I couldn't be arsed to walk all the way up to the banqueting hall just to discover that you were in your living quarters asleep in bed.'

'How do you know I'm here?'

'A shrewd guess.'

'Did you sleep well, Baron?'

'No, I've been up all night working on this fucking . . . Listen, I've modified the machine.'

'Ah, good. This is indeed good news.'

'It is, my friend. I've recorded Gigi's brain patterns and induced them into your traitorous assistant's brain. Miss Hocks is now a nymphomaniacal heterosexual sex fiend.'

'Excellent! I'm on my way.'

'Before you go, come down here and see what you think of Miss Hocks.'

'Will do, Baron.'

'I'll see you in a minute.'

'No, give me two minutes. Make that three minutes. On second thoughts . . . '

'I'll see you when I see you, my friend.'

'That's stating the obvious, Baron. I mean, you can hardly see me before you see me, can you?'

'True, but . . . '

'Look, we're wasting time. I'm on my way. Or I will be, once you get off the phone and let me get off my bed. And have a shower and dress and . . . '

'I'll see you when you're ready.'

'And not before.'

'Or after.'

After washing his giant cock and balls in the shower, the Professor hurriedly dressed. *Miss Hocks, transformed into a nympho?* he mused, leaving his living quarters. This was just what he'd been waiting for. His penis stiffening in anticipation of slipping into his assistant's tight cunt, his heavy balls rolling, this was what he'd worked towards for three long years.

Dashing through the banqueting hall as Kirsty complained of an aching bum and Lucifer groaned, Snide sprinted through the corridor and leaped down the stone steps to the dungeon. At last, Miss Hocks would beg to be fucked, he mused, his cock solid, straining his zip to bursting point. First her mouth, then her cunt, then her bum, then her cleavage, then her . . . *God, life's just wonderful!*

Walking across the lab as the phone rang, the Professor eyed Penny's naked body tied over the bench – her incredible clitoris protruding delightfully from her gaping sex crack below her exposed bottom-hole. It was high time she had another good anal rogering, he mused, grabbing the receiver. The agents in a row, tied over the bench with their rounded buttocks jutting out, their small brown portals defenceless – it was high time they all had a damned good anal spunking!

'Hallo,' he said, pressing the receiver to his ear, wondering who was calling this time.

'Who are you?' a woman asked.

'Who are *you*?' Snide returned.

'You rang me just now.'

'No, I didn't.'

'Yes, you did. I dialled one four seven one and got your number.'

'I haven't called anyone. Stop wasting my time.'

'You must have called me. Who are you?'

'Listen, madam – I haven't called anyone!'

'Someone called me from your phone. I dialled one four . . . '

'I don't care what you dialled. Stop wasting my time and . . . '

'Is there anyone else there who might have called me?'

'There might be, there again, there might not. Look, I'm busy – you have no right to disturb people. Jesus F. Christ, I could have been having a wank!'

'What?'

'Imagine it, the first spurt of spunk spurts, and then the bloody phone rings. There's nothing worse than an interrupted orgasm.'

'My God, you're vile!'

'The spunk still spurts, but the throbs just don't happen. All that wanking terminating in a stalled orgasm . . . What a waste of a good spunking.'

'You're obscene!'

'I do my best. Why don't you go and bring yourself off

with a cucumber instead of ringing people and accusing them of ringing you?'

'My God, I have never heard such disgusting . . . '

'You'll hear worse in a minute. Er . . . How's this? Why don't you shove a cucumber up your arsehole and finger your wet cunt hole?'

'I'll report you to British Telecom!'

'I'll report *you* to British Telecom, madam! Nuisance calls are illegal.'

'And so is disgusting language. What's your name?'

'Pope Brian Eric the third and a half.'

'I'll get on to British Telecom straight away.'

'While you're on to them, tell them to fuck off.'

'Oh!'

'And tell them that if they send me another bill, I'll stuff it up their corporate arsehole.'

Banging the receiver down as the Baron chuckled, Snide turned to Miss Hocks, flashing her a salacious grin as he eyed her straining bra, her sex-bulged panties. If the Baron had completed the alpha-wave transference properly, the woman would beg for a fuck the minute she laid eyes upon the Professor's magnificent penis. It would be rather nice if she also had lesbian tendencies, he mused, picturing her with her tongue up a young schoolgirlie's dripping sex hole. More than nice, it would be absolutely amazingly fucking brilliant!

'Has the transformation transformed you, Miss Hocks?' he asked, standing before the woman.

'My name's Gigi,' she returned firmly. 'I'm a government agent posing as a mobile hairdresser.'

'I think you've overdone it, Baron,' Snide murmured, gazing longingly at Rebecca's rounded buttocks and ima-gining his penis rammed deep into the dank heat of her bowels. 'But at least we now know that Gigi is an agent. That just leaves those two horny little tarts, Rebecca and

Kirsty. I'm sure one of them is a real hairdresser, but which one?'

'A discovery we'll no doubt discover sooner or later,' the Baron murmured.

'Let's hope we discover the discovery sooner rather than later. Tell me, Miss Hocks . . . I mean Gigi. Do you fuck?'

'I'm a hairdresser.'

'Yes, but do you fuck?'

'I cut hair.'

'Hairdressers are allowed to fuck as well as cut hair. You do have a cunt, don't you?'

'I cut hair.'

'Christ, this is all I need. Baron, Lucifer's been in the banqueting hall all night with his cock stuck up Kirsty's bum. Would you be good enough to help him to retrieve his member while I rape Miss Hocks and shag her rotten?'

'Shag her rotten what?'

'Her rotten cunny.'

'Of course, my friend. By the way, the alpha-wave helmet now acts as a satellite dish. When I've dislodged the butler's cock from the tart's arsehole, I'll take the helmet up to the turret and aim it at an innocent young girl who might be passing by. There again, she might not be so innocent – or passing by.'

'Excellent!'

'Snip, snip! Let me go!' Rebecca cried, struggling to lift her naked body off the bench.

'And me!' Angelica rejoined. 'You can't treat us like this, you must let us go!'

'I've been here all night! Gigi hissed. 'Unless you free me now . . .'

'All shut up!' Snide returned angrily. 'You're to be fucked and spunked in turn, so you might as well accept it.'

'If you dare to . . . ' Rebecca began.

'Each of you will have your bum fucked, spunked, fucked and spunked again, and then severely whipped! Now, be quiet!'

Grabbing a bottle of depilatory cream from the shelf as the Baron left the lab, the Professor placed a large bowl on the chair and filled it with the cream. Turning to Miss Hocks, he tore her knickers off and forced her to sit in the bowl, chuckling wickedly as she struggled to escape the despicable man. 'Too late!' Snide laughed uncontrollably, plunging his hand into the bowel and massaging the cold cream into her hairy mons, her succulent vaginal lips. 'You're to be a schoolgirlie again!'

Lashing the woman to the chair with a length of rope, he ripped her bra from her firm breasts and gazed longingly at her darkening areolae, her elongated nipples. Whether the brain patterns had turned her into a nympho or not, she was going to have the Professor's cock spunking up her fanny, and that was that! *I'll not wait a second more than I have to*, he promised himself, painfully twisting and pulling her brown milk teats.

'Professor Snide!' she gasped as he pulled her nipples harder, her breasts becoming taut cones of flesh. 'You cannot do this sort of thing, it's against the law.'

'Fuck the law,' he grinned. 'And fuck you.'

'When the government gets to hear about this, you'll be hung for treason.'

'I'm already hung like a horse, so what the hell? You're to be severely punished for working for the government, Miss Hocks.'

'You're the one who'll be severely punished, and my name is *not* Miss Hocks.'

'Bollocks!' he chuckled, gagging the woman's mouth with a pair of cunny-dripping panties he happened to come across. 'Right, while the cream's doing its job, I think I'll whip these delightful girls' bottoms.'

'Don't you dare!' the three prisoners cried in unison as Snide grabbed the whip from the torture chamber.

'OK, I'll move along the line and give you all one lash each, and then start at the beginning again. I reckon twenty or so lashes should cream your cunts up ready for my horse cock.'

Gigi was the first in line, the first to have her naked buttocks lashed by the thin leather tails. Yelping, her body jolting as the stinging pain permeated her rounded bottom orbs, she turned to face Rebecca, noticing the fear mirrored in the girl's wide eyes. 'Argh!' Rebecca screamed as the tails bit into her pale bottom globes, a loud cracking sound reverberating around the dungeon. Next in line was Angelica. She'd already had a taste of the whip, her buttocks and shaved vaginal lips bearing the thin pink weals as a stark reminder of the earlier merciless thrashing.

'Please, not again!' she cried as the whip lashed her tensed bum cheeks.

'Again and again and again!' Snide chortled, moving back along the line to Gigi. 'Lash number two!' he grinned, bringing the whip down with a deafening crack.

'Argh!' the girl cried, her rounded buttocks twitching as the leather tails struck her pale flesh.

'You're my little schoolgirlies and you've been very naughty. Number two for Rebecca!'

'Argh! Snip, snip!'

'And number two for Angelica!'

'Argh!'

Lowering the whip to his side as the Baron wandered down the stone steps, Snide sensed that something was very wrong. Had the man managed to yank Lucifer's cock out of Kirsty's bum hole? he wondered, noticing anxiety mirrored in his eyes. Or had he snapped the butler's cock off?

'Call it a sixth sense, Baron,' he finally said. 'But I sense that my senses are sensing that something's very wrong. Does that make sense or is it nonsense?'

'Indeed, it does make sense. You have sensitive senses, my friend.'

'So, what's wrong?'

'The doorbell rang and I went to see who it was . . . I seem to have allowed a man into the castle.'

'You allowed a man into the castle?'

'As I opened the doors, he rushed in and dashed across the banqueting hall. I've searched everywhere, but I can't find him.'

'Shit, and double shit! He could be anyone and he could be anywhere up to anything. Anyone, anywhere, anything, anytime.'

'Yes, I realize that, He's obviously a spy, in hiding somewhere waiting until we've gone to bed so that he can search the castle.'

'OK, I'd better go and look for the sneaky bastard. You carry on whipping the prisoners' beautiful bottoms. Oh, Miss Hocks should be done by now.'

'Done, my friend?'

'She's sitting in a bowel of depilatory cream. Her fanny hairs should have dropped off by now.'

'Right, I'll clean her up and inspect her womanly crack.'

'She'll no longer have a womanly crack, she'll have a schoolgirlie crack. Did you manage to yank Lucifer's cock out of Kirsty's bum?'

'No, my friend. Sadly, it would seem that his cock is to remain embedded within the girl's bottom-hole for good. Till death do them part.'

'Poor old Lucifer, forever arsed off. Oh well, I'd better go and search for this man, whoever he is.'

Making his way to the banqueting hall, Snide pondered on the intruder. He reckoned that the man had been sent by the government to discover the fate of the missing agents. But there was no immediate panic: it was one thing getting into the castle, and another getting out. Crossing the banqueting hall, the Professor grinned at Kirsty as she complained about the butler's cock being stuck up her bottom all night.

'You'll have to be patient,' he said as he passed her. 'I have far more important things to worry about.'

'But . . .'

'I'll order a take-away curry later.'

'No!'

'OK, I'll use plastic explosive.'

'No!'

'In that case, bollocks!'

Leaving the hall, the Professor searched the keep. Apart from the headless lady who tried to sexually assault him by grabbing his cock, there was no sign of anyone, least of all the mysterious man. The castle was a big place, he could be hiding anywhere, Snide mused, escaping the grasps of the deadly woman and walking to the north wing. Having searched all the wings, including his own living quarters, he climbed the winding steps to the turret.

'Who are you?' he asked, approaching a middle-aged man dressed in green cords, brown brogues and a green checked shirt.

'Er . . . Who are *you*?' he returned, his bushy eyebrows raised.

'I own this castle. My name's Snide, Professor Sexton Snide.'

'Johnson, Tom Johnson,' the man replied.

'What are you doing here? What do you mean by dashing into my castle and hiding up here? Are you an escaped convict?'

'Certainly not, I'm a psychiatrist. I've been sent here to determine the extent of your insanity.'

RAY GORDON

'Just about everyone here is insane, if not completely mental. Excluding me, of course. Who sent you?'

'The Department of Mental Health. Under the Mental Health Act, I have the power to certify you insane – if I so wish. I'm open to bribes, of course.'

'Really? Egg and chips.'

'I'm sorry?'

'Egg and chips. What do you make of that meaningless and completely out-of-context statement?'

'I'd say that you're hungry, Professor.'

'Wrong, it's a sign of acute clinical insanity.'

'Is it?'

'Of course it is. People don't usually say *egg and chips* in the middle of a conversation, do they?'

'No, I suppose not.'

'Imagine that we're talking about the weather and I say, *womb*. What would you think?'

'I'd think that your mother had a troubled pregnancy.'

'Wrong again. It would be a subconscious outburst in response to my mother's infertility.'

'Your mother was infertile?'

'Yes, from childhood. Toast and marmalade.'

'Professor, I have the power to . . . '

'And under the Castle Trespassing Act, I have the power to torture you to death.'

'You can't do that to people.'

'I *can* and *will* do what I like. I don't believe that you're a psychiatrist, Mr Johnson. You wrongly interpret egg and chips and wombs, so I reckon you're a government agent.'

'A government . . . What on earth makes you think that?'

'I can smell fishy agents a mile off, not that you're wearing panties.'

'How do you know about my . . . my little fetish?'

'You *are* wearing panties?'

164

'Well, yes.'

'Skimpy silk panties or stained, schoolgirlie navy-blue knickers?'

'The latter.'

'Interesting.'

'What's your interest in schoolgirls, Professor? Are we like-minded perverts?'

'I just love their tight, hot, juicy-wet . . . Of course we're not like-minded perverts. I have no interest in schoolgirls whatsoever. Like-minded perverts, indeed. Ovaries! Would you care for tea and custard creams?'

'Oh, thanks very much.'

'Wait in the gunpowder room, over there behind that oak door. I'll be back in a minute.'

'You're too kind.'

'Fallopian tubes!'

Locking the door as the man wandered into the gunpowder room, Snide rubbed his hands together. *Another agent out of the way!* he reflected happily as he left the turret and descended the winding steps. There was no way Johnson could escape, not unless he had some explosives or an axe or a chainsaw or a sawn-off shotgun – which he didn't. *I must do something about Lucifer's cock.*

Taking stock as he returned to the banqueting hall, Snide ruminated on his prisoners. Hairdresser one, Gigi – not yet fucked or shaved, but she'd had her buttocks whipped. Hairdresser two, Rebecca – whipped, but not fucked and spunked. Hairdresser three, Kirsty – well fucked, spunked, and tied to the chair with Lucifer's cock stuck up her arse. Schoolgirlie Angelica – fucked, whipped and shaved. Penny, the Inspector's daughter – shaved, given a three-inch clitoris, fucked rotten and whipped. There was still a lot of fucking to be done, Snide reflected, gazing at Kirsty's brown ring gripping the base of Lucifer's cock.

'Sir,' Lucifer groaned. 'Sir, I really can't stay like this for much longer.'

'Neither can I!' Kirsty rejoined. 'My bum really hurts!'

'There's nothing I can do about it,' Snide said. 'As it is, I have a man up on the turret and several girls in the dungeon. Hairdressers, schoolgirls, psychiatrists, policemen's daughters . . . I can't take much more of this. Shit, now the bloody phone's ringing. I'll screw your cunt in a minute, Kirsty. A fucking great multiple orgasm might squeeze Lucifer's cock out of your bum.'

'No!'

'Yes!'

Grabbing the receiver, Snide frowned as a man introduced himself as the Prime Minister. The fascists must have received the ransom note, he mused – and the painted peas. This was make-or-break time. If the government gave in to his demands, he'd be left in peace, if not . . . *An all-out war!*

'This is an honour,' Snide said.

'Thank you, Professor.'

'No, I mean, it's an honour for you, Prime Minister.'

'Oh, I see. I have about my person a clitoris and two nipples.'

'How odd!' Snide laughed. 'Are you saying that you're a woman?'

'Pardon?'

'Do you have a fanny or a cock?'

'Do you realize to whom you are speaking?'

'Yes, the PM – Mr Pre Menstrual, Mr Penis Masturbator, Mr . . . By the way, I didn't vote for you.'

'I'm sorry to hear that, Professor.'

'I'm not. Fucking fascists. How come you have a clitoris and nipples?'

'You sent them to me.'

'Ah, the mouldy peas . . . I mean, they belong to one of your agents. At least, they did before I cut them off.'

'Do you realize that it's against the law to remove women's nipples and clitorises?'

'I have a licence, I'm a licensed clitectomist and nipplectomist.'

'How convenient. Which agent did the aforementioned erectile pudenda belong to?'

'How many agents have you sent to destroy me?'

'Er . . . Only the one. Is she still alive?'

'Of course she is, but not for much longer. OK, my demands are . . . '

'I don't succumb to terrorism, Professor.'

'Who said anything about terrorism?'

'Cutting women's clitorises and nipples off is tantamount to terrorism.'

'Fucking bollocks! It's nothing of the sort. Right, I want a helicopter and . . . '

'What for?'

'I've seen it in films, the baddies always demand a helicopter.'

'Professor, I'm ringing to tell you that we are *not* going to succumb to your demands. You will be dealt with by the SAS who, as we speak, are on their way to your castle.'

'The SAS? Do you honestly think that the SAS are capable of . . . '

'I don't think, Professor – I *know*!'

Banging the phone down, the Professor turned as the Baron wandered into the hall. The man was looking pleased with himself, Snide observed. *Good news, at last?* He doubted it very much! Focusing on Kirsty's open vaginal entrance as the Baron stood before the girl, Snide wondered whether to sell her to the PM. With a sexy little plaything to keep him occupied, he might call the SAS off. No, his wife would never agree to it.

'We must release one of the prisoners,' the Baron murmured pensively.

'We can't do that!' Snide returned. 'Release one of the . . . Good God!'

'I've set the machine up on the turret, along with the helmet. I need a girl to test the device on.'

'Test it? What devilish plan have you planned, Baron?'

'I've recorded my brain patterns, my friend. We'll release one of the girls and, as she runs away from the castle, I'll aim the helmet at her. If the machine works, she'll return to the castle.'

'Why will she?'

'Well, because I want to be here and, with my brain patterns, so will she.'

'What about me?' Kirsty asked. 'I'll run away.'

'How can you run away from the castle with the butler's cock stuck up your arse?' Snide chortled. 'It's a physical impossibility. OK, Baron, go back to the turret and I'll release the Inspector's daughter. You can test the machine on her.'

'Perfect, my friend!'

'Not really, but it'll do.'

Dashing down to the dungeon as the Baron raced up to the turret, Snide released Penny, informing her that she could return to the village in the state she'd arrived – naked. Ignoring the other prisoners as they begged for their freedom, he grabbed the whip and gave each girl's bottom orbs a good lashing. Yelping as the leather tails cracked loudly across their crimson buttocks, their naked bodies jolting, they again demanded to be released.

'Released?' Snide echoed, discarding the whip and leading Penny up the steps. 'I can't release naked girls with beautiful cunts, tight arseholes and wonderful titties!'

'Please!' Rebecca cried. 'Snip, snip!'

'*You*, of all the prisoners, Rebecca? Good God, you haven't been cunt-fucked or bum-fucked yet!'

'No!'

'Yes!'

Leading Penny through the castle, Snide opened the doors and told her to go home. Watching as she ran down the hill, her weal-lined naked buttocks bouncing, he prayed for the machine to work. As she grew smaller with distance, he frowned, wondering what had gone wrong. 'Ah, ha!' he grinned as she stopped and turned. Heading back to the castle, her three-inch clitoris protruding from her young, shaved sex crack, waving from side to side, she smiled as she approached the doors.

'Hallo, my friend!' she beamed.

'Oh, er . . . It's good to have you back, Penny . . . I mean, Baron,' he smiled.

'It's good to be back. I could do with a sexy young girl to play with: any suggestions?'

'With your beautiful penis, I'm sure you'd be able to satisfy young Kirsty. She's in the banqueting hall with the butler's cock stuck up her back passage. Why don't you fuck her?'

'Yes, I think I will.'

Leading the naked girl to the double-bum-fucking chair, Snide watched excitedly as she knelt between Lucifer's legs and positioned her erect clitoris between Kirsty's gaping cunny lips. Unzipping his trousers as Kirsty began protesting, he moved behind the chair and shoved his knob into her mouth to keep her quiet.

'I really can't abide shouting,' he murmured, sinking his purple plum deeper into her hot mouth as she moaned through her nose. 'OK, push your clitoris . . . I mean, push your cock up her fanny.'

'Sir, what's going on?' Lucifer asked from beneath the chair.

'Nothing for you to worry about, Lucifer. We're just abusing Kirsty's naked body to gratify our debased sexual cravings. Can you manage another bum-fucking, terminating in a bowel-spunking?'

'I'll do my best, sir.'

'Good man. I reckon that if the girl has a few massive orgasms her bum muscles will squeeze your cock out.'

'I do hope so, sir.'

Watching Penny slip her solid three-inch clitoris deep into Kirsty's well-juiced cunt, Snide grinned. This really *was* a new angle on lesbian sex! he reflected as the pink, pencil-like shaft drove fully home, the girls' fleshy cunny lips pressing together. *A clitoris fucking a cunt? Weird in its weirdness!*

It might be an idea to have Penny slip her penis-lookalike clitty up one of the prisoners' bums, he mused in his rising debauchery. Wondering whether the gamma-ray machine would extend the girl's clitoris to six inches, he withdrew his cock and drove his swollen, egg-size glans deep into Kirsty's hot mouth again. And if the machine was able to thicken the clitoral shaft by a few inches . . . *Christ, a cunny crack with a life-size cock sticking out of it!*

Penny plunged her clitoris in and out of Kirsty's tightening cunt as Lucifer propelled his rock-hard cock into the girl's bottom-hole, the wonderful gasping sounds of sexual satisfaction reverberating around the banqueting hall. Snide's penis swelling within Kirsty's wet mouth, his orgasm approaching, he grabbed the girl's head and drove his huge knob to the back of her throat. Quivering as her three orifices were abused, crudely penetrated as Penny's fingers massaged her solid clitoris, Kirsty attained her mind-blowing orgasm.

Gobbling on the Professor's cock for all she was worth, she moaned through her nose as her climax peaked and his sperm gushed, bathing her sweeping tongue. Penny's clitoris pulsating within the girl's vaginal sheath, she let out a long low moan of pleasure as her orgasm erupted. Grunting and groaning from the bench beneath the chair, Lucifer thrust his hips, driving his orgasming knob deep into Kirsty's bowels as his spunk jetted.

'God, she's good!' Snide breathed, his swinging balls bashing Kirsty's face as he thrust his spunking knob in and out of her hot mouth.

'There's nothing I like more than spunking up a girl's cunt!' Penny cried, repeatedly pumping her three-inch clitoris into the tethered girl's tightening pussy hole.

'Spunking?' the Professor chuckled. 'Oh, er . . . yes, I see what you mean.'

'I still can't get my cock out of her bum, sir,' Lucifer complained, desperately trying to withdraw his spent organ from the girl's gripping anal duct.

'Shit and double shit!'

'I hope not, sir!'

Finally slipping his dripping penis out of Kirsty's mouth, the Professor knelt beside Penny and eagerly watched as she rocked her hips, driving her clitoris in and out of the girl's creamy vaginal duct. This really was a session of rampant filth! he reflected as the two girls' swollen and very wet pussy lips slapped together with a delicious squelching sound. But what to do about Lucifer's cock?

'Ah, debauchery at its highest!' the Baron grinned as he approached the lewd scene. 'Or its lowest.'

'Baron, I'm pleased to say that the machine worked perfectly,' Snide enlightened his friend. 'The girl came back to the castle and demanded a fuck.'

'That's exactly the way I think,' the Baron ruminated. 'She obviously has my brain patterns in their entirety. I suggest we induce my alpha-wave patterns into the Inspector's brain the next time he approaches the castle.'

'Better still, we could induce your alpha-wave patterns into the Inspector's . . . Ah, you've just said that.'

'Indeed I have, my friend.'

'By the way,' Snide said, climbing to his feet as Penny thrust her clitoris into the gasping girl's cunny hole with a loud squelch. 'The SAS are on their way.'

Walking across the hall, the Baron gazed out of the window and rubbed his chin meditatively. He was no doubt devising a devilish plan, the Professor mused, standing by the man's side. The SAS weren't to be mucked about with: if they commandeered the tanks, they could easily blow the castle to pieces. But could they defend themselves against Lucifer's karate bollock-chops? There again, Lucifer would have to have his own cock chopped off before he could leave the castle and do his bollock-chopping.

'OK,' the Baron murmured. 'I have to return to London.'

'To London?'

'That's where I came from, my friend.'

'Yes, but what about the SAS?'

'That's exactly my point.'

'Is it?'

'Of course.'

'Oh, I see. Actually, I don't see.'

'My friend, I came from London bearing important news.'

'Yes, I know.'

'And I now have to return to London'

'I don't understand, Baron.'

'Strangely, neither do I. I'll be in touch.'

Watching the Purple Baron leave the castle, Snide frowned. This was all he needed in his needy time of need. But what could he do? Turning to see Penny slipping her solid, cunny-dripping clitoris into Kirsty's gasping mouth, he decided to have a wank. It always helped to masturbate and shoot his spunk over the floor during times of great mental confusion.

Hauling his erect penis out of his trousers as he made his

way to the dungeon, he wondered what the Baron had done with Miss Hocks. Her fanny hair gone, it was high time she made his dream come true by opening her legs and begging to be fucked rotten. *Fucking is better than wanking*, he reflected. *Well, sometimes,* he ruminated, his cock waving from side to side as he descended the steps to the dungeon.

'Miss Hocks!' he called, pulling his foreskin back as he entered the lab. Looking about him, wondering where the woman had got to, he wandered into the rack chamber. 'Ah, there you are,' he said, eyeing her shaved fanny as she lay chained to the rack. 'Tell me, what do you think of my magnificent penis?'

'Who is Miss Hocks?' she asked, pulling on her bonds, trying to free her naked body.

'Er . . . you are. Or, you were. Actually, this is all very confusing. I'm never quite sure who's who. Ah, that's right, you're Gigi the hairdresser.'

'No, she's not!' Gigi called from the lab. 'I'm Gigi the bloody hairdresser!'

'Shut up, girl! If you're not careful, you'll be Gigi the well-fucked! OK . . . er, who am I? Ah, yes, I'm Snide.'

'Professor, unless you release me and allow me to . . . ' Miss Hocks began.

'Christ, not again! Moan, moan, bloody moan! Enough whingeing, let's have a look at your hairless cunt.'

Parting the woman's fleshy outer hillocks, Snide grinned as a wicked and severely debauched idea came to mind. Grabbing his King Dong vibrator from the shelf, he switched the device on and pressed the rounded end between the woman's gaping outer labia. Squirm and protest as she did, there was nothing she could do to halt the violation of her virginal pussy hole. *Three long years!* the Professor reflected, his cock swelling in anticipation of entering her tight cunny. *Three long fucking, fuckless years!*

'Stop it!' Miss Hocks cried as the vibrator drove deep into her tight cunt.

'Stop it?' Snide echoed. 'But I've only just started.'

'Please, not my pussy!'

'Where would you like it then, up your bum?' he chuckled.

Now there's a thought!

'Yes, up my bum,' she whispered sheepishly.

'What?'

'Up my bum.'

This was a turn-up for the library books, the Professor mused. Gigi must have some kind of peculiar fetish concerning her hot, tight bottom-hole. Probably some lesbian-induced fixation she picked up in her early teens, he pondered, imagining a naked netball team prancing around the pitch. *Hairless cracks, tightly closed in youth . . . Fuck me!* Perhaps she'd been introduced to cucumbers by a lesbionic and dangerously debauched PE mistress. *Oh, to be PE Mistress!*

Slipping the vibrator out of the woman's hot vaginal duct, Snide parted her tensed buttocks and pressed the cunny-wet end of the buzzing shaft against her brown anal iris. Gasping as he pushed and twisted the plastic phallus, Miss Hocks lifted her head, her pretty face grimacing as her anal sphincter muscles yielded to the rounded tip of the intruding dildo. The well-lubricated shaft slipping into her rectal duct, opening her tight sheath, she whimpered, her body shaking uncontrollably as the pink rod glided into her bottom tube.

'God, that's heavenly!' she cried, her head flopping back onto the rack as the vibrations permeated her quivering pelvis. 'Ah, yes! More, give me more!' Propelling the plastic shaft into her spasming anal canal, Snide twisted the vibrator, the sensations waking the secret nerve endings deep within the girl's abused bottom. 'Yes!' she cried again, her delicate brown tissue stretched tautly around the buzzing vibrator. 'More! Give me more!'

So this was the real Gigi, Snide reflected, gazing at the gasping girl's dishevelled hair as she tossed her head from side to side. For some reason, the brainwave transference had been incomplete, he mused. Gigi was obviously a rampant nympho, but Miss Hocks didn't have Gigi's inhibitions to keep her sexual desires secret. Knowing what the young Gigi was really like, Snide knew that she'd soon be writhing in orgasm once he'd stuffed his horse-like cock up her beautiful anal sheath.

'Oh, please! More, more!' Miss Hocks begged as Snide drove the eight-inch shaft deeper into her anal duct. Her mouth open, her eyes rolling, she gasped in her exquisite pleasure as the Professor grabbed another vibrator from the shelf and drove it into her tight cunt. Three long years, and now his assistant was begging for more. This was more like it! he thought happily, wondering whether she'd appreciate his knob spunking in her mouth.

Rebecca, Angelica and Gigi shouting from the lab, demanding to be released, the Professor decided to force them into lesbian sex after he'd dealt with Miss Hocks. It was a shame that the Baron wasn't around to help with the debauchery. But no matter: Snide was more than capable of defiling as many young girls who came his way, or who came across his face – more, even.

'Right, that's it!' Rebecca shouted. 'When I get out of here, snip – I'm going to see to it that you're locked up and the key thrown away! Snip, snip.'

'You'll never get out of here, snip or no snip!' Snide chuckled, moving along the rack.

'Keep going!' Miss Hocks whimpered as the Professor rammed the two vibrators in and out of her lust ducts. 'More! Faster, faster!'

She was ripe for a mouth-fucking, he reflected, grabbing the base of his cock with his free hand and pressing his purple-headed warrior against the woman's gasping mouth. Lifting her head, she eagerly swallowed half the length of his gigantic organ, his pulsating knob buried somewhere deep within her hot throat as she clamped her lips and gums tightly around his massive shaft.

'Bloody hell!' he breathed, still unable to believe that his prudish assistant was not only enjoying two vibrators up her sex holes, but was committing the beautifully vile act of sucking his cock to orgasm. All he had to do now was induce Gigi's alpha-wave patterns into his other prisoners, and he'd have his very own harem.

His spunk suddenly gushing from his pulsating glans, bathing the girl's snaking tongue as he withdrew his saliva-dripping shaft and drove into her again, he gasped and grimaced in his coming. His copious flow of sperm seemingly never-ending, he filled Miss Hocks's cheeks until her mouth overflowed, the opaque liquid running in rivers down her flushed face. Swallowing the gushing sperm as the vibrators transmitted delightful ripples of pleasure through her contracting womb, her own orgasm gripping her naked body, she moaned through her nose. Her eyes rolling as she flew to her sexual heaven, she gobbled on the Professor's orgasming glans for all she was worth as he thrust the plastic phalluses in and out of her spasming ducts.

This really was something else, Snide mused, gazing at the woman's erect nipples, her chocolate-brown areolae. She'd undoubtedly enjoy the nipple clamps, and the vaginal lip clamps, and the anal speculum, and the vaginal cucumber, and a tit-thrashing, and a buttock-caning . . . The lab would never be the same now that Miss Hocks had been transformed into a sex-starved, sex-crazed, sex-mad sexpot of a sexy nymphomaniac!

'Keep sucking!' he breathed, his pulsating knob pumping out the last of his spunk. 'God, you've got a beautiful mouth!'

176

Her body becoming rigid as her orgasm peaked, she sucked out the remnants of the Professor's oozing sperm. Her climax beginning to wane at last, she repeatedly swallowed and sucked, desperate for more sperm. Running his hand along his veined shaft, Snide squeezed the remaining sex liquid out of his slit before slipping his spunk- and saliva-dripping cock out of her mouth. Gasping in the aftermath of her incredible climax, her naked body shuddering uncontrollably as the vibrations transmitted through her quivering womb, Miss Hocks finally relaxed as the ripples of sex faded.

'Well, you certainly enjoyed *that*,' the Professor smiled, dragging the hot plastic shafts out of her inflamed sex sheaths. Switching the vibrators off, he gazed at the girl juice issuing from her open cunt hole, trickling down between her buttocks. Her anal entrance well-lubricated, her rectal sheath hot and ready, now was the time to slip his giant cock deep into her bum and spunk her bowels.

Releasing her feet, he pulled down the chains hanging from the ceiling and clamped the ends to her ankles. Turning the handle on the wall, her feet parting and rising high into the air, her naked body moving down the rack, her buttocks positioned over the end of the wooden planking, he grinned and rubbed his hands together. Her feet high above her head, he eyed the neat rosebud of her fully exposed bottom-hole nestling between her open buttocks. *Perfect!* he chuckled inwardly, taking his erect penis in his hand and standing at the end of the rack.

'And now for a bum-fucking!' he laughed, pressing his bulbous knob against her cunny-juiced brown portal.

'God, yes!' she gasped as his glans slipped past her sphincter muscles and drove into her hot rectal duct, her brown ring hugging the base of his purple crown. 'Ah, that feels good! This reminds me of Julia.'

'Who's Julia?'

'A girl at school.'

'What? She had a cock?'

'No, her father was a nurseryman – he grew cucumbers.'

'You had a lesbian relationship?' the Professor asked, sliding his penis in and out of the girl's rectal tube.

'Yes, several.'

'You're bisexual?'

'Yes.'

'Perfect!'

Gigi was the ideal candidate! he ruminated, pondering on a harem of bisexual sexmad girlies at his disposal. Lesbian licking, anal fucking, cunny-fucking, cocksucking, buttock-whipping . . . A lifetime of perverted sex lay ahead. But the SAS were on their way, he mused, driving the entire length of his baseball-bat-size penis into his writhing assistant's bowels. His heavy balls resting against her taut buttocks, he pondered on Lucifer. The butler was no use to anyone with his cock stuck up Kirsty's bottom, and what with the Purple Baron doing a runner . . .

'Oh, my bum!' Miss Hocks whimpered, jiggling her hips as her muscles tightened, her rectal tube gripping the Professor's mammoth organ. 'Really give it to me. Fuck my arse!'

'God, you're insatiable,' Snide murmured, yanking her vaginal lips wide apart and focusing on the wet, pink flesh surrounding her open sex hole.

'With your beautiful cock, I think you're the man for me.'

'I *know* I am,' he returned confidently.

'Prove it, Professor – *prove* that you're the man for me.'

Words of sheer sexual bliss, he ruminated, forcing four fingers into her vaginal cavern. *Prove it? I'll bloody well prove it!* he thought, driving his fingers further into her drenched cunt, her outer love lips stretched tautly around his knuckles. Twisting and pushing his hand, he finally managed to slip his fist into her bloated vaginal cavern. Her pink outer labia

178

gripping his wrist, he withdrew his rock-hard penis and drove his swollen glans deep into her tightening anal cylinder again.

'God!' she cried, her young cunt spasming, gripping his clenched fist. 'Oh, God!' Ramming his penile shaft in and out of her burning bottom-hole, his fist pistoning her inflamed cuntal sheath, her naked body jolting, the Professor gasped as she whimpered in her crude pleasure. His spunk jetting again, his massive balls draining, he pumped his fruits deep into the very core of her naked body as she reached her own mind-blowing, fist-fucking, arse-screwing-induced climax.

Screaming in her ecstasy, her head rolling from side to side as she rode the crest of her earth-shuddering multiple orgasm, the chains clanking loudly, she rocked her hips, taking the entire length of the Professor's horse-like penis deep into her dank bowels. 'Oh, my arse,' she whispered in her sexual delirium. 'Fuck my arse, really fuck my arse. God, my beautiful cunt. Oh, oh, my cunt.'

Spraying the last of his sperm into the semi-conscious woman's anal core, Snide finally stilled his rock-hard cock, his swollen knob absorbing the heat of her fiery rectal cavern. His heaving balls rolling, already filling with spunk for the next orgasmic gushing, he pulled his juiced fist out of her tight cunt. Her sex hole squelching, her outer lips slapping together, she shuddered in her debauchery. Crying out as he withdrew his cock from her abused anal sheath and staggered across the rack room, she lay quivering in her sexual abandonment.

'Oh, Professor!' she breathed, apparently finding a second wave of lust as she lifted her head. 'I want you again, spunking up my bum again.'

'Christ, give me a minute or two to recover!' he returned, zipping his trousers. 'I'll prove that I'm the man for you, but give me a minute.'

A massive explosion resounding throughout the castle,

Snide looked up at the ceiling. Either Lucifer had retrieved his cock and was up the turret firing at someone, or he was . . . *He was what?* Snide pondered, dashing up the stone steps. The windows in the banqueting hall shattering as another explosion reverberated throughout the castle, he knew that the worst had come – the SAS had arrived.

'What the fuck . . . ' Lucifer cried as another explosion shook the very foundations of the castle, his cock still embedded deep within Kirsty's anal tract as Penny drove her erect clitoris into the girl's yawning cuntal opening.

'OK, Professor Snide!' a man bellowed through a loud hailer. 'This is the SAS! The castle is surrounded. Open the doors or we'll huff and we'll blow your house down!'

'Fuck and quadruple fuck!' the Professor spat. 'I blame you for this, Lucifer!'

'*Me*, sir? But . . . '

'Well, that's it – the end is nigh,' Snide sighed as another explosion rocked the castle. 'I wonder what Sir Walter Raleigh would have done?'

'Lit a cigarette, sir?'

'More than likely. Alexander Graham Bell?'

'Phoned for assistance, sir?'

'Undoubtedly. John Logie Baird?'

'Watched the *News At Ten*?'

'Rasputin?'

'Had a wank, sir?'

'There's a thought! We shall wank on the beaches, we shall wank . . . No, we're fucking well doomed. I'll plead clinical insanity, Lucifer.'

'And I'll plead penile dementia, sir. Satan, hear us in our time of need!'

'What *are* you talking about?'

'I'm asking for help, sir.'

'I'm the one who needs help!' Kirsty cried. 'My bum

really hurts and I don't want a girl's deformed clitoris up my cunt!'

'Shut up, girl!' Snide returned. 'Can't you see that we're in a state of siege?'

'Sorry.'

'You will be! No cannon, no gunpowder, no balls . . . Bollocks!'

'Might I suggest that we die with honour, sir?'

'No, you might not suggest that we die – with or without honour.'

'Professor Snide, this is the SAS! You have until sundown to come out with your hands up!'

'Fuck and treble fuck! I'm going to throw the psychiatrist over the turret wall. It won't help, but it'll be fun. I'll see you later.'

'What about my bum?' Kirsty asked.

'Fuck your bum!'

Chapter Eight

Standing atop the windswept turret, Professor Snide gazed across the rolling hills. Sundown was a long way off, he observed, looking up at the bright sun – there was time to save the castle, but how? Turning his attention to the alpha-wave machine, he pondered on the Baron's modification to the helmet. It had worked on Penny, so why not try it on the SAS?

Leaning over the wall, he noticed a group of men milling around by a clump of trees. The alpha-wave machine contained the Baron's brain patterns, he reflected, focusing on a massive rocket launcher partially concealed by the trees. Aiming the helmet at the SAS would . . . What *would* the Baron's brain patterns do to the men? Perhaps they'd come to the castle in search of a young girl to fuck, each believing that they were the Baron.

'Let me out!' the psychiatrist yelled, hammering on the gunpowder room door.

'Shut up! You're liable to have yourself certified insane for shouting like that!' the Professor snapped, aiming the helmet at the group of men and flicking the switch on the control panel.

'You can't keep me locked in here, Professor!'

'Of course I can.'

'You're mad!'

'I'm completely, absolutely, thoroughly, unequivocally, utterly and totally bonkers.'

'My God!'

'OK, here goes,' he murmured, flicking another switch. The men looked about as if totally confused before they finally made their way towards the village. What was in their minds, the Professor had no idea, but at least the bastards were leaving. Watching as they disappeared, he wondered where they were going. To rape the postmistress? *What the fuck?*

Turning to the gunpowder room door as the psychiatrist began hammering and shouting again, the Professor wondered what to do with the distraught man. Chuck him over the turret wall? If Lucifer was free, he could karate chop the man's bollocks off. Lucifer and Kirsty, and now the psychiatrist . . . More bloody problems!

Grabbing the alpha-wave machine and dashing down the winding steps, a wicked plan was forming in the Professor's deranged mind. If he was going to be thrown out of the castle, he'd be prepared for the future – take the horny girlies with him. The state might well snatch the castle, but they weren't having the girlies!

In the lab, he gazed at his delectable prisoners, their naked bodies tied over the bench, their rounded buttocks perfectly projected for a damned good anal rogering. The three pairs of buttocks weal-lined, beautifully crimsoned from the merciless lashing, they deserved another damned good thrashing. But not yet.

In some respects, things were looking up, the Professor reflected as he readied the machine. Miss Hocks was stretched on the rack with her fanny shaved, her bottom-hole positioned for an anal fucking. Rebecca, Gigi and Angelica were tied over the bench, ready for whatever perverted abuse came to mind. Penny was fucking Kirsty with her three-inch clitoris, and Lucifer . . . *Poor old Lucifer*, he mused, placing the helmet on Gigi's head as she hissed her threats and protests – forever arse-cocked. Slapping Gigi's naked buttocks as she shook the helmet off her head, his anger rising, he grabbed the whip.

'How dare you struggle!' he bellowed, lashing her naked buttocks with the thin leather tails. 'Unless you keep still and allow me to record your brain patterns, I'll shove a marrow up your arsehole!'

'A marrow?' she echoed huskily, as if excited by the notion.

'Yes, a fucking great marrow.'

'Ooh, that sounds . . . I mean, you just dare to abuse my bottom!'

'I'll abuse your mouth in a minute. Look, all I want to do is record your brain waves so that I can transform the other girls.'

'Transform them?'

'We don't want to be transformed!' Rebecca and Angelica cried in unison.

'Shut up! You'll all be transformed, and that's the end of the matter!' he returned.

'Transformed into what?' Gigi asked.

'They'll all be like you, think the way you do. They'll enjoy anal sex, perverted lesbian sex . . . '

'I *don't* enjoy that sort of vile and disgusting, perverted filth!'

'Of course you do, Gigi. I know all about you, your vile, filthy, corrupt, disgusting and perverted sexual desires and practices. Now keep still, otherwise I won't shove anything up your bum.'

Her body unmoving as Snide plonked the helmet on her head, she was obviously hoping that he'd abuse her bottom-hole, force a cucumber or a marrow deep into her anal shaft. But it was the Professor's cock she was going to have shoved up her bum, as well as carrots, bananas, candles, vibrators, pumpkins . . . *Pumpkins? That reminds me*, he mused, eyeing her small brown hole as he flicked the switch and recorded her alpha-wave patterns. *Penny's clitoris, enlarged to the size of a fucking great cock, and shoved right up Gigi's arsehole!*

'OK, all done,' he finally said, switching the machine off. 'Now I have your brain patterns, I can turn any girl into a rampant, nymphomaniacal, bisexual, dirty, perverted, filthy little . . . '

'Hang on!' she broke in. 'I'm not that bloody bad!'

'You will be, my horny little tart – you will be!' *That's a thought*, he mused, eyeing the computer.

Hooking the helmet up to the computer, the Professor brought Gigi's brain waves up on the screen. Gazing at the patterns, he massaged the girl's brown portal, noting one particular peak rising, indicating the pleasure derived from the anal stimulation. Driving his finger into the dank sheath of her rectal duct, he watched the peak rise with her increasing pleasure.

Slipping his finger out of her tight anal duct, he noted that the peak diminished. Slapping her naked buttocks, another peak diminished, indicating her displeasure. Making a mental note of the two peaks, he focused on several other peaks, each one representing a particular erogenous zone, a sexual preference.

'You don't like being spanked, do you?' he asked.

'No, of course I bloody don't!'

'How about this?' he smiled, forcing four fingers into her vaginal cavern.

'Stop it!' she returned, a third peak falling, signifying her dissatisfaction.

Sitting at the keyboard and grabbing the mouse as Rebecca and Angelica demanded their freedom, Snide highlighted the group of peaks representing Gigi's sexual likes and dislikes. Amplifying each peak was sure to send her libido soaring, he reflected – and she'd beg for perverted sex. Sending the modified patterns back to the alpha-wave machine, he rubbed his hands together as he pondered on the result.

Gigi would be the same person but, he hoped, she'd be oversexed in the extreme, delighting in every aspect of crude sex. This was the answer, he mused, operating the controls and inducing the patterns into the girl's brain. Finally removing the helmet, he stood behind her naked body, focusing on her tightly closed anal inlet nestling between her firm buttocks. The time had come to test her response.

'Do you like this?' he asked, slapping her rounded buttocks as hard as he could with the palm of his hand.

'Ah, yes!' she cried as he spanked her again, a loud smack echoing around the lab. 'More, more!'

'And what about this?' he grinned, forcing four fingers into her tightening cunt.

'Ah, ah! That's beautiful! Push your hand right up me!' she whimpered, her tethered body quivering uncontrollably, her girl juice flowing in torrents from her bloated vaginal cavern. 'Your fist, I want your fist right up my lovely cunt!'

This was incredible, he reflected, forcing half his hand into the girl's drenched vaginal cavern. With the modified brain patterns, Miss Hocks was going to be the perfect sexpot, and Rebecca and Angelica and Penny and Kirsty . . . Into everything and anything, the girls would be ever-ready for crude and extremely debauched sex!

Withdrawing his hand from Gigi's cunny, he placed the helmet on Rebecca's head and induced the modified alpha-wave patterns into her brain. Eyeing her pert bottom-hole, he couldn't wait for her to beg him to spunk her bowels, to fuck her cunt, to sperm her mouth . . . A group of sex-crazed girlies at his disposal? *God, life's great!*

Inducing the patterns into Angelica's brain, he focused on her bottom-hole, small, brown, tightly closed, inviting . . . There was something about girls' bottom-holes that he found fascinating. The secret entrance to their tight rectal ducts, to their bowels, the thought of their anal rings gripping the base of his solid cock . . . Yes, there definitely was something fascinating about girls' bottom-holes!

'OK,' he murmured, removing the helmet. 'Now I have three sex-mad, sex-crazed sexpots to play with!'

'My bum!' Angelica cried. 'Please, I want your lovely cock right up my tight bumhole!'

'Snip, snip – I'm first!' Rebecca breathed, her bottom wiggling.

'What about me?' Gigi asked. 'I want you first!'

'Calm down, girls. You'll all enjoy the pleasure of my fucking great cock spunking your tight bums, just be patient.'

'I want you *now*!' Rebecca ordered the Professor. 'Snip, snip! Give it to me *now*!'

'No, me first!' Angelica cried.

'No, me!' Gigi bellowed.

This was brilliant, Snide thought, whipping his solid penis out of his trousers and pulling his foreskin back. A row of naked girls begging to have their bums fucked! What more could a pervert want? A bottom-tonguing might be interesting, he mused, imagining his tongue exploring inside the girls' anal ducts. *The more perverse, the better!*

Eyeing his bulbous purple knob, he stood behind Gigi, the first in line for a good anal rogering. Parting her tensed buttocks, opening her anal valley, he pressed his swollen plum against her exquisite brown tissue, pushing and twisting his shaft as she fervently begged him to enter her. His knob finally slipping past her tight brown ring, absorbing the heat of her inner flesh, he shuddered.

'God, your bum's tight!' he gasped.

'And your cock's big!' she whimpered as his shaft drove into her rectal tube, bloating her pelvic cavity.

'What about me?' Rebecca complained. 'Snip, snip.'

'You're next, my horny little tart!'

'And then me!' Angelica rejoined.

'Yes and then you, my dirty young schoolgirlie.'

The Baron was missing out on the fun, Snide reflected, again pondering on his friend's inexplicable departure. *All the more bottoms for me!* he chuckled inwardly, watching his veined shaft sink into the quivering girl's spasming rectal duct, her brown ring stretched tautly around his horse-like cock. Grabbing her shapely hips and withdrawing his member, her brown tissue clinging to his penile rod, pulling away from her anal crease, he drove into her again.

'I've never known anything like it!' Gigi gasped, her naked body jolting as he repeatedly withdrew his penis and propelled his swollen glans deep into her tightening arse.

'I have!' he laughed, slapping her buttocks with his palm. 'This is what Satan made girls for.'

'Satan?'

'Yes, he made young girlies like you for one reason and one reason only – to be severely arse-fucked!'

His spunk finally issuing from his knob-slit, he rammed his rod in and out of Gigi's twitching bottom-hole. His heavy balls swinging, slapping her swollen vaginal lips as he continued the crude arse-fucking, taking her to her sexual heaven, he increased the pace of his rhythm. 'Argh! Argh! Argh! Argh!' he grunted with each violent thrust of his solid cock, pumping the last of his spunk into her brimming duct as she whimpered in her coming.

Finally withdrawing his spent member with a loud sucking sound, her buttocks closing, concealing her sperm-dripping anal portal, Snide reeled backwards across the lab. This was more like it! he reflected, leaning against the wall to steady his trembling body. Horny young tarts demanding a good buggering, what could be better?

Zipping his trousers as the other girls demanded a good

anal fucking and spunking, he knew that he'd have to recover before complying with their crude requests, would have to wait for his member to rise again. Grabbing a length of rope and staggering up the stone steps, ignoring the girls' futile pleas, he made his way to the banqueting hall to find out whether Lucifer had managed to extract his cock from Kirsty's arsehole.

'Professor Snide!' Kirsty snapped as he entered the hall and stood before the double-bum-fucking chair. 'Professor Snide, I demand that you remove your butler's cock from my bottom-hole and release me this minute!'

'Anything else?' he smiled.

'Yes, you can also tell this weird girl to remove her weird clitoris from my fanny!'

'Problem number one, the butler's cock is his own business: it has nothing to do with me. Problem number two, Penny has a mind of her own, and if she deems it necessary to fuck your cunt with her clitoris, the prerogative's hers. Problem number three . . . '

'Problem number one is that, unless you release me, you'll find yourself in jail.'

'Problem number six . . . er, how many problems are there?'

'You have only one problem, Professor – the prospect of jail!'

'And you have only two problems, Kirsty – the problem of your cocked bumhole and the problem of your clitted cunny-hole.'

'Sir, may I be so bold as to suggest plastic explosive?' Lucifer asked.

'No, you may not. OK, I'm going to tie this rope to your ankles and pull you off the bench. Hopefully, during the pulling process, your cock will slip out of her bum.'

'I do hope so, sir.'

'Penny, do you mind withdrawing your clitoris from Kirsty's fanny so I can de-cock her arse?'

'Only if I can fuck her after the butler's got his cock out of her bum.'

'You can do what you like to her after the butler's got his cock out of her bum.'

Tying the rope around Lucifer's ankles as Penny slipped her clitoris out of Kirsty's cunt and moved aside, the Professor dragged the other end across the hall, pulling for all he was worth. The butler's body moving along the bench, his cock anchoring him, he groaned as his penis stretched. Ignoring his protests, Snide pulled harder on the rope, the butler's cock elongating but still remaining lodged within the complaining girl's bottom-hole.

'It's no good,' the Professor sighed. 'It won't come out.'

'Try again,' Kirsty whined. 'I can't stay like this any longer.'

'OK, one more try, but I don't hold out much hope.'

Pulling on the rope again, the bum-fucking chair glided across the floor as the Professor gave one almighty yank. 'Argh!' Lucifer cried as his penis popped out of the girl's bum like a cork out of a bottle, the report echoing like a gunshot around the hall. 'That fucking hurt!' Staggering to his feet, Lucifer massaged his sore penis before zipping his trousers.

'Christ! Your bum's something else!' Snide grinned, focusing on the sperm gushing from the girl's gaping anal portal.

'Never again am I going to have anyone fuck my bum!' she returned angrily as Penny knelt before her, her pink clitoral shaft erect, ready for anal penetration.

'Wrong, my friend!' Penny chuckled. '*I'*m going to fuck your bum!'

'No!'

'Yes!' Snide laughed. 'Yes, yes, yes!'

'No, no, no!'

Turning to Lucifer as Penny parted Kirsty's buttocks and managed to drive her solid clitoris into the tethered girl's inflamed anal canal, Snide told him about the psychiatrist locked in the gunpowder room. Lucifer's only suggestion was to karate chop the man's bollocks off, a suggestion that Snide was about to go along with until the phone rang.

'Professor Snide,' he replied.

'Major Dastardly-Williams here.'

'Dastardly-Williams?'

'Colonel-in-Chief of the Special Air Service.'

'Colonel? But you just said Major.'

'Did I? Oh well, not to worry.'

'Whoever you are, I don't need your special hair services – I have more than enough hairdressers as it is.'

'Hair services? What the devil are you talking about, man?'

'I have no idea, Captain.'

'Captain? Now look here, Snide – my men have returned to HQ demanding lewd sex with young girls.'

'Really, Colonel . . . Major?'

'What the dickens have you done to them?'

'I haven't touched any young girlies. Well, not recently. Not for at least ten minutes . . . ten years.'

'My men, you blithering idiot!'

'Men? Are you suggesting that I've sexually interfered with men's naughty bits? Do you need a mobile hairdresser?'

'A mobile . . . Listen to me, Professor.'

'I am.'

'You are what?'

'Listening to you.'

'You've done something dastardly to my men. I want them returned to their normal state.'

'Something dastardly, Major Dastardly-Williams? But, surely, they *are* normal men. I mean, men demanding lewd sex with young girls is perfectly normal in my cookery book.'

'There's something very wrong with the workings of your brain, Professor.'

'Yes, I know. Actually, I have a resident psychiatrist. A psychiatrist who resides.'

'I'm not surprised!'

'I'd better go and ask him for some group sex . . . I mean, group therapy. It's been nice talking to you, Lieutenant. Goodbye.'

'But . . . '

Replacing the receiver, Snide pondered again on having Lucifer karate chop the psychiatrist's bollocks off. The psychological approach might be better, he mused. Leave the man in the gunpowder room until he went completely and utterly insane and then . . . Or use the alpha-wave machine and transform him into a lesbian.

'Sir, shall I karate chop the psychiatrist's bollocks off?' Lucifer asked, chopping the air with the edge of his hand.

'No, we'll leave him in the gunpowder room for the time being. What I *would* like you to do is go down to the clump of trees at the foot of the hill and bring back the rocket launcher.'

'Rocket launcher, sir?'

'The SAS left it there. It's bigger and presumably more powerful than ours. Go and get it and set it up on the turret.'

'Right away, sir.'

Pondering on his problems as Lucifer left the castle, Snide rubbed his chin. The SAS had been dealt with temporarily, he reflected, but it was time to make some concrete plans for the future. Three long years, and now Miss Hocks was a sex-crazed nympho. All the girlies had been transformed into sex-crazed nymphomaniacs, except for Kirsty. Once Penny had finished screwing the girl's bum with her three-inch clitoris, he'd induce the modified patterns into the girl's brain and she could join the harem. But there was the psychiatrist to deal with, and the government . . . Concrete plans had to be made forthwith.

'I wish my penis was bigger,' Penny complained as she rocked her hips, her erect clitoris sliding in and out of Kirsty's inflamed bottom-hole.

'Your wish is about to come true, Cinderella!' the Professor replied, a wicked idea coming to mind. 'Follow me to the lab and I'll give you the biggest clitoris . . . I mean, the biggest penis you could ever imagine.'

'Really?' she giggled, slipping her pencil-like organ out of Kirsty's anal duct and leaping to her feet.

'Let us repair to the lab!'

'Is it broken?' she frowned.

'No, but it's rather untidy.'

'Let me go!' Kirsty cried as they left the hall.

'No!'

'Yes!'

This was no way to deal with the problems, the Professor mused, leading the girl down to the dungeon – but to suck a clitoris the size of a penis would be exquisite. Trying to picture the massive pink protrusion emerging from the top of the girl's sex crack, he pondered on the wisdom of taking photographs and selling them for a huge profit. Better still, sell the girl's naked body to perverted men for crude sex. Recalling the Baron's words, he grinned. *You could earn a fortune from such a machine.*

'That's just what I intend to do,' he breathed.

'What is?' Penny asked, standing by the bench and admiring Gigi's rounded weal-lined buttocks, her delectable anal crease.

'Er . . . Nothing. Right, sit on the chair and I'll give you the biggest clitty . . . the biggest *penis* ever.'

'Fuck my bum!' Rebecca cried.

'Wait!'

As Penny sat down, Snide grabbed the gamma-ray box and knelt between her parted feet. Her buttocks over the edge of the chair, her enlarged clitoris protruding from her gaping sex slit, he placed the box between her thighs, her pink pleasure shaft entering the hole. Switching the device on, the vacuum sucking her erectile clitoral protrusion deep into the box, he looked up at her pretty face.

'When the buzzer sounds and the light flashes, your penis will be ready for inspection,' he smiled.

'Ooh!' she gasped. 'It feels heavenly!'

'Just think, Penny . . . I mean, Baron. You'll be able to fuck each girl in turn, shove your clit . . . your *cock* up each hot, tight bottom-hole in turn.'

'I can't wait!' she squealed, the vacuum building as he switched the gamma ray on.

'Neither can I!'

Ignoring the prisoners' demands to be arse-fucked and clit-sucked, Snide again pondered on the SAS. As the government weren't going to give in to his demands, the SAS would undoubtedly send another wave of men to wreak havoc and . . . *Fuck the SAS*. Asking Penny to hold the box in place, he leaped to his feet and grabbed the ringing phone.

'What is it?' he snapped, becoming increasingly irritated by the continual interruptions.

'Professor, it's DI Peel.'

'Oh, Inspector. You haven't heard from me for some time.'

'Heard from you . . . You mean, you haven't heard from *me* for some time.'

'That's what I said.'

'No, *you* haven't heard from *me*, as in, *I* haven't called *you* for some time.'

'I know you haven't, Inspector.'

'Er, right. I'm calling to inform you that . . . '

'Didn't I call you?'

'No, Professor – *I* called *you*.'

'What did you call me? I hope you haven't been calling me names.'

'Professor, please stop playing childish games. The reason I'm calling is to inform you that the SAS are on their way to . . .'

'They've been.'

'What?'

'The SAS, they came, they went – and they didn't conquer.'

'Came and went?'

'They called in for morning coffee, which I thought most polite of them.'

'Morning coffee? I think we've got our wires crossed, Professor. I'm talking about the Special Air Service.'

'Yes, run by Major Dastardly-Williams.'

'Dastardly-Williams came to see you?'

'For morning coffee.'

'I know nothing about this.'

'Fuck me!'

'I *beg* your pardon?'

'Er . . . I've just made a terrible faux pas. Dastardly-Williams ordered me to keep quiet about his unwelcome visit. He said that I should tell no one and also instructed me not to tell anyone else.'

'But the SAS were sent to capture your castle and bring you to trial.'

'I find that most odd, Inspector. Dastardly-Williams told me that his men were going to capture the village police station and bring *you* to trial.'

'*Me*? There's obviously been some sort of mix-up. I'd better get on to my superior and get this sorted out.'

'Yes, I think you had. By the way, have you had any luck with your daughter?'

'No, the aliens still have her.'

'If I were you, Inspector, I'd suggest to your superior that the SAS sort the aliens out rather than raid your police station.'

'Yes, I think I will. Her mother misses her terribly.'

'Misses her what?'

'Her daughter.'

'What? You mean to say that her mother's lost her daughter, too?'

'Obviously, both her mother and her father have lost their daughter.'

'This is despicable. How many daughters have gone missing?'

'Just mine.'

'And her mother's?'

'My daughter, and my wife's.'

'Your wife's daughter as well? Good God!'

'What? Are you feeling all right, Professor?'

'I really don't know. What with everyone's daughters going missing, I really don't know how I feel.'

'Yes, well . . . I'll be in touch.'

'OK, Inspector. I do hope the missing daughters turn up. I'm sure their parents must be fraught with worry, if not distraught.'

'Yes, I'm sure they will. Good day, Professor.'

Watching Penny writhe in sexual ecstasy as the box sucked on her elongated clitoris, Snide rubbed his chin pensively. If the Inspector believed that aliens had taken not only his daughter but the other missing girls, the little sex pots could forever remain in the castle to be enjoyed at will. No one would come looking for them, not if they thought that the girls were on Mars or Venus – or up Uranus.

The prisoners had to be well hidden, he reflected. Should the castle be raided, there must be no sign of the young beauties – not one pair of girl-stained panties, not one bra or even a tell-tale pubic hair. The secret tunnel was a good hiding place to stash the girlies, but it was dark and dank – not ideally suited for fresh young maidens with hot juicy cunts, tight anal sheaths, firm rounded titties . . .

'Any chance of something to eat?' Rebecca asked, turning her head and gazing at the Professor.

'Only my cock!' the Professor sniggered.

'We're all starving.'

'Sex-starved or food-starved?'

'Both.'

'Fucking bollocks, I'm not a bloody chef. You'll have to wait until my butler gets back, he'll cook something.'

'Ah, God!' Penny gasped as the gamma-ray box sucked her clitoris to orgasm. 'Oh, my cock!'

'Your cock?' Angelica frowned, lifting her head and looking at the writhing girl.

'Er . . . Take no notice,' Snide smiled. 'She thinks she's a . . . Just take no notice.'

As Penny fell off the chair and writhed in ecstasy on the floor, her clitoris slipped out of the hole in the box. Gazing wide-eyed at the massive pink protrusion, the Professor could hardly believe it. Seven inches long and as thick as the thickest penis, Penny's clitoris would make medical history – it would make anal fucking history.

Kneeling between the girl's splayed thighs, Snide examined her clitoral dildo. Her outer lips stretched, held wide apart by the broad base of the 'penis', her sex hole was completely bared. Scrutinizing her smooth, glistening clitoral shaft, wondering whether she could actually fuck herself with her massive 'cock', he leaned forward and licked the sensitive tip. Taking half the organ into his mouth as the girl writhed and gasped in her agonizing pleasure, he rolled his tongue round the twitching head.

'Oh, God!' she cried, parting her legs further as he slipped three fingers into the wet heat of her yawning vaginal cavern. 'God, I'm coming already!' Her naked body trembling uncontrollably, she gripped the Professor's head, clutching his unruly hair and pulling him down on her pulsating sex rod. Her vaginal juices streaming down his hand as he thrust his fingers in and out of her spasming cunt, she rocked her hips, driving her clitoris deep into his gobbling mouth as she attained a massive orgasm.

'I'm there!' she screamed, her face flushing, her nostrils flaring. Wondering what it was like to have a cunt and a penis-lookalike clitoris, the Professor imagined Penny screwing Gigi's fanny while he screwed Penny's pussy hole. Better still, he could screw Penny's arse while she screwed Gigi's fanny. There again . . . The beautifully disgusting permutations were endless!

Her orgasm finally waning, Penny breathed heavily, her head rolling from side to side as her body began to calm. Slipping her gigantic clitoris out of his mouth, the Professor watched the protrusion slowly deflate and finally lie limp, snuggling between her gaping pussy lips. She really was something else, he mused, dragging his drenched fingers out of her hot sex duct. What the Inspector would say if he were to see his daughter now, he dreaded to think! *Fuck the Inspector!*

'I want it up my bum!' Rebecca called as the Professor climbed to his feet.

'And you're going to *have* it up your bum,' he grinned, eyeing Penny's clitoris as it began to twitch and stiffen. 'Penny . . . I mean, Baron, would you do the honours?'

'I'd be only too delighted, my friend,' she grinned, leaping to her feet and standing behind Rebecca, her insatiable clitoris fully erect.

'I want it, too,' Angelica breathed, wiggling her buttocks.

'And me,' Gigi rejoined.

'All right, all right,' the Professor said. 'You'll all have a bum-fucking if you're patient. OK, let the fun commence!'

Watching Penny position her solid clitoris between Rebecca's parted buttocks, the pink, rounded tip pressed against the girl's anal eye, the Professor grinned as his penis stiffened within his tight trousers. Once she'd slipped her sex pole into Rebecca's bum, he'd slip his cock into Penny's bum and spunk her bowels. His cock spunking up her arse, her clit pulsating in orgasm up Rebecca's arse . . . Things were looking up – right up!

As the rounded end of the girl's huge clitoris drove into Rebecca's anal sheath, both girls gasping in their pleasure, the Professor whipped his horse-like penis out of his trousers and yanked his foreskin back. His swollen purple knob glistening in the light, he moved behind Penny and parted her firm buttocks, exposing her brown anal portal as she drove her giant clitty deep into Rebecca's tight rectal duct.

Pressing his bulbous glans against Penny's tight anal ring, his knob suddenly sucked into her hot rectum, he gasped. 'Ah! Your bum's the tightest I've ever known!'

'And so's hers,' Penny breathed, her cunny lips slapping Rebecca's buttocks as she repeatedly withdrew her clitoris and drove it back into the girl's rectal sheath.

'Is that a dildo?' Rebecca asked, her naked body rocking.

'No, it's my cock,' Penny replied.

'But . . .'

'Don't ask questions,' the Professor broke in. 'Just enjoy it.'

'God, I'm enjoying it all right! Oh, my bum!'

'Oh, my clitty!'

'Oh, my cock!'

'Oh, my God!' the Baron gasped as he entered the lab.

Turning, the Professor gazed in disbelief at his friend. Dressed in a red miniskirt, stockings and red stilettos, his white blouse straining to contain his full bra, the Baron's red glossed lips furled into a salacious grin. Slipping his penis out of Penny's tight bottom-hole, the Professor stood before the man, his cock deflating as he frowned.

'Er . . . Baron, why are you dressed as a woman?' he asked. 'Do you have a leaning towards transvestism?'

'It's a disguise, my friend,' the Baron replied, hoisting his false tits up.

'But I thought you'd returned to London?'

'It was a ploy. I left the castle and walked to the railway station. Slipping into the Ladies, I disrobed a female toiletee, causing her great anguish in the process, and donned her clothes and returned here.'

'But . . . '

'The enemy believe I caught the London train, so I can now move about safely, infiltrate their ranks and . . . '

'Dressed as a woman?'

'It's the perfect disguise, my friend. Although I have difficulty walking in my rather tight panties, it's the perfect disguise.'

'Are they silk?'

'Red silk, and so tight that my balls swell out on either side of the crotch and my knob sticks out of the top.'

'Amazing.'

Turning and looking at Penny as she screamed, reaching her mind-blowing climax, her erect clitoris shafting Rebecca's tight bum hole, the Professor pondered on the Baron's disguise. Transvestism was intriguing, he mused, imagining wearing a pair of tight silk panties. Entering ladies' toilets dressed in a miniskirt would be fascinating: there were bound to be some very interesting sights – and sounds! There was something about female toilets that was absolutely fascinating, he reflected – but there was no time for such illegalities now.

'What's your plan, Baron?' he asked, slipping his penis back into his trousers and tugging up the zip.

'I plan to masturbate and cream my silk panties.'

'There's one major flaw in your plan, Baron.'

'You mean, I've overlooked something?'

'Yes. I used the alpha-wave machine on the SAS. They've gone.'

'How does that affect my wanking and sperming in my red silk panties?'

'It doesn't.'

'Thank God for that.'

'Before you cream your panties, I have to inform you that the psychiatrist is still locked in the gunpowder room. What we should do with him, I really don't know.'

'Fear not, my friend, for I have a plan so wicked, so devious, that . . . '

'But you haven't thought of it yet?'

'On the contrary, I've planned my plan meticulously.'

'What *is* this plan, Baron?'

'I shall bring the psychiatrist down here and force him to endure perverted sex with our prisoners.'

'Fuck me!'

'No, thank you. I shall return forthwith!'

As the Baron tottered up the stone steps in his miniskirt, the Professor turned and watched Penny slip her clitoris out of Rebecca's inflamed bottom-hole and stagger backwards across the lab. As the girl rested on the chair, her firm breasts heaving as she breathed heavily in the aftermath of her incredible coming, he decided that it was time to use his prisoners for sex so debased, so vile and perverted, so filthy and disgusting . . .

'No more pussyfooting,' he breathed pensively, wondering what perverted acts to instruct his girls to commit. Releasing each girl, helping them off the bench, he stood them in a row, scrutinizing their pert breasts, their curvaceous young bodies. They'd lick each other's clitties to orgasm, he decided. Finger each other's tight cunts and drink the flowing juices, finger each other's hot bottom-sheaths, suck on each other's erect nipples and . . .

'You must let me go!' the psychiatrist yelled as the Baron dragged him down the stone steps. 'You don't understand, I . . .'

'Please be quiet!' the Baron ordered his prisoner, standing the man before the row of naked girls.

'You are to be forced into acts of perverted and highly illegal sex,' the Professor grinned. 'OK, girls, strip him – and sexually abuse him!'

'Please, you don't . . .'

'Silence!' the Baron bellowed.

Grinning as the girls stripped the struggling psychiatrist, Snide waited in anticipation for the humiliation and degradation to begin. Desperate for crude sex, the young beauties would suck his cock, knead his balls, rub their naked bodies all over him and bring themselves off. That was the way to treat interfering psychiatrists, he mused as the man's trousers were yanked down his legs, exposing his limp cock hanging over his hairy ballbag.

'You don't understand!' the prisoner protested again as his cock was eagerly grabbed by three hands.

'I understand only too well,' Snide replied. 'You've come here to establish the extent of my clinical insanity and, for your sins, you'll be sexually abused by my naked girlies.'

'No, I'm not really a psychiatrist.'

'Don't tell me that you're a mobile bloody hairdresser!'

'No, I'm the Prime Minister.'

'The . . .'

Frowning at the man, Snide rubbed his chin. There *was* some resemblance, he pondered. But why would the PM dash into the castle disguised as a psychiatrist? No, he was talking bollocks, just trying to gain his release with his pathetic story. He was no more the PM than Snide was a moralistic, wholesome, upright pillar of the community!

'You can't be the PM because he phoned me while you were locked in the gunpowder room.'

'That was my colleague. He . . . '

'If you're the PM, then I'm a nun's sex crack!' the Professor chuckled as Rebecca wanked the man's stiffening cock and sucked on his purple knob.

'Please, I have to return to Number Ten!'

'Forget Number Ten, it's number sixty-nine you'll be having. You're going to come in the sexpot's mouth, and that's the end of the matter.'

'But my wife . . . '

'You can come in your wife's mouth later.'

'Professor, I am the leader of the government. You cannot . . . '

'In that case, you'll be punished for your fascism. The whip, I think. Yes, ten lashes across each buttock. And then a ball-whipping followed by a cock-spanking.'

Pulling the stripped man to the floor, the naked girls sat astride his writhing body, rubbing their open cunts over his face, his solid cock. Angelica's girlie juice trickling over his heaving balls, Gigi's cunny cream running down his face, they began gasping in their pleasure. Grabbing his cock, Angelica guided his knob deep into her tight cunt, bouncing up and down, his swollen glans battering her young cervix as she rode him to her orgasm.

'Please!' he gasped through a mouthful of Gigi's wet cunny flesh. Grinding her clitoris into his mouth, silencing him, Gigi rocked her hips, delighting in the sensations emanating from her pulsating pleasure bud. Kneeling either side of the man, Rebecca and Penny grabbed his hands, forcing his fingers into their drenched sex sheaths, gasping as their juices of lust ran down his wrists.

'A few hours of enforced and terribly illegal sexual abuse should be punishment enough!' the Professor sniggered.

'Indeed, my friend,' the Baron smiled, hoisting his false tits up. 'Might I ask where Miss Hocks is?'

'She's on the rack, stripped, chained, and ready for an anal fucking.'

'In that case, I suggest that we . . . '

'Fucking bollocks, there's the phone again.'

Walking to the bench, Snide grabbed the receiver, massaging his solid cock as he wondered who was interrupting the proceedings this time. *It might be an idea to have the phone disconnected,* he reflected as heavy male breathing emanated from the receiver. Mr Brass from ARSE, Mother Horgasm, Inspector Peel . . . Now there was a perverted sexual phone pest making orgasmic sounds down the phone!

'Who the fuck is this?' he finally asked. 'What the fuck do you think you're doing?'

'Sexton, is that you?'

'Of course it's fucking me. Who the fuck are you?'

'Sorry, it's your old friend . . . '

'Spaz, what the hell do you mean by breathing heavily and making orgasmic noises down my phone?'

'I was having a quick wank while I . . . '

'Why do you always wank when you're on the phone?'

'Because I usually call up dirty-girlie lines and listen to them fingering themselves while I bring myself off.'

'Good God, is there no end to your perversity?'

'I hope not!'

'What did your wife say about your spunked trousers?'

'I told her it was double whipping cream.'

'You should have got her to lap it up. Anyway, I'm busy right now.'

'Sorry, I dialled the wrong number. I wanted Saucy Sexy Suzie.'

'Saucy Sexy Suzie? Jesus F. Christ!'

'I'll call you later.'

'Much later, I hope. In fact, I hope you never call . . . '

'Sexton, shut up!'

'Sorry.'

'God, I'm coming! Bye!'

Banging the phone down, Snide cursed as it rang again. 'Fuck me, what the shitting hell is it?' he asked, grabbing the receiver again. 'Can't you have a wank without ringing me?'

'Have a *what*, Professor?' Peel asked surprisedly.

'Oh, Inspector – I'm sorry about that, I was fantasizing.'

'You have a strange telephone manner.'

'Yes, it was my upbringing – fucking perverted nuns. Er . . . How can I be of persistence . . . assistance?'

'I've just received news from someone on the inside.'

'What, a gynaecologist?'

'A gynae—? No, someone who works in the government. Apparently, the PM went off on a highly secret mission and hasn't been seen since. I just wondered whether, seeing as you have peculiar connections with the SAS and the government, you might know something about it?'

'I know nothing about Prime Ministers, other than the fact that they're all lying fascist bastards who love the idea of reducing the age of consent for vile homosexual sex, they want to ban cannabis, they want to ban duty-free booze and fags and put the ferries out of business, they want to put up taxes, they want cars off the road – and they talk a load of fucking bollocks.'

'Professor, you really must stop swearing over the telephone.'

'Who the fuck votes for those lying fuckers?'

'Well, I just thought I'd ask about the PM.'

'The fucking Trotskyist, Marxist, Leninist, Thatcherite bastard fucking cunting voters, that's who votes for them.'

'I'll call you later, when you've sorted out your political views.'

'Fucking welfarist pigs! Socialist fucking capitalist bastards!'

'Goodbye, Professor.'

'I blame the BBC.'

'The BBC? What on earth have they to do with . . . '

'Totalitarian, dictating, money-grabbing fucking bastards!'

'Goodbye, Professor.'

'Fucking communists!'

Slamming the phone down and turning to look at the man on the floor as the girlies raped him, Snide pondered on his true identity. *Shit, he must be the fucking PM!* he concluded, scratching his head and wondering what to do with him. But what a hostage! With the PM held prisoner in the castle dungeon, Westminster wouldn't dare make one move – they were bollock snookered. But there'd be trouble, he knew – big trouble!

'From your obvious confusion, I take it that you're not into politics, my friend?' the Baron asked, adjusting his tight panties.

'Fuck politics, what are we going to do about the Prime bloody Minister?'

'Nothing.'

'Nothing?'

'We'll keep him here, in the dungeon. No one will know where he is and, from the way he's been leading the country, I doubt that anyone will care.'

'Good thinking, Baron. In fact, bloody good thinking. OK, let's raid the nunnery.'

'Why raid the nunnery?'

'Well, we can fuck a few nuns, drink wine, blaspheme and . . . '

'You have a devious mind, my friend.'

'Thank you, Baron – coming from you, that means a lot to me. But, apart from blaspheming and the like, I want to see Sister Elizabeth. I never did get to fuck her.'

'Right! To the nunnery!'

Chapter Nine

Leaving for the nunnery, the Professor opened the castle doors to find himself facing a young couple. The attractive girl seemed distraught, her long blonde hair dishevelled, her face flushing as she nervously wrung her hands. The man appeared angry, frustrated, his expression pained as he gazed at Snide and the Baron.

'Can I help you?' the Professor asked.

'I believe . . . ' the man began hesitantly. 'Er, I believe you have ways of transforming prudish women into real women.'

'From where did you obtain this wholly incorrect and completely wrong information?'

'Ah,' the Baron murmured, shoving his hand up his miniskirt and adjusting his tight panties. 'That was my idea.'

'What idea?'

'I placed an advert in a magazine, my friend. I thought you might make some money from your machine so I . . . '

'I see,' the Professor grinned, eyeing the pretty girl's long shapely legs, the slight swell of her pink blouse concealing her small breasts. 'That's a bloody good idea: I'm glad I thought of it. So, you're here to be transformed into a real woman?' he asked, smiling at the girl.

'Yes, it's . . . it's what Jack wants,' she replied nervously, hanging her head in her embarrassment. 'He says it'll be worth spending five hundred pounds to . . . '

'Fuck what Jack . . . I mean, is it what *you* want?'

'Well, I don't know. I suppose I am rather shy and prudish and puritanical and strait-laced and moral in the extreme.'

'Fear not, my lovely, for you've come to the right place! You'll be unprudished, unpuritanicaled, unlaced and demoralized forthwith. Baron, grab the bastard's money . . . I mean, take the money from Jack while I escort our client to the lavatory . . . to the *laboratory* to defile her.'

'Can't I go with her?' Jack asked, handing over a wad of notes, his eyes frowning as he noticed the stubble on the Baron's chin, the false breasts sagging around his stomach.

'Go with her?' Snide echoed, grabbing the girl's hand and yanking her into the castle. 'Of course you can't go with her. If there's any defiling to be done, I'll do it. Clear off and . . . I mean, come back in an hour or two, preferably three. In fact, never come . . . '

'My friend,' the Baron interrupted Snide before he put his foot in it. 'Take the girl down and I'll see that Jack comes back later.'

Leading the girl to the dungeon, Snide pondered on his guest's curvaceous young body. About eighteen years old, tall and slim with an angelic air about her, she was worth an anal poking, that was for sure. Once she'd been transformed into a dirty, filthy, disgusting little tart, Jack would be over the moon – and he'd be all over her writhing naked body! But the Professor would have to take her for a test run before returning her to her young man: he'd have to ensure that she fucked rotten.

Not wanting an audience, Snide left the girl in the corridor and peered into the lab, instructing the girls to drag the struggling PM into the torture chamber and close the door. Waiting until the lab was clear of all signs of debauchery, he took the young girl's hand and led her down the stone steps to her fate – to her peril.

210

'Right,' he said, plonking her on the chair as the PM's groans resounded around the torture chamber. 'This won't take long. My name's Snide, by the way – Professor Sexton Snide.'

'Lydia,' she smiled, her hands clasped in her lap.

'OK, Lydia. Tell me, do you . . . '

'What's that noise?' she asked, looking at the torture-chamber door as the PM's groans of ecstasy grew louder.

'I've got the builders in. They're refurbishing the castle,' he lied, locking the oak door. 'Tell me, do you masturbate?'

'Oh!' she gasped, her wide eyes reflecting shock as she gazed in disbelief at the Professor.

'Let me put it another way: do you finger your cunny hole and massage your clitty to massive orgasms?'

'Finger my . . . Professor, I really don't think you should be asking such dreadful questions of an innocent girl such as I.'

'Dreadful questions? What's dreadful about them? All I want to know is, do you bring yourself off?'

'Bring myself off? Are you sure that you're . . . '

'Lydia, do you want to be a normal girl?'

'I *am* normal.'

'Jack doesn't seem to think so.'

'He's *ab*normal.'

'In what respect?'

'He wants me to . . . to do disgusting things.'

'Oh, you mean, he wants to fuck your mouth and spunk down your throat?'

'Professor! How do you know what he . . . '

'Because any normal man *would* want to fuck your mouth and spunk down your throat. OK, I'll just slip this helmet onto your head and, within minutes, you'll be stripping off and begging me to tongue-fuck your dripping cunt-hole.'

'I will not!'

'Of course you will.'

Flicking the switch as wails of female orgasm emanated from the torture chamber, Snide felt his cock stiffen as he gazed longingly at his client's shapely thighs. His heavy balls rolling and heaving, he wondered which vile and disgustingly perverted act to ask the girl to perform once she'd been transformed into a rampant, whorish nymphomaniac. Strip her and shave her cunt? Yes, that would do for starters!

'OK,' he smiled, flicking the switch and removing the helmet. 'How do you feel?'

'I'm not sure,' she replied, looking about the lab in her disorientation. 'I don't seem to feel any different.'

'I'll put you to the penis test,' he grinned, dragging his massive cock out of his trousers and fully retracting his foreskin. 'OK, suck me off.'

'Suck you . . . My God, I've never seen such a big penis!'

'Do you like it?'

Without answering, she leaned forward and grabbed the broad base of his solid veined shaft. Opening her pretty mouth, she sucked his huge glans inside and rolled her wet tongue around the succulent purple plum. Breathing heavily through her nose as she closed her eyes, she moved her head back and forth, repeatedly taking his silky-smooth glans to the back of her throat.

This was incredible! the Professor reflected, his penis twitching, his knob throbbing beneath her sweeping tongue. Within a couple of minutes, he'd transformed the prudish girl into a sex-starved, sex-crazed nympho! Five hundred pounds? Easy money! Perhaps he could do a deal with the PM, transform his wife into a filthy tart in return for calling the SAS off.

'Hang on,' he said, pulling away, his saliva-dripping knob leaving her cock-hungry mouth. 'Before I spunk down your throat, I want you to take all your clothes off.'

'Oh, I can't wait!' she giggled, standing and ripping her blouse open, the buttons flying in all directions.

'Fuck me, neither can I!'

Eagerly watching the girl toss her blouse to the floor and unhook her bra, the Professor's eyes widened as she peeled the white silk cups away from her firm breasts. Topped with chocolate-button nipples, her youthful mammary globes were small but delightfully formed. If her cunny was in proportion, it would be wonderfully tight! he reflected as she tugged her skirt down her long legs.

Kicking her shoes and skirt aside, she stood in her ballooning red panties, gazing at the Professor as she slowly pulled the flimsy garment down. She was obviously revelling in her striptease act, gently easing the material down just enough to expose her unfurling blonde pubic hair. A little further, and the top of her tightly closed sex crack came into view. His eyes transfixed on her alluring pinken slit, Snide waited in anticipation, his solid cock sticking out of his trousers, his knob swollen.

'Do you masturbate?' he asked her again as she slowly dragged her panties down her firm thighs, her rubicund inner cunt lips coming into view.

'No, I've never masturbated,' she grinned, her succulent sex lips unfurling.

'Lie on the couch over there and masturbate for me.'

'I'm . . . I'm not sure how to do it,' she replied, her panties falling down around her ankles.

'Come, I'll show you.'

Leading the girl across the lab as she kicked her panties off her feet, the Professor pondered on the idea of charging her for masturbation lessons. *Better not push my luck!* Reclining on the couch, her thighs spread wide, her pussy slit gaping, she ran her finger up and down her pink sex valley. *Instinct?*

Snide mused as she located her clitoris, running her finger round the erect protrusion.

'Ah, that's nice!' she breathed, massaging her sex button faster.

'Don't neglect your cunt,' he said, kneeling on the floor between her open legs. 'It's most important to finger yourself during masturbation. You must finger your wet, hot, tight, well-creamed, juicy . . . '

'I've never put my finger in my . . . in my vagina,' she murmured, slipping her hand beneath her left thigh, her fingers opening her dripping vaginal entrance.

'You'll love it, I assure you. I speak from experience, I'll have you know. I've spent a lifetime fingering girls' cunts. That's it, push your fingers deep into your hot cunt.'

'Oh, ah! God, that's heavenly!' she gasped, easing half her hand into her drenched vaginal cavern.

Tweaking her nipplettes as she massaged her solid clitoris and fingered her hot sex duct, his twitching cock pointing skywards, the Professor couldn't contain himself any longer. Pulling her hand out of her squelching pussy, he licked and sucked the girlie juice from her slender fingers. She tasted nice, extremely nice. In his rising debauchery, he decided to get her to taste her flowing honeydew.

Ramming three fingers into her tightening vaginal canal, he scooped out her warm cream. As he offered his hand to her gasping mouth, she sucked on his dripping fingers, delighting in the taste of her vaginal lubricant. Again, he scooped out her girlie liquid and slipped his fingers into her mouth, the aphrodisiacal taste driving the girl wild as she massaged her clitoris faster.

Pressing his massive knob between her gaping vaginal lips, he drove his shaft deep into her tight cunt, her smooth stomach rising as her pelvic cavity bloated. Whimpering as she continued her clitoral massaging, she looked down at her outer labia, forced wide apart by his massive penis.

'God!' she breathed as he withdrew his well-juiced cock and thrust into her young vaginal sheath again. 'God, I've . . . I've never known anything like it!'

'Jack's five hundred was well spent,' he grinned, pulling her fleshy outer lips up and apart, exposing her pulsating clitoris to her vibrating fingertips.

'I've never had an orgasm,' she confessed, her clitoris swelling, her cunt tightening around his veined shaft.

'You've never . . . Good God!'

Watching her masturbate as he fucked her, Snide wondered whether Lydia would become a regular visitor to the castle. Unfortunately, Jack was young and very good-looking: he'd be able to satisfy her insatiable thirst for rampant sex. There again, if the Professor were to suggest that Lydia should visit the castle once a week for libido boosters . . .

Grinning as a wicked idea came to mind, he thrust his penis in and out of her squelchy vaginal canal as she fervently massaged her swollen clitoris. This was the plan of all plans, he mused, scrutinizing her beautiful body, her small firm tits adorned by long erect nipples. A wonderfully tight cunt, perfectly formed outer love lips and delicious inner folds . . . This was the master plan.

If Jack wasn't able to satisfy the girl, if his libido inexplicably diminished, she'd *have* to return to the castle for crude sex. Simplicity itself! he reflected. Connect the alpha-wave machine up to the computer, plonk the helmet on Jack's head, and reduce his libido. The poor man would shun her sexual advances, rebuff her when she stood naked before him demanding that he tongue-fuck her wet girlie crack.

Lydia's wailing breaking the Professor's reverie, his heaving balls slapping her rounded buttocks, he repeatedly drove his twitching cock deep into her young cunt. Increasing his fucking motion, he gasped as his glans pulsated and his spunk finally coursed along his solid shaft and gushed from his orgasming knob.

'Coming!' he cried as she arched her back, her own climax griping her naked body, sending electrifying ripples of sex through her contracting womb. Again and again he pummelled her hot cervix with his pulsating knob, filling her vaginal cavern with his copious sperm as she massaged her throbbing clitoris and gasped in her first coming.

'I don't want it to stop!' she wailed, her lubricious sex juices issuing from her bloated cunt, mingling with the Professor's sperm and spraying her inner thighs. His drenched shaft emerging from her hot duct and driving into her quivering body as his climax rolled on, he pumped his fruits deep into her young lust tube to the accompaniment of her cries of sexual satisfaction 'I want to come forever!' she sang, her naked body rocking with the beautiful cervical battering.

Now *there* was a thought, Snide mused. Perpetual orgasm? Was it possible to achieve and endure a perpetual orgasm? Apart from the possibility that it might end in death, the notion was fascinating. A permanent erection would be interesting, he reflected. Satisfying girl after girl with an ever-erect cock was something to be worked on, but not now. There was Jack to deal with, the PM . . .

That's another thought, Snide mused, ramming his cock deep into the girl's cunt, the last of his spunk jetting from his throbbing knob, bathing her young cervix. Plonk the helmet on the PM's head and turn him into a communist. No, perhaps not!

'Don't stop! Keep fucking me!' Lydia demanded the gasping Professor as her orgasm peaked, her naked body shaking violently. 'Oh, your cock! Your beautiful cock! Ah, my cunt!'

'Jesus F. Christ!' he gasped, lifting her legs high into the air and thrusting his gigantic member into her spasming sex sheath. 'You're insatiable!'

Her legs over his shoulders, he continued his cervical pummelling, her outer labia swelling between her parted thighs, her inner lips dragging along his veined shaft, her stomach rising and falling with every beautiful thrust of his horse-like penis. His wet cock finally beginning to deflate, he slowed his rhythm, gently sliding his organ in and out of her inflamed cunt as she massaged the last pulses of orgasm from her sex nodule.

'Again!' she cried as he slipped his spent member out of her sperm-drenched vagina. 'Fuck me again!'

'You'll have to wait until I've recovered,' he said, lifting her legs off his shoulders and clambering to his feet.

'No, I want you *now*!'

'Lydia, you don't seem to understand that my cock . . . '

'I don't want to understand your cock! I just want it up my cunt, fucking me!'

A permanent erection was definitely a priority! Snide reflected as Lydia fervently massaged her clitoris, determined to bring out another shuddering orgasm. Zipping his trousers as the PM cried out in what sounded like a massive sexual climax, Snide hooked the alpha-wave machine up to the computer. Jack's demise was nigh! he reflected – the destruction of his libido was nigh!

Dashing up the stone steps as Lydia whimpered in her coming, Snide again pondered on his wicked plan. He'd tell Jack that the alpha-wave machine would bring him and Lydia sexual compatibility, attune their brainwaves for a perfect sex life. Jack would leave the castle with no interest in sex and . . . No, decreasing his sex drive would do the trick, there'd be no need to completely eradicate the man's libido and leave him totally asexual.

'Ah, Baron,' the Professor smiled as he wandered through the castle's doors and joined the man by the moat. 'I see you're standing by the moat.'

'You're most observant, my friend.'

'Thank you. I've transformed the girl into a raving nymphomaniac and taken her for a test run.'

'Excellent. I'm sure the advert will bring many clients, and plenty of money.'

'I'm sure it will. But there's something else the advert will bring.'

'What's that?'

'A never-ending stream of girlie visitors to the castle, all demanding to have their beautiful cunnies well screwed and spunked.'

'But their partners will . . . '

'I have a devious and highly illegal plan in mind.'

'What is this plan?'

'Their partners will find that their libido has mysteriously diminished, disappeared even – leaving the girlies frustrated in the extreme and desperate for my throbbing cock and jetting spunk.'

'What is this devilish plan, my friend?'

'A plan so evil, so demonic, so debased, so wickedly sinful, so . . . Ah, here comes Jack. I'll explain the highly illegal details later, Baron. In the meantime, I'll take Jack down to the lab and rip his bollocks off.'

'Has it worked?' Jack asked eagerly as he approached.

'Admirably!' Snide grinned. 'Follow me and you can fuck for yourself . . . see for yourself.'

Leading his gullible victim to the dungeon, the Professor wondered what the man's reaction would be when he discovered Lydia naked on the couch, fingering her fanny and vigorously masturbating her clitty to orgasm. He'd obviously be delighted and want to give her a good vaginal rogering there and then. Perhaps he should be allowed one last fuck before his sex drive waned.

'My God!' Jack cried, bounding down the steps into the lab and gazing in disbelief at Lydia as she thrust her fist in and out of her sperm-brimming fanny and massaged her swollen clitoris. 'What a transformation!'

'Indeed,' the Professor grinned. 'Sit on the chair and I'll attune your brainwaves with Lydia's.'

'I don't need your treatment. There's nothing wrong with *my* sexual urges.'

'I realize that, Jack. But, in order to find compatibility with Lydia, you'll have to be in tune with her bizarre sexual needs and desires. You must bear in mind that she's now into anything and everything, sexually speaking. I won't go into the sordid details: suffice it to say that my machine will tune you into her wavelength.'

Plonking the helmet on the man's head as he sat on the chair, Snide brought Jack's alpha-wave patterns up on the computer screen. Identifying the peaks representing the man's excessive libido, Snide grabbed the mouse and reduced Jack's sex drive. Grinning wickedly as Lydia relaxed after another incredible orgasm, Snide finally removed the helmet. Evil though it was, his plan was brilliant!

'Oh, Jack!' Lydia grinned, parting her drenched vaginal lips and exposing her sperm-dripping sex hole, her ripe clitoris. 'Come and fuck me like you've never fucked me before.'

'Not now, Lydia,' Jack replied, rising to his feet.

'Please, you must fuck me!'

'Later, maybe. Let's go home.'

'I know!' she beamed, leaping off the couch. 'We can fuck on the grass, beneath the evening sun!'

'I don't know, Lydia. I'm not really into that sort of thing.'

'But . . .'

'Er . . . Lydia,' Snide broke in, passing the girl her torn blouse. 'If ever you feel the need to return to the castle, please don't hesitate. In fact, it might be an idea to return now and then so I can monitor your progress.'

'Come on, let's go,' Jack whined, making his way up the steps.

Watching Lydia dress as Jack mooched off, Snide rubbed his hands together. He'd have plenty of money and dozens of girlies demanding crude sex. What more could a man want? But the government were marring his plans, cramping his style, and he didn't like that. They'd have to be dealt with once and for all.

'I'll see you again, I hope,' he grinned as Lydia finished dressing.

'You'll see me again, all right!' she beamed, holding her blouse together as she made her way up the steps.

'I hope all goes well with Jack.'

'So do I. It's strange, he's always been incredibly over-sexed, and now . . .'

'He'll be OK. I'll bet he drags you into the bedroom the minute you get home.'

'He'd better!'

Placing the helmet on his head as the girl left, Snide recorded his own alpha-wave patterns, concentrating his thinking on the way he'd like the country to be run. This was going to be fun, he mused, finally removing the helmet and switching the machine off. What the Prime Minister would do when he returned to Number Ten, he dreaded to think!

Right, now for the PM! Snide chuckled inwardly. Unlocking the torture chamber door, he gazed at the lewd scene. The PM's wrists cuffed to the steel rings in the wall, his pubic hair shaved off, his balls in Angelica's mouth, his purple knob licked and sucked by Rebecca and Gigi . . . This was hardly punishment! the Professor reflected as the man's spunk spurted, splattering the pretty girls' faces.

'That's adultery!' Snide chuckled. 'What your wife will say, I dread to think!'

'Please!' the man gasped, the last of his sperm shooting from his orgasming knob and running down Angelica's sex-flushed face. 'I have to return to Number Ten!'

'All right girls, when you've lapped up his spunk, bring him into the lab and tie him to the chair.'

Returning to the lab as the girls licked the spunk from the PM's hairless balls, Snide eyed the helmet, pondering on his next move. Kirsty had to be released, she'd been bound to the double-bum-fucking chair for long enough. At some stage, Penny would have to contact her father. Girls, girls, girls, he mused, deciding to hold a merciless whipping session as the PM was dragged into the lab.

'Professor!' the PM cried. 'You cannot keep me here and force me to endure perverted sex with these disgusting young women!'

'I don't intend to keep you here,' Snide returned as the girls tied the man's naked body to the chair.

'I've had naked girls sitting on my face, I've been forced to commit the highly illegal act of anal intercourse, I've had to put my tongue into their vaginas, I've . . . '

'Stop complaining. You can leave in a couple of minutes.'

'What are you doing?' the struggling man asked as the Professor placed the helmet on his head.

'Calming you down before you leave. Just relax, this won't take a minute.'

'I do not need calming down!'

'Of course you do, you're verging on clinical insanity!'

Flicking the switch, inducing his alpha-wave patterns into the Prime Minister's brain, Snide ordered the girls to release Miss Hocks. The woman had been on the rack for long enough, he reflected. Apart from that, it was high time she benefitted from the modified brain patterns, bringing her in line with the other sex-crazed girls. Her fanny shaved, it was also time for her to experience the delights of crude lesbian sex – and a damned good buttock-whipping.

'OK,' Snide said, removing the helmet and releasing the PM. 'You'd better get dressed and then return to Number Ten.'

'Yes, I . . . I will,' the man replied hesitantly, his head spinning.

'What plans do you have for income tax, Prime Minister?'

'Er . . . I'm going to abolish income tax. All Inland Revenue buildings will be destroyed and all their employees sacked.'

'What about duty on alcohol?'

'Abolished!'

'I'm pleased to hear it. Right, get dressed and bugger off.'

Prime Minister's question time would be interesting, Snide mused as the man dressed. No income tax, no duty on alcohol: with those and all the other suggestions and ideas he'd induced into the PM's brain, the country would be a great place to live. But more important was the Professor's future, the clients arriving to have their wives and girlfriends transformed into shameless tarts, the rampant sex sessions, the endless supply of fresh, juicy cunts and cash . . .

Leading the confused PM up the steps as the girls helped Miss Hocks stagger out of the rack chamber, the Professor decided to release Kirsty. The poor girl had been mouth-fucked, arse-fucked, fanny-fucked, cock-fucked, clitoris-fucked . . . All the girls would be rounded up and kept in the dungeon, stored in the torture chamber for sessions of rampant sex. Life was looking good, he mused, closing the doors behind the PM and walking into the banqueting hall.

'Ah, we think alike,' he said as the Baron released Kirsty.

'Indeed we do, my friend – juicy cunts, firm titties, tight bottom-holes . . . We think alike, all right. Like-minded perverts!'

'No, I mean, releasing Kirsty. It's just what I had in mind. Where's Penny?'

'She seems to have disappeared.'

'She's escaped!' Kirsty cried as the Baron dragged her aching body upright. 'She's gone to get help!'

'Of course she hasn't!' Snide returned. 'She's one of us.'

'She's gone to get her father,' the girl grinned. 'We had a long talk, and I convinced her that she should turn against you and . . . '

'She has your brainwave patterns, Baron,' Snide murmured pensively, turning to face the man. 'There's no way she'd drop us in it.'

'That's true, but . . . '

'But what?'

'I've had a theory for some time now.'

'Bloody hell! A theory?'

'I'll tell you about it later. In the meantime, I suggest we transform this little beauty into a dirty, filthy, disgustingly rampant little tart of a nymphomaniacal whore.'

'Into a what?' Kirsty echoed, massaging her inflamed vaginal lips.

'Into a sex machine!' Snide laughed uncontrollably. 'Do it, Baron! Take her down and do it!'

'Forthwith, my friend – forthwith!'

'And shave her cunt!'

'Will do!'

'No!'

'Yes!'

Chuckling as the Baron dragged the struggling girl across the hall, Snide clapped his hands. Things were looking up . . . Or were they? Shaking his head, he looked at the shattered windows and realized that all was far from well. With the money rolling in, he'd have no trouble having the windows repaired, but if the SAS attacked the castle again . . . Grabbing the ringing phone, he was surprised to hear Sister Elizabeth's voice.

'Professor, you have to help me,' she said softly.

'What's the matter?' he asked. 'How may I be of help during your time of dire need?'

'I've tied a nun to a bed. I've had my wicked way with her, but . . . I can't release her because she's going to tell the Reverend Mother what I've done.'

'A precarious predicament, if ever there was one – or two. I'll come over to the nunnery and give the aforementioned tethered nun a hand . . . Give you a hand.'

'There's a drainpipe by the window on the first floor at the side of the building. Climb over the wall in the lane, go through the wood and cross the grass, and you'll see me at the window. I'll look out for you.'

'I'll be there shortly, or sooner, even.'

'Oh, thank you. If the Reverend Mother . . . '

'Fear not the evil wrath of the Satanic woman, for I am your knight in shining armour.'

'Are you?'

'Well, not exactly. I shall repair to the nunnery forthwith!'

Wondering why it was taking Lucifer so long to nab the rocket launcher from the clump of trees at the foot of the hill, the Professor left the castle and made his way to the nunnery. The Reverend Mother Horgasm was another problem, he reflected, wondering what to do with the woman. 'Shame she hasn't got any bollocks!' he chuckled, bounding down the hill. 'I suppose Lucifer could karate chop her tits off!'

Finally reaching the nunnery, he climbed over the ten-foot flint wall and hid in the undergrowth. It was high time a few nuns were fucked to seal their faith in the Devil, he mused, wondering whether nuns wore knickers. *Do they masturbate?* he pondered, imagining the naked nuns sprawled across the alter with church candles up their tight cunnies.

'Satan, I offer thee my cunt!' he chuckled, noticing the Reverend Mother hovering by the entrance to the building as he neared the edge of the wood. 'I'd like to offer *her* cunt to the Devil,' he murmured pensively, waiting until the old hag had gone before dashing across the grass. *If she's got one!*

Reaching the huge Victorian building, he made his way round the side of the nunnery and crouched behind a clump of hydrangeas at the base of the drainpipe. 'So far so good,' he breathed, looking up at Sister Elizabeth leaning out of the window. Shinning up the drainpipe, hoping no one would spot him, he managed to climb through the window into the six-bedded dormitory.

'Good grief!' he gasped, eyeing a gagged, naked nun tied to a bed, her feet on the floor either side of the bed, her thighs wide, a massive candle emerging from her bloated pussy hole.

'I don't know what to do,' Elizabeth whispered. 'Ever since I visited your castle, I've been trying to get my hands inside the nuns' knickers.'

'I know the feeling!'

'I can't help myself. I have this overwhelming urge to suck their nipples.'

'I know the urge!'

'And I have this powerful desire to push my tongue up their hot vaginas.'

'I know the desire!'

'And I have a terrible craving to lick their bottom-holes.'

'I know the craving!'

'And I have a longing to spank their beautiful buttocks.'

'I know the longing!'

'And I have a constant yearning for orgasm.'

'I know the yearning!'

'And I have an unquenchable thirst for . . . '

'I know the unquenchable . . . Enough of feelings, urges, desires, cravings, longings, yearnings and thirsts. I have a plan.'

'A plan, Professor?'

'You know, a scheme, an idea, a . . . '

'Yes, I know what a plan is.'

'Then why ask?'

'No, no . . . What *is* your plan?'

'Ah, I see. Do I have one?'

'I don't know.'

'Of course I do, it's in my trousers.'

'The plan?'

'No, my cock. Right, enough of plans and cocks – we must sexually abuse the naked nun.'

'I've already done that.'

'*I* haven't!'

Settling between the nun's splayed legs, the Professor slipped the wet candle out of her inflamed cunt, watching as her swollen outer lips closed. Parting her fleshy folds, revealing the entrance to her young vagina, he examined the glistening pink flesh surrounding her open lust hole. Her sex valley creamy-wet, her clitoris swollen, he parted her love lips further and peered into her drenched sex duct. Licking his lips as he eyed the opaque liquid streaming from her inner nectaries, he gently massaged her swollen clitoris, grinning as her smooth stomach quivered.

His penis solid, aching for the wet heat of her young sex sheath, he leaned forward and licked her vaginal crack, lapping up her oozing juices of arousal as she squirmed and writhed. She tasted nice, he mused, his tongue entering her hot sex duct – creamy, juicy, sexy. Breathing in her female sex-scent, he drove his tongue further into her tight cunt, lapping up her copious juices.

226

'Professor!' Elizabeth whispered urgently. 'Professor, there's no time for this!'

'There's all the time in the world,' he replied through a mouthful of wet girlie flesh.

'There isn't!'

'Then let's *make* time.'

'The Reverend Mother's floating around. If she comes in here and . . .'

'If she comes in here, I'll rape her.'

'No!'

'Yes!'

Kneeling between the struggling nun's legs, Snide slipped his erect penis out of his trousers and pulled his foreskin back. Wide-eyed, the tethered nun lifted her head and looked in horror at his bulbous purple knob hovering threateningly above her defenceless sex hole. Ignoring Elizabeth's protests, he positioned his swollen glans between the nun's dripping inner lips, lubricating his torpedo with her cunny juices in readiness for vaginal penetration. Forcing his massive purple bulb into her sex opening, her inner lips spreading wide, he slowly moved forward, his shaft entering her tight duct.

'Ah, yes!' he gasped, driving his rod deep into her tight cunt. His swollen knob resting against the soft hardness of her wet cervix, her fleshy sex lips hugging his broad cock, he withdrew his glistening organ and thrust into her again. Her cunny juices flowing in torrents as he pistoned her vaginal cylinder, the squelching sounds of sex reverberating around the dormitory, he pummelled her hot cervix with his weapon head, taking her to her sexual heaven.

'Tight, hot, and beautifully wet!' he gasped, his heavy balls battering her tensed buttocks.

'Professor, someone's coming!' Elizabeth cried, holding her hand to her open mouth as footsteps neared.

'*I'll* be coming in a minute!' he chuckled, the old iron bed creaking as he thrust his penis in and out of the writhing nun's vaginal sheath.

Fucking the nun for all he was worth, his heavy balls swinging, his knob bloating her vaginal cavern as she arched her back in her obvious arousal, the Professor grunted with each forceful thrust of his solid cock. She was a good fuck, he mused, increasing his pace as her naked body trembled and her eyes rolled. Were all nuns a good fuck? he wondered. Living a life of celibacy, apart from rampant masturbation sessions with church candles, they were bound to be a good fuck.

His sperm finally coursing along his veined shaft and jetting from his pulsating knob, he propelled his massive organ deep into her spasming cunt with a vengeance. 'Ah, ah!' he gasped, his gushing sperm filling the nun's vaginal cavern, the squelching noises growing louder as the blend of spunk and girlie come spurted from her bloated pussy, spraying his swinging balls. As the nun tossed her head from side to side, moaning through her nose as she reached her enforced climax, the door flew open, banging the wall with a dull thud. Sister Elizabeth dived beneath a bed.

The Reverend Mother Horgasm stood with her hand to her open mouth, her eyes wide beneath her starched wimple as she stared in horror at the blatant debauchery. Momentarily stunned, unable to utter one word as the Professor drained his massive balls, she leaned against the wall to steady her sagging body.

'My God!' she finally gasped as the Professor withdrew his massive penis from the nun's brimming cunt, spunk dripping from his slit and trickling over her black pubic bush. 'Oh, my God!'

'Bloody hell fire!' Snide cried, leaping off the bed with his cunny-dripping cock sticking out of his trousers.

'Professor Snide, what *do* you think you're doing?'

'Er . . . I was just . . . '

'Release the poor child this instant!'

'It's not what you think,' he smiled sheepishly.

'What is it, then?'

'Well, we were just . . . '

'Just what?'

'Playing around, having some fun, a laugh.'

'Never have I witnessed such wicked and sinful debauchery!'

'It wasn't wicked, or sinful debauchery,' he grinned, his huge penis hanging from his flies, glistening in the light. 'It was . . . '

Dashing across the room, the Reverend Mother released the quivering nun and removed the gag from her pretty mouth. Helping the girl to her feet, she gazed in horror at the sperm and girlie juice issuing from her inflamed vaginal opening and streaming down her inner thighs. The orgasmic blend pooling on the floorboards, Mother Horgasm ordered the girl to cover her naked body.

'It was rape, wasn't it?' she asked as the girl grabbed her habit from the next bed.

'Don't be silly!' Snide laughed, winking at the girl. 'Of course it wasn't rape!'

'I'm asking Sister Mary!' the Reverend Mother hissed, her clenched fists embedded in her ample hips. 'Well, *was* it rape?'

'I . . . ' the girl stammered.

'Answer me, child!'

'Can't you see that you've sent her into shock?' Snide broke in. 'You've frightened her into a state of severe vaginal shock.'

'*Me?* It's pretty obvious that *you*'re the one who's shocked her.'

'No, I only fucked her . . . I mean . . . '

'My God, you despicable man!'

'Er . . . Well, I suppose I'd better get back. I have things to do and do to things.'

'You're not going anywhere, Professor. I intend to call the police and have you arrested for gross indecency, rape, and . . . Put your penis away!'

'Oh, sorry. It has a habit of slipping out.'

'A habit of slipping . . . How did you get in here?'

'Through the door, as you did. Right, I'll be off. I have the shopping to do, and I must go to the bank, pay the phone bill and . . .'

'Sister Mary, go and call the police.'

'She can't call the police, not when she's in severe shock,' Snide said, edging towards the door.

'Come back here!'

Fleeing the room, the Professor ran down the corridor and bounded down the huge oak staircase as the Reverend Mother chased after him, screaming and shrieking. Opening the main door, he sprinted across the grass to the woods, dashing through the undergrowth until he reached the wall. 'That was close!' he breathed, clambering over the wall and jumping onto the road. 'Fuck me, I could have been struck down!'

Making his way back to the castle, he pondered on the Reverend Mother. She'd call the police, he knew, but at least he'd saved Sister Elizabeth from the wrath of the old bat. He was pretty sure that the raped nun wouldn't drop Elizabeth in it. After her enforced fucking resulting in a massive orgasm, she'd probably go creeping to the castle in search of the Professor's magnificent cock for another damned good vaginal rogering.

Wondering how the PM was getting on as he ambled up the cobble path to the castle, he imagined the man being certified insane when he proposed abolishing income tax and duty on alcohol. It was all good fun, he mused, stopping to take in the view. The huge orange sun setting over the Forest of the Dead, there was no sign of the tanks, no SAS men milling around, but it was only a matter of time before DI Peel made an untimely appearance.

Sitting on the soft grass, he contemplated the situation, the alpha-wave machine, his harem. Placing an advert was a brilliant idea, but how many girls could the Professor fuck? Lydia would be a regular visitor to the castle, and what with his team of live-in sex-crazed nymphomaniacs . . . A permanent erection was the answer, he mused. Was it possible to modify to the gamma-ray box?

'Problems,' he sighed, finally rising to his feet and turning towards the castle.

'You think *you*'ve got problems?' a soft female voice murmured.

'Oh, Sister Mary!' he exclaimed, turning on his heels to face the behabited young nun. 'You made me jump.'

'Sorry. I thought I'd come and find you after the lecture I got from the Reverend Mother.'

'What did she say?'

'I couldn't tell her that you'd raped me because . . . Well, I didn't want to get you into trouble. After my deflowering, as she put it, I'm to be defrocked – thrown out of the nunnery.'

'Oh, I'm sorry to hear that. I feel terribly responsible, Mary.'

'And so you should. Mind you, I did rather enjoy . . . Well, you know.'

'So did I! Where will you go? What will you do?'

'I was wondering whether I could stay with you, just until I . . .'

'Of course you can.'

'There's a slight problem.'

'What's that?'

Facing a clump of bushes and waving her hand, Mary

turned and looked at the Professor, anxiety mirrored in her dark eyes as five nuns emerged from the foliage. This was another turn-up for the dirty books, Snide mused as they approached. Led by Sister Elizabeth, giggling and nudging each other, the fresh-faced nuns stood in a row before the Professor.

'Is there room for us?' Elizabeth asked.

'Fuck me! I mean, of course there is. Er . . . Why have you all left the nunnery? What are you doing here?'

'Well, after hearing about Mary's experience with you, we thought . . . we thought it might be nice if we were forcefully and crudely deflowered.'

'Come back!' the Reverend Mother cried, lifting her habit as she ran up the path. 'You'll all return to the nunnery this minute, or there'll be real trouble!'

'Christ, let's get out of here!' Snide gasped, dashing towards the castle with the nuns in tow.

Reaching the doors, he ushered the little beauties into the castle as the Reverend Mother came panting up the hill, shouting and screeching like a woman possessed. The old hag needed a damned good anal rogering: that might shut her up for a while. *On second thoughts!* Closing and locking the doors, he breathed a sigh of relief as he gazed at the young beauties.

'That was a close shave!' he grinned as the Baron emerged from the banqueting hall. 'Talking of close shaves . . . '

'Good grief!' the Baron cried, gazing at the flock of excited nuns. 'What have we here?'

'I'll explain later,' Snide said as the Reverend Mother hammered on the doors. 'Right, let's eat and then retire for the night. What with one thing and another, it's been quite a day.'

'Where will we sleep?' Mary asked, pulling her habit over her head, revealing her curvaceous naked body.

'In the east wing, the wing that faces west. Actually, it faces east-west but . . . To be accurate, it faces slightly more to the south than . . . What the fuck am I talking about? You'll all sleep with me in my living quarters.'

'Lucifer has set the rocket launcher up on the turret, my friend,' the Baron said, adjusting his bulging miniskirt as the other nuns removed their habits and stood naked before the men.

'Professor Snide!' DI Peel yelled, banging on the door.

'Fuck!'

'Professor, open the door this instant!'

'Double fuck!'

'I have a search warrant, Professor!'

'Treble fuck!'

'There are six of us,' Elizabeth smiled, cupping her firm breasts in her hands and tweaking her erect nipples.

'Sextuple fuck!'

Chapter Ten

'Another day, another fuck,' the Professor grinned, relaxing on his bed next to the Baron with two naked nuns gobbling his swollen knob.

'Indeed, my friend,' the Baron murmured, his bulbous glans sucked to the back of Sister Mary's throat as another two nuns licked and nibbled his rolling balls.

'This is better than being stuck in the nunnery,' Elizabeth smiled, her pink tongue eagerly lapping up the hot girl juice flowing from Mary's open sex hole.

'Excuse me, sir!' Lucifer called, knocking on the locked door.

'What it is?'

'DI Peel is here to see you.'

'Fuck it!'

'He's in the banqueting hall.'

'Double fuck it! OK, I'll be there in a minute.'

Talk about no peace for the wicked! Snide reflected, his knob slipping out of the nun's mouth as he leaped off the bed. Hurriedly dressing, he left his living quarters, swearing to kick Lucifer in the balls for inviting the Inspector in. Penny must have gone running to her father and told him about the dungeon and . . . The butler should have known better, he reflected as he raced to the banqueting hall. *I'll tear his ball bag clean off for this!*

'Ah, good morning,' Peel said, his expression reflecting suspicion as he eyed the Professor with disdain.

'Good morning, Inspector. What can one do for one?'

'Why are the windows smashed?'

'An alien attack. Bloody Martians.'

'I see. Why wouldn't you open the doors last night?'

'Open the doors? I'm sorry, I'm not with you.'

'When I was banging and shouting, why wouldn't you let me in?'

'Banging and shouting? I know nothing of the alleged incident.'

'I thought as much.'

'How much?'

'As much.'

'Have the aliens returned the missing daughters?'

'No, not yet.'

'Thank God for that! I mean . . . '

'I have a warrant to search the castle, Professor.'

'You've already searched the castle.'

'That was before.'

'Before what?'

'Before six nuns were seen entering the castle. I believe them to be in hiding.'

'Six nuns in hiding?'

'You raped a nun in the nunnery, and then six nuns were seen entering your castle.'

'There's obviously been a mistake, Inspector. I have never raped a nun in my life, and as for nuns in hiding . . . '

'The Reverend Mother Horgasm rang me and told me of the exodus of the nuns. When I arrived at the castle, the Reverend Mother informed me that the nuns had followed you into the castle. You ignored my demands to be allowed into the castle, as you did hers, and . . . '

'I did hear the Reverend Mother banging on the doors, but I couldn't let her in because she was in a state of manic depression.'

'Manic depression?'

'She was fine one minute, talking about the beautiful summer evening, and then she flipped. She went out of her mind, psychotic, and began ranting and raving about a hallucination she'd had in the nunnery.'

'A hallucination?'

'She saw a man raping a naked nun tied to the bed. When she approached the bed, the man and the nun disappeared into thin air. I suggested that she lay off the vodka for a while, and then she started going on about breaking into the off-licence.'

'I see.'

'There's another thing, Inspector. The Reverend Mother has abducted a young girl.'

'How do you know this?'

'She was mumbling to herself about a girl she has imprisoned in the nunnery. She was saying something about chaining the girl to the wall and sexually abusing her. I'm sure it was a figment of her deranged mind, but I thought it best to tell you.'

'If this is true, it's extremely serious, Professor.'

'I agree. She also said that Penny was . . .'

'Penny?'

'That's the girl's name.'

'Are you sure?'

'Positive. She said that Penny was naked and chained to the wall, and that the monks from the monastery were taking turns to bugger her.'

'My God!'

'I have also discovered a most disturbing fact.'

'Go on.'

'The nunnery is the HQ of the aliens.'

'*What?*'

'I have it from a very unreliable source that the Reverend Mother is a Martian.'

'Never!'

'You'd better believe it.'

'Who is this unreliable source?'

'He's with MI5, his code name is Brown Sauce.'

'Brown Sauce? Right, I'd better get on to the super about this. Before I go, I'd better take a quick look round.'

'What for?'

'As I have a warrant, I'd better check the castle over. I don't want the super thinking me incompetent.'

'Fuck. I mean . . . OK, have a quick look round, Inspector. Er . . . Why don't you start at the top and work your way down?'

'Yes, I'll start with the turret. I know the way.'

'Of course.'

This was becoming serious, Snide mused as Peel made his way to the turret. With six naked nuns in his living quarters and a flock of sex-crazed nymphomaniacs in the dungeon, this was becoming *more* than serious. Had Lucifer dug the lion pit, it would have been easy to dispose of the interfering sleuth. There was only one thing for it, he decided, dashing to his living quarters. If the nuns dressed in skirts and blouses, and the Baron donned his women's clothing, Snide could pretend that they were visitors to the castle.

Instructing the naked girls to go to Lucifer's wardrobe and find the necessary clothing, the Professor enlightened the Baron about Peel's unwelcome visit. Rubbing his chin as the man hurriedly donned his miniskirt and blouse, Snide wondered where Penny had got to. It would seem that she hadn't gone running to her father with tales of debauchery, so where was she? *Fuck Penny!*

'What the hell are we going to do with the girlies in the dungeon?' the Baron asked, hoisting his false tits up.

'I don't know. More to the point, what the hell are we going to do with the girlies in the dungeon?'

'A good question, my friend.'

'What is?'

'The one you just asked.'

'It's a good question, but we need a good answer.'

'Answers don't come easily, good or otherwise.'

'Otherwise what?'

'Otherwise we'll be in real trouble.'

'God, you're right there! I've got it! Let's think of an answer, and then dream up the question.'

'How do you mean?'

'For example, the answer is, cook a meal.'

'Cook a meal?'

'What was the question, Baron?'

'I have no idea.'

'I'll tell you. I'm hungry, what shall I do?'

'Cook a meal.'

'Exactly! Don't you see how easy it is having the answer and then thinking of the question?'

'Er . . . No, not really.'

'OK, the answer is – dress the girlies as men.'

'What?'

'That gives us the question, which was, what do we do with the girlies in the dungeon?'

'Dress them as men.'

'Exactly! God, is there no end to my brilliance? Here's another one. The answer is, murder the Inspector to death. OK, what was the question?'

'Er . . . What do we do with the Inspector?'

'That's right! This is what's called lateral thinking, we're actually literally thinking laterally. Or are we actually laterally thinking literally?'

'I'm afraid I'm lost, my friend.'

'OK, the answer is, you're standing in my living quarters. The question, obviously, was – where are you?'

'Where am I?'

'You said you were lost and, by using lateral thinking, I came up with the answer, which then allowed me to determine the question. You were lost and I found you. OK, the answer is . . . '

'Kill the Inspector?'

'No, we dress the girlies as men. Right, you go and find the nuns and dress them as men and I'll nip down to the dungeon with some of my clothes. Show the nuns around the castle. A guided tour, OK?'

'Right you are, my friend.'

Grabbing a pile of trousers and shirts as the Baron left, Snide made his way to the dungeon, praying for the Inspector not to appear before the scene was set. With the Baron showing a bunch of women around the castle and the Professor giving several men a guided tour, the Inspector would be stumped. This really was the plan of all plans, he reflected, bounding down the steps into the lab to discover a mass lesbionic orgy taking place.

'OK, girls!' he called. 'Enough licking, fingering and massaging – I want you to dress in these clothes and then follow me upstairs.'

'Trousers?' Rebecca frowned, licking pussy juice from her succulent lips.

'The castle is being searched by Inspector Peel. He's looking for a flock of missing nuns and . . . Don't worry about that now, just dress in these clothes.'

'I've never dressed as a man before!' Angelica beamed, slipping her fist out of Gigi's vaginal canal.

'I need sex!' Miss Hocks cried, massaging her inflamed pussy slit.

'What do we do with Kirsty?' Snide asked, noticing the girl chained to the rack.

'The Baron has transformed her,' Gigi said, clambering to

her feet with vaginal cream trickling down her inner thighs. 'She's one of us now.'

'Excellent! OK, all dress and then meet me in the banqueting hall.'

The stage set, the players almost ready, Snide wandered upstairs to the hall to await the Inspector's arrival. Although this was the plan of all plans, it was only a short-term solution, he knew. In the long term, the Inspector would be back with more allegations of raped nuns and missing daughters. The alien scam wouldn't fool Peel for long. Once he'd been to the nunnery and questioned the Reverend Mother, he'd discover that she was no more a Martian than Snide was an upright pillar of the community.

'Shit, now what?' the Professor groaned as the phone rang.

'Snide here,' he said, grabbing the receiver.

'Professor, it's Jack.'

'Oh, Jack. Er . . . How are things?'

'I haven't slept all night. Lydia's been wanking me, sucking me, rubbing her cunt all over me . . . '

'I'm so pleased to hear it. Your money was well spent, Jack, don't you agree?'

'Yes, but . . . '

'But what?'

'Well, I don't seem to have the urge any more. I've lost all interest in sex.'

'A perfectly normal reaction, Jack. What with Lydia's unquenchable thirst for filth, it's quite normal for you to . . . '

'She's left me. She says that she wants a real man.'

'She'll be back, don't worry.'

'I think she's on her way to see you.'

'Excellent! I mean . . . If she turns up here, I'll fuck her. Er, I'll send her home.'

'OK, thanks.'

'You're most unwelcome, Jack.'

Replacing the receiver, Snide rubbed his chin. The plan had worked admirably: no doubt Lydia would soon arrive demanding an anal fuck. But how many girls could the Professor service? Six nuns, Gigi, Rebecca, Kirsty, Angelica, Miss Hocks, Penny . . . Where *was* Penny? he wondered. She'd been more than happy with her penis look-alike clitty, so why run away?

Again pondering on a permanent erection, the Professor smiled as Peel wandered into the hall. The man was frowning and rubbing his chin, obviously deep in thought as he stared at the Professor. Turning as the Baron led a group of young men into the hall, Peel scratched his head.

'This is the banqueting hall,' the Baron said in a high-pitched voice, hoisting his tits up. 'Henry the something or other would have dined here before taking one of his wives to the east wing to fuck her . . . I mean, to sleep.'

'Professor,' Peel said, standing before Snide as the Baron rambled on. 'Professor, there's a rocket launcher atop the turret.'

'Yes, I'm well aware of that,' Snide replied.

'What's it doing there?'

'It's to combat alien attacks. The government gave it to me to help in the war against the Martians.'

'I see. What's all this, then?' he asked as the besuited girlies appeared, led by Gigi who looked every bit a man.

'Another guided tour. They're a group of businessmen from London.'

'There's something not quite right here, but I can't put my finger on it.'

'Not quite right, Inspector?'

'It's all too innocent. Guided tours, no sign of anything untoward, and you say that the Reverend Mother Horgasm is a Martian.'

'Yes, that's right. By the way, what happened to the

ruthless thief who escaped from the prison on the wild and windy moor?'

'Ruthless thief? Oh, er . . . Captured and returned to prison. I'll check your laboratory next, Professor.'

'Yes, of course.'

So far, so good, Snide pondered as the sleuth wandered off. But enough of police and guided tours and all that bollocks. The minute the Inspector left, Miss Hocks would have the modified alpha-wave patterns induced into her brain, completing the harem of sex-crazed nymphos. The nuns didn't need the alpha-wave machine: with their rampant sex drive, all they needed was constant fucking, licking, fingering, sucking, knobbing . . .

But Sister Elizabeth still had the Professor's brain patterns. She'd have to be transformed, turned into a bisexual sex-crazed whore at the earliest opportunity. Once Peel had gone, Elizabeth would be dealt with and all the girls would have their fannies shaved, their nipples clamped, their buttocks whipped and . . . Excluding Penny, there were eleven girls in the castle – more than enough for . . .

'And these broken windows are the result of an attack by the Druids,' the Baron enlightened the men as he led them around the hall, bringing the Professor back from his daydream.

'Baron, the Inspector's in the lab. You can cut the guided tour bit,' Snide said.

'But I'm enjoying myself.'

'And so am I,' Gigi smiled. 'There's nothing like a guided tour, especially dressed as a man.'

'I want sex!' Miss Hocks gasped, massaging her sex crack through her trousers.

'Later, Miss Hocks,' the Professor said, eyeing the woman's breasts billowing her shirt. 'We'll all have a rampant session of perverted sex when the Inspector's gone. I need some fresh air – carry on with the tour.'

Ambling through the castle doors, Snide breathed in the fresh morning air. It was another lovely day, a perfect day for wandering into the village and nabbing a horny, miniskirted teenage girl. There was still no sign of the tanks, he mused, adjusting his stiffening penis as he recalled Clarissa sitting on the wall with her thighs wide apart. No SAS, no tanks . . . There was only DI Peel to contend with.

Noticing a distant figure walking up the path towards the castle, he shielded the sun from his eyes, trying to make out who it was. It was a female, he mused, eyeing the girl's short skirt. Perhaps Penny had decided to return. No, it was Jack's sex-crazed bird, he observed as she approached. No doubt she wanted a damned good fanny-licking and cunt-fingering and mouth-spunking and anal fucking . . . She *would* have to arrive just when Peel was searching the castle!

'Good morning, Lydia,' the Professor grinned, eyeing her nipples clearly defined by her tight T-shirt.

'I've left Jack,' she announced, standing before Snide with a large bag slung over her shoulder.

'Yes, he rang me earlier with the sad news.'

'He has no interest in sex whatsoever. I just don't understand it, he's changed beyond belief.'

'He'll come off . . . come round. He's probably having it off today . . . having an off day.'

'Professor, I'm here because I desperately need sex.'

'Don't we all!'

'I want you to fuck me – hard.'

'How hard?'

'Very hard. Fuck me as you've never fucked before.'

'The castle's rather busy at the moment, full of nuns and police . . . '

'Come down to the forest, I want you to fuck me beneath the trees.'

'Well, put that way, I don't see that I have a choice.'

'No, you don't. Come on, let's go.'

Following the blonde nymph down the cobble path, Snide felt his penis fully stiffen as he eyed her shapely thighs, her firm buttocks billowing her tight skirt. She was in for the fuck of her young life, he decided, wondering how tight and hot her anal duct was. With the modified brain patterns, she'd no doubt enjoy a damned good buttock-whipping with a tree branch, and even a tit-thrashing.

Entering the forest, his heavy balls rolling, he followed the girl into a clearing, gazing at her curvaceous young body as she dropped her bag to the ground and tore her clothes off. Unhooking her bra, she peeled the silk cups away, revealing her firm breasts topped with huge elongated nipples. Bending forward and slipping her red panties down, exposing her inflamed sex crack, she stood up with her feet wide apart and grinned at the Professor.

'I'm rather sore,' she said, looking down at her sex slit, her hair veiling her pretty face like a curtain of gold silk. 'I've been masturbating for hours.'

'I know the feeling.'

'I want you to behave like an animal.'

'No problem!' he grinned, whipping his trousers and shirt off.

'No, I mean . . . I want you to pretend to be a dog.'

'A dog? I'd rather pretend to be a horse.'

'OK, that'll do. Get on all fours and I'll ride you.'

On his hands and knees, his huge balls swinging between his thighs, he grinned as Lydia sat on his back with her feet either side of his naked body. Her gaping cuntal crack pressed against his skin, he could feel her juices of lust oozing from her open sex hole and trickling over his back. Rocking her hips, she massaged her inner sex flesh against his spine, whimpering as her clitoris throbbed and swelled.

'I like riding horses,' she gasped, flinging her head back. 'Especially bareback.'

'Obviously!' the Professor chuckled as she reached behind her naked body and slapped his buttock.

'Come on, Blackie! Take me for a ride through the forest!'

Riding the Professor with a vengeance, rocking her hips and grinding her open cunt into his spine, Lydia wailed her appreciation as her clitoris pulsated and her sex milk flowed. 'Coming!' she cried, her fingernails digging into his back as her well-juiced cunt glided over his spine. 'God, I'm coming already!'

The Professor's cock solid, in dire need of a tight fanny, a wet mouth, a hot anal duct, he reached beneath his naked body and fully retracted his foreskin. Focusing on his purple plum, his swinging balls, he knew exactly where his veined shaft was going – right up her bottom-hole! But first he'd spunk her pretty mouth, and then her dripping cunt. *God, life's good!*

'I'm done!' Lydia cried, her quivering body lolling to one side. 'Oh, my cunt!' Falling to the ground, her thighs splayed, she lay on her back massaging the last ripples of sex from her swollen clitoris. 'God, I was so desperate to come. Your machine didn't just increase my libido, it sent it sky-high!'

The alpha-wave machine was quite an invention, Snide reflected, watching the girl slip three fingers into her inflamed pussy hole. *Imagine inducing the patterns into the Reverend Mother's brain! God, no!* Young girls, yes, but not old hags. There again, it might be fun to see the Reverend Mother in an acute state of sexual arousal.

Fuck Mother Orgasm! Crawling over Lydia's trembling body, the Professor was about to spear her open cunt with his solid organ when she moved down, positioning her head beneath his swinging penis. Her pretty mouth open, his knob brushed against her succulent lips as she poked her tongue out and tentatively licked his swollen glans. She was teasing him, he knew, as the tip of her tongue lightly touched his knob-slit. His shaft twitching, a tremor running through his fully-laden balls, he breathed deeply as her tongue tasted his salty plum.

'You're to be milked before you fuck me, Blackie!' she giggled, grabbing the base of his penis and sucking his swollen knob into her wet mouth.

'God, that's good!' he gasped. 'But I'm a horse, not a cow.'

'I'll milk you all the same,' she said huskily, running his glans over her pretty lips.

Wanking his erect shaft as she gobbled on his bulbous knob, she kneaded his heavy balls with her free hand, breathing deeply though her nose as she savoured his salty plum. Where she'd got the horse idea from, the Professor didn't know. Surely, she hadn't been down on the farm and . . . No, of course she hadn't! There again . . .

'What a beautiful cock you have, Blackie,' she breathed, slipping his silky-smooth glans out of her wet mouth and licking his rock-hard shaft.

'All the better to fuck you with,' he smiled.

'And what big balls you have.'

'All the better to spunk you with.'

'Wait a minute, you're a horse not a wolf.'

'Oh, my mistake. God, I'm going to come!'

'No, you mustn't!' she cried clambering out from beneath his body. 'My bum, you must fuck my bum!'

Grinning as she knelt down with her head on the ground, her alluring buttocks jutting out, he moved behind her naked body. His massive organ waving from side to side, his full balls swaying, he focused on her gaping vaginal lips, the opaque liquid streaming from her pink sex hole. As he was about to drive his solid knob deep into her cunt to lubricate his weapon for anal penetration, he noticed a gnarled stick lying on the ground. A buttock-thrashing was in order, he decided, grabbing the stick.

'Argh!' she cried as the stick struck her pale buttocks with a loud crack.

'Like it?' he asked, whacking her tensed orbs again.

'Oh, yes! Thrash me! Thrash me as you would a naughty schoolgirl!'

This was more like it, he chuckled inwardly, lashing her pert buttocks again and again. Imagining her to be a schoolgirlie as he thrashed her naked bottom, he pictured a pair of navy-blue knickers pulled down to her thighs. *Christ, I could be arrested for what I'm thinking!* A gymslip, white ankle socks, navy-blue knickers well creamed and stained with fresh girlie juice . . . *Stop it, stop it!*

The nuns would receive a damned good buttock-whipping, he decided, and the dungeon girlies. There'd be a mass whipping session terminating in multiple orgasms and lashings of anal spunking. There'd be cunny spunking, mouth spunking, cleavage spunking, nipple spunking, bottom spunking . . .

'Please!' Lydia cried, her buttocks burning a fire-red as the stick repeatedly struck her twitching anal globes. 'Please, fuck my bum!' Discarding the stick, Snide walked towards her on his knees, positioning his bulbous glans between her gaping love lips. Running his knob up and down her open sex valley, lubricating his torpedo in readiness for vaginal penetration, he suddenly drove into her tight cunt.

'God, yes!' she sang as his shaft impaled her drenched vaginal sheath.

'After a few hard cunny thrusts, I'll force my horse cock up your beautiful arsehole!' he chuckled in his debauchery.

'Now, I want you up my bum now!'

'Christ, you can't wait, can you?'

'*Now*, fuck my bum *now*!'

'All right, all right!'

Withdrawing his dripping penis, Snide splayed Lydia's burning buttocks, revealing her small brown hole, the portal to her inner core. Grabbing his solid shaft and pressing his swollen glans against her rectal iris, he moved forward, his cunny-juiced knob forcing her anal rosebud open. Gasping as his purple bulb entered her inlet and sank into her tight lust duct, she projected her buttocks further. Delighting in the crudity of the lewd act, she reached between her parted thighs and grabbed his heavy balls as his shaft slowly sank deeper into her rectum.

'God, you're so big!' she breathed as her brown portal opened to capacity, stretching tautly around his veined rod.

'And you're so tight!'

'More, more! Oh, ah! Give me more!'

His penis gliding into her anal sheath as she kneaded his heaving balls, he grabbed her hips and pushed half his length into her quivering body. Again, she demanded more, insisting that she could take his entire cock into her bottom. Pulling on her hips, his shaft sinking deeper into her anal core, to his amazement, he completely impaled her on his granite-hard organ. Her delicate anal ring gripping the base of his shaft, he slowly withdrew and rammed into her again.

'Oh, God!' Lydia breathed as Snide's knob massaged the dank inner flesh of her bowels. 'God, it's heavenly!'

'You have the most beautiful arse I've ever fucked!'

'And you've got the biggest cock I've ever had up my arse. In fact, the *only* cock!'

Ramming his penis in and out of the girl's spasming anal duct, the Professor could hold back no longer. His glans swelling and pulsating against her velveteen inner flesh, his sperm gushing from his knob-slit, pumping deep into her bowels, his pubic bone smacking her quivering buttocks, he shuddered in his incredible coming. Lydia was the finest anal fuck ever, he reflected, thrusting his giant cock into her bottom-hole with such force that her cries of sexual ecstasy resounded throughout the forest like those of a howling coyote. She'd be a regular visitor to the castle, there was no doubt about it!

Watching his sperm-glistening penis repeatedly withdraw and drive into her tightening anal duct, he focused on her stretched brown ring. The delicate tissue clinging to his shaft as his cock glided out of her rectal tube, as if trying to suck his organ back into her quivering body, he dug his fingernails into her buttocks and drove his knob deep into her bum again. Painfully yanking her weal-lined globes apart, opening her bottom crease, he continued to pump his sperm into her brimming bowels until she collapsed to the ground, exhausted in her coming.

'Please, no more!' she cried as he lay on top of her with his cock embedded deep within her inflamed lust sheath. 'Please, I must rest!'

'God, so must I!' he panted, his huge balls wedged between her rounded bum cheeks as she writhed beneath him.

'Oh, Professor! Never have I known anything like it!'

'It's a shame poor old Jack's out of the picture.'

'Thinking back, he was never really *in* the picture. And now that his sex drive is zero, he doesn't stand a chance of being in a sketch, let alone an oil painting.'

'I must say it's rather odd that he went off you like that. I'd have thought he'd have been all over you. An extremely attractive, beautiful, sexy girl like you, I'd have thought . . . '

'Oh, thank you. You certainly know how to flatter a girl.'

'I also know how to fuck a girl!'

'Professor, may I ask you something?'

'Oh, sorry, you want me to get off you.'

'No, no. Do you have anyone special in your life?'

'Special? There are about a dozen . . . Er . . . No, not really. Why?'

'I just wondered. Can you manage it again?'

'Manage what again?'

'To fuck my bum.'

'Yes, of course!'

'You're so manly, strong, amazingly well-hung, virile, potent, powerful, sexually energetic . . . '

'Compliments will get you everywhere! OK, on your knees again with your bum sticking out, and I'll give your bowels a second spunking.'

Taking her position as the Professor took his weight off her naked body, she reached between her thighs and grabbed the base of his shaft, holding his penis in place as she jutted her buttocks out. Withdrawing his cock, he propelled his swollen knob deep into her rectum, beginning the second anal fucking of the session. Again and again he drove his solid cock deep into her tightening arsehole, delighting in the sensations of crude sex as she writhed and whimpered in her lewd ecstasy.

His second coming approaching, his knob pulsating, the Professor tried to hold back to prolong the girl's pleasure. 'Ah!' he gasped as he lost control, his spunk jetting from his orgasming knob, bathing the illicit coupling of penis and arsehole. Grabbing her shapely hips, fucking her arse like a man possessed, his second load of sperm filling her bowels, he again pondered on a permanent erection. *Sheer bliss!*

Imagining taking one girl after another with his ever-erect penis, fucking a row of beautiful bottom-holes, he focused on the girl's brown anal tissue clinging to his glistening cockshaft. There had to be a way to modify the gamma-ray machine, he mused as his spunk pumped from his knob. The machine had permanently increased the size of his penis, so why not . . .

'What's going on here?' a deep male voice bellowed.

'Oh! Er . . . ' Snide gasped, looking up to see a burly man in a checked shirt wielding an axe. 'Who are you?'

'The woodcutter. Who are you?'

'Er . . . This is Little Red Riding Hood and I'm . . . '

'Little Red Riding Hood?'

'Yes, she was on her way to see Granny Smith when . . . '

'Are you the wolf?'

'He's a horse,' Lydia said, lifting her head and gazing at the man through a curtain of long golden hair.

'A horse fucking Little Red Riding Hood's arse? You're mixing up Black Beauty and . . . '

'Wait a minute, what business is it of yours?' Snide asked, slipping his flaccid penis out of the girl's sperm-brimming arsehole. 'You can't interrupt people when they're having it off. It's unethical, impolite, discourteous . . . '

'You're breaking the forest rules.'

'Fucking bollocks!'

'The Forestry Commission rules clearly state that there'll be no fucking in the forest.'

'That's a load of bollocks!'

'Section ten, rule fifteen – sexual intercourse is not permitted within the forest.'

'What about the birds and the bees? And the deer and foxes and hedgehogs and badgers and . . . '

'The rule applies only to human beings.'

'I told you,' Lydia broke in as she sprawled out on the soft grass with her thighs wide apart, her pinken sex slit gaping. 'He's a horse.'

'If he's a horse, then I'm a donkey.'

'In that case, you'd better fuck me.'

'Why?'

'Because I love being fucked by donkeys.'

'That's against the law. And besides . . . '

'Wait a minute,' Snide interrupted the man. 'What have you got against fucking? I always thought that burly lumber-jacks were real men, red-blooded males into fucking and just about anything and everything sexual.'

'That's a myth. Us lumberjacks aren't burly, red-blooded heterosexuals.'

'You're not? What the hell are you, then?'

'Cross-dressers, for starters.'

'Fuck me!'

'Is that a request?'

'Certainly not! Bugger me, you come here and . . . '

'Is *that* a request?'

'There's something very wrong with you.'

'There's nothing wrong with me. I suggest you leave the forest before I exert my authority and arrest you for commit-ting the act of sexual intercourse within the forest.'

'All right, all right! Come on, Lydia, let's get out of here.'

'Why don't you hit him?' she asked as she sat up.

'Because he's bigger than me. Well, in some respects.'

Fuming as he dressed, the Professor decided to have Lucifer karate chop the man's bollocks off at the earliest opportunity, if not sooner. *Fucking bastard!* he cursed inwardly, watching Lydia tug her skirt up her long legs. A damned good session of perverted sex beneath the trees ruined by a cross-dresser was *not* conducive to the fulfilment of the Professor's rampant sexual desires.

'Right, let's go,' he sighed as the lumberjack disappeared into the trees.

'Who does he think he is?' Lydia asked, grabbing her bag and shaking her long blonde hair loose.

'I don't know who *he* thinks he is, but *I* think he's a wanker.'

'You haven't spermed up my cunt yet,' she complained.

'Later, my horny little tart – later.'

'I need to come again.'

'You'll have to wait. What are your plans?'

'I'll go and see Jack, give him one more chance to fuck me.'

'And if he won't?'

'I'll come back and see you.'

'Excellent!'

Leaving the clearing, the Professor led the girl through the trees to the path. She was right, he reflected as they emerged from the forest into the bright sunlight, he'd not spermed up her cunt. He'd let her down, left her unspunked, unmouth-fucked, uncleavage-fucked – and desperate for another orgasm. This was no way for the infamous Professor Sexton Snide to behave. If word got out that he'd left a sexy young tart begging for a fanny-fucking, desperate to come, he'd be a laughing stock among perverts worldwide. The woodcutter had to die a gruesome death, that was for sure!

'Right, this is where we part company,' Snide said, eyeing the girl's dishevelled long hair.

'I suppose so,' she sighed, massaging her pussy crack through her skirt. 'Bloody woodcutter, I didn't even have the chance to use this,' she said, taking a huge cucumber from her bag.

'Jesus F. Christ!' he gasped. 'What else have you got in your bag?'

'This,' she smiled, pulling out the biggest vibrator he'd ever seen. 'And this, and this.'

'A rubber hose and . . . Clothes pegs?'

'For my nipples.'

'*Bloody* woodcutter! Come to the castle whenever you like, Lydia. And bring your goodies bag with you.'

'I will. Professor, I'd like to . . . Never mind.'

'You'd like to what?'

'Nothing. I'd better be going.'

'OK, keep in touch.'

'I will. Bye.'

Ambling up to the castle, the Professor wondered whether DI Peel had completed the search and left. It was about time the interfering sleuth was dealt with once and for all, he mused as he reached the doors. Missing nuns, missing daughters, missing village girls . . . It was time the Inspector went missing – permanently! And the bloody woodcutter!

'Ah, Lucifer!' he beamed as the butler opened the doors. 'How are things?'

'Not at all good, sir.'

'Not at all good?'

'The Inspector . . . He has six habits.'

'Sex habits? The filthy pervert!'

'Habits, as in nuns' habits. They were on the floor, by the wall over there.'

'Shit! Where are the habits now?'

'The Inspector took them away as evidence, sir.'

'Fuck me! I blame you for this, Lucifer!'

'*Me*, sir?'

'You should have noticed the habits this morning, if not last night. The nuns ripped them off when they arrived, and they've been there all bloody night.'

'Where, sir?'

'Where the Inspector found them.'

'He hasn't found the nuns.'

'The habits, you fool!'

'Oh, I see. He won't necessarily put two and two together, sir.'

'Of course he won't, he'll put six and six together – six habits and six missing nuns. I'll have to think of something. In the meantime, go down to the forest and find the woodcutter.'

'The woodcutter, sir?'

'A big burly bloke with an axe. Find him and chop his bollocks off.'

'Yes sir.'

'And bring his bollocks back here as proof of the de-bollocking. That's what the wicked witch had the woodcutter do to Snow White.'

'Is it?'

'Something like that.'

'I thought it was Sleeping Beauty and the . . . '

'Just do it, Lucifer! Wicked witches and sleeping beauties, indeed.'

'Yes, sir.'

Now there was going to be real trouble, the Professor reflected, watching Lucifer chopping the air with the edge of his hand as he left the castle. Six missing nuns, and six habits discovered in the castle . . . What more proof did Peel need? There again, he hadn't discovered the nuns. Habits were one thing but, until he found the nuns, the evidence was circumcisional.

Wondering where everyone had got to, the Professor made his way down to the lab, mumbling about woodcutters, wicked witches and sleeping beauties. 'Snow White had seven cocks to stuff up her cunt, and I've got a dozen cunts to stuff my cock up,' he murmured, entering the deserted laboratory. 'Mirror, mirror on the wall, who's got the biggest cock of all? I fucking well have!' he chuckled.

Looking around the lab, he wandered into the rack chamber and then looked in the torture chamber. 'Where the fuck is everyone?' he breathed, bounding up the stone steps. Naked girls were like policemen, he reflected – whenever you wanted one, there was never one around. Walking through the banqueting hall, he searched his living quarters. 'Baron, where are you?' he called, returning to the hall and scratching his head.

'Now what?' he sighed, grabbing the ringing phone. 'Snide speaking.'

'Professor, ve have vays of making you talk,' a woman with a heavy German accent said.

'Ways of making me talk? Who the fuck is this?'

'Ve vant your machine, Professor.'

'My machine?'

'Ve vant your machine to create ze perfect male, ze perfect German male.'

'Bollocks, you can't have it.'

'Ve can, and ve vill have ze machine. I vill make a deal.'

'Fuck off!'

'Ze return of ze girlies in exchange for ze machine.'

'You've got my girlies?'

'Ve have ze girlies and ze Purple Baroness.'

'Baroness?'

'Ze old lady vith ze stubbly chin.'

'Bollocks!'

'Nein bollocks!'

'I have two, actually.'

'Silence! You vill bring ze machine to ze forest at midnight, or ze girlies and ze Purple Baroness vill die!'

'Listen to me, you Kraut-faced bitch! You are not having my machine!'

'Professor, Professor – you do not seem to understand. Your girlies vill die ze horrible death unless you give me ze machine.'

'Who the hell are you?'

'My name is Fräulein Gretel Ballhousen, I am ze Commandant of ze Vomen's Sexual Front. Ve need males, ze perfect males vith ze big dicks.'

'The Commandant of the . . . I don't care if you're the common cunt of the women's fucking clitorises, you are *not* having my machine.'

'Your girlies vill die unless you bring ze machine to ze forest at midnight!'

257

Hanging up, the Professor rubbed his chin, wondering how the bitch had managed to nab not only the girlies but the Baron. Assuming she'd not arrived unaccompanied, he pondered on the mass kidnapping. A German gang after his machine? The notion was feasible, but it was more likely to have something to do with Inspector Peel or the government.

'Where was Lucifer at the time?' he murmured, wondering what to do. 'And where the hell's Penny?' About to return to the forest to find the Krauts, he noticed a piece of paper pinned to the wall with a knife. ' "You vill bring ze machine to ze forest at midnight, or ze girlies vill die!" Fuck me, she means it!'

Chapter Eleven

With midnight approaching, the Professor paced the laboratory floor. No phone calls, no visitors, no word from Fräulein Gretel Ballhousen . . . Wondering how the German cow had heard about his machine, he pondered on the magazine advert. Perhaps she'd seen the ad and . . . 'Jack?' he breathed. If Jack was working with the Kraut, then so was Lydia.

'Sorry I've been so long, sir,' Lucifer said as he wandered down the steps.

'Lucifer! Christ, it's good to see you!'

'Oh, thank you.'

'Everyone's gone, the girlies, the Baron . . . '

'Yes, they were taken by a gang of foreign women earlier today.'

'What?'

'I was returning to the castle from the chemist when I saw the Baron and the girls being marched away at gunpoint.'

'Why the fuck didn't you tell me?'

'You didn't ask, sir.'

'I didn't ask? Fuck me!'

'I'd rather not, sir.'

'I don't mean literally! Bloody hell, Lucifer, you can be really thick at times. Our entire stock of fresh, juicy girlies stolen, and the Baron, and you didn't bother to tell me?'

'I'm terribly sorry, sir.'

'And so you should be, it's incompetence in the extreme.

Remind me to rip your cock off and stuff it up your arse later.'

'I'll make a note of it.'

'I wonder why they didn't take the alpha-wave machine?'

'Perhaps they were disturbed, sir.'

'You'll be disturbed in a minute! Did you get the wood-cutter's bollocks?'

'No, I couldn't find him.'

'Where the hell have you been, then?'

'I came across a small cottage in the forest, sir. It was a lovely little place with a thatched roof and climbing roses wending their way around the small oak door and neat rows of geraniums and pansies lining the path and . . . '

'Fuck the flowers! Did you go inside?'

'Yes, I did. There was a table with bowls of porridge and . . . '

'Have you been on the vodka again?'

'No, sir.'

'I don't believe you. What happened next?'

'I went upstairs and there was this horny girl with long golden locks on a small bed and . . . I was about to fuck her when . . . '

'Don't tell me, the three bears came back.'

'No, sir, not three bears.'

'Who, then?'

'A German woman with a machine-gun. I had to climb out of the window and shin down the drainpipe.'

'A German woman?'

'Gretel.'

'Gretel? Christ, why didn't you put two and two together?'

'How do you mean, sir?'

'The cottage is obviously their hideout.'

'Whose hideout?'

'The women who nabbed the girlies and the Baron.'

'There were no girlies there, sir.'

'I've had enough of woodcutters and witches and Goldi-locks and . . . '

'And bowls of porridge, sir?'

'Bowls of . . . Shut up, I'm thinking!'

'Yes, sir.'

The girlies and the Baron were obviously being held close to the cottage, Snide mused as he paced the floor again. Fräulein Gretel Ballhousen and her band of hopefully loose women were obviously waiting at the edge of the forest by the path to take delivery of the machine. If the Professor entered the forest from another direction and located the cottage . . . *Gretel?* he pondered. *Hansel and Gretel?* A cottage, a wood-cutter, bowls of porridge . . .

'We must go to the cottage,' he said, bounding up the steps. 'Do you remember where it is?'

'I think so, sir.'

'Don't you know?'

'Well, yes.'

'Good. Under cover of the night, we should be able to creep through the forest and, if we're lucky, find the Baron and the girlies. Grab a couple of machine-guns from the turret and meet me outside.'

'Outside the cottage?'

'Outside the bloody castle!'

'Yes, sir.'

Hansel and Gretel were German, he pondered, leaving the castle. Fairy tales? What was the connection between the woodcutter and Gretel? *Curiouser and curiouser*, he mused, looking up at the silvery moon as Lucifer emerged from the castle wielding two machine-guns. *All I need now is a Che-shire-bloody-cat grinning at me!*

'OK, let's go,' Snide said, grabbing a gun and closing the doors.

'Ready when you are, sir.'

'Are you?'

'Yes, sir.'

'It's always down to me, isn't it?'

'I'm not with you.'

'Everyone depends on me. You're ready when I am. Why can't you be ready before me?'

'I *am* ready.'

'You said you were ready when I was. Never mind, let's go.'

Walking down the grassy hill, well away from the cobble path, they finally entered the foreboding Forest of the Dead. 'I believe it's this way, sir,' Lucifer said, the moon giving just enough light as they trekked through the trees. Following his butler, Snide kept his ears open for noises – twigs cracking underfoot, the whimpers of enforced female orgasm and the delicious squelching sounds of rampant sex. Wherever the girlies were being held, they'd undoubtedly be tied up, and there'd be an armed guard. But a bunch of German women with hairy armpits weren't going to get in Snide's way.

'There, sir,' Lucifer whispered, placing his hand on the Professor's shoulder and pointing to a clearing. 'You see, the cottage.'

'Yes, I see the cottage,' Snide murmured. 'The front door's open, but where are the girlies?'

'Look, sir, there's movement! Over there, to the left of the cottage.'

'Christ, it's the Baron and the juicy girlies.'

'And there are a couple of women guarding them.'

'OK, this is the plan.'

'What is, sir?'

'Don't interrupt. What we'll do is cause a diversion. If you shoot me, they'll come running over and . . .'

'But you'll be dead, sir.'

'Shit, I hadn't thought of that. I mean . . . I was only joking, you fool. Shoot me, indeed. Good grief, do you really think . . . Let's stop talking bollocks. Creep round to the other side of the cottage and throw a few stones into the bushes over there. They'll go and take a look, and then I'll sneak into the cottage.'

'What for, sir?'

'I want to fuck Goldilocks.'

'What, now?'

'Why not?'

'If you say so, sir.'

'I do say so. OK, off you go.'

What with DI Peel, the government, and now the German women, things weren't looking at all good, the Professor reflected as Lucifer crawled through the undergrowth. Although, once the girlies and the Baron had been released, he'd make concrete plans to deal with the protagonists once and for all. First things first, he mused, his cock stiffening as he imagined fucking Goldilocks to orgasm.

Sneaking into the cottage as the women went to investigate the rustling in the bushes, he cautiously made his way up the narrow staircase to the bedroom. Eyeing a young blonde, her naked body tied to the smallest of three beds, her eyes closed, he placed his gun on the dressing table. Young and extremely attractive, the girl appeared to be sleeping. Who'd be the better fuck? he wondered. Sleeping Beauty or Goldilocks?

Her thighs wide, her feet hanging down either side of the bed, her cuntal crack gaping, her small rounded breasts topped with elongated milk buds, Goldlocks was a delectable little beauty. Any naked girl tied to a bed like that deserved a good fucking, there was no question about it. Tied to a bed or not, she deserved a good fucking!

Moving closer to the bed as he unzipped his trousers and hauled his python-like penis out, he focused on her pinken sex folds. Protruding from her gaping vaginal slit, her inner love lips glistened alluringly in the light. Opaque liquid trickling over her rubicund sex flesh, running down between her parted buttocks, she was obviously ripe for a damned good fucking.

This was a stroke of luck, he mused, climbing onto the bed with his bulbous knob hovering over the downy blonde pubes covering her sex mound. Pulling his foreskin back as she stirred and let out a sigh, he glanced around the room. No one around, and Goldilocks ready for a damned good fucking? This was either luck, or a trap!

'Oh, what are you doing?' she gasped, her pretty mouth hanging open, her sky-blue eyes wide.

'Sorry about this,' he smiled, parting her fleshy vaginal folds. 'It's just that I can't help myself when I come across pretty young blondes tied to beds with their legs wide open and their cunts inviting my fucking great cock.'

'You can't do this!'

'Of course I can.'

'My boyfriend will be back any minute!'

'Your boyfriend?'

'Yes, he's gone out for some fresh air.'

'Don't talk bollocks! What's your name?'

'Goldie.'

'Ah, the infamous Miss Goldilocks!'

'No, Goldie Smith.'

'Goldie whatever you are, you're going to be severely fucked.'

Positioning his bulbous knob between the struggling girl's pinken inner folds, the Professor drove his shaft deep into her tightening vaginal sheath, impaling her curvaceous young body on his massive flesh rod. She was so wet, her pussy juices squelching and spurting from her bloated cunt as he thrust his cock deep into her hot duct, that he wondered whether she'd recently been fucked. If so, by whom? he pondered, lowering his head and sucking her erect nipple into his mouth. *Daddy Bear?*

Mouthing her milk teat as he forced his horse-like cock in and out of her tightening pussy hole, he ignored her futile protests, battering her wet cervix with his gigantic knob. His weighty balls slapping her rounded buttocks as his glistening penile shaft repeatedly emerged and drove into her youthful cunt, he shuddered as he felt the beginning of his orgasm.

'God, I'm going to spunk up your cunt!' he gasped, her solid milk bud slipping out of his mouth. 'I'm . . . I'm coming already!'

'No, you mustn't spunk up me!' she cried, desperately trying to free herself.

'I have no choice!'

'No!'

'Yes!'

His sperm coursing along his twitching shaft and jetting from his orgasming knob, he rammed his cock into her tight vaginal cavern with a vengeance. Reaching her enforced climax, her pulsating clitoris massaged by his pistoning shaft, her body shaking violently, she tossed her head from side to side. Her long blonde hair veiling her sex-flushed face as she rode the crest of her orgasm, her stomach rising and falling with every cervix-pummelling thrust of the invading penis, she whimpered in her incredible coming.

'God, it's beautiful!' she cried, arching her back and raising her hips to meet his thrusts. 'Oh, I'm there! Oh, God!'

'Jesus F. Christ! There's nothing I like better than spunking up a young girl's . . . '

'Who's been fucking in *my* bed?' someone growled from the doorway.

'Bloody hell!' Snide gasped, his sperming cock slipping out of the girl's cunt as he leaped off the bed and turned to face the shadowy figure. 'Who the fuck are *you*?'

'Oh, Professor!' Penny breathed. 'I . . . I didn't realize it was you, my friend. What are you doing here?'

'Fucking Goldilocks!' he gasped, wanking his cock and shooting the rest of his sperm over the polished floorboards. 'Or I was.'

'Don't make a mess on the floor!'

'Oh, sorry. What are you doing here?'

'I'm on a mission.'

'So was I, the missionary position.'

'What's going on?' Goldie asked, raising her head and focusing on Penny.

'We can't talk here, not in front of her,' Penny whispered, taking the Professor's arm as he tugged his zip up. 'Come on, let's go.'

'What about me?' Goldie cried. 'You can't leave me half fucked!'

'The three bears will be back soon!' Snide laughed, grabbing his gun as Penny dragged him out of the room. 'Perhaps Daddy Bear will give you one up your bum!'

Creeping out of the cottage and slipping into the forest, Snide crouched behind a clump of bushes with Penny. Keeping his head low as the two German women sat on the grass rolling cigarettes, he turned to Penny, again wondering what she was doing skulking around the forest and sneaking into the cottage. Perhaps she was a spy? he mused, eyeing her naked inner thighs and recalling her penis-lookalike clitoris. *Perhaps she wants a fuck?*

'OK, what's all this about?' he whispered.

'It's a long story,' she smiled, sitting with her legs crossed, the light of the silvery moon shining on her bulging red panties that strained to cover her massive clitoris. 'What with talk of aliens, mobile hairdressers, and the police investigating you, I thought I'd do some investigating of my own.'

'Do you still have the Baron's brain . . . I mean, who are you?'

'The Purple Baron. Who do you think I am, Cinderella?'

'Er . . . no one. I mean, obviously you're someone.'

'Of course I'm someone. How could I be no one?'

'I don't know. I suppose if you weren't anyone you'd be . . . I really must stop talking bollocks.'

'I couldn't agree more.'

'Neither could I. So, what's all this about?'

'I knew about the tanks so I left the castle and searched the forest.'

'What did your search reveal?'

'I saw you with a girl, doing wonderfully dreadful things to her.'

'I couldn't help myself.'

'Obviously not!'

'Did you see the woodcutter?'

'I did, my friend. Why did you mention Little Red Riding Hood to him?'

'It seemed fitting.'

'He asked you whether you were the wolf, which I found odd.'

'Again, it's fitting. Woodcutters, wolves, Little Red Riding Hood . . . It all fits.'

'Maybe, but it got me thinking. I discovered that he's not a woodcutter: he's a spy.'

'I thought as much, or as little. How do you know he's a spy?'

'I followed him to the cottage, my friend. He was talking to a German woman about the big bad wolf. A few minutes after that, I saw your butler shinning down the drainpipe, mumbling something about Goldilocks. That's when I began to fit the jigsaw together. A woodcutter, Goldilocks, a big bad wolf, a woman calling herself Gretel . . . '

'Come to think of it, the SAS said that they'd huff and they'd puff and . . . '

'Exactly.'

'And when your father first came to see me he mentioned a big bad wolf.'

'I was wondering what all the fairy-tale stuff was about so I hid beneath one of the cottage windows and eventually learned the answer.'

'Which is?'

'The whole thing has been set up by the government. They're calling it *Operation Big Bad Wolf* – the wolf being you.'

'*Me?*'

'The police were after you, and the government agents, and the people from the so-called Ministry of Castles and Dungeons, and the SAS – not to mention the German woman.'

'I didn't mention her. What are they trying to do?'

'Initially, the police were investigating missing village girls and strange goings-on in your castle. When word got out about your machine, things began to hot up and government agents were sent in.'

'Who told them about the machine?'

'Miss Hocks, of course. The government want your machine, and they'll go to any lengths to get it.'

'Government agents, a band of Germans kidnapping my girlies, the SAS . . . Why not just go to the castle and take the machine? It would be easy enough, wouldn't it?'

'From what I overheard, there are *real* Germans after your machine. Gretel's no more German than I'm French.'

'Or I'm Dutch.'

'You're not Dutch.'

'I was just reinforcing your statement.'

'Oh, right. Anyway, the idea of Gretel and her gang is to confuse any real Germans who might turn up on the scene.

You see, your machine must remain secret from the world. If the world powers knew about it, they'd all be after it and . . . '

'Rather like James Bond in *Goldfinger* where he . . . '

'No, not really.'

'I still don't see why the government don't just take it.'

'Because you'd start shouting your mouth off. The idea was to capture you when they raided the castle, but you weren't around. It's one thing taking the machine, but they'd have to nab you as well.'

'Simultaneously. Or at the same time, even. Christ, the Krauts are shooting at the bushes! What the hell's going on?'

'They're probably miffed because, while you were in the cottage, your butler released the girls.'

'Great!'

'They've obviously discovered that the prisoners have escaped.'

'Their wrath has been roused.'

'Indeed, my friend. Come on, we'd better get back to the castle before . . . '

'Penny . . . I mean, Baron. Why are you on my side?'

'Because you've given me the biggest cock a man could want.'

'Cock? Oh, I see what you mean.'

'Come, we must repair to the castle!'

'That reminds me, I must repair to the castle and repair the shattered windows – and the ballcock in the upstairs toilet. But the first thing I'm going to do is take you down to the lab and erase the Baron's brainwave patterns and . . . '

'Come, my friend – we're wasting time.'

'I'll come later. We'd better go, we're wasting time.'

Creeping through the forest, Snide pondered on Penny's revelation, wondering whether to believe her or not. Operation Big Bad Wolf? Germans after his machine? It was possible, but he'd learned to trust no one. The best way to

deal with Penny was to chain her to the rack and stretch the
truth out of her. In fact, it was high time all the girls were
stretched, shaved, whipped and fucked senseless.

Leaving the forest and making their way up the grassy hill
to the castle, Snide noticed the tall stooping frame of his
butler lurking by the doors. Lucifer had done well, he
reflected as he approached the man. Managing to release
the girlies, he'd done very well – but not well enough. *Time
for a bollocking!*

'Lucifer!' the Professor yelled, standing before the man.
'Why did you leave me in the cottage?'

'I heard wails and cries of orgasmic lust and thought it best
not to disturb you, sir.'

'I'll disturb *you* in a minute. Fuck me, I could have been
captured and shot to death! Murdered, even!'

'Let's get inside,' Penny said as machine-gun fire
resounded throughout the forest. 'It's not safe out here.'

'Good thinking, Baron,' the Professor grinned, opening
the doors.

'Baron?' Lucifer echoed.

'Don't ask awkward questions, Lucifer!' Snide returned,
entering the castle and locking the doors. 'OK, where's the
Baron?' he asked, propping his gun up against the wall.

'I'm here,' Penny said.

'No, I mean . . . Lucifer, where is he?'

'She's . . . I mean, he's standing next to you, sir.'

'No, the other one.'

'The other one?'

'You know.'

'You mean, there are two Barons?'

'No, you fool! You released the girls, right?'

'Yes, sir. I escorted them back here and took the liberty of
locking them in your living quarters.'

'And the man that was with them?'

'Man?'

'In the forest, tied to a tree.'

'Oh, *that* Baron. I couldn't get to him, sir. He was tied up some way from the girls and . . . '

'He's still there?'

'I can't see him from here, of course, but I would imagine that he's still there.'

'Fuck and quadruple fuck! Why the hell didn't you . . . '

'We must make plans,' Penny interrupted the Professor.

'Yes, plans to release the Baron.'

'But I'm the Baron.'

'No, I mean . . . God, I can't take much more of this fucking bollocks. Lucifer, take Penny . . . take the Baron down to the lab and induce the modified alpha-wave patterns into her brain . . . *his* brain.'

'Yes, sir.'

'I don't want to be modified!' Penny wailed as Lucifer grabbed her by her tits and dragged her away.

'You'll *be* modified and that's the end of the matter.'

That would solve *that* little problem, the Professor reflected as the screaming girl was bundled down to the lab. *Two Barons, indeed!* It would be interesting to see what she thought of her clitoris once she'd been transformed into a sex-crazed, dirty, filthy tramp of a bisexual nymphomaniac, he mused. But, in the meantime, there was work to do – namely, the release of the Baron.

To return to the Forest of the Dead was the best plan, he reflected as he grabbed his gun and opened the doors. The last thing the so-called Germans would expect immediately after the escape of the girlies was the release of the Baron. The Professor would rescue his old friend if it was last thing he did, and he'd spray the cottage with bullets until the place fell to the ground in a heap of rubble. After he'd nabbed Goldilocks, that was.

'Ah, Professor!' DI Peel grinned as Snide left the castle.

'Oh, Inspector! You made me jump. Er . . . What are you doing here at this time?'

'What I'd like to know is, what are *you* doing with a machine-gun?'

'I'm going grouse shooting.'

'Grouse shooting? But . . . '

'Grouse? Did I say grouse?'

'Yes, you did.'

'I'm so sorry, I meant mouse . . . No, I didn't. Louse, as in woodlouse.'

'You're going to shoot a woodlouse with a machine-gun?'

'Woodlice, it's the only way to get rid of the pesky things.'

'Most odd. Professor, I discovered six habits in your castle earlier today. How do you account for that?'

'I'd say that you were searching the castle and you found the habits.'

'No, how do you account for that fact that they were in the castle?'

'Oh, I see. Er . . . We're putting on a play called . . . called *The Wicked Nuns of the Wicked Nunnery.*'

'A play?'

'Yes, the local amateur theatrical society are . . . '

'I'll check with the local society. It's been brought to my attention that my daughter was going into the forest to do some snooping around.'

'Really? Who brought this attention to your attention?'

'My daughter. She rang me from a call box.'

'There are no call boxes in the forest.'

'She rang me from the village before she went to the forest.'

'A clever move on your daughter's part, Inspector – but what has this to do with me?'

'My daughter called herself the Purple Baron. I knew it was her because I recognized her voice.'

'How recognitiative of you, but I still don't see where I come off . . . come in.'

'Neither do I, yet. Something else has been brought to my attention.'

'You're very attentive, I must say.'

'Thank you.'

'Not at all.'

'I've learned that the Prime Minister has taken leave of his senses.'

'Taken leave? Where did he go?'

'Mentally speaking, Professor. He's of a deranged mind.'

'Fascinating, but I really must dash. Was there anything else?'

'One last thing. My men raided the nunnery and . . . '

'Was that wise?'

'In view of the fact that you told me that the nunnery is the aliens' headquarters, I believe it was most wise. We have the Reverend Mother Horgasm in custody.'

'An excellent move, Inspector!'

'Thank you. We'll be interrogating her in the morning.'

'She'll lie, of course.'

'Yes, I'm well aware of that.'

'There's only one way to deal with these aliens: you have to strip them naked and examine their bottom-holes.'

'I *beg* your pardon?'

'To prove that the Reverend Mother is an alien, check her bottom-hole. She should have two if she's a Martian.'

'Two bottom . . . '

'And two vaginal canals. Check her clitoris, you should find that she hasn't got one.'

'Right, thanks for the tip.'

'Not at all, Inspector. I like to be of assistance to the boys in blue when I can.'

'You have a fine community spirit. Well, I leave you to your woodlouse shooting.'

'Woodlice, the plural. Let me know how you get on with the Reverend Mother.'

'I will. Goodnight, Professor.'

'Goodnight.'

Slinging his gun over his shoulder and dashing down the hill before the sleuth asked any more questions, the Professor slipped into the forest. The release of the Baron was of paramount importance, he reflected, creeping through the trees towards the cottage. With the girlies having escaped, no doubt the Krauts would have stepped up security. A diversion was called for, he decided as he approached the cottage. It might have been an idea to bring Lucifer along to karate chop a few clitorises off, he reflected, hiding behind the bushes and gazing at the armed women guarding the Baron.

'I thought you might return!' Gretel growled, standing behind the Professor with a gun pointing at his head.

'Oh! Er . . . Good evening,' he smiled, rising to his feet as she grabbed his gun. 'What a lovely night for a walk in the forest. A walk in the Black Forest!' he chuckled. 'Black, as in dark.'

'A walk in ze Dead Forest!' she returned.

'Yes, quite. Actually, I know that you're not really German.'

'Of course I am German! Come, you go to ze cottage for ze torture.'

'Torture? Can't we have coffee and biscuits instead?'

'Nein! You have ze torture!'

Walking to the cottage with Gretel's gun digging in his back, the Professor waved at the Baron. He'd let his friend down, he knew as he was ushered into the cottage and ordered to climb the stairs. At least the girlies were safe, he reflected – but for how long? Surely, Gretel would have her band of women raid the castle and grab not only the girls but Lucifer and the machine.

'Remove all your clothes!' Gretel snapped as they entered the bedroom.

'Good evening, Goldie,' the Professor said, smiling at the naked girl tied to the bed. 'We meet again.'

'You fool!' she hissed. 'You let your cock rule your head!'

'Indeed, I do. But we had a good fuck, did we not?'

'You should have released me!'

'Enough!' Gretel stormed. 'Remove all your clothes!'

Unbuttoning his shirt, the Professor wondered what horrendous torture he was going to have to endure. Perhaps he'd be forced to tongue-fuck Goldilocks, or drive his solid cock up her tight bottom and spunk her bowels. By the evil look in Gretel's dark eyes as he dropped his trousers, he thought not! What was the worst thing that could happen? he pondered, kicking his shoes and trousers aside and standing before the women with his magnificent cock hanging halfway down his thighs.

'Ah, you have ze gros cockenhousen!' Gretel grinned, eyeing his huge member.

'Yes, it *is* rather big,' he replied proudly, praying that he wouldn't have to fuck the woman. *Now that really would be the ultimate torture!*

'You have ze big balls, nein?'

'No, only two.'

'Two are enough for me. Make your cockenhousen stiff.'

'How?'

'Have a vank and make it stiff.'

Running his hand up and down his veined shaft, his member hardening as he eyed the sperm and girlie juice oozing from Goldie's yawning vaginal slit, the Professor wanked his cock to a full erection. Standing with his magnificent organ pointing to the ceiling, his heavy balls swinging, he tried not to imagine Gretel naked. There was one sure way to deflate his penis, and that was to picture the woman's naked body!

'Now you vill put your cockenhousen in ze girl's mouth,' she instructed him.

'In her mouth?' he echoed, wondering what sort of torture the wonderfully debauched act was supposed to be.

'Down her throat! Hurry!'

'All right, all right!'

'Now! Put it in ze girl's mouth now!'

Clambering onto the bed and kneeling beside Goldie's pretty face, the Professor grabbed his cock, pulling his foreskin right back and offering his glans to her partly open mouth. 'Suck it!' Gretel bellowed. 'Suck ze cockenhousen!' Opening her mouth, the girl sucked on the Professor's purple plum, closing her eyes as she savoured his salty knob. Moving forward, pushing his meaty length deeper into her hot mouth, the Professor withdrew and drove into her again.

If this was torture, he'd happily endure hours of it! Mouth-fucking fanny-fucking cleavage-fucking, bum-fucking . . . What finer way to spend a night? This was just what he needed. And there was one thing Goldilocks needed, he observed, eyeing the blonde down covering her sex mound, her fleshy outer lips. A thorough fanny-shaving!

'You vill sperm over her face,' Gretel instructed the Professor, moving closer to the bed. 'I vant to see you sperm over her face.'

'This is a strange way of torturing someone,' Snide grinned, his cock twitching as the girl rolled her tongue over his swollen knob.

'Torture begins later. You vill sperm her face before your balls are tortured.'

'My balls?' he gasped.

'Your balls, your cockenhousen, your knob . . . You vill be tortured until you sperm again.'

That sounded OK, he mused, his spunk almost ready to pump up his shaft and jet from his pulsating glans. Death by orgasm? It sounded like a cocktail, or a chocolate pudding. 'God!' he gasped as he slipped his orgasming knob out of the girl's gobbling mouth. His sperm shooting from his slit, he wanked his shaft, sustaining his orgasm to shrieks of delight from Gretel.

Squeezing her eyes shut as the sperm flew through the air and showered her pretty face, Goldie poked her tongue out, capturing the opaque liquid and swallowing her prize. His spunk splattering her cheeks, her golden hair, he massaged his swollen knob, still sustaining his orgasm.

'You vill vank faster!' Gretel ordered the Professor.

'Christ, I'm doing my best!' he gasped, wanking the sperm from his throbbing knob.

'It is not good enough! Faster!'

Increasing his masturbating rhythm, his sperm shooting from his purple knob, splattering Goldie's face and running down her neck, the Professor positioned his glans over her mouth. Wondering what he'd be forced to do next as the copious flow of spunk shot from his slit, he watched Goldie lick her lips, trying to lap up every drop of sperm raining down from his swollen glans. Her pink tongue snaking down her chin, capturing the opaque liquid, she was quite a girl, he reflected, wondering how hot and tight her anal sheath was. If Gretel fucked off somewhere, he could . . .

'OK, now finger her fanny!' Gretel bellowed, watching the last of the Professor's spunk shoot from his purple knob as she was joined by two teenage accomplices. Eyeing the attractive, machine-gun-wielding girls as they gazed in awe at his magnificent cock, Snide hoped he'd be forced to fuck the little beauties. This was better than saving the Baron, he

reflected. Fucking girls' mouths was far more fun than . . .
But the Baron was his friend, and he'd already let him down
once. Sperming girls' mouths and fingering their fannies was
one thing, but the Baron had to be rescued.

As Gretel ordered the two women to strip, Snide clambered off the bed. Once the women were in a state of severe
sexual arousal, he'd make his move. If Gretel became excited
by the debauchery to the extent where she was oblivious to
her surroundings, he'd have no problem slipping out of the
room. As he sat back down on the bed and parted the girl's
succulent vaginal lips, he supposed he should rescue Goldilocks. After all, she was as much a prisoner as the Baron. Or
was she?

Forcing three fingers into Goldie's tight cunt, the Professor
watched the two girls toss their blouses to the floor and
unhook their straining bras. No doubt they were preparing
for a rampant fucking, he mused, his fingers squelching in
Goldie's well-juiced vagina. An ever-erect penis was definitely the answer, he decided, focusing on the girls' elongated
nipples as they leaned forward to tug their wet panties down.

Continuing his fanny-fingering, he watched the girls pull
their panties down their shapely thighs. Their pussy lips
adorned with well-trimmed black pubes, their pink sex cracks
gaping, they were ripe for a damned good fucking. Grinning
as one girl knelt down and licked the other's fanny slit, Snide
prayed for Gretel to join in the lesbianism, giving him the
opportunity to make his escape.

'You vill lick her until she is vell creamed,' Gretel
instructed the girl. 'Ven she is ready, ze Professor vill fuck
her cuntenhousen.'

'Yes, Fräulein,' the girl replied, pushing her tongue into
her gasping friend's vaginal sheath and lapping up her
flowing juices.

'What are you going to do with me?' Goldie asked.

'You vill commit dreadful lesbian acts vith ze girls.'

'I won't!'

'You vill! You vill also lick my cuntenhousen.'

'Never!' Goldie cried as Gretel began stripping.

It would be a shame to leave without fucking the lesbians, Snide mused, forcing another finger into Goldie's juiced pussy duct. But the Baron's release had to be secured before enjoying the delights of lesbian-fucking. Eyeing the naked fat Kraut, and wishing he hadn't, the Professor wondered whether he could perform for the lesbians in front of such an ugly sight!

'Now you vill lick me,' Gretel instructed the girl kneeling on the floor. 'Leave her cuntenhousen and lick mine.'

'Yes, Fräulein,' the girl replied obediently, kneeling before Gretel and parting the woman's full vaginal lips.

'Ah, zat is good!' Gretel gasped as the girl's tongue entered her drenched vagina. 'You vill both lick me until I come.'

With Gretel swaying in her debauched pleasure, her eyes closed as the girls' tongues attended her sex crack, the time had come to make a run for it, the Professor decided. Yanking his drenched fingers out of Goldie's cunny hole, he slipped off the bed and moved cautiously towards the door. His clothes in a heap beneath one of Gretel's feet, he'd have to leave the cottage naked, but he'd be safe enough in the dark. Holding his finger to his lips and winking at Goldie, he crept out of the room with his massive cock dangling between his thighs.

It was a warm night, he reflected, descending the stairs with his heavy balls swinging. He'd not have a problem sneaking back to the castle naked, as long as DI Peel wasn't lurking! Or the woodcutter, for that matter! Imagining the burly man axing his cock off, he left the cottage and crept towards the Baron.

'You're naked, my friend,' the Baron remarked as Snide released him.

'I couldn't get my clothes,' the Professor whispered as cries of female orgasm emanated from the cottage. 'I see you're still dressed as a woman.'

'Yes, my panties are killing me.'

'Come on, we must return to the castle fifthwith.'

'What about the fat Kraut? Aren't we going to take her prisoner?'

'You must be joking!'

'I see your point, my friend.'

'As I said, I couldn't get my clothes.'

'Not that point. I meant . . . '

'We're wasting time by talking bollocks. I suggest we leave now.'

'If not sooner.'

'Or before.'

Stealing through the forest with the Baron, Snide wondered what Gretel would do with Goldilocks. Pondering on returning to the cottage later and releasing the girl, he pictured her naked body. She had a beautiful cunt, a cunt worth rescuing, not to mention fucking and spunking. But the fat Kraut would have to be dealt with before any cunny rescuing plans were put into action. She wouldn't give up until she'd got her fat hands on the alpha-wave machine, that was for sure. She had to be done away with, permanently. Had Lucifer dug a lion pit . . .

'Look, my friend!' the Baron gasped, pointing at the castle. 'If I'm not mistaken, that's the fat Kraut standing by the doors – and she's naked.'

'My God, it's the fat Kraut standing by the doors – and she's naked! How the hell did she get here before us?'

'I have no idea.'

'Perhaps she's an alien. She might have access to a flying saucer and . . . Christ, I really must stop talking bollocks.'

'Indeed, you must. This is no time to be talking bollocks.'

'No time at all. I suggest we stop talking bollocks and do something constructive.'

'Or something *de*structive, such as kill the Kraut.'

'It's a brilliant plan, Baron, but I don't have a gun.'

'Damn and blast!'

'I've got it. I'll shoot her with my cock.'

'With your cock?'

'I'll wank and shoot her with sperm.'

'I don't think that's a good idea. The sight of your erect penis throbbing in orgasm might rouse her craving for debauched sex.'

'Apart from that, it might turn her on. OK, we'll return to the cottage, grab my gun, and Goldilocks, and then come back and kill the fat Kraut.'

'An excellent idea, my friend.'

Trekking through the forest, Snide again wondered how Gretel had managed to get to the castle so quickly. But, however she'd done it, at least she was out of the way. Her young lesbian accomplices wouldn't present a problem: they were probably on the floor writhing in ecstasy – leaving the way clear to release Goldilocks and grab the gun.

'It'll be nice to have my clothes back,' the Professor whispered as they approached the cottage.

'It'll be nice to get out of this miniskirt and these ball-cutting panties once we're back at the castle.'

'That's a thought.'

'What is?'

'Shit, I've forgotten what I was going to say.'

'Who are you?' a young girl in a party dress asked as she leaped out of the bushes.

'Fuck! Er . . . Who are *you*?' the Professor gasped, eyeing her rounded breasts billowing her white dress.

'My name's Alice. I'm looking for the tea party.'

'Tea party? Christ, a woodcutter, Little Red Riding Hood,

Gretel, Goldilocks, the Big Bad Wolf . . . What the fuck's going on in this forest?'

'There's a party tonight,' Alice smiled. 'Why are you naked?'

'Because I'm the Mad-bloody-Hatter.'

'Where's your hat?'

'Where's my . . . Jesus F. Christ! Everyone's insane!'

'Insanity rules!'

'How old are you?'

'Sixteen. See you at the party!' the girl giggled, skipping into the bushes.

'Fuck me backwards!'

'I think I know what's going on, my friend,' the Baron murmured pensively as he pulled his panties out of his anal crease.

'I'm pleased someone does.'

'I think I'm dreaming.'

'What?'

'This is all a dream.'

'Of course you're not bloody dreaming! We're talking bollocks again. Let's go.'

Entering the cottage, the Professor led the Baron up the narrow stairs to the bedroom to discover that Goldilocks and the lesbians had gone. The ropes snaking across the ruffled bed, the sheet stained with girlie juice and sperm, there was no way any of this had been a dream. *Curiouser and curiouser*, he mused, grabbing his clothes from the floor and tugging his trousers on.

'They've gone,' he said, buttoning his shirt as he turned to the Baron.

'That's stating the obvious, my friend.'

'Obviously. Now what do we do?'

'I don't know.'

'The answer is to find Goldilocks, so what's the question?'

'You're talking bollocks again.'

'So I am, Baron. I wonder who that Alice girl was?'

'Her name's Alice.'

'I know that, but who was she? There's something afoot, I can smell it.'

'You'd best put your shoes on. I suggest we gatecrash the tea party.'

'Good idea. OK, I've got my gun – let's go.'

Creeping downstairs with the Baron in tow, Snide froze as he stared at the two naked lesbians blocking the front door. Wielding machine-guns, they ordered him to drop his gun and go into the lounge. This was a fine mess, he reflected, having no choice other than to comply with their demand. And this was an even finer mess! he mused as the Baron followed him through the doorway.

'Ve meet again!' Gretel grinned, standing by the fireplace.

'How the hell do you move around so quickly?' the Professor asked.

'Silence! You vill be sexually tortured for your insolence.'

'Where's Goldilocks?'

'Ze voodcutter has her.'

'I don't know why you're pretending to be German.'

'I am *not* pretending. OK, clothes off.'

'Not again!'

'You vill do as you are told. Unless you vish to die.'

'I have no wish to die, madam,' the Baron said. 'And I have no wish to remove my miniskirt and blouse.'

'You are a strange lady. You talk like a man.'

'I *am* a man.'

'Filthy pervert!'

'You can talk!' Snide chuckled. 'Christ, the way you carried on with those lesbians . . . '

'Silence! Take ze prisoners up to ze bedroom,' she instructed the girls. 'Strip them and chain them to ze valls. I am going to remove their balls.'

'You can't do that!' Snide returned, clutching his full scrotum.

'I can and I vill. I shall go to ze castle tomorrow and get ze machine, killing anyone who gets in my vay. Take them up and strip them!'

The fat Kraut wasn't joking! the Professor mused as he climbed the stairs with the Baron. Followed by the gun-wielding lesbians as he entered the bedroom, he reckoned that this was the end. The only chance they had now was Lucifer, if he wasn't drunk! But the butler wouldn't be prepared for Gretel's visit and, knowing him, he'd open the doors to the Kraut and let her in. The machine would be lost, the girlies taken away . . . *Fuck and treble fuck!*

Chapter Twelve

The sun rising over the castle, Lucifer stirred in his bed as Beethoven emanated from his radio alarm. Fondling his erect penis, he pondered on the girlies, wondering whether the Professor would allow him a session of debauched sex with the horny tarts before beginning the day's duties. There was nothing like a little cunny-licking and fanny-fucking to begin the day, he reflected as he climbed out of bed.

Eyeing his solid penis and heavy balls in the full-length mirror, he contemplated borrowing the gamma-ray machine to increase the size of his organ. It wasn't fair that the Professor should enjoy a horse-like penis, he ruminated, turning to face the radio as he heard something about the Prime Minister.

'His plans to abolish income tax and duty on alcohol have shocked the government,' the news reader droned. 'And the unprecedented step of certifying the Prime Minister insane and placing him in a secure unit for the mentally ill has shocked the nation.'

'Interesting,' Lucifer breathed, wandering into the bathroom and taking a shower. The Professor's antics were getting out of hand, and he wondered what his crazy boss would do next. Send all Inland Revenue employees to the firing squad? 'Anarchy rules!' he chuckled, lathering his rock-hard cock with soap. His penis twitching, his bulbous knob swollen, he contemplated having a quick wank, but decided to save his spunk for one of the girlies' gobbling mouths.

He'd get his hands on one of the naked beauties when the Professor wasn't around, and get his cock up her well-juiced cunny.

Leaving the shower and dressing, he finally emerged from his room and made his way to the Professor's living quarters – his penis painfully erect within his tight trousers. Finding the girls naked, sitting around the lounge enjoying their breakfast, he thought it odd that the Professor wasn't entwined in lust with one of the little sexpots. It was most unusual for the Professor not to enjoy eating pussy and drinking cunny milk for breakfast.

Was this the opportunity he'd been waiting for? he wondered, eyeing one of the nuns as she lay sprawled across the sofa with her creamy cunny crack gaping. Focusing on another girl as she lay on the floor with her thighs wide, a banana protruding from between her swollen pussy lips, he thought he was going to cream his trousers. It was best to see what the Professor was up to before enjoying a hot, creamy banana! he decided.

Locking the door as he left the room, he searched the dungeon, checking the torture and rack chambers before climbing the winding steps to the windswept turret. Something was wrong, he knew as he checked the gunpowder room. There'd been no word from the Professor, no cries of female orgasm emanating from the dungeon late into the night, no sounds of a whip lashing taut buttocks . . . Something was very wrong.

Casting his eyes over the forest, he instinctively knew that the Professor and the Baron were out there, probably in the cottage, and he could only assume the worst. Wondering whether to rescue Professor Snide or appease his aching cock, he imagined two nuns sucking and licking his swollen glans. It was a hard choice, very hard!

Walking to the banqueting hall, he gazed at the ringing

phone, trying to fight the urge to force one of the girls attend his erect penis, gobble his knob and drink his sperm. But he knew the consequences should he abuse the girls without the Professor's permission, and non-surgical removal of his bollocks wasn't something he fancied – especially before breakfast!

'Professor Snide's residence,' he said, grabbing the phone.

'This is DI Peel, who's that?'

'It's me.'

'Who's me?'

'Lucifer, the butler.'

'Ah, right. May I speak to the Professor?'

'I'm afraid he's been unavoidably deranged . . . detained.'

'Do you know something that I don't?'

'I know several things that you don't.'

'Such as?'

'I know the colour of my silk panties.'

'The colour of your . . . What I mean is, do you know something about the Professor that I don't?'

'Yes, I know how big his cock is.'

'His whereabouts, man!' the Inspector yelled.

'He keeps his whereabouts in his underpants.'

'Why do you have a fascination with the Professor's genitalia?'

'I don't, Inspector.'

'Let's start again. Do you know where the Professor is?'

'He disappeared last night.'

'I saw him just before he went lice shooting. I wonder whether he's still . . . '

'I can't see from here.'

'I realize that! Did he tell you when he planned to return?'

'He didn't say when he'd be back because he didn't tell me that he was going. He'd hardly say when he was coming back if he'd not said he was going out.'

'When are you expecting him to return? You must have a rough idea?'

'Sadly, I'm not expecting to return.'

'Right, as this conversation is obviously going nowhere, I'll go to the forest and find them.'

Replacing the phone, Lucifer decided to take a trip to the forest himself. About to grab the rocket launcher from the turret, he realized that he could hardly blow up the cottage knowing that the Professor and the Baron might be inside. Taking a machine-gun instead, he left the castle, pondering on his plan. Wiping out the Krauts single-handed wouldn't be easy, but nothing was impossible.

Creeping through the trees towards the cottage, his cock harder than ever, he stopped, again wondering whether to have a quick wank to appease his craving for orgasm. Finally succumbing to his soaring libido, he placed the gun up against a tree and hauled his cock out of his trousers. It was no good going into battle with a rampant erection and his balls heavily laden. Apart from anything else, it wasn't conducive to concentrating on the job in hand.

'Ah, that's good!' he breathed, rolling his foreskin back and forth over his pulsating glans. 'There's nothing like a wank.'

'What are you doing?' Alice asked as she emerged from the bushes and gazed in awe at Lucifer's huge cock.

'Oh! Who are you?' Lucifer gasped, hurriedly concealing his penis.

'I'm Alice. Are you wanking?'

'Er . . . No, of course I'm not. You shouldn't be roaming the forest, Miss.'

'I've been to a party.'

'In the forest?'

'Yes, it was great. We danced and drank and smoked dope and fucked and . . . '

'You fucked?'

'Of course! Mind you, the dormouse wasn't much good. Do *you* fuck?'

'Well, yes.'

'Come on then.'

'You want me to fuck you?'

'As hard as you can,' she grinned, pulling her dress over her head. 'Really give it to me.'

There was something strange about the girl, Lucifer mused as she ripped her bra away from her firm breasts. Firstly, it wasn't usual to be met by girls in the forest who stripped off and demanded a good fucking. Secondly, it was rather odd to have a tea party in the forest. Thirdly, a dormouse couldn't very well . . . *A dormouse?* This had to be a trick, he decided as she ripped her knickers off, revealing her shaved, school-girlie-lookalike vaginal lips, her creamy pinken slit.

'I don't want to fuck you,' he said, although his twitching penis told him otherwise as he gazed at her inner petals protruding from her pink girlie slit.

'You *don't* want to fuck me?' she frowned, parting her fleshy vaginal lips and exposing her ripe clitoris to his wide eyes.

'No, I don't just fuck willy-nilly.'

'Oh. In that case, I'll be on my way.'

'I was talking to Gretel earlier,' he said, going for broke and watching for her reaction.

'But aren't you . . . '

'She instructed me to grab the machine from the castle.'

'Ah, you're on our side!'

'Of course.'

'Hang on. She told me that she was going to the castle this morning to . . . '

'A change of plan. What are your instructions?'

'I'm to radio the cottage should anyone approach.'

'You have a radio?'

'Yes, don't you?'

'I . . . I lost it.'

'Gretel will give you another one. I'm sorry I stripped off and went on about fucking, but I thought you were a friend of Snide's. What's your code name?'

'Er . . . Hansel.'

'The superior?'

'Am I? I mean . . . Yes, I am.'

'Why don't you know what my instructions are if you're . . . '

'I was testing you, making sure that you really are Alice. As you'll appreciate, I can't be too careful. For all I know you might be Christopher Robin's sister-in-law. Did Gretel tell you to fuck anyone who approaches the cottage?'

'She told me to use my body to delay people.'

'Well, as we're on the same side, I suppose I could fuck you.'

'Great!'

Eyeing the little beauty's hairless pussy lips as she reclined on the forest floor with her thighs wide apart, Lucifer slipped his erect penis back out of his trousers. Pulling his foreskin back, displaying his purple knob, he pondered on the girl as she ran her finger up and down her creamy-wet pussy crack. Alice, Gretel, a tea party, a dormouse, a woodcutter, a cottage, bowls of porridge . . .

This was Lucifer's chance to get into the Professor's good books by discovering all there was about the fairy-tale scam and blowing the gaff on the Krauts. But he'd have to play it by ear, he mused, sitting beside Alice. Prise information out of the girl without her discovering that he knew absolutely nothing.

'You have a nice cunt,' he smiled, leaning over and licking the full length of her drenched sex valley.

'And you have a nice cock,' she replied huskily, grabbing his solid member.

'Tell me, what's Gretel going to do with the Professor and the Baron?'

'Once the government have the machine, they'll be imprisoned for life. Mmm, I like your finger up my Cheshire.'

'Up your Cheshire?'

'Cat, up my pussy. How come you don't know the plan?'

'I do, it's just that I keep changing it.'

'You keep changing it?'

'I was on my way to the castle to get the machine when the woodcutter stopped me. He told me that Gretel's already got the machine so I changed the plan – we're all to pull out.'

'No one told me that.'

'That's odd. Where's your radio?'

'In the bushes, over there. Perhaps I should call in and . . . Oh, oh, that's nice! God, how I love fingers stretching my cunt open!'

'You have a lovely cunt, Alice. When did you shave?'

'One of the agents shaved me – one of the mobile hairdressers. When Gretel grabbed the girls from the castle, she realized that the hairdressers had been subjected to the Professor's weird machine and . . . Ah, yes! Finger-fuck me faster!'

'What the . . . ' DI Peel gasped as he stumbled across the lewd scene.

'Ah, Inspector!' Lucifer grinned. 'Er . . . I've captured one of the aliens. You'd better take her in for torturing . . . I mean, for questioning.'

'Good man!' Peel beamed, rolling the struggling girl over and cuffing her hands behind her back. 'Er . . . Why do you have your penis out?'

'It was a ploy.'

'Get off me!' Alice cried.

'A ploy that worked very well. Right, come on my beauty – it's the cells for you!'

'No!'

'Yes!'

Chuckling as the Inspector dragged Alice into the bushes, Lucifer zipped his trousers and grabbed his gun. The first thing to do was find the radio, he mused, searching the bushes she'd pointed to. It was a shame that he'd not had the chance to glean more information out of her, he reflected, crawling beneath a bush – and a greater shame not to have fucked her tight cunny!

'Ah, there it is!' he breathed, grabbing the radio and switching it on. 'Gretel, are you there?' he asked.

'Who is zis speaking on ze radio?' she bellowed.

'This is . . . this is Hansel.'

'This is an honour, sir!'

'Is it?'

'But of course. Vhat are your instructions?'

'You're to pull out immediately.'

'Jawohl! Oh, I was forgetting – I can cut the German crap now.'

'The machine is now in the hands of the government. You must pull out and leave the Professor and the Baron in the cottage. They'll be picked up later.'

'Yes, sir.'

'Leave the cottage immediately.'

'I'll see you back in London, sir.'

'Will you? Ah, yes, of course. See you later.'

That was easy enough! he reflected, slipping the radio into his pocket and heading towards the cottage. Release the Professor and the Baron, and then return to the castle and have a damned good banana breakfast followed by a rampant anal rogering of one of the girls was the best plan, he decided. What with the enemy returning to London, there'd be plenty of time to prepare for the next onslaught of so-called Krauts, he mused, hiding behind the bushes as Gretel and her girls left the cottage. And plenty of time to fuck the girlies' bottom-holes!

'OK, come out with your cocks up!' he called, entering the cottage and dashing up the stairs once the coast was clear.

'Lucifer!' Snide beamed, his naked body hanging from chains fixed to his wrists.

'I am here to save you, sir,' the butler grinned triumphantly as he released the men.

'You timing's perfect,' the Baron said. 'The Germans have just left.'

'Yes, I told them . . . '

'There's no time for explanations, Lucifer. We must repair to the castle sixthwith and make sure the machine is . . . '

'Gretel and her girls have returned to London, sir. And Alice . . . '

'Have they got the machine?'

'No, sir – the machine is safe.'

'You've done well, Lucifer!' the Professor praised his butler as they left the room and bounded down the stairs. 'You can tell me everything on our return to the castle.'

'Aren't you both going to put your clothes on?'

'There's no time for such English pleasantries. Come on!'

Running through the forest with Lucifer and the Baron close behind, the Professor decided to give all the girls the buttock-thrashing of their young lives in way of celebration. With the Krauts gone, and no sign of the SAS, things were looking up again. But the machine would have to be well hidden, possibly in the secret tunnel. Every precaution had to be taken in case the real Germans showed their faces.

Nearing the castle, his huge penis swinging between his legs as he sprinted up the hill, he chuckled wickedly as he reached the doors. His ultimate goal was near, a lifetime of abducting young village girls, rampant sessions of naked-buttock-thrashing, cunny-fucking, bottom-fucking, mouth-fucking . . .

'OK,' he panted, closing and locking the doors once the Baron and Lucifer were inside. 'Lucifer, hide the machine in the secret tunnel.'

'Yes, sir. Er . . . There's some bad news.'

'Bad news? What have you done now?'

'I inadvertently allowed Penny to escape before I'd had a chance to induce the modified brain patterns . . . '

'Fuck me! OK, not to worry. Baron, if you'd be so good, construct a lookalike machine and leave it in the lab.'

'Of course, my friend. I can see your plan clearly.'

'Where is it?'

'In your head, presumably.'

'You can see inside my head?'

'No, I mean . . . '

'We're talking bollocks again, Baron.'

'I agree.'

'Right, we still have DI Peel to worry about. What with the nuns' habits he found here, and his missing daughter, it won't be long before he returns and asks more searching questions.'

'First things first, my friend. I'll go and construct a lookalike machine.'

'That's a brilliant idea.'

'Thank you.'

As Lucifer and the Baron left, Snide decided to take a walk into the village. Although he had enough girls to keep him in perverted sex for years, there was something about abducting young village girls that fascinated him. It might be fun to go to the library and deface a few books, he mused, leaving the castle. Or break the deafening silence by hurling crude comments at the prudish librarian!

In a wicked mood, he trotted down the cobble path, the morning sun warming him as he passed a pregnant woman walking her Alsatian. *She's been fucked and spunked!* he chuckled inwardly, imagining her with her legs open, a huge cock driving in and out of her wet cunt. *I wonder whether the dog . . .* 'Don't be disgusting,' he murmured.

Passing the village school, he stopped to watch the girlies playing netball. His insatiable thirst for crude sex getting the better of him as he leaned against the fence, he massaged his stiffening penis through his trousers. Eyeing their white ankle socks, their firm, shapely thighs revealed by their incredibly short pleated skirts, he imagined their navy-blue knickers. They'd undoubtedly be stained and damp with teenage cunny juice, stretched tightly over their fresh, swollen pussy lips. He reckoned he could easily sell their cunny-scented knickers for twenty pounds a pair, if he could get his hands on them. *A nice little earner!* he mused as the scowling PE mistress walked over to the fence.

'What are you doing?' she asked, placing her fists on her curvaceous hips.

'Watching the match,' he replied, his arousal obvious from the huge bulge in the crotch of his trousers.

'I know who you are,' she said with a hint of anger. 'You're Doctor Sex from the castle.'

'What of it?'

'I know what you're thinking.'

'Are you a mind-reader?'

'I don't have to be!'

'Tell me what I'm thinking.'

'You're looking at the girls and thinking about their . . . '

'Thinking about their what?'

'I can't say it.'

'Shall *I* say it?' he chuckled.

'No, just go away and leave us alone.'

'I'm thinking about their beautiful pussy lips, their wet girlie cracks and ripe clitorises and . . . '

'You're an evil man! Go away before I . . . Oh!' she gasped as he pulled his solid penis out and rolled his foreskin back. 'Oh, my God!'

Laughing as she fainted, Snide tucked his cock into his trousers and wandered off. Passing what was left of the village stores and post office, he laughed again as he recalled the shock registered on the woman's face. There was nothing like being extremely crude and flashing his cock at PE mistresses. *I should have had a wank and spunked in front of her!*

'Excuse me,' an attractive young woman said, stopping the Professor in his tracks as he neared the library. 'Can you tell me where the castle is?'

'The castle?' he echoed, wondering whether she was another mobile hairdresser. 'I know nothing about castles.'

'Professor Snide's castle.'

'Ah, *that* castle. I can tell you where it is, but he's away at the moment.'

'Oh, no.'

'He's on a school trip with a netball team. I mean, he's on holiday. What was it you wanted to see him about?'

'Is he a friend of yours?'

'I've met him once or twice but I don't really know him.'

Noticing the swell of her firm breasts billowing her tight blouse, the outline of her nipples pressing against the white material, he imagined his erect penis nestling in her cleavage, her tits crushing his veined shaft as he spunked her pretty neck. She was definitely ripe for a fucking, he decided, coming up with a wicked and highly illegal plan.

'I'll take you to the castle,' he smiled. 'The Professor's butler might be able to help you. He might also be of assistance to you.'

'That's very good of you,' she smiled.

'I know it is. Come on, I'll show you the way.'

Walking down the street, Snide led the woman to the village green. There was something fishy about her, he mused. And it was surely more than coincidence that she had happened to stop him and ask where the castle was. *Another agent?* he pondered. There were so many people after the machine that it wouldn't be at all surprising if she was working for some government or other.

There was no way she was going anywhere near the castle, he decided, walking across the grass to the wooded area edging the green. Once under cover of the trees, he'd pull her knickers down and finger her wet cunny and then sperm her mouth and then screw her fanny and then roger her anal duct and then . . . *First things first*, he reflected – *discover who she is and what she wants.*

'I would have thought there'd have been a road leading to the castle,' she said, her blue eyes frowning as she followed the Professor through the undergrowth.

'This is a short cut,' he replied, entering a small clearing. 'There *is* a road, but it would take an hour or more to go that way. Shall we rest here for a minute?'

'Rest? But we've only just started.'

'I have a bad leg, I have to rest it.'

'Did you break it?'

'No, I stepped on the end of my cock and twisted my ankle.'

'The end of your . . . '

'The edge of the kerb.'

Eyeing her bulging red panties as she sat with her chin resting on her knees, her tight short skirt having ridden up as she'd sat down, the Professor felt his penis stiffen, his full balls heave. Sitting opposite her, trying to conceal his rampant erection, he wondered where to begin the questioning. Ask her outright? he pondered. No, it was better to chat about the weather or some other mundane crap before launching into searching questions.

'Have you come?' he grinned. 'I mean, have you come far?'

'From London,' she replied, her succulent lips smiling.

'I couldn't live in London. The noise, the traffic . . . '

'I'm used to it. I grew up in London, I've lived there all my life.'

'Travelling all the way from London, you must have something very important to tell the Professor.'

'Yes, I have.'

'It's a shame he's away.'

'It must have been a last-minute decision to go on holiday because my boss told me that Professor Snide was at his castle yesterday.'

'Who's your boss?'

'I shouldn't really say anything, but . . . I work for Doctor Gender. He runs a research centre.'

'What does he research?' *Girlie cracks?*

'It's rather embarrassing, actually.'

'That's OK, I don't embarrass easily.'

'The research is to do with penis size and development.'

'Penis size and . . . What on earth does that have to do with the Professor?'

'Word has it that Professor Snide has developed a machine that increases the size of the male penis.'

'It could hardly increase the size of the *female* penis!'

'No, I suppose not.'

'It sounds interesting. Is that what you want to see him about?'

'Yes. Well, no. You see, the idea was that I should make an excuse to get into the castle and then try to get the plans for the machine.'

'Devilish, I must say. You have no qualms about lying, then?'

'I'm a natural-born liar.'

'That's amazing, so am I.'

'What a coincidence. Can you tell me anything about Professor Snide?'

'I've heard that he's an uncontrollable sex maniac.'

'My God!'

'His insatiable thirst for perverted sex rules his life. Does that excite you?'

'No, of course it doesn't.'

'I thought it might wet your knickers.'

'Wet my . . . That's disgusting!'

'I'm sorry. You see, I'm a sex maniac . . . I mean, a sexologist. I'm used to talking frankly to women about vaginal lubrication.'

'A sexologist? Oh, well, in that case . . . '

'My name's Roger, by the way.'

'I'm Sandy.'

'Sandy by name, randy by nature.'

'Pardon?'

'Nothing. I might be able to help you get my hands up your . . . get your hands on the plans for this machine.'

'Really?'

'I know the Professor's butler quite well. Well, not that well. In fact, only fairly well.'

'Are you feeling well?'

'Perfectly well. Well, fairly well. I could get you into the castle, but . . . '

'To be honest, I've made several terrible mistakes recently. I've lost the company a lot of money and my boss is on the verge of firing me. If I could get the plans . . . '

'I'd need something in return.'

'I'm that desperate, I'd do anything.'

Really? 'Take your knickers off.'

'What?'

'Take your knickers off.'

Her face flushing, her mouth hanging open, she was obviously stunned by his lewd request. But if she really was that desperate for the plans, she'd hoist her short skirt up and pull her knickers down. It wasn't much to ask, the Professor reflected. After all, he only wanted to look at her pussy. For starters, anyway!

As she stood up and lifted her skirt, the Professor grinned. Another conquest, he mused, eyeing again the triangular patch of her bulging red panties covering her full sex lips. It might be an idea to have her strip and then hide her clothes, he mused, his mind brimming with wicked ideas. She could hardly leave the woods naked, and she'd no doubt do anything and everything to get her clothes back.

'Take all your clothes off,' he instructed her.

'*All* my clothes? But you said . . . '

'I'm like the wind, I've changed my mind.'

'You can't go around asking women to strip.'

'Why not?'

'Well, it's unethical.'

'Sod ethics!'

'But . . . '

'I can get you the plans, Sandy. One word with the Professor's butler, and the plans will be yours.'

'What if someone comes?' she asked, her face turning crimson as she slipped her shoes off and unzipped her skirt.

'No one will come, we're safe enough here. There again, I might . . . '

'It won't end there, will it? I mean, once I'm naked you'll . . . '

'Your boss will be delighted if you return with the plans, Sandy. You'll be the flavour of the month, and the year.'

'I can't do it. I can't strip in front of a stranger.'

'It's entirely up to you. Start with your skirt and blouse and take it from there.'

Watching as she tugged her skirt down her long legs and unbuttoned her blouse, the Professor again wondered whether she was an agent. She might well strip naked in the line of duty, he ruminated as she slipped her blouse over her shoulders and stepped out of her skirt. She might even fuck in the line of duty!

But if she *was* an agent, she'd have known who he was – and she'd hardly have asked him for the plans. Perhaps she had some hare-brained scheme up her sleeve, he pondered – or up her skirt. The safest way to play it was to assume that she was an agent, he decided, his penis twitching as he gazed longingly at her bulging panties. Disregard her story about a research centre and treat her as if she was a government agent.

'You have a very nice body,' he remarked, focusing on her deep cleavage.

'May I dress now?' she asked, folding her arms over her firm breasts.

'You're not *un*dressed yet.'

'Please, I . . . '

'Tell me, are you married?'

'No, no, I'm not.'

'Boyfriend?'

'No, not at the moment.'

'You surprise me. An attractive young woman such as you, I'd have thought you'd have several men on the go.'

'About the plans . . . '

'Bra and panties, Sandy. You know it makes sense.'

Reaching behind her back, she unhooked her bra and peeled the silk cups away from her pert breasts. Her nipples elongating in the cool air of the woods, her areolae darkening, she gazed at the Professor. Her face flushed, embarrassment reflected in her blue eyes, a tear ran down her cheek. Was this part of her training? he wondered. Turning on the tears, looking for compassion . . . Yes, it was undoubtedly part of her training as an agent.

'You have very nice tits,' he remarked crudely, focusing on her brown milk teats.

'Please, don't be coarse.'

'I can't help it, it's in my nature. Right, let's have a look at your cunt slit.'

'Do you *have* to be so vulgar?'

'Yes, I do. Come on, I only want to see your fanny crack.'

'Please, I . . . '

'Pull your knickers down and open your cunt and show me your lust hole.'

'No, I'm not going to . . . '

'OK, no plans.'

Biting her lip, her long blonde hair cascading over her pretty face as she leaned forward, she eased her panties down her shapely thighs. Her pinken cunny slit barely concealed by her scanty blonde pubes, her inner labia protruding from her young sex valley, she really was ripe for a damned good fucking. But a little more humiliation was in order first, he mused. Degrade her in the extreme before forcing his horse-like penis deep into her tight cunt and spunking her cervix.

'Turn round and stand with your feet wide apart,' he ordered her as she stepped out of her panties. 'That's it, now bend over and touch your toes.'

'No, I'm not going to . . . '

'Do it, Sandy. If you want my help, you'll do exactly as I tell you.'

'But it's obscene.'

'You don't have to tell *me* that!'

His dark eyes wide as she hung her head and touched her toes, he gazed at her outer sex lips swelling alluringly below her beautifully rounded buttocks. Her pinken inner lips unfurling, he wondered whether the obscenity of her lewd act was turning her on. He very much doubted that she'd ever displayed her cunny crack like that before. But this was nothing!

'You have a very nice cunt,' he murmured. 'OK, reach behind your legs and pull your cunt lips apart.'

'No! What do you think I am?'

'Do it, Sandy!'

'I have never known anyone as crude as you!'

'Come to think of it, neither have I!' he laughed. 'OK, pull your cunt lips open and show me your sex hole.'

Her slender fingers tentatively creeping behind her firm thighs, she parted the swollen hillocks of her outer love lips just enough to expose her fleshy inner folds. 'Keep going,' the Professor murmured, kneeling behind her and focusing on the small bridge of skin running between her two lust ducts. Easing her sex lips further apart, exposing the glistening pink flesh surrounding her yawning vaginal mouth, she looked at the Professor between her legs.

She was no doubt wondering what he was going to do as he licked his lips and moved closer to her crudely bared sexual centre. But *he* knew only too well! Planting a kiss on her naked buttock, he ran his tongue over the smooth skin of her bottom orbs. 'No!' she cried as he licked the length of her anal crease, his tongue dangerously close to her exposed anal inlet. Ignoring her protests, he parted her buttocks and licked around the sensitive skin surrounding the secret portal to her rectal duct. Quivering as his tongue teased her delicate brown tissue, she made a futile attempt to pull away.

'Don't you like it?' he asked, grabbing her hips and pushing his mouth into her bottom crease.

'No! Please, I've done as you asked.'

'Has anyone ever licked your bumhole before?'

'No!'

Moving down her anal valley as she sobbed her protests, his tongue snaking around her crudely bared vaginal entrance, he tasted her flowing sex juices. She didn't move away as he thought she would when he drove his tongue deep into her drenched cunt. Although she wriggled and complained, she did nothing to halt the beautiful violation of her femininity.

'Open your cunt as far as you can,' he ordered her, lapping up the creamy juices flowing from her inner nectaries. Complying, she pulled her vaginal lips further apart, the pink flesh surrounding her cuntal entrance forming a cone, stretched to the limit. Eyeing her urethral opening, the stalactite-like remains of her hymen, he drove his tongue into her hot sex cavern again.

Sucking out her juices of arousal, his tongue snaking over the drenched inner walls of her young vagina, he pressed his thumb into the rosebud of her tight bottom-hole. 'No!' she screamed, making a suspiciously perfunctory effort to pull away as his thumb sank deeper into her hot anal duct. Squirming and gasping as he massaged her velveteen rectal flesh, her lust juices flowing in torrents from her open cunt, she whimpered as her arousal soared.

All women were basically sex-starved whores, Snide reflected. All it took was a tongue up their wet cunts and a thumb forced into their tight arseholes and they were writhing in ecstasy. But it was a shame that they had to be forced or blackmailed into enjoying sex. They loved having their cunts attended by tongues, their bottom-holes penetrated by thumbs, so why didn't they just open their legs and beg for sex? Women moved in mysterious ways, he reflected – as did Miss Hocks before her enforced transformation.

Sandy's naked body quivering uncontrollably, the Professor decided that the time had come to give her what she wanted, what all women craved – a tongue-induced orgasm. Moving down, his tongue sweeping over her solid clitoris, he knew she was succumbing to her carnal desires as she wailed her appreciation. Yanking her cunny lips further apart, her pinken flesh almost at tearing point, she blatantly offered her femininity in its entirety to the Professor.

'God, don't stop!' she screamed as her clitoris swelled and pulsated beneath his caressing tongue. At last, she'd reached the point of no return. It wasn't that women didn't enjoy crude sex, the problem was coercing them to pull their knickers down and taking them to the point of extreme arousal where they begged for it. Sobbing and protesting one minute, and then gasping in ecstasy? They certainly did move in mysterious ways!

Sinking his thumb deeper into her anal canal, he twisted his hand, pushing three fingers into her gaping cunt, delighting in her cries of pleasure as she neared her climax. Massaging her inner vaginal flesh, inducing her cunt milk to issue from her bloated sex canal, he felt his penis twitch and his knob swell. After a damned good multiple orgasm, he'd spunk up her cunt and then fuck her pretty mouth and then screw her tight arsehole and then . . .

'Coming!' she sang as her cunt poured out its creamy love juices. 'God, I'm . . . I'm coming!' Her naked body shaking violently as her orgasm erupted within her throbbing clitoris, she swivelled her hips, grinding her drenched vaginal flesh into the Professor's face as her cries of sexual satisfaction resounded throughout the woods.

Sustaining her orgasm with his sweeping tongue, his thrusting fingers and thumb, he decided that she'd endure a buttock-thrashing with a rough tree branch before he fucked her senseless. As she was undoubtedly an agent, she deserved a merciless thrashing – and an arse-sperming. There again, all young women deserved it!

'Oh, oh!' she whimpered as her orgasm rolled on, her sex juices pouring from her bloated cunt and running down the Professor's hand. 'Ah, I've never come so much in all my life!' she cried as her pleasure peaked, her naked body quivering like a leaf in the wind. Her fleshy love lips swelling, her sex folds turning ruby-red, her thighs twitching, she wailed as she rode the crest of her orgasm 'Please, don't stop!' she sang, her cunt spasming, gripping his thrusting fingers and spurting out more orgasmic cream.

Sucking on her clitoris, her wet fanny flesh pressed against his face, Snide mouthed and licked her pulsating nodule, sustaining her crude pleasure. Pressing his thumb deeper into her tightening anal sheath, he continued to lick and suck her swollen clitoris until her knees sagged and she crumpled to the ground.

His thumb still embedded deep in her anal canal, his fingers sucked into her inflamed cunt as she lay on her stomach writhing in the aftermath of her massive climax, he massaged the last ripples of sex from her inflamed lust holes. Gasping as he finally withdrew from her hot sheaths, she lay trembling on the ground, her long blonde hair dishevelled, matted with the perspiration of orgasm.

She was ready for a buttock-whipping, Snide mused, grabbing a gnarled branch bearing dozens of leaves. Her head turned away, her tousled hair veiling her face, she knew nothing of her impending thrashing as he knelt beside her and raised the branch above his head. Bringing it down across her pale buttocks with a loud swish, he grinned wickedly as her young body convulsed and her buttocks tensed.

'Argh! No!' she screamed as the branch struck her taut anal globes again. 'Please, no!'

'Yes!' he chuckled, sitting astride her back and pinning her down.

'Argh! God, no!'

306

'God, yes!'

Lashing her burning buttocks as she wriggled and squirmed beneath him, Snide watched the weals fan out across her reddening flesh, delighting in her plight as she begged pathetically for mercy. Her screams reverberating throughout the woods, the birds fluttering from the trees as he continued the cruel thrashing, her buttocks began to turn a fire-red.

'Please, no more!' she sobbed, trying to push the Professor off her back as the branch lashed her quivering bottom again.

'You'll soon come to like it!' he chuckled in his wickedness.

'No! I can't take any more!'

'Of course you can!'

The gnarled twigs of the branch biting into her burning flesh as he persisted with the cruel beating, the Professor decided that the time had come to pierce her tight bottom-hole with his massive penis. Giving her one last lash, her burning bottom globes twitching uncontrollably, he discarded the branch and climbed off her trembling body.

Tugging his solid cock out of his trousers as she lay sobbing on the ground, he knelt between her parted thighs with his bulbous knob hovering over her gaping anal crease. Oblivious to his obscene plan as he leaned forward, his swollen glans nearing the yawning entrance to her vaginal duct, she was about to haul her exhausted body up when he drove his weapon head deep into her sex-juice-flooded cunt.

'No!' she screamed as he completely impaled her on his granite-hard lust rod. 'God, no!'

'God, yes!' he laughed, withdrawing his well-juiced cock and driving into her spasming cunt again. 'Christ, you're so wet!'

'Please! Please let me go!'

'I haven't spunked you yet!'

'No, I don't want to be . . . '

'All women want to be spunked. What's the matter with you?'

'This is rape!'

'It's fucking beautiful!'

Gasping as he shafted her tight vaginal sheath, her naked body trembling, she began whimpering in her enforced pleasure. Once he'd screwed her to orgasm, he'd slip his cock out of her pussy and drive his knob deep into her bowels. She'd like that, he mused, battering her creamy-wet cervix with his bulbous glans. Well, *she* might not, but *he* would!

Crying out as her orgasm erupted within her throbbing clitoris, she begged for more. 'Harder! Faster!' she sang as he fucked her. 'God, I'm there!' Her swollen love lips gripping his glistening shaft as he repeatedly drove his cock into her quivering cunt, Snide felt the beginning of his own orgasm stirring. Slipping his cock out of her hot vagina, he pressed his cunny-wet knob against the brown tissue surrounding her anal entrance and thrust his hips forward.

'No!' she screamed as his knob drove past her defeated sphincter muscles and glided into her rectal duct. 'Please, not there!' Ignoring her sobs, he forced his erect penis into her tight anal tube, her brown ring gripping his wet shaft as he completely impaled her. Withdrawing, he thrust into her bottom again, her naked body shaking violently as the sensations of debauched sex permeated her inner core. Grabbing her hips and pulling her up until she was on her knees, he drove into her again and again, her naked body rocking as he arse-fucked her with a vengeance.

'Oh, God!' she whimpered, her head on the ground as he propelled his penis head deep into her bloated bowels. 'God, I've never . . . '

'Never had your arse fucked?' he chortled.

'Oh! Ah! Ah, it's . . . it's heavenly!'

'Here it comes!' he cried as his sperm coursed along his veined shaft. 'Ah! Here comes my spunk!'

His glans swelling, throbbing in orgasm, his sperm jetted from his slit, bathing the illicit coupling. On and on he thrust his cock deep into her arse, filling her hot bowels with his seed to the accompaniment of her cries of debased pleasure. All women should have their arses regularly fucked and spermed, he reflected, yanking her buttocks wide apart. All women should be mouth-fucked, cunt-fucked, arse-fucked, whipped and . . .

'Please, don't stop!' she screamed as her body rocked and her neglected clitoris pulsated in orgasm. 'God, I can feel your sperm inside me!'

'I'll give you another bottom-thrashing in a minute!' he gasped, the last of his spunk issuing from his orgasming knob.

'No!'

'Yes!'

Her naked body finally collapsing to the ground, she breathed heavily as the Professor lay on top of her with his cock embedded deep within her arsehole. Her anal ring gripping the base of his organ, her bowels bloated, she quivered as he gyrated his hips, massaging her inner flesh with his spunk-wet knob.

She was a right little beauty, he reflected as she let out long low moans of pleasure. But she was also an agent, and agents should be punished for their wickedness with a damned good bum-thrashing. And so should schoolgirlie netball players! His weight on his hands as his mind filled with highly illegal thoughts of perverted sex, he lifted his body to withdraw his spent cock.

'Fuck, it won't come out!' he breathed, recalling Lucifer's cock jammed up Kirsty's bum.

'Ouch!' she cried as he lifted his body again, the vacuum building within her rectal sheath. 'Please, take it out!'

'I can't! The bloody thing's stuck!'

'Argh! You must take it out!'

'Fuck me, I know that!'

'Quickly!'

'I'm doing my best!'

'God, it feels as if my insides are being sucked out!'

Again and again he tried to slide his cock out of her anal tube, but his stubborn organ remained lodged firmly up her tight bum. This was all he needed, he reflected as he stilled his body and listened to twigs snapping underfoot. To be caught with his cock up a girl's sperm-brimming arse wasn't exactly what he'd planned!

'Let's go this way!' a young girl squealed.

'Ooh! I just love eating my packed lunch in the woods!' another cried.

'Fuck me!' Snide gasped as their voices grew louder.

'For Christ's sake, pull it out!' Sandy gasped.

'Come on, I think there's a clearing over here!' one of the young girls called excitedly. 'I hope Miss Turnpike doesn't catch us. You know how cross she gets when we sneak out of school at lunch time.'

'Fuck and quadruple fuck!'

Chapter Thirteen

'Where have you been, sir?' Lucifer asked as the Professor staggered into the castle at three in the afternoon. 'We've been looking everywhere for you.'

'I had a spot of bother in the woods. To be exact, I had a fucking great problem with a young woman and two virginal . . . I won't go into that. Suffice to say that I've committed a highly illegal act which is probably punishable by death, or worse.'

'Goodness me!'

'My sentiments entirely. What's been happening in my absence?'

'*Everything!* DI Peel was here mumbling about aliens and nuns' habits and the local amateur theatrical society. He was also complaining about missing nuns, raiding the nunnery, the church suing him for raping the Reverend Mother . . . '

'Oh, God!'

'A man calling himself Mr Brass called. He was a bit of an anorak type, kept going on about arses and aliens.'

'Christ!'

'And then that man from the village came storming into the castle.'

'What man?'

'Clarissa's father.'

'Shit!'

'It seems that he's going to take the law into his own hands and deal with you himself, whatever that means.'

'Double shit!'

'Jack came here looking for you.'

'Jack?'

'Lydia's . . . '

'Bollocks, what did he want?'

'Something about you having destroyed his libido, sir. He's going to sue.'

'Fuck! I hope you've no more bad news for me.'

'I'm afraid I have. Gretel rang.'

'Oh?'

'She said something about you having duped her and your life won't be worth living.'

'Cunts! Anything else?'

'She said that she'd have your bollocks for breakfast, stuff your cock up your arsehole, and . . . '

'Anything else apart from that?'

'There's one last thing, sir.'

'Go on.'

'Major Dastardly-Williams rang. He asked me to tell you that the SAS are on their way to destroy the castle.'

'Fuck me!'

'Is that legal, sir?'

'No, it's bloody not! How are the girlies?'

'Hot, tight, wet . . . '

'Have you . . . '

'Er . . . I took the liberty of keeping them on the boil, so to speak.'

'You fucked them?'

'Well, I kept them well-creamed.'

'You fucked them?'

'I sort of . . . '

'Lucifer!'

'Yes, sir – I did fuck them.'

'Bastard!'

'I'm sorry, sir. I just thought that they might dry up if they were neglected.'

'Dry up, indeed!'

'There is *some* good news. Several young couples have called in response to the advert.'

'Ah, that's more like it!'

'I've devised a booking system for the clients. The first woman's due to arrive for treatment at eleven tomorrow morning.'

'Excellent! Where's the Baron?'

'In the lab, sir.'

'Right, I'd better go and see how he's getting on. The girls must be severely punished for allowing you to fuck them. Bring them down to the rack chamber, one at a time, and I'll give them the buttock-whipping and tit-thrashing of their young lives.'

'Any preference as to which girlie should be punished first?'

'Yes, Miss Hocks will do for starters.'

'Yes, sir.'

Bounding down to the lab as Lucifer went to grab Miss Hocks, the Professor pondered on the problems. By installing the alpha-wave machine atop the turret, he could fend off any would-be attackers, but for how long? He could easily turn the second wave of SAS men into nancies or sex-crazed perverts, but the day would surely come when he would lose the battle. The government were another major worry. Even if they got their hands on the lookalike machine, they'd soon realize what had happened and come back for the real device.

'I told Lucifer to hide this!' the Professor said angrily, gazing at the alpha-wave machine as he leaped down the steps to the lab.

'That's the fake, my friend,' the Baron smiled proudly. 'The real machine's hidden in the secret tunnel.'

'That's amazing! It certainly had *me* fooled!'

'Apart from looking like the real machine, it works – to an extent.'

'To an extent?'

'It lights up and buzzes and . . . Well, to all outward intents and purposes, it's just like the real thing.'

'Excellent!'

'I'm going to put it on the table by the doors: it's the ideal place for a thief to find it. I've also constructed another machine based on your gamma-ray box. It's over there, on the bench.'

'What does it do?' Snide frowned, gazing at the box.

'I've not tested it yet but . . . It's a sex-change machine.'

'*What?*'

'By recording the physical make-up of a female, the molecular structure can be induced into the male body and . . . '

'It'll turn a man into a woman?'

'If it works, yes.'

'Jesus F. Christ!'

'Hopefully, it will also work in reverse.'

'Fuck me! Bloody hell, that's brilliant! We must test it thirdwith.'

'Indeed, we must. I thought we might use your butler as a guinea pig.'

'Turn him into a woman?'

'Why not?'

'That's a thought. Christ, we could fuck him . . . her.'

'It might be dangerous, my friend. Changing the molecular structure of his physical body will transform him into a woman but, mentally, he might still be a man.'

'Should that turn out to be the case, we'll use the alpha-wave machine to turn him into a sex-crazed nympho.'

'Yes, I had thought of that, but . . . '

'No buts! He's bringing Miss Hocks down for a naked buttock-whipping and tit-thrashing. We'll sit her on the stool and record her feminine molecular structure and . . . '

'There's no need for a helmet, my friend. All I have to do is point this transducer at her, and her molecular structure will be recorded.'

'So, you then point the thing at Lucifer and . . . '

'Exactly. But there might be other problems . . . '

'Fuck other problems, just do it.'

As Lucifer descended the stone steps with Miss Hocks in all her naked glory, Snide rubbed his hands together gleefully. If the Baron's machine worked, DI Peel could be turned into a woman. The SAS could be turned into women and . . . *Better still, I could turn myself into a woman with a real cunny and tits!* Pondering on the fun he could have as the Baron discreetly aimed the transducer at Miss Hocks and recorded her molecular structure, the Professor noticed his butler climbing the steps.

'Er . . . Hang on, Lucifer. I might be needing you,' he said, winking at the Baron. 'Miss Hocks, would you wait in the rack chamber?'

'Only if you fuck my arse and cream my bowels,' the woman grinned, provocatively licking her succulent lips.

'Of course I will! I'll be with you shortly. On second thoughts, I'll be with you sooner than that. Sooner than you think, or I think.'

'Just be quick!' she said huskily, running her hands over her rounded breasts and tweaking her erect nipples.

Closing and locking the door as she slipped into the chamber, Snide turned as the Baron aimed the device at Lucifer. Would the butler instantly sprout tits and a fanny? he pondered. Would he look like Miss Hocks? If something went wrong, he might become asexual! What if the molecules became mixed up and he ended up with his face between his legs and a pussy on his head? *The true definition of a cunt-head!* the Professor laughed inwardly as the Baron flicked the switch.

Instantly becoming a clone of Miss Hocks with well-rounded breasts billowing his shirt, the butler looked about the lab. It seemed to have worked, but there were tests to be carried out, Snide mused. A damned good fanny-fucking was the finest test of all! And a clit-licking and an arse-knobbing and . . .

'Er . . . Miss Hocks,' the Professor said, smiling at his butler. 'In the name of devilish science, would you please remove all your clothes?'

'I can't think why I'm dressed as a man,' the clone frowned, unbuttoning her shirt and tugging her trousers down her shapely legs.

'My God!' the Baron gasped as her full breasts and perfectly formed vaginal slit came into view. 'You know what this means, my friend?'

'Your machine works.'

'Yes, but the potential! For example, when DI Peel is here we'll make sure that the real Miss Hocks is with him all the time, not once out of his sight. Meanwhile, the other Miss Hocks slips into the village and robs the bank.'

'Ah, so Miss Hocks is banged up for robbery and the other one isn't.'

'No, no. Neither woman will be done for robbery because the Inspector will be a witness to the fact that she was here all the time.'

'So, not knowing that there are two, he'll think . . . '

'Exactly!'

'I have a better idea!' Snide laughed. 'Turn me into a woman, and I'll find out what it's like to be fucked rotten by a bloody great cock.'

'Later, my friend. Before we do anything, we must examine our creation.'

Scrutinizing the woman's body as she kicked her trousers aside, the Professor knelt before her and instructed her to part her full pussy lips. Complying, she pulled her fleshy folds apart, revealing her ripe clitoris, the wet entrance to her sex duct. Her fanny was perfect, he observed. But, with two identical women milling around the castle, there might be grave problems.

'Security,' he murmured, looking up at the Baron.

'Security?'

'If anyone discovers what we've done, the whole thing will be blown sky-high. Reverse the process and bring Lucifer back. When we need a second Miss Hocks, we'll use the machine again.'

'Good idea,' the Baron replied, flicking the switch.

'Will that be all, sir?' Lucifer asked. 'Oh! Er . . . I seem to be naked!' he gasped, looking down at his limp cock snaking over his hairy balls. 'I do apologize, sir. Er . . . Where are my clothes?'

'Worry not, Lucifer!' the Baron laughed. 'We used hypnosis to play a little trick on you.'

'It wasn't hypnosis,' the Professor corrected his friend. 'It was . . . '

'Hypnosis,' the Baron repeated, winking at Snide.

'Ah, yes – that's what is was.'

'Oh, I see,' Lucifer murmured, obviously perplexed.

'Dress, Lucifer, and then go about your duties,' the Professor said, grinning as he eyed the man's limp cock.

This was incredible, Snide pondered as the butler dressed. But things were getting out of hand. What with his living quarters full of naked women, Gretel on her way back to have his bollocks for breakfast and shove his cock up his arse, Major Dastardly-Williams sending the SAS in to destroy the castle, DI Peel investigating aliens and nuns' habits, Mr Brass from ARSE on the loose, Clarissa's father on the rampage,

Jack searching for his lost libido . . . Again, he realized that he had to make concrete plans for the future, decide on what he wanted, long-term, and go for it.

'Baron, I've been thinking,' he said, formulating an evil plan in his wicked mind as Lucifer finished dressing and climbed the steps. 'Is it possible to surround the castle with a force field?'

'What sort of force field?'

'Is it possible to modify your machine and surround the castle with a force field that would affect anyone approaching, instantly changing their sex?'

'I don't see why not, my friend. I'll get to work on it straightaway.'

'Good, good. In the meantime, I'll give Miss Hocks the buttock-whipping and tit-thrashing of her life. Er . . . Ignore any screams you might hear coming from the rack chamber.'

'Of course.'

'I'll see you later, much later. In fact, I might never . . . Sorry, I slipped into bollock mode again.'

'Excuse me, sir,' Lucifer said, standing at the top of the steps. 'There's someone here to see you.'

'Who's someone?'

'Somebody.'

'Someone or somebody?'

'Both, I suppose.'

'Fuck it! Just as I was about to sexually abuse Miss Hocks!'

Pushing past the butler and making his way to the doors, Snide decided that he'd had enough of the continual interruptions. Mobile hairdressers, policemen, nuns, Germans, women stopping him in the street . . . Nothing but interruptions, he reflected angrily. Whoever this was would have their balls ripped off, or their tits – or both! *Concrete plans*, he again mused as he reached the doors. The time had definitely come to decide what he wanted, and then go for it.

'Yes?' he asked, opening the doors to an elderly lady dressed in a shawl and headscarf. 'What the hell do you want?'

'Like a juicy red apple, deary?' she grinned, clutching the fruit in her wizened hand.

'I'd like a juicy . . .'

'Go on, take a bite,' she said, offering him the apple.

'I'm not hungry.'

'Have it later, deary.'

'I intend to!' he chuckled, taking the apple. 'Now get out of here and leave me in peace.'

'You'll be in peace all right!' she chortled as she scurried away.

Fuck off!

Closing the doors, Snide gazed at the apple, wondering why the old bat had bothered to walk all the way up to the castle to give him the fruit. 'Senile old hag,' he breathed, placing the apple on the hall table as someone hammered on the doors.

'Now what do you want?' he asked, yanking the doors open. 'I told you to go away and . . . Oh, Inspector Peel. How awful . . . how lovely to see you.'

'Likewise, I'm sure, Professor. May I come in?'

'Come where you like, in or out.'

'Pardon?'

'Come in, come in.'

Closing the doors as the sleuth entered the castle, Snide turned and gazed at the man. *Concrete plans?* How could he make plans, concrete or otherwise, with the Inspector regularly visiting the castle? If the man had his daughter back, he might keep away for a while, but he'd soon return complaining about nuns' habits and aliens.

'I have some grave news,' Peel began.

'The graveyard hasn't been attacked by aliens, has it?'

'The graveyard? No, no, I have some grave news – some bad news.'

'Oh, that's a relief.'

'It would seem that the SAS are on their way to destroy your castle.'

'How do you know this? How did you come across this delicate and no doubt highly secret information?'

'I've been doing some digging around.'

'Intriguing.'

'I've been left in the dark for too long, Professor – and I don't like it.'

'Your fear of the dark probably stems from a dreadful childhood experience.'

'I don't mean I'm frightened of the dark. My superiors have told me virtually nothing about the government's involvement with you and your castle. There have been so-called alien attacks, my daughter's been abducted, and there are the nuns who . . . As I said, I've done some digging around.'

'And?'

'There *are* no aliens, Professor.'

'That's good news.'

'The Reverend Mother Horgasm is as honest as the day is long, a perfectly normal human being – and the nunnery is nothing more than a nunnery.'

'I'm so pleased.'

'I'm not. After I stripped her and checked her for two bottom-holes, two vaginal canals and no clitoris, she's suing me for rape.'

'Oh, that *is* bad news.'

'Indeed it is. You've been lying to me all along, Professor. Anyway, I don't see why you're pleased. The SAS are on their way to . . .'

'Yes, so you said.'

'You don't mind? Your castle is about to be wiped off the map and you . . . '

'No one's wiping anything off the map, Inspector.'

'I know about your plans, Professor.'

'I have no plans.'

'No? What about surrounding the castle with a force field?'

'Er . . . What are you talking about?'

'There's a mole, Professor – I know everything.'

'A mole?'

'Yes, a mole.'

'In that case, you'll know where your daughter is.'

'I haven't discovered my daughter's whereabouts, as yet. But I *do* know that the missing nuns are here, and three agents posing as mobile hairdressers and another posing as a schoolgirl and . . . '

'I don't know who this mole is, but they've been leading you down the garden path, Inspector.'

'I think not. Obviously, I can't reveal the mole's identity, but I trust him or her implicitly.'

'Don't you know the mole's sex?'

'Of course I do. So, the tables have turned, Professor. I suggest you return my daughter, release the nuns and agents, and . . . '

'Inspector, let me tell you something,' Snide said, placing his hand on the man's shoulder and leading him into the banqueting hall.

This was quite a predicament, he mused as Peel gazed at the double-bum-fucking chair. *A mole?* Miss Hocks was clean, he reflected – although extremely dirty sexually speaking! It had to be one of the girlies: the only two men were Lucifer and the Baron and they were OK. But all the girls had been transformed into rampant tarts, they'd hardly be feeding the Inspector information. And besides, Peel would have known about his daughter had there been a mole in the castle. *Where's Penny got to?* he wondered, facing Peel.

'There *is* no mole,' Snide smiled.

'Oh, yes, there is. How else would I know about the force field?'

'I'm going to tell you something of a highly secret nature, Inspector,' Snide said mysteriously. 'Your digging around has obviously revealed some information, but only a little. I shouldn't say anything, but . . . I'm working for MI5.'

'*You?* You're working for MI5?'

'Yes. You've stumbled across something big, bigger than the both of us.'

'I haven't fallen over.'

'Stumbled across, as in discovered. We're working on an international . . . No, I can't reveal such sensitive information. But I'll tell you this – unless you stop interfering, you might find yourself disappearing without a trace.'

'But . . . '

'Even your Superintendent knows nothing about our activities. The castle is our headquarters and . . . The alien scam, the Reverend Mother being a Martian, the nunnery being the HQ . . . It was all designed to put you off the scent, Inspector. To be honest, the problems you've caused MI5 have been horrendous. Tell me, how did you know about the force field?'

'I sneaked into the castle and overheard you talking about it.'

'I must tighten up security.'

'The doors were open so I just walked in.'

'I see. Right, I'll have to report this to my superiors. I suggest that you go about your normal duties in the village and keep well away from the castle.'

'Yes, I will. But . . . '

'There are no buts, Inspector.'

'But, my daughter . . . '

'We're doing our best to get her back. She was taken hostage by . . . As I said, we're doing our best.'

'My God, I didn't realize that . . . '

'No, obviously not. Say nothing to your Superintendent. If he asks you to investigate me or the castle, pretend to go along with it. Report back to him as usual and tell him that you've searched the castle and questioned me and that everything's OK.'

'Right, will do. I suppose your story about the local amateur theatrical society was another ploy?'

'Was it?'

'There is no such local society.'

'Ah, yes. Er . . . This is a big one, Inspector. So big that . . . I've said enough as it is. Right, you'd better get back.'

'Yes, I will. And thank you for enlightening me, Professor.'

'I had no choice. Right, off you go.'

Rubbing his hands together as the sleuth left the castle, Snide punched the air with his fist. 'That's the best scam yet!' he chuckled. But he knew that his scams only served to keep Peel away for a while. The time would come, yet again, when the man returned with his accusations and allegations. There was only one way to deal with not only the Inspector but all the interfering bastards – and that was by using the machine.

'What's my ultimate aim?' Snide murmured, gazing at the shattered windows in the banqueting hall. *Sex? Money? Sex and money?* There were too many people involved. The Baron seemed to have installed himself permanently in the castle. Not that the Professor minded, but he did like his privacy now and then. The renegade nuns had moved in and taken up residence, as had Miss Hocks and the girlies. Although they were the harem, offering sex as and when Snide wanted it, it would be costly to feed and keep them.

Apart from the residents, too many people knew about the

machine. *Perhaps the Baron's advert wasn't such a good idea,* he reflected, recalling Lucifer's booking system for the clients. With a continual flow of couples visiting the castle, not to mention agents, the place would end up like Piccadilly Circus! 'A concrete plan,' he again pondered as the phone rang. 'It's time I had *that* bloody thing ripped out!'

'Yes!' he bellowed as he grabbed the receiver.

'Sexton, it's me.'

'Spaz, how are you?'

'Fine, fine. Listen, my au pair eventually turned up.'

'Oh, good.'

'Apparently, she'd been sleeping in the forest.'

'Sleeping in the forest?'

'With a man she's taken up with – a Mr Potter. Anyway, what with pillow talk and all that bollocks, she discovered one or two interesting things.'

'Such as?'

'Potter had been sent to your place to . . .'

'Yes, I had my butler attack him in the forest, chop his bollocks off and leave him tied to a tree.'

'According to Helga, he still has his bollocks. But that's beside the point. He told her that he was sent to your place to take you off somewhere, the idea being that you'd never be seen again.'

'He sounds like a nice chap. What else have you found out?'

'I don't know what the fuck's been going on at your castle but, from what I overheard when he was fucking Helga in the toilet earlier, he's a double agent.'

'Go on.'

'He's working for the Germans *and* the British government. Is this making any sense to you, Sexton?'

'All the sense in the world! Where is he now?'

'He's staying here, at my place.'

'Kill him.'

'What?'

'Kill him, bump him off, do away with him, brown bread . . . '

'Hang on, hang on. Before I go murdering anyone, what's all this about? What's the SP?'

'It's a long story, Spaz. Basically, I've invented a machine – and everyone's after it.'

'Fuck me, it must be some machine!'

'It is, believe me.'

'Whatever this machine does, Potter wants it – and he wants it bad. He told Helga to visit you and steal the machine.'

'Thanks for the tip-off, Spaz.'

'She left some time ago, she'll be there shortly.'

'Fuck, as soon as that?'

'Fuck her when you like.'

'I will, Spaz – I will! OK, I must dash.'

Banging the phone down, Snide rubbed his chin and paced the floor. 'I must stop rubbing my chin and pacing the floor,' he murmured, wondering when Helga would arrive. If he gave her the opportunity to steal the lookalike machine, the Germans would keep away for a while. But, again, the plan would only serve as a short-term solution – the Germans returning as soon as they discovered that they'd been duped.

'Talking of being duped, Gretel's after my bollocks,' he breathed.

'Lucky old you,' Sister Elizabeth smiled as she entered the hall in all her naked glory.

'Ah, Sister – how are you? How are your juicy bits?'

'Professor, the girls and I have been talking and . . . Well, we're not getting enough sex.'

'What with all the problems, neither am I!'

'We need a man, several men.'

'Several men? Look, I can't think about this now. Just hang on for a while, be patient and bear with me.'

'That's exactly what we want.'

'What is?'

'You bare, naked, denuded, starkers . . . '

'You'll have all the sex you want once I've sorted out one or two problems, I promise you.'

'All right, we'll give you twenty-four hours to get your act together – and your cock.'

'OK, OK. Go and give the girlies a good licking out to keep them quiet for a while.'

'All right, but you only have twenty-four hours.'

More bloody problems! Snide mused as the girl wandered off, her rounded buttocks inviting a thrashing. Deciding to instruct Lucifer to chain the girls in the dungeon in case they took a trip to the village in search of cocks, he cringed as the doorbell rang. This was Helga, he knew as he walked across the hall – Helga the terrible. She needed a damned good tit-whipping, he reflected – and a buttock-thrashing and . . . No, it was best to play along with her, give her the opportunity to steal the lookalike machine.

'Ah, Helga!' he beamed as he opened the doors. 'It's nice to pee you . . . to see you.'

'It will be nice to see yours also as well,' she smiled, stepping into the castle.

'I'm sure it will!'

'I am visiting you, Professor.'

'Yes, I can see that.'

'I am soon to return to my own country.'

'That'll be nice for you.'

'It will being very nice.'

'Where have you been, Helga? Professor Spasm told me that you'd disappeared.'

'I was coming in the forest.'

'How nice for you.'

'May I be seeing your equipment?'

'Of course!' he sniggered, unzipping his trousers and hauling his penis out.

'Not that!' she shrieked.

'Don't you like it?'

'I am not liking horses, I am liking your machine.'

'Ah, the alpha-wave transference machine,' he grinned, concealing his stiffening penis and zipping his trousers.

'Yes, that is the one. I am taking a grave interest in your machine. I am liking to examine it.'

'There are one or two things I'd like to examine, Helga – namely your sweet pussy and . . . '

'My pussy is no more being examined!'

'No pussy examining, no machine examining. The choice is yours, my little beauty.'

'You'll have me . . . How do you say? You'll have me over a barrel.'

'Indeed I will! I'll tell you what, come and take a look at my new chair.'

'A chair?'

'Yes, it's a special chair. Come on, it's in the banqueting hall.'

'I am not wanting to see a chair, Professor.'

'Of course you are.'

Before she made her escape with the fake machine, she was to endure a damned good bum-fucking, Snide decided, leading the young girl into the hall. A cucumber shoved up her tight anal duct was in order, and then a tit-whipping and a bloody good buttock-thrashing and . . . Working for that bastard-face Potter, the double-crossing bitch was going to pay dearly!

'This is not a chair,' Helga said, frowning at the contraption.

'It's a special chair designed to relax the body,' the Professor smiled, taking her hand. 'Give it a try. Sit down and recline and you'll see how relaxing it is.'

'I am not wanting relaxing.'

'Of course you are.'

'This is a trick, Professor. You are not wanting to examine my pussy, I am knowing that you are wanting to look up my holes.'

'This has nothing to do with your holes, you silly girl!' he chuckled, forcing her to sit on the chair. 'That's it, now recline and relax.'

'But I am going downside up!'

'Upside down, Helga. You really must practise your English.'

Grabbing her feet, Snide raised and parted her legs, clamping her ankles in the stirrups before she realized what he was up to. Gazing at the swell of her red silk panties as he yanked her skirt up over her stomach, he felt his penis stiffen in readiness for the inevitable fucking. *Anal or vaginal?* he pondered, eyeing her girlie crack clearly outlined by the tight material of her panties. *Both!*

Struggling as he pulled her damp panties to one side, revealing her yawning pussy crack, she protested wildly as he slipped his finger between her soft pinken folds and drove it deep into her hot cunt. Her feet in the stirrups, her thighs wide, there was no way she could save herself as he tore her panties away from her sex slit and tossed the garment to the floor.

'Let me go!' she screamed as he slipped a second finger into her creamy vaginal sheath.

'No pussy-fingering, no machine examining!' he laughed, parting her fleshy outer lips with his free hand.

'I am not wanting pussy-fingering!'

'No, but I am!' he chortled, whipping his massive penis out of his trousers.

328

Massaging her inner sex flesh with his fingers, inducing her cunt milk to flow in torrents, he knew she was ripe for a fucking as her vaginal muscles spasmed and tightened. Slipping his fingers out of her well-juiced sex duct, he positioned his bulbous glans between her gaping inner love lips, grinning as she squirmed and spat expletives.

'Let the fucking commence!' he cried, forcing his solid member deep into her tight lust sheath. 'Ah! Hot, tight, wet, juicy, creamy . . . God, how I've missed your beautiful cunt!'

'No! You are being too big!'

'And you are being bloody tight!'

Watching her wet inner lips dragging along his glistening shaft as he withdrew his cock, he drove into her again, jolting her young body. Withdrawing his rock-hard member until her pink petals lovingly hugged his swollen knob, he again propelled his weapon head deep into her tight sheath. Stretching her fleshy outer lips apart, he focused on her ripening clitoris. Wondering when she'd last enjoyed a massive orgasm as her sex nodule visibly swelled and her juices of arousal trickled over his swinging balls, he wondered how many times she could come.

A contest might be fun, he mused, increasing his rhythm as she began shuddering and gasping. Use the King Dong vibrator on each girl's clitoris in turn and count their orgasms, the winner to enjoy a double mouth-fucking terminating in a double throat-spunking. This was what life was all about, he reflected, his massive organ pistoning her squelching vaginal tube. Entrapping young girls and fucking their beautiful cunts and mouths and bottom-holes . . . This was his goal.

'I am going!' Helga cried as her cunt tightened around his pistoning cock. 'Oh! Oh, I am going!'

'You're not going until you've come!' he laughed, his

heavy balls slapping her tensed buttocks as he repeatedly rammed his throbbing knob into her tight sex duct.

'I am going before I come!'

'You might not know whether you're coming or going, but I'm coming!'

His spunk coursing along his twitching shaft and jetting from his knob-slit, again and again he propelled his cock into her spasming vaginal sheath. Reaching her own climax, Helga whimpered as her womb contracted and her young body shook violently. Her cunt milk spewing from her bloated sex hole as her orgasm peaked, she tossed her head from side to side, crying out in her debauchery as her brimming cunt overflowed with the blend of sperm and girlie-come.

Perverted sex, money, debauched sex, more money and more sex . . . *That* was the concrete plan, the Professor reflected as he battered the girl's creamy cervix with his bulbous knob. To eat, drink and sleep vile sex was his aim – and no one was going to get in his way. DI Peel, the SAS, the so-called Germans . . . No one was going to halt the debauchery.

'Oh, my pussy!' Helga gasped as her second climax erupted within her pulsating clitoris. 'I am going again!'

'A permanent erection,' Snide thought aloud as the last of his spunk jetted from his orgasming glans, bathing the illicit union.

'I am going again, do me harder!'

'I'll do your bum in a minute!' he chortled, massaging her erect clitoris with his fingertips. 'And your mouth and your tittie cleavage!'

Finally withdrawing his spent member as Helga shuddered in the last ripples of her orgasm, the Professor sat back on his heels, gazing at the creamy liquid oozing from the girl's inflamed lust hole. Eyeing the delicate brown tissue surrounding the portal to her rectal duct, he again pondered on a permanent erection. Imagining fucking twenty girls one after the other, and then fucking them again, he grinned as his cock restiffened and his mind swirled with thoughts of highly illegal acts.

'Here we go again!' he cried, parting Helga's buttocks and pressing his spermed knob against her anal iris.

'No, you must not do me there!' she protested as his glans stretched her brown tissue open and slipped into the welcoming heat of her anal sheath. 'Please, you must not . . . '

'Yes!'

'No!'

Driving his solid cock deep into her tight rectal passage as she wiggled and squirmed, he forced three fingers into her drenched cunt. Massaging her solid clitoris with his free hand, taking her to another enforced orgasm, he looked at her pretty face. Her cheeks flushed, her mouth open, her nostrils flaring, he knew she was enjoying every minute of the debauchery. All females, young and old, enjoyed a damned good session of rampant sexual abuse, he reflected as he fucked her arsehole. And a naked-buttock-thrashing and a tit-whipping and . . .

'That's not fair!' Elizabeth cried as she entered the banqueting hall and gazed at the lewd scene. 'I didn't give you twenty-four hours to fuck *her*!'

'I'll fuck who I like!' Snide chuckled, gazing at the naked nun.

'In that case, so will I!'

Standing with her thighs either side of Helga's head, Elizabeth bent her knees, her open cunt slit settling over the girl's gasping mouth. Gyrating her hips, sliding her yawning cunny crack back and forth over Helga's face, she began gasping in her lewd act. This was more like it, Snide mused, his wide eyes transfixed on the cunny juice running down the au pair's flushed face. A cock up her arse, fingers up her cunt, and a fanny forced over her mouth . . . This was what perverted sex was all about!

'No!' Helga finally managed to scream through a mouthful of juicy cunny flesh.

'Yes!' the Professor chuckled, driving his knob deep into her hot bowels.

'Ah, yes!' Elizabeth gasped as her clitoris swelled and pulsated within Helga's wet mouth.

'My God!' the Reverend Mother Horgasm cried as she entered the hall.

Ignoring the woman as she ranted and raved, Snide continued fucking Helga's tight bottom sheath, his second coming nearing as his swollen knob massaged the girl's inner anal flesh. As Elizabeth cried out in the grips of her orgasm, the Reverend Mother fainted, her habit concealing her ample body as she collapsed to the floor in a heap. That would keep the old hag quiet for a while, Snide chuckled inwardly as his spunk shot from his throbbing knob, lubricating his pistoning shaft.

'Tongue my cunt!' Elizabeth gasped. 'Tongue-fuck my cunt!'

'Christ, you're wet!' Snide breathed, eyeing the nun's cunny juices streaming down Helga's grimacing face. 'I'll drink your cunt milk when I've spunked her arse.'

'No, *she* must drink it.'

'I must not!' Helga protested as Elizabeth's gaping cuntal valley momentarily left her mouth. 'I must not be drinking . . .'

'That's it, force your cunt over her mouth to shut her up!' Snide grinned as Elizabeth's gaping vaginal crack silenced the au pair.

Finishing his anal fucking, the last of his spunk oozing from his swollen knob, the Professor dragged his deflating penis out of the girl's well-spermed rectal sheath and slipped his fingers out of her burning vagina. Watching Elizabeth rock her hips, her swollen clitoris gliding over Helga's gasping mouth as she sustained her climax, he pondered on the Reverend Mother. *The doors must have been left open*, he mused, wondering what to do with the interfering woman when she came round.

'God, my cunt!' Elizabeth shrieked as her orgasm peaked, her lust juices spewing from her vaginal opening and drenching Helga's face. Rolling his foreskin back and forth over his silky-smooth glans, the Professor pondered on giving Elizabeth a bloody good anal rogering. She was certainly in the mood for a rectal fucking, but he'd not finished with Helga yet. The girl was to endure the anal speculum before she escaped from the castle with the fake machine.

'I'll teach her to side with Potter,' he murmured, rising to his feet and making his way to the lab as Elizabeth wailed her appreciation for the au pair's gobbling mouth. Deciding as he bounded down the stone steps, to stick the vaginal speculum up the au pair's bum and stretch her rectal duct to at least four inches in diameter, he asked the Baron how he was doing.

'Very well, my friend,' the man grinned. 'The force-field machine is almost ready for testing.'

'Excellent! When will it be ready for testing?'

'Soon.'

'As soon as that?'

'Indeed. But I have to warn you that there are dangers involved.'

'Dangers?'

'Transforming men into females is all very well, but . . . '

'Let's not talk about dangers, Baron.'

'Why not?'

'It's boring. I suggest we talk about perverted sex and

dripping cunt holes and pulsating clitorises and spunking knobs and . . . '

'There are other things in life,' the Baron murmured, adjusting the machine with a screwdriver.

'Yes, you're right. There are tight bumholes and erect nipples and schoolgirlie spanking and creamed knickers and . . . '

'OK, I'm ready for testing.'

'You want me to test you?'

'No, the *machine*'s ready. I'll take it up to the turret and try it out on a passer-by.'

'It might be an idea to test it on someone walking past the castle.'

'Good idea. I'll see you later.'

'Much later, Baron. In fact . . . Shit, there I go again!'

As the Baron lugged the machine up the steps, Snide grabbed the vaginal speculum from the bench and slipped it into his pocket. Pondering on stretching Helga's bottom-hole wide open with the device, he rubbed his chin as another wicked idea came to mind. *Three cocks up one bumhole?* Nothing was impossible! he reflected. With the butler beneath the girl and the Baron on top, their cocks embedded in her anal canal, he could then slip his horse-like cock between the Baron's legs and shove it right up her bum. *A three cock bum fuck!* 'First things first,' he murmured, picturing Helga's anal portal stretched open by the speculum, her inner flesh exposed.

Looking around the lab for his King Dong vibrator as Elizabeth's cries of sexual ecstasy resounded around the castle, he felt his massive penis stiffen again. Another anal fucking was in order to lubricate the au pair's bum sheath with spunk before using the speculum. Elizabeth's anal ring could do with a damned good stretching, he ruminated as she cried out in sexual ecstasy again. And then Helga would have

334

her clitty vibrated to orgasm and then Elizabeth would have her anal duct vibrated and then . . .

'Right!' he beamed, grabbing the vibrator and bounding up the stone steps. 'Sexual abuse, here I come!' Making his way through the corridor, he dashed to the banqueting hall, his cock now solid within his trousers, his heavy balls rolling. Entering the hall, he tugged his zip down and dragged out his erect member.

'OK, I'm going to . . . ' Gazing in astonishment at the empty double-bum-fucking chair, he looked around the hall. 'Where the hell are they?' he breathed, zipping his trousers and placing the vibrator on the table. Scratching his head, he went to his living quarters, wondering whether the nun had taken Helga there for the other girlies to finger-fuck and tongue to orgasm. 'I don't believe it!' he gasped, gazing around the lounge. 'Where *are* they?'

Searching the castle for his harem, he finally made his way up to the windswept turret to find the Baron. This was crazy! he thought, noticing the machine lying on the flagstones. 'Baron, where are you?' Doing his best not to rub his chin again, he checked the gunpowder room before returning to the banqueting hall.

Something was afoot, he knew as he called out for Lucifer. Had the real Germans kidnapped everyone? he pondered, turning to the chair and looking at the straps hanging from the stirrups. Perhaps the SAS had moved in and done their dirty deed. One minute the castle was full of girlies with juice cunny cracks and tight bottom-holes, and the next – nothing!

'Fuck!' he spat, turning and gazing out of the shattered windows. 'Fuck and treble fuck!'

Chapter Fourteen

Pondering on the mysterious disappearance of the girlies, and of the Baron and Lucifer, Professor Snide climbed out of bed and gazed out of the window at the early-morning sun rising above the forest. Had the Germans been the culprits, he'd have heard from them by now. They'd have also taken the fake machine that was still on the table where the Baron had left it.

'Curiouser and curiouser,' he breathed, stepping into the shower and lathering his stiffening penis. Rolling his foreskin back and forth over his swollen glans, he pondered on having a quick wank before beginning the day. His heavy balls swinging, he ran his hand up and down his veined shaft, his rock-hard cock twitching in response, his knob pulsating as he thought of the school netball team.

Suddenly coming up with a theory, he turned the tap off and grabbed a towel. Sadly, there was no time for wanking and spunking, he reflected, his penis deflating as he dried himself. With everyone in the castle disappearing, there was no time for anything – and there were no girlies to fuck! 'Christ, I'm cuntless!'

The Baron's force-field machine must have malfunctioned, he mused. Instead of turning everyone into Miss Hocks lookalikes, it had somehow zapped their molecular structures, and they'd all disappeared. Having been in the dungeon when the Baron had switched the machine on, the Professor hadn't been affected by the force field.

'That's got to be the answer,' he murmured, hurriedly dressing and making his way to the turret. Wondering, as he climbed the winding steps, whether he could reverse the process, he leaped onto the windswept turret and gazed at the machine. Wondering too why the red light was flashing, he cast his eyes over the controls. He knew, as he switched the machine off, that flicking the wrong switch or turning the wrong control might forever banish everyone to the realms of non-existence.

'At last, my friend!' the Baron cried, almost stopping the Professor's heart.

'Christ!' Snide gasped, turning to face his friend. 'What the . . . where the fuck did you come from?'

'Nowhere.'

'Nowhere?'

'I didn't exist – not physically, anyway.'

'Bloody hell!'

'A small adjustment is required. When I switched the thing on, my molecular structure was broken down and I dematerialized.'

'Lucifer and the girlies disappeared, too.'

'They'll be back now.'

'Thank God for that. I couldn't live in a cuntless castle.'

'No normal man could live without a cunt, my friend.'

'Or abnormal. But this is brilliant, Baron – we can make Peel disappear, and the SAS and . . . '

'No, it's too dangerous. Allow me to adjust the machine and we'll stick to our original plan.'

'Better still, we'll stick to our original . . . Oh, you've just said that.'

'Indeed.'

'Where have you been, Baron? I mean, what was it like having no body?'

'Terrible. I was in dire need of a wank, but I had no cock.'

'Jesus F. Christ! I was in dire need of a wank but there was no . . .'

'There's no time to lose, my friend.'

'That's right, there was no time to wank.'

'The machine must be up and running before our unwelcome visitors visit us.'

'Bloody visitations. OK, I'll leave you to do your stuff and go and check on the others.'

Returning to the banqueting hall, Snide discovered Elizabeth rubbing her dripping vaginal flesh over Helga's open mouth – and the Reverend Mother lying on the floor in a heap. Dragging the behabited woman across the hall, he opened the castle doors and rolled her limp body outside. The last thing he needed was the old hag coming round and ranting and raving again!

'Let me in!' she cried as he closed the doors and turned the key. 'Let me in this instant or you'll find yourself in serious trouble!' Ignoring her, he returned to the banqueting hall to carry on where he'd left off – to spunk Helga's arsehole and then stretch her anal canal open with the speculum.

The Baron's machine had great potential, he reflected as the phone rang. To have people disappear into thin air was the answer to all his problems, despite the Baron's opinion. Deciding to get his hands on the machine when the Baron wasn't around and then zap a few people's molecular structures, he lifted the receiver.

'Snide,' he said as Elizabeth cried out in the grips of another massive lesbian-induced orgasm.

'Professor, this is DI Peel.'

'Fuck me! I mean . . . Good morning, Inspector.'

'I disagree, Professor – it's far from a good morning. I've discovered that you don't work for MI5 any more than I do.'

'Don't you?'

'Don't I what?'

'Work for . . . '

'Stop playing games, Professor. I've had enough of yo
duping me. I made a right fool of myself by . . . I won't g
into that. Suffice to say that my men are on their way to you
castle to arrest you.'

'How considerate of them, I'll put the kettle on.'

'They won't be wanting tea.'

'Don't you allow them a tea break? Surely, you don'
expect your men to work without a tea break, Inspector?'

'Tea breaks have nothing to do with your imminent arrest
You'll be tried for treason and . . . '

'That's most unreasonable. For what reason is this trial fo
treason?'

'Attempting to overthrow the government.'

'I've not attempted to throw anything at the government

'You won't think it so funny when you're hung publicl)
Professor.'

'I'm very well hung privately, thank you. Right, I'll put th
kettle on and wait for your men to arrive. I wonder whethe
they all take sugar?'

'They'll be there within minutes so don't think you've tim
to escape.'

'How many minutes?'

'Two or three.'

'As soon as that?'

'As soon as that. I'll be in the cells awaiting your arriva
Professor.'

'It'll be nice to see you again. Er . . . Have you heard fror
your daughter?'

'No, I haven't. God only knows where she is. By the way
Alice is with MI5 – she'll be testifying.'

'Alice?'

'The naked girl who was in the forest with your butler. Th
end is nigh, Professor Snide.'

'Shit, I'm doomed! Er . . . Goodbye, Inspector.'

Everything depended on the Baron's force field, he pondered as he replaced the receiver. If the machine failed, ruination would fall upon him like a ton of shit. 'Fuck!' he spat as Elizabeth wailed in the beginnings of another shuddering orgasm and a loud knock sounded on the doors. 'Double fuck!' *Perhaps it's the old hag.* Rushing to the doors and sliding the heavy bolt across, he made his way to the turret and told the Baron of the arrival of the unwelcome visitors.

'I'm not ready,' the Baron said, prodding the machine with a screwdriver.

'Don't worry about turning them into women, just make them disappear up their own arseholes.'

'We might *all* disappear up their own arseholes, my friend.'

'Argh! Perish the thought!'

'Exactly. I need ten minutes, that's all.'

'And I need a damned good fuck.'

'There's no time for fucking.'

'Fuck. I just hope the doors keep them at bay until you're ready.'

'They will, I'm sure. Leave now.'

'Leave? Where shall I go?'

'Anywhere, just leave me to work.'

Returning to the castle doors, the Professor shook his head as Peel's men hammered and shouted, demanding that he let them in. Her tongue stuck up Helga's well-spunked fanny, Elizabeth was no help whatsoever, and the other girlies were no doubt frigging each other off in his living quarters. 'Where the hell's Lucifer?' he murmured as the phone rang yet again. Dashing into the hall, his head beginning to ache, he grabbed the receiver.

'I'm busy!' he snapped.

'I'd like to speak to Professor Snide's butler,' a young woman said.

341

'His butler?'

'We have a mutual friend, my name's Sandy.'

'Ah, yes. Er . . . This is the butler speaking.'

'Great. I met a friend of yours, his name's Roger.'

'Good old Roger. How is he?'

'Apart from the fact that he raped me and left me naked in the woods with two young girls, he's fine.'

'Rape and pillage . . . That sounds like old Rog!'

'Listen, he told me that you could get the plans for the Professor's machine.'

'Ah, yes – he rang me about it. I suggest that you come here this evening and meet me. The Professor will be out, so I'll have my glans . . . I'll have the plans waiting for you.'

'Great! About seven?'

'Perfect.'

'Thanks. I'll see you later.'

'Like a lamb to the slaughter!' he chuckled as he replaced the receiver and made his way to Lucifer's room. Once he'd lured the unsuspecting Sandy into the dungeon, he'd strip her and whip her buttocks and fuck her cunt and spunk her bum and wank down her throat and . . .

'Lucifer, are you in there?' he asked, hammering on the locked door.

'Er . . . No, I'm not.'

'Where the hell are you, then?'

'In the forest, sir.'

'In the . . . Wait a minute, how come I can hear you if you're in the forest?'

'Ventriloquism, sir. My mother taught me how to throw my voice.'

'I'll throw your cock unless you fucking well let me in!'

Peering into the room as the butler edged the door open an inch or so, Snide frowned. There was a strong fragrance in the air, a fragrance that reminded him of aroused girlies, of damp navy-blue knickers, of young hairless pussy cracks. Trying to push the door open further, he ordered Lucifer to stand back or be crushed to death.

'I can't, sir. My foot's stuck and . . . '

'You'll have your knob stuck in a minute, stuck right up your arse!'

'Er . . . I have company, sir,' Lucifer confessed, his face grimacing as he leaned on the door to close it.

'Company? Who's in there?'

'A friend, sir.'

'Don't talk rubbish, you know as well as I do that you don't have any friends. Let me in this instant or . . . '

Leaning on the door as Lucifer moved aside, the Professor crashed into the room and fell to the floor. Dragging himself up, he brushed his dishevelled hair back with his fingers and kicked the man in the bollocks as hard as he could.

'Argh!' Lucifer moaned, holding his crotch.

'You incompetent fool!' Snide spat. 'Goldilocks! What are you doing here?' he gasped, eyeing the pretty girl standing in the corner of the room. 'And why are you naked?'

'I'm visiting,' she replied, proudly cupping her firm, rounded breasts in her hands.

'Visiting? Naked girls don't visit strange butlers.'

'I do.'

'Obviously! Lucifer, what's the meaning of this debauched scene of wanton filth?'

'She came to borrow some porridge, sir.'

'Borrow some . . . A lame excuse if ever there was one. Good God, I can smell her cunny a mile off. You've been fucking her, haven't you?'

'Only a little, sir.'

'I've a good mind to fire you! Good grief, the castle's being raided by Peel's men, not to mention the Reverend Mother,

the SAS are on their way – and you're fucking the arse off
Goldilocks!'

'Not her arse, sir.'

'Shut up and get down to the doors. If the men break in,
karate chop their bollocks off.'

'Yes, sir.'

'And don't fail me! If you do, you'll find that you have no
bollocks.'

'What about me?' Goldie asked as she reclined on the bed
with her thighs parted, her creamy pinken sex slit gaping.

'Don't be so silly, you haven't got any bollocks.'

'I mean, what are you going to do with me?'

'I'm going to severely deal with you in a most severely
severe manner!' Snide returned as the butler made his escape.

Closing and locking the door, the Professor hauled his
erect cock out of his trousers and grinned at his prisoner.
She'd been a good fuck in the cottage, he recalled, eyeing her
well-juiced vaginal slit. But this time she was going to endure
far more than a mere vaginal fuck. Taking the speculum from
his pocket, he hid the device behind his back and instructed
the girl to roll over.

'You'll have it from behind,' he said as she lay on her
stomach, exposing her perfectly rounded buttocks, her alluring anal crease.

'Not my bum!' she cried, parting her thighs as wide as she
could.

'Of course not. My God, as if I'd do such a despicable thing
to a young girl. All I'm going to do is to fuck your sweet
cunny hole and spunk your cervix.'

'Your butler's already done that.'

'Filthy pervert, I'll have his bollocks ripped off for his
wanton behaviour.'

Kneeling between her shapely thighs, Snide parted Goldie's firm buttocks and eyed the small brown portal to her

rectal core. *I'll teach her a lesson!* he chuckled inwardly, pushing the end of the speculum against her delicate anal tissue. *One quick shove should do it.* The stainless-steel device driving deep into her tight rectal duct, her young body jolted.

'Argh! What's that?' she screamed, lifting and turning her head.

'Nothing special,' he chuckled, squeezing the levers and stretching her brown hole open.

'Argh! Take it out!'

'No.'

'Yes!'

The speculum was so designed that the levers were to one side, allowing access to the patient's vaginal canal or, in this case, the victim's rectal sheath. 'Perfect,' he murmured, her anal tissue yielding as he squeezed the levers. Peering into her dank rectal sheath as she writhed and squirmed on the bed, his mind swirling with wicked ideas, he ignored her futile protests and opened her bumhole further.

'Beautiful!' he chortled, gazing in awe as her brown ring expanded to capacity. Unable to restrain himself, he slipped three fingers into her open duct and massaged her hot inner flesh. Delighting in her protests and screamed expletives as she struggled to escape, he forced another finger deep into the dank heat of her bloated anal cavern.

With Peel's men hammering on the castle doors and the SAS on their way, this wasn't really the time for a rampant session of anal abuse, Snide reflected. But his insatiable thirst for crude sex had once again got the better of him. There again, things weren't *too* bad, he mused. If the Baron wasn't able to turn the men into women, Lucifer would chop their bollocks off, so there was no real need for concern.

'Stop it!' Goldie cried as the Professor pistoned his fingers in and out of her spasming anal passage. 'You can't do this!'

'I *am* doing it,' he returned. 'And unless you tell me who you really are, I'll stretch your bum open further.'

'You know who I am! I'm Goldie Smith.'

'Goldie Smith, my arse! Your arse, rather. Where do you live?'

'In the forest, with the woodcutter. Argh! Take your fingers out!'

'You're an agent, I know it.'

'Only for Tupperware.'

'Bollocks, you're a government agent working for the government.'

'Of course I'm not!'

'Right, I'm going to fuck your arse and spunk your bowels.'

'No!'

'Yes!'

Withdrawing his fingers, Snide slipped his solid knob into Goldie's open hole, his shaft gliding deep into her hot lust duct as she wriggled and protested wildly. A damned good buttock-whipping would do the young filly good, he ruminated, his knob embedded deep within the dank heat of her bowels, his heavy balls pressing against her swollen vaginal lips. Goldie Smith, Goldilocks . . . She'd reveal her true identity if he had to fuck and whip her arse until she passed out!

'No, your cock's too big!' she complained as he withdrew his huge penis and drove into her open bottom-hole.

'All the better to fuck you with!'

'This is illegal!'

'Excellent!'

Squeezing the speculum levers, he opened her inflamed anal sheath further, grinning as she spat her threats. There was nothing like a damned good anal fucking with the aid of a speculum, he thought, shafting her velveteen duct with his massive organ. It might be an idea to invite the local school netball team to the castle and use the device on the young girlies' bottom-holes, he mused – and that of the PE mistress!

'God, I'm coming already!' he gasped, his swollen knob throbbing as he shafted her tight anal duct. 'Here it comes!' His spunk jetting from his orgasming glans, filling her hot rectal sheath, he fucked the little beauty for all he was worth. Delighting in her screams as his swinging bollocks slapped her swollen vaginal lips, he repeatedly rammed his spunking cockhead into her brimming bowels, at last taking her to her shuddering climax.

'Oh, oh!' she gasped, reaching beneath her stomach and massaging her pulsating clitoris. 'Oh, I'm . . . I'm coming!' On and on the Professor drove his horse-like penis deep into her bloated rectal tube until his heavy balls had drained and his shaft began to deflate. Making his last thrusts, he finally collapsed over her quivering body, grinning as she masturbated her young clitty, sustaining her climax.

'Christ, that was something else!' he breathed as she finished herself off, her naked body writhing beneath his. 'I don't suppose you know where Snow White hangs out? I wouldn't mind giving her one up her arsehole.'

'Ah, yes!' Goldie cried as her orgasm peaked, her pulsating clitoris solid beneath her vibrating fingertips.

'You do?'

'Ah, yes! Yes!'

'Where?'

'Oh, my cunt!'

'She lives up your . . . '

Leaping off the girl as a huge explosion shook the castle, his cock leaving her anal sheath with a loud sucking sound, Snide zipped his trousers and dashed out of the room, locking the door behind him. He had no idea what the hell was going on as he raced through the banqueting hall, wondering where

Helga and Elizabeth had got to as he passed the cunny-stained double-bum-fucking chair. It wouldn't be Peel's men, he was sure. They might be armed with handguns but not with rocket launchers, hand grenades and bazookas! It was probably the bloody SAS, he mused as he met his butler by the doors and asked him what had happened.

'An explosion, sir,' the man smiled, swigging from his hip flask.

'Jesus F. Christ, I gathered that much! Who the fuck did it?'

'The SAS, sir. I was atop the turret just now with the binoculars and I spied them lurking near the trees at the foot of the hill. It would appear that they have another rocket launcher and . . . '

Another explosion rocking the castle as the naked girlies gathered around the Professor, Snide reckoned that the end had come. 'To the dungeon!' he cried. 'We'll be safe enough down there!' Leading the way, he wondered what the Baron was up to. He'd obviously been unable to get the machine working, he reflected as another explosion ripped through the castle.

'Fuck me!' he spat, locking the dungeon door once the girlies and Lucifer were in the lab. 'The fucking fascist bastards seem to have us hemmed in.'

'May I suggest something, sir?' Lucifer asked as the phone rang.

'No, you may not!' Snide returned, lifting the receiver. 'Who is it?' he bellowed. 'What the fuck do you want?'

'Exactly that!' a girl giggled.

'Exactly what?'

'A fuck!'

'Who is this? How dare you use obscene fucking language over the fucking telephone!'

'It's me, Lydia. Having a bad day, Professor?'

'Oh, Lydia. Yes, as it happens, I am.'

'I just thought I'd call to let you know that Jack's joined a monastery.'

'What? He's become a monk?'

'Yes.'

'Thank God for that! Look, I have to go – call me another time.'

'OK, I'll pop in for an arse-fuck when I'm passing.'

'Great, I'll look forward to it – if I'm still in the land of the living.'

'What do you mean?'

'Nothing. I have to go.'

Replacing the receiver, Snide decided to go up to the turret and find out what the Baron was doing. Another explosion reverberating throughout the castle, something had to be done – and quickly! Dangerous or not, the machine would have to be used to zap the bastards and make them disappear. Zap the SAS, and Peel and his men, and . . .

'Baron, what the fuck's going on?' he asked as he stepped onto the turret.

'A minor problem,' the man replied without looking up from the machine.

'Minor? Don't you mean a fucking major bollocking problem?'

'Just give me ten minutes.'

'You said that fucking hours ago.'

'Grab the binoculars and see what's going on.'

Focusing on the rocket launcher at the foot of the hill, Snide shook his head in disbelief. There were at least thirty or forty men milling around, and another dozen or so moving up the hill towards the castle. This was definitely the end, he was sure as a rocket flew over his head, narrowly missing the turret.

Pondering on his mistakes, he realized that he should never

have allowed the nuns to move in, or nabbed village girlies or got involved with Sister Elizabeth or . . . Hindsight was as much good as a teenage girl without a cunt, he reflected – what was done was done. Turning as Lucifer appeared in the turret doorway, he suddenly had an idea.

'The only way out is to give them the alpha-wave machine,' he murmured.

'Sir, may I make a suggestion?' Lucifer asked.

'No, you may not. Baron, I'm going to give them the alpha-wave machine, and the gamma-ray box – it's the only way.'

'Is that wise, my friend?'

'It's far from fucking wise but I don't see that I have a choice.'

'Sir, may I . . . '

'Shut up, Lucifer! Right, I'll go get the machine from the secret tunnel.'

Leaving the turret and making his way down the winding steps, Snide rubbed his head. This was indeed a sad day, he reflected as he approached the banqueting hall. But he could always construct another alpha-wave machine, and an improved gamma-ray box. And there were plenty of girlies in the world, all ripe for picking and fucking and . . .

'Ve meet again!' Gretel grinned, wielding a machine-gun.

'How the hell did you get in here?' Snide asked, glancing at the locked doors.

'I have my vays. You vill get ze machine and come with me.'

'Come with you? Perish the thought! I'd rather have a damned good wank than . . . '

'You vill do as you are told or your balls vill be tortured off!' she snapped, taking the red apple from the table by the doors.

Watching as she took a bite, Snide recalled the old hag dressed in a shawl. *Like a juicy red apple, deary?* There was an unremarkable resemblance, he mused as Gretel turned green and collapsed to the floor. 'There's nothing like a taste of your own medicine, *deary!*' he chuckled, dragging the woman into the banqueting hall. Wondering how she'd managed to get into the castle as he heaved her onto the double-bum-fucking chair, he placed her ankles in the stirrups.

'That'll keep you quite for a while!' he chuckled, trying to recall whether it was a kiss from Prince Charming or a chunk of apple falling out of Snow White's mouth that had saved the girl. 'Mirror, mirror on the wall, who's got the biggest tool of all? I have!' he laughed, grabbing Gretel's gun and making his way to the secret tunnel.

Eyeing the alpha-wave machine, he sighed. There had to be another way, he reflected, leaving the machine in the tunnel and pushing the stone wall back into place. *To sacrifice years of work* . . . 'No, I won't do it!'

Returning to the banqueting hall as another explosion shattered what was left of the windows, he suddenly came up with the plan of all plans – a motherfucking plan of plans. Racing up to the turret, he grabbed his butler by the lapels and ordered him to get the machine from the tunnel.

'But, sir . . . ' Lucifer began.

'Do it, Lucifer! Take it down to the lab and set it up on the bench.'

'You have a plan, my friend?' the Baron asked as Lucifer left the turret.

'Indeed, I do. How are you getting on with your machine?'

'Nearly there.'

'Right, a change of plan. Bring it down to the lab.'

'But . . . '

'I've captured Gretel, and I've come up with the mother-fucking plan of motherfucking plans!'

'But . . . '

'Trust me, Baron – trust me!'

RAY GORDON

Returning to the lab, Snide rubbed his hands together and cleared the bench to make a space for the machines. This was a long shot, he ruminated as the girls chatted excitedly. If it failed, then he was done for! No more girlies' wet cunts, no more tight bottom-holes, no more buttock-whipping or mouth-spunking or . . .

'Helga escaped,' Elizabeth enlightened him, tweaking her erect nipples as she leaned against the bench.

'Fuck me!'

'Mmm, I'd love to!'

'Not now! Christ, we're under attack and you want a fuck?'

Shaking his head as he wondered how many more problems he could take, he ordered the gaggle of girlies to wait in the torture chamber as Lucifer descended the steps. Instructing the man to place the machine on the bench and then bring Gretel down to the lab, he pondered on Helga. But there was no time to worry about the girl. Besides, she'd probably returned to Professor Spasm.

'What are you doing, Lucifer?' he snapped.

'Standing here, sir.'

'I told you to go and get Gretel!'

'Is she here?' the butler asked, obviously perplexed.

'Of course she is. I'd hardly tell you to get her from the hall if she wasn't fucking well there!'

'No, sir – I suppose not.'

'Quickly, time is of the essence! Go, go, go!'

'Yes, sir.'

Switching the alpha-wave machine on, he placed the helmet on his head and recorded his own brain patterns. Chuckling wickedly, he removed the helmet and hooked the machine up to the computer, erasing all memories of the machines, abducting village girlies, raping nuns, abusing the Inspector's daughter, and any other incriminating thoughts.

'OK,' he beamed as the Baron lugged his machine down

352

the steps. 'Set it up here and get it going as quickly as you can. The force-field idea was fucking useless, so use the transducer as you did before.'

'I was almost there,' the man complained. 'If you'd given me another ten . . . '

'Let's stop talking bollocks and get to work, there's very little time.'

'Of the essence, my friend?'

'Of the essence.'

As the Baron settled at the bench and began tinkering with his machine, Snide rubbed his chin pensively. *I really must stop rubbing my chin!* The girlies were safe enough in the torture chamber, Goldilocks was locked in Lucifer's room . . . Frowning, he again wondered where Penny had got to. He'd not seen the girl since they'd returned from the cottage and Lucifer had dragged her down to the lab. 'Fancy letting her escape,' he murmured under his breath as the butler lugged Gretel down the steps.

'Right, bung her on the chair,' he said as Lucifer staggered across the lab.

'She's very heavy, sir,' the man complained, dumping the woman on the chair.

'That's because she's fucking fat.'

'Is she dead?'

'I hope not! Baron, how are you doing?'

'I do believe I'm there, my friend.'

'Excellent! OK, aim the transducer at me and record my molecular structure.'

'What's your plan?'

'Just do it.'

This was the only hope, Snide reflected as the Baron aimed the transducer and fiddled with the machine. If this failed, all was doomed. Another explosion rocking the castle, he shook his head, praying for his plan to work.

'All done,' the Baron smiled.

'OK, now point the thing at Gretel and turn her into me.'

'Ah, I now see your plan!' the Baron grinned, aiming the transducer at the fat woman. 'You're going to send the clone down the hill and . . . '

'Exactly! The enemy will believe that I've given myself up and leave us in peace.'

'But they'll still want the machine.'

'I have another plan, Baron. A plan so wicked, so devious, so evil, so dastardly, so ingenious . . . Fuck me, I must stop talking bollocks. OK, clone the fat Kraut!'

Stripping off as the Baron fiddled with the controls, the Professor placed his clothes on the bench. This was the ultimate solution, he was sure as he fondled his horselike cock. With the clone in custody, the enemy believing they'd won, he'd be left in peace to carry on with his perverted ways. *The first thing I'll do is rape the prudish librarian! And the PE mistress and the netball team and . . .* Grinning as the machine whirred and Gretel turned into a second Professor Snide, he began ripping her clothes off.

'God, she's . . . I mean, *he*'s you!' Lucifer gasped in disbelief.

'Yes, he is,' Snide grinned. 'Help me to dress him in my clothes.'

'Is she . . . is *he* drugged?' the Baron asked.

'Yes. If I'm right, all I have to do is remove the chunk of apple from his mouth, like this, and . . . Ah, he's beginning to come round! We must hurry!'

Plonking the helmet on the clone's head once Lucifer had finished dressing the man, Snide flicked the switch, inducing the modified alpha-wave patterns into his brain. Standing up and staggering around the lab, the clone reeled as the helmet fell off his head and he regained full consciousness.

'Go down the hill and give yourself up!' Snide bellowed, hiding behind the bench.

'Yes, give myself up,' the clone echoed, climbing the stone steps.

'Why are you hiding?' Lucifer asked.

'I didn't want to confuse him. Had he seen me, he'd have wondered why there are two of us and . . . Fuck that! OK, once he's reached the SAS, we should be in the clear. I say we celebrate by whipping and fucking the girlies' bums!'

'My friend,' the Baron said pensively. 'Your plan is brilliant, but the Inspector is bound to come here.'

'Why?'

'To search for his daughter, among other things. And what about the girlies?'

'What about them?'

'They'll know that you're still here, they'll know your secret.'

'And Goldilocks,' Lucifer rejoined.

Pacing the floor, the Professor knew that his friend was right. It would be too risky having a dozen or more people knowing the truth. He'd never be able to go down to the village and nab horny teenage girls or hurl abuse at the PE mistress or whisper crude comments to the prudish librarian. *Let alone fuck her!*

'Sir, your client will be here soon,' Lucifer said.

'Shit, I'd forgotten about that.'

'When she arrives, shall I say that . . . '

'Don't answer the door. She'll soon give up and go away.'

'What was your wicked, devious, evil, so-dastardly and ingenious plan?' the Baron asked as the Professor climbed the stone steps.

'The modified brain patterns . . . The clone knows nothing about the machines or abducted girls. He won't break under torture because he knows nothing.'

'Brilliant! But there are still major problems, such as the Inspector and . . . '

'I have some thinking to do. I'm going to my living quarters for a while.'

Flopping onto his bed, Snide pondered on a life locked in the castle, never able to venture outside or receive visitors. Once news broke of 'his' arrest and imprisonment, he'd become a prisoner in his own castle. 'Fuck it!' he spat, realizing that the state would nab the castle once they believed him to be locked up. 'My plan was far from fucking brilliant!' Reaching to the bedside table and grabbing the ringing phone, he was surprised to hear Penny.

'Where are you?' he asked.

'In the village, my friend.'

'Christ, you still have the Baron's alpha wave . . . '

'I'm calling to tell you that everyone's moving out. The police, the SAS . . . They're all leaving.'

'Yes, that's because . . . God, what a mess.'

'Why, what's the problem?'

'I can't tell you. Look, you'd better come here so that I can reinstate your . . . Just come here, OK?'

'What do you want to do?'

'You'll have to go home to your parents at some stage.'

'My parents have long since gone, my friend – you know that.'

'Shit! Not the Baron's . . . Come up to the castle, OK?'

'OK, give me half an hour.'

Replacing the receiver, the Professor sighed. 'A free man but imprisoned for life in my own body.' He could quite easily clone himself as someone else, but who? To become another Baron wasn't what he wanted, and he certainly didn't want to look like Lucifer! *A woman?* he pondered. Cloning himself as another man *or* woman wouldn't stop the state from nabbing the castle.

'I've got it, my friend!' the Baron beamed as he burst into the room.

'Got what?'

'It's just turned up at the castle doors.'

'Not another income tax demand?'

'No, your wife.'

'My wife? Christ, I haven't seen Christine for years!'

'She's been searching for you for the last five years and, now she's found you, she's staking a claim in the castle. She's the answer to all your problems.'

'She caused me so many problems that I . . . '

'This is the answer, my friend!'

'There are far more problems than you realize, Baron.'

'Everyone believes you to be in custody, right?'

'Yes, but I can't show my face. The fascist pigs will take my castle, even if I clone myself. I'm doomed.'

'No, no, you're not. I've locked your wife in the rack chamber. I took it upon myself to strip her and chain her to the rack, of course.'

'Did you fuck her?'

'Only a little: I couldn't restrain myself. Listen, you are to become a clone of your wife.'

'What? If I do that, what will she do? We'd have to bump her off.'

'No, we wouldn't.'

'If only we had a lion pit.'

'We can turn your wife into another Helga, my friend.'

'Wait a minute, Helga's returning to her own country soon. She'll be thousands of miles away so . . . '

'Perfect!'

'So the cloned Helga could stay here and . . . '

'No, we let her go.'

'But . . . '

'Your wife will be herself, but in Helga's body.'

357

'She'll go to the police!'

'And say that you stole her body and gave her another one? Hardly!'

'Good point, she'd be arrested for clinical insanity. So, being my wife, I'd be free to . . . But the state will still want the castle.'

'We'll cross that bridge when we come to it. Come on, we've work to do.'

Following the Baron to the lab, Snide pondered on the idea. His wife was a goodlooker, he reflected, and she used to be a good fuck – before she caught him shagging the arse off their neighbour's teenage daughter! *A stake in the castle?* he pondered. He'd thought she'd long since given up trying to get her hands on his money. Women moved in mysterious ways, he reflected. Christine was about to move with a damned good whipping and fucking, and there'd be nothing mysterious about it!

'Ah, Christine!' he beamed as he entered the rack chamber and gazed at her naked body.

'Sexton! That man raped me!' she cried, scowling at the Baron as he ambled into the chamber.

'Of course he didn't, he just fucked you a bit.'

'Let me go, for God's sake!'

'Oh, no. Oh, no, no, no, no!'

'Yes!'

'No! Your visit was most timely, Christine,' he grinned, rubbing his hands together as he scrutinized her firm breasts, her well-spermed vaginal crack. 'Just what the doctor ordered – Doctor Sex, that is!'

'What are you going to do with me?'

'Nothing, nothing at all. Apart from steal your body.'

'Steal my body? My God, what evil lurks in your evil mind? I always knew there was something very strange about you.'

'You didn't know the half of it.'

'You're going to kill me, aren't you?'

'Don't be so silly, Christine – I don't kill people! You're to have a new body, the body of a healthy young girl with firm titties and the tightest cunt ever.'

'No!'

'You'll be pleased with your new body, I assure you.'

'What will I tell my friends? They won't recognize me and . . . '

'Tell them that you've had a make-over. Right, we're wasting precious time. Baron, your machine, please.'

'Certainly, my friend!'

Lugging the device into the rack chamber, the Baron aimed the transducer at the woman and recorded her molecular structure as Snide rubbed his hands together gleefully. Helga would have to have her structure recorded before she left the country, he mused, but that wouldn't present a problem. And he was sure that his wife would be more than pleased with a fine, curvaceous teenage body!

'All done,' the Baron said, breaking the Professor's reverie.

'Right, go over to Spasm's place and, without Helga realizing, record her molecular structure.'

'I don't know where he lives.'

'I'll take you,' Lucifer said, materializing in the doorway.

'Good man!' Snide beamed. 'While you're gone, I'll spend a little time alone with Christine.'

'No!'

'Yes!'

Pressing his finger between her gaping vaginal lips as she writhed and struggled, he forced it deep into her sex sheath. This was a turn-up for the Doomsday Book, he reflected – no contact with Christine for years, and then his finger stuck right up her hot cunt! But this was only the beginning of the session of rampant sexual abuse. She was to be severely punished for . . . For what? he pondered. For complaining when he'd shagged the arse off their next door neighbour's daughter, for denying him illegal sex as and when he'd wanted it, for identifying him as the flasher at the church fête, for . . . Shit, for being his bloody wife!

Forcing another finger into her tightening lust hole, his penis stiffening, he decided to fuck her before the merciless whipping session commenced. She'd never enjoyed sex, his cock spunking up her tight cunt – and he very much doubted that she'd enjoy his new horse-like penis rammed up her honeypot. But *he* would!

'I have a surprise for you,' he grinned, his fingers slipping out of her wet cunt with a delicious sucking sound.

'And *I* have a surprise for *you!*' she spat. 'I'm going to the police and . . . '

'No one's going to the police, Christine,' he broke in, hauling his erect penis out of his trousers. 'What do you think of this?'

'My God! What . . . what have you done to it?'

'Made it bigger. All the bigger to fuck you with!'

'No!'

'Yes!'

As he was about to climb onto the rack and force his penis deep into her vaginal duct, Lucifer appeared in the doorway and let out a little cough. Now what? Snide wondered, noticing anxiety mirrored in the man's eyes as he turned to face him. More problems, no doubt!

'That was quick!' Snide breathed. 'How on earth did you get to Professor Spasm's and back in such a short time?'

'As luck would have it, Helga came here to say goodbye.'

'Excellent! Where is she?'

'The Baron recorded her molecular structure and told her to fuck off out of it.'

'Most civil, I must say.'

'Sir, there's a slight problem.'

'Go on.'

'DI Peel is heading this way.'

'Fuck and treble fuck!'

'Ready when you are!' the Baron grinned as he dashed across the lab with his machine.

'Right, there's no time to lose!' Snide said, zipping his trousers. 'Do your stuff, Baron!'

Recording Christine's molecular structure as the Professor and Lucifer looked on, the Baron flicked a switch and changed the woman into a clone of Helga. Aiming the transducer at the Professor, he again flicked the switch, instantly turning him into Christine.

'Who are you?' he asked, grinning at Snide.

'I'm me, Sexton Snide.'

'Ah, I *did* have the right setting. I wasn't sure whether the transformation would give you her mind or not. By the way, you can have your body back at the flick of a switch.'

'Fucking brilliant!'

'What's happened to me?' Christine asked, lifting her head and gazing at her teenage body, her firm breasts. 'God, I'm . . . '

'You're bloody lucky!' Snide chuckled, fondling his new tits and tweaking his erect nipples. 'I think I'll have a go with my King Dong vibrator, I've always wanted to know what it's like for a woman.'

'Sir . . . I mean, Miss,' Lucifer grimaced. 'DI Peel . . . '

'Ah, right. OK, chuck Helga out . . . I mean Christine, and I'll receive my visitor in the banqueting hall.'

'I suggest you don your wife's clothes first, my friend.'

'Good idea, Baron' he replied, grabbing the woman's dress and tugging it over his head. 'I can hardly receive the Inspector if I'm naked. Lucifer, you'd better give her some clothes before you throw her out.'

'Right away, sir.'

'And then hide the machines in the secret tunnel.'

'Yes, sir.'

'And be fucking quick about it! OK, Baron – to the banqueting hall!'

Racing up the stone steps with the Baron in tow, Snide hurried to the hall. Rubbing his hands together as he paced the floor, he could hardly wait to see Peel. No doubt the man was still searching for his daughter, he mused, recalling the girl's incredible clitoris. There were still a few loose ends to tie up, not least reinstating Penny's alpha-wave patterns. But all was going well, so far.

'Do you realize what this means?' he asked the Baron as a loud knock sounded on the doors.

'Yes, it means someone's knocking on the door.'

'No, no! It means that I can enjoy perverted sex as a man or a woman.'

'Yes, of course.'

'I'm in prison, and yet . . . '

'I'll answer the door.'

'Oh, right.'

Grinning as the Baron showed DI Peel into the hall, the Professor adjusted his hair and donned a sweet smile. Deliberately showing his deep cleavage as the man stood before him, he held out his hand and introduced himself.

'Mrs Snide?' the Inspector echoed.

'That's right. I've come here to stake a claim in my husband's castle.'

'Oh, I see. I didn't realize he was married.'

'Separated, actually.'

'Ah, yes. Er . . . Would you mind if I searched the castle?'

'Of course I wouldn't mind, Inspector. What are you looking for, exactly?'

'My daughter. Your husband . . . Well, it's a long story. I'll begin at the top: I know my way around.'

'Certainly.'

'I'll check on . . . ' the Baron began. 'Er . . . I'll go with the Inspector.'

'Right you are.'

Watching Peel leave the hall, Snide mused on having a cunt. Shoving his hand up his dress, he slipped his fingers between his fleshy vaginal lips and massaged his clitoris. Easing a finger deep into his creamy vaginal sheath as the phone rang, he thought about female masturbation. *Cucumbers, candles, vibrators, lesbian sex, cocks . . . Now there's an idea!*

'Snide . . . I mean, Professor Snide's secretary,' he said, pressing the receiver to his ear.

'Is the Professor there?' a woman asked.

'No, he's been unavoidably detained. To whom am I speaking?'

'This is Miss Nipplewart, Headmistress of the village school. I'm calling about an illegal incident that took place between the Professor and two of my girls in the woods.'

'Headmistress, before you continue, might I suggest something?'

'Yes?'

'Fuck off!'

Banging the phone down, Snide punched the air with his fist. At last, the future was looking good, he pondered. The best of both worlds, a cock or a fanny as and when he wanted – the future was looking brilliant! There was no way that the government would try and nab the castle, he was sure. With Mrs Christine Snide residing in the castle, the PM locked in a mental home and the clone in prison, the castle was safe enough.

'Ah, Inspector!' he grinned as the man walked across the hall. 'That was quick.'

'There's no point in searching the castle. The Professor's in custody, so my job's done. As for my daughter . . . '

'I heard that she'd gone missing.'

'No doubt she'll turn up when she's ready.'

'I'm sure she will, Inspector.'

'Well, I'd better get back to the station. Good day, Mrs Snide.'

'Good day, Inspector. Oh, and . . . '

'Yes?'

'Nothing.' *Fuck off!*